THE DARKNESS WE FELL INTO

also by P. Hartwell

Cailleach's Embrace

The Last Inhale

The Sacred Island

Beneath West Seneca

Time in Kilkenny

Brotherhood in Grease and Dust

The Hollow Axle

The Guardian's Hunger

THE DARKNESS WE FELL INTO

Some shadows pull you under.
Others set you free

P. HARTWELL

The Darkness We Fell Into

Cover art and design by P. Hartwell

ISBN: 978-1-969929-18-2

Dedication

For the ones who survived what should have broken them— who rebuilt themselves from fractured memories and quiet courage. For every heart that learned to trust again, even when the shadows whispered otherwise. And for those still searching for the truth in their own darkness—may you find the light that refuses to let you go.

1
The Scent of Cinnamon and Rain

Four in the morning is its own kind of quiet. Not peaceful — just empty, the way a room feels after someone's left it. Amber had learned to live inside that emptiness. She'd made it her whole personality, really.

She pressed the heel of her palm into the dough and felt it push back, warm and yielding, and for a fleeting second, the jagged knot of wire beneath her ribs uncoiled. Flour dusted her wrists, a fine pale coating that made her look like she was disappearing into the countertop. Which, honestly? Not the worst idea she'd had.

Six months in Cherry Creek. Six months of four AM starts and measured cups of flour and the soft, reliable smell of cinnamon filling the Roasted Bean's kitchen like a promise she could actually keep. She had a routine. She had a counter to lean on and an oven that didn't lie and a town small enough that nobody looked too hard at a girl who didn't want to be looked at. That was the whole plan, and it had been working just fine.

She shaped the cinnamon rolls in silence, listening to rain tap against the back window. It was early October, and Cherry Creek had decided to skip whatever gentle version of fall might exist and jump straight into cold, gray, relentless. The kind of weather that pressed down on your shoulders and dared you to try and feel optimistic.

Amber was not feeling optimistic. But she was feeling productive, which was close enough.

By six-thirty, the display case was stocked. Cinnamon rolls glistening with glaze, blueberry scones lined up in rows, a lemon loaf she'd made on a whim because she'd had extra zest and needed something to do with her hands at three in the morning when the nightmare woke her up again. She didn't think about the nightmare. She thought about the lemon loaf. She turned the sign on the door from CLOSED to OPEN and watched the rain streak down the glass in long, cold rivulets.

The first real customer of the morning came in just after seven.

She heard the bell above the door and glanced up from the espresso machine with the automatic smile she'd practiced until it felt nearly real. The man who stepped inside was tall enough that he had to duck slightly under the low wooden beam over the entrance, and he shook the rain off his jacket in one efficient motion, like he did everything with that same economy of effort. Broad-shouldered under a faded flannel shirt, dark blond hair damp and pushed back from his face, jaw carrying a couple days of stubble that was starting to lean toward actual beard territory. He had a scar through his left eyebrow — thin, pale, old — and eyes that were some particular shade of blue that made Amber think of winter lakes.

He was looking at her the way people look at something they recognize, and she had never seen him before in her life.

Okay.

She kept the smile in place. "Morning. What can I get you?"

He stopped at the counter and looked at the display case with absolutely no expression, then looked back up at her. "Black coffee. And one of those." He nodded toward the cinnamon rolls.

"Good choice." She meant it. Those were the best thing she made, and she wasn't modest about it. She poured the coffee, plated the roll, set it all on the counter and told him the total. He pulled a crumpled bill from his jacket pocket and laid it on the counter, and when she picked it up to make change, their fingers brushed — just barely, just for a second — and her whole nervous system had the audacity to short-circuit over that.

She dropped the coins into his palm. He didn't move immediately. "These yours?" he said. He meant the rolls.

"I made them, yeah."

Something shifted in his expression. Not quite a smile. More like the idea of one passing behind his eyes. "They're good," he said, like he'd tried one already. Like he knew. He picked up his coffee and the plate and moved to a table by the window, and Amber stood behind the counter and very deliberately did not watch him.

She watched him a little.

He ate the cinnamon roll slowly and drank his coffee and looked out at the rain, and there was something about the stillness of him that made her uneasy in a way she couldn't name. Most people fidgeted. Checked their phones, shifted in their seats, made small talk with whoever was nearby. He just sat there like he was completely comfortable taking up space, like the quiet didn't bother him at all. Like he was used to waiting.

She turned back to the espresso machine. *Stop it.*

Lila arrived at seven forty-five in a burst of wet caramel curls and polka-dot rain jacket and the particular energy of someone who had strong opinions about everything and was not planning to keep them to herself.

"Lord, it is disgusting out there," she announced, shaking her umbrella at the doormat. Her amber eyes swept the room, landed on the man by the window, and she got this look on her face — eyebrows up, lips curved, a silent *well, well* that she somehow broadcast without making a sound. She cut behind the counter and leaned close to Amber. "That's Dalton Vale."

"I don't know who that is," Amber said quietly.

"He's got the garage on Route 9. Grew up here, left for the military, came back." Lila arranged this information with the practiced efficiency of someone who had cataloged every soul in a three-county radius. "Doesn't come in here much. Doesn't come most places much, honestly. Kind of a whole situation."

"A situation."

"A whole one." Lila glanced over again. "He's looking at you." "He's looking out the window."

"Same direction, honey."

Amber made a point of not checking. She restocked the napkin holder with great focus and purpose.

When she looked up a few minutes later, Dalton Vale was gone. The table was cleared. His coffee cup sat rinsed in the bus tub — he'd done that himself, which surprised her — and the plate held nothing but a faint smear of glaze. She hadn't heard him leave. Hadn't heard the bell over the door, hadn't heard his boots on the floor, nothing. He'd just stopped being there.

"See?" Lila said sagely. "A whole situation."

Amber's shift ended at two. The rain had softened to a fine, persistent mist by then, the kind that got into your collar and the back of your neck and made everything smell like wet pavement and leaves going to rot. She gathered her bag from the back room, said goodbye to Lila, who was already deep in conversation with a couple of regulars, and pushed out the side door into the alley.

Her car was parked around the corner on the narrow strip of lot the bakery shared with the hardware store next door. She'd been meaning to get the rattle in the front end checked. She'd been meaning to do a lot of things. There was a whole list of things she kept meaning to do, and she was getting to all of them slowly, in the order of least terrifying first.

She was fishing her keys out of her bag when she saw it.

The envelope was tucked under the windshield wiper on the driver's side. Small, white, slightly damp. The kind of plain, standard envelope you could buy anywhere, in any quantity, completely untraceable. She'd seen enough crime documentaries to know that.She'd also seen enough of her own life to feel, before she even touched it, what this was.

Her hand didn't shake. She'd gotten good at that. She pulled the envelope free, turned it over. No name on it. No postmark. She slid her thumbnail under the seal and opened it.

Inside was a photograph.

Her front door. Her building, the blue-gray siding she'd memorized from the outside every night when she came home, the little potted plant she'd put on the step because she'd read somewhere that small acts of domesticity helped with anxiety. The photo was taken at night, from across the street or maybe from further down the block — close enough to be specific, far enough to be patient. And on the back, in thick charcoal strokes that pressed almost through the paper: *I found you.*

The mist kept falling. A car rolled past on the street without slowing. Somewhere down the block, a dog barked twice and stopped.

Amber stood very still and breathed through her nose and did not fall apart. She'd gotten good at that too.

Six months. Six months of careful, quiet, deliberate nothing. She'd changed her name on everything she could change it on. She'd told no one where she'd moved. She'd built this little careful life out of flour and routine and the particular mercy of a town that minded its own business, and somehow, somehow, it hadn't been enough.

She turned the photograph over again and looked at her front door in the dark and thought: *they were standing right there.*

Her stomach turned over, slow and cold. She put the photograph back in the envelope. She put the envelope in her bag. She unlocked her car and got in and sat there with the heat running and her hands flat on her thighs until her pulse came back down to something manageable.

She thought about calling someone. She thought about it the same way she'd thought about it for two years — seriously, briefly, and then she remembered the detective in Albany who'd looked at her across his desk and said, *we just don't have enough to go on*, and the thought passed.

She started the car and drove home through the mist and didn't cry, because crying was a thing she allowed herself between two and four in the morning when there was nothing else to do with it, and not in parking lots in broad daylight where anyone could see.

She made it back to her apartment, locked the deadbolt and the chain, and stood in her kitchen with her coat still on and made herself a cup of tea she didn't drink. The afternoon light was flat and gray through the window. She looked at the potted plant on her front step through the peephole — she'd drilled one in at knee height and one at normal height, because she was thorough like that — and the plant sat there exactly as she'd left it, small and stubborn and alive.

I found you.

She pressed her forehead against the door and closed her eyes. The wood was cool against her skin. She breathed in and out and thought about the cinnamon rolls and the rain and the particular quiet of four in the morning when the whole world was still asleep and nothing bad had happened yet. She tried to hold onto that. She was pretty good at holding onto things.

What she kept coming back to, though, when she was honest with herself, was the man at the table by the window. Dalton Vale, with his still, patient quality and his winter-lake eyes that had looked at her like he already knew her name before she said it. She didn't know what to do with that. She didn't know if it was comfort or warning or something in between — just that it had felt like both at once, which was not a combination she had any idea how to process.

She thought about the way he'd rinsed his own cup and left without making a sound, and the way his fingers had barely touched hers over the coins and how her whole body had registered it like a static shock. She thought about how, when she'd looked up and found him gone, her first feeling had been something she was not going to examine too closely because it had been awfully close to disappointment.

Pull yourself together, Rowan.

She went to her bedroom and sat on the edge of the bed and pulled the envelope out of her bag and looked at it one more time. The handwriting was the same as the one she'd gotten in Albany, two years ago, the one the detective had said they couldn't trace. Same pressure. Same charcoal. Same economy of words, like he'd thought about exactly what would land hardest and used only that.

He'd found her in six months.

She put the envelope in the shoebox in the top of her closet, behind the spare blanket, next to the two others she'd been hoping were the last. She pushed the closet door shut. She went back to the kitchen and picked up her tea and stood at the window and watched the rain start up again in earnest, coming down heavy and silver now against the street below, turning everything soft at the edges.

Out on Route 9, somewhere past the edge of town, a garage sat dark against the weather. She knew that now. She knew his name, and she knew he drove a truck, and she knew he took his coffee black and didn't leave crumbs.

She didn't know why that felt, at the end of a day that had cracked open beneath her, like the only solid thing she'd touched.

But it did. It absolutely did, and she hated herself a little for it, and she watched the rain and waited for morning the same way she always did —one breath at a time, hands wrapped around something warm, not looking too hard at what was coming next.

2

Broken Seals

The rattle in her front end had gone from mildly annoying to genuinely alarming somewhere between Tuesday and Thursday, and by Friday morning, Amber had run out of excuses to ignore it. She'd been putting off the garage the same way she put off everything that required interacting with a stranger in a confined space — methodically, creatively, and with diminishing success.

Vale's Garage sat on Route 9 like it had grown there, a low concrete building with two bay doors and a hand-painted sign that had seen better decades. A rusted-out pickup on blocks occupied the gravel lot beside it, and the smell of motor oil drifted all the way out to the road. She pulled in just before eight, killed the engine, and sat there for exactly three seconds before she made herself get out.

The first bay door was open. She heard him before she saw him — the metallic clank of a wrench, the scrape of something shifting against concrete. She stepped into the shadow of the bay and found a pair of boots sticking out from under a chassis. Long legs in worn denim, a strip of bare forearm visible where the flannel had ridden up, the whole thing slicked with grease and effort.

"Hello?" she said.

The boots stilled. Then a rolling sound, and Dalton Vale slid out from under the car on a creeper board, squinting up at her against the gray morning light. His dark blond hair was pushed back from his face, a smear of grease cutting across one cheekbone, the collar of his henley dark with sweat at the base of his throat. He looked like a man who worked hard and didn't think twice about it, and her throat went embarrassingly dry.

"Amber." He said her name like he'd been expecting her. Not surprised, not formal. Just — like he knew where she'd end up.

"My car's making a noise," she said, because that was the reason she was there, and she was going to stick to it. "A front-end rattle. It gets worse when I brake."

He sat up off the creeper in one fluid motion, wiping his hands on a rag that was already beyond help. His eyes moved past her to her car in the lot, and she watched him take it in the same way he'd taken in everything — quiet, thorough, like he was reading it.

"Pull it into the other bay," he said. "I'll take a look."

She did. He was under it inside of four minutes, and she stood to the side with her coffee cup and tried not to watch the way his arms moved. She watched anyway. The muscles in his forearms shifted under the skin when he reached for tools, and there was a scar on his right elbow that looked old enough to have a story she'd probably never hear. The whole scene had this particular quality of early morning competence that she found deeply, inconveniently attractive.

He was out from under in less than ten minutes. He stood, tossed the rag over his shoulder, and looked at her with that flat, considering expression she was already starting to recognize.

"Your front sway bar link's shot," he said. "Both sides. Rotors are showing wear too. I can do the links today, but I'll need to order the rotors." He paused. "You been driving on this?"

"It only started rattling a couple weeks ago."

"The links have been going longer than that." The way he said it wasn't accusatory, exactly, but it had that quality of someone who was accustomed to other people not noticing things they should have noticed.

"I've been busy," she said.

"I'll get the links done by noon." He moved toward the workbench, already done with the conversation on his end, apparently. "You need a ride to work, I'll drive you."

"You don't have to do that."

"I know." He didn't look up from the parts he was sorting. "I'll drive you."

It wasn't phrased as an offer, exactly. It wasn't phrased as anything except a fact, and she stood there for a second trying to find a reasonable objection and coming up empty. So she got in his truck.

The cab smelled like motor oil and something underneath it — leather, maybe, or the cold mountain air that had followed him in from the morning. The seat was worn soft, the dashboard spare, no air freshener or fast food wrappers or any of the usual human detritus. He drove the way he did everything else: direct, unhurried, not filling the silence with noise.

She looked out the window at the trees going bare along Route 9 and told herself the quiet was just quiet, not charged, not full of things neither of them was saying. She was wrong, obviously. The silence in that cab was practically a presence of its own, sitting between them on the bench seat like a third passenger with opinions.

"How long have you had the garage?" she asked, because apparently she was going to talk into it after all.

"Came back three years ago," he said. "It was my dad's before." "You grew up here?"

"Yeah." A pause. "Left at eighteen. Came back when I needed somewhere to be." He said that last part like it cost him something, or maybe like it was just the plainest true thing he knew how to say about it.

She understood that, actually. She understood it better than she'd like to admit, and she turned back to the window before he could see it on her face.

He dropped her at the bakery without ceremony, and she climbed out and almost said something real to him — she could feel it sitting in her chest, some unguarded thing pressing at the back of her teeth — but she just said thank you, and he nodded, and that was that.

The morning rush was easier when she was busy. Busy was good. Busy meant her brain had somewhere to go that wasn't the envelope in the shoebox in her closet or the way Dalton Vale's jaw tightened when he said *I'll drive you* like he'd already decided and was just letting her catch up.

Lila arrived at nine, slid behind the counter in a cloud of perfume and polka dots, and took one look at Amber's face.

"Okay, what happened?" "Nothing. Car trouble."

"Uh-huh." Lila began refilling the pastry display, but her eyes were doing that thing where they tracked Amber with the focused patience of a woman who had extracted confessions from far more resistant people. "And who fixed said car trouble?"

"Dalton Vale. It's his garage, I dropped it off."

Lila set down a blueberry scone with exaggerated care. "He drove you in, didn't he."

"He offered."

"Honey, Dalton Vale does not *offer* things." She leaned on the counter, voice dropping to the conspiratorial register she reserved for real information. "He hasn't driven a woman anywhere in this town since Jamie Forsythe's car broke down in a snowstorm in 2021 and he gave her a lift to the hospital because she was in actual labor. And that was purely because he was the only one on the road." She paused for effect. "He's never once asked anyone out. Not once. The women in this town have tried — believe me, I've watched it happen — and he just looks at them like they said something in a language he doesn't speak."

"Maybe he just doesn't date," Amber said. She was wiping down the espresso machine and working very hard on sounding uninterested.

"It's more than that." Lila's voice softened a little, like she was handling something careful. "He came back different. Whatever he did in the military— and nobody knows exactly what, because he doesn't talk about it and the discharge papers might as well be redacted — it changed something. He keeps to himself. He fixes things and takes care of his property and he's always real decent when you run into him, but there's this..." She trailed off, searching. "Wall, I guess. Like he decided he was done with something and he's real firm about it."

Amber thought about the silence in the truck cab. The way he'd looked at her car before he even got close to it, like he was assessing risk. *I'll drive you.*

"What was the discharge for?"

"Nobody knows. That's the thing." Lila straightened, shrugging. "He doesn't owe anybody an explanation, and he clearly knows it. Which is either admirable or suspicious depending on your mood." She gave Amber a pointed look. "What's your mood?"

"I don't have a mood. I have a car getting fixed."

"Sure you do." Lila smiled, not unkindly. "Go check your locker. I think there's a jacket you left in there last week, and your break's in ten."

Amber went to the staff room in the back, which was barely a room — a narrow corridor with lockers and a coat rack and a folding chair that nobody ever actually sat in. She spun her combination, pulled the locker open, and reached for the jacket on the hook.

She saw it before she touched it.

It was sitting on the shelf above the hook, propped against the back wall of the locker like it had been placed there deliberately, with care. A single lily, dried and pale, the petals gone papery and faintly translucent at the edges.

White. The exact shade of the arrangement at Marcus's funeral. She knew because she'd stood in front of those flowers for forty minutes not understanding how someone she'd loved could be in a box twenty feet away, and the image had gone straight into the part of her brain that kept things she'd never asked to keep.

Her hand went still on the locker door. The jacket was right there, close enough to touch. She didn't touch it. She didn't move at all for a long, strange moment, her mind doing that thing it did when something was very wrong — going preternaturally quiet, like it was rationing resources.

He's been in here. Not just watching from a distance, not just leaving notes on windshields. In here. In this building, in this room, at her locker. He knew her combination or he'd broken it, and he'd stood in this three-foot corridor and set that flower on the shelf and walked back out through the kitchen, past the ovens, through the space where she worked every morning at four AM with her back to the door.

The walls got closer. She noticed that the way you notice a temperature change — sudden, total, physical. The air turned thin and her pulse went loud in her ears, and she pressed her back against the lockers across from hers and made herself breathe, made herself count, made herself stay in her body instead of going somewhere small and unreachable the way it wanted to. The strip of fluorescent light above her buzzed softly. She focused on that. On the buzz, on the cold metal of the locker at her back, on the fact that she was standing up and breathing and she was fine, she was fine, she was —

She was not fine. She pushed through the staff room door, through the kitchen, and out the back into the alley, and the cold air hit her face like a slap that she was honestly grateful for. She put her hands on her knees and breathed. The brick wall of the building across the alley was close, maybe eight feet, close enough to feel like it was leaning in. A dumpster. A stack of flattened cardboard. The smell of coffee grounds and wet concrete.

She didn't hear him approach. She just became aware, gradually, that she wasn't alone in the alley.

Dalton was standing at the alley entrance, not touching her, not speaking. He had her car keys in one hand. He'd probably come to drop them off, she realized distantly. The links. He'd finished the links.

He took in her posture — hunched forward, hands on her knees, hair falling over her face — and something in him went very still. He crossed the distance between them slowly, the way you'd approach something you didn't want to startle, and he crouched down just slightly to get level with her and held out the keys.

"Here," he said. Low. No inflection that would require her to perform anything back at him.

She took the keys. Her hand was shaking. She watched it shake like it belonged to someone else.

He didn't ask what happened. He didn't say anything at all. He just straightened and stood close enough that she could feel the warmth coming off him in the cold alley air, and after a moment he reached down and wrapped both his large hands around hers — keys and all — and held them. Not squeezing. Not moving. Just steady, warm, present, like ballast.

The shaking started to slow.

She kept her eyes on the brick wall across from them and breathed through her nose and let the warmth of his hands work its way into her fingers, up her wrists, into the ice that had settled in her chest. He didn't rush her. He didn't ask her to explain or look at him or be okay on any particular schedule. He just stood there, solid as the concrete under her feet, and waited.

After a while — she didn't know how long — the shaking stopped.

She should tell him. The thought moved through her, slow and serious. She should tell him about the lily, about the locker, about the photograph under her windshield wiper, about the shoebox in her closet with three envelopes in it. He was right here. He was holding her hands in an alley and not asking for a single thing in return, and some stupid, hopeful part of her wanted to hand it all over to him like he could fix it the way he'd fixed her sway bar links — methodically, quietly, without drama.

But she'd done that once before. She'd told someone she trusted and then she'd spent two years living with what trusting people could cost.

She pulled her hands back gently, and he let her go without hesitation.

"Thank you," she said. Her voice came out steadier than she expected. "For the car. And for — " she gestured vaguely at the space between them, at whatever had just happened.

"You don't have to thank me." He looked at her like he was weighing something, and for one long second she thought he was going to ask anyway — *what happened in there, what are you running from, who found you* — but he didn't. His jaw shifted. He looked at the end of the alley instead. "Keys work fine. Rotors will be in by Monday."

"Okay," she said. "Monday."

He held her gaze for a moment longer than strictly necessary, that particular blue sharpness of his eyes doing the thing where it felt like being read. Then he nodded once, turned, and walked back down the alley toward the street, his footsteps quiet on the wet concrete, disappearing around the corner before she'd fully processed that he'd been there at all.

She stood in the cold and looked at her car keys and thought: *he was already here. Before I even came out. Before I could have called him.*

She turned that over for a moment, studying it from a few different angles.

Then she went back inside, because the morning wasn't done and neither was she, and because there was a dried white lily sitting in her locker and she needed to figure out what to do about it, and falling apart in the alley was only going to help for so long before she needed something more than warmth and steadiness and a pair of careful hands.

She needed to remember that safety and danger could wear the exact same face. She'd learned that lesson already, at a cost she was still paying.

She just wished it didn't feel quite so much like both lived in that particular shade of winter-lake blue.

3
The Midnight Baker

The festival order was her own fault, really. She'd said yes without doing the math, which was a rookie mistake for someone who'd survived on careful calculations for two years. Forty-eight mini loaves of rosemary focaccia, three dozen honey-glazed croissants, and enough cinnamon pull-apart rolls to feed the better half of Cherry Creek — all of it due by seven AM Saturday, which meant she was standing in the Roasted Bean's back kitchen at midnight on Friday with flour on her forearms and the radio playing softly enough that she could hear the street outside.

The street was quiet. That was fine. Quiet was fine.

She told herself that every ten minutes or so, and it almost worked.

The kitchen was hot — the ovens had been running since eight and the ventilation in the old building was a suggestion more than a system. She'd shed her hoodie an hour ago and was working in a tank top now, her hair twisted up and pinned with a spare pencil, a thin sheen of sweat at the back of her neck. The smell in there was good, at least. Yeast and warm butter and the faint sweetness of honey, the kind of smell that lived in your clothes for days and you didn't mind at all. She pressed the heel of her hand into the focaccia dough and felt it push back, elastic and alive, and let the rhythm of it do what it always did: slow her brain down to something manageable.

She'd been at it long enough that her shoulders ached. She rolled them back, reached for the olive oil, and felt it then — that particular prickling along the back of her neck that she'd learned not to dismiss.

She looked up slowly.

The storefront windows were dark squares from this angle, the street beyond them barely lit by the single working lamp on the corner. She couldn't see much. That was the problem. Anyone standing in that

darkness could see her perfectly — lit up and oblivious, moving around in a tank top with flour on her arms like she'd forgotten how exposed glass made you.

She hadn't forgotten. She'd just gotten comfortable, which was somehow worse.

Her hand found the rolling pin on the prep table beside her. Heavy ceramic, solid enough to do real damage, and she'd picked it up in this exact kitchen for this exact reason before she'd ever consciously decided to. She set it close, within reach, and went back to the dough. Her ears were working now, cataloging every sound — the creak of the building settling, the low hiss of the oven, the faint drip of the sink faucet she'd been meaning to report.

The knock made her hand clamp around the rolling pin before she'd even registered the sound fully.

Three beats. Deliberate. The back door.

She stood there for a second, not breathing, her pulse doing something unhelpful behind her ribs. Then a voice came through the door, low and unmistakable.

"It's Dalton."

She exhaled. Set the rolling pin down. Crossed to the door and opened it, and there he was — tall and slightly damp from the mist that had been hanging over the street all night, his flannel open over a gray henley, a set of keys dangling from two fingers.

"Your car's done," he said. "Rotors came in early. I saw your light."

She stepped back to let him in, because the alternative was standing in the doorway having a conversation where the whole town could theoretically hear it, and she was too tired for that kind of performance. He came in, ducking slightly out of habit even though he cleared the frame by a couple of inches, and stopped just inside the door.

The kitchen was small. She hadn't fully accounted for how small it would feel with him in it.

"You're alone out here," he said. It wasn't a question.

"I'm aware." She set the keys on the counter and went back to the focaccia, because the dough wasn't going to work itself and she needed something to do with her hands. "The order's due at seven. I'm fine."

He didn't leave. She could feel him standing behind her, and she was acutely aware of the tank top, the bare skin of her shoulders, the fact that the kitchen was warm enough that the air pressed close and every scent in the room had gotten more concentrated — yeast and honey and, underneath it, something that was distinctly him. Cinnamon, leather, the clean mineral edge of cold night air he'd carried in on his jacket.

She kept working the dough. He moved to lean against the counter along the opposite wall, and she could see him in her peripheral vision, watching her with his arms crossed, that quiet, flat attention he gave everything.

Most people got uncomfortable being watched. She'd expected to. Instead it made her hands feel steadier, which made no logical sense and she decided not to examine it.

"You bake when something's wrong," he said, after a while.

She paused for half a second, then kept going. "I bake because I have forty-eight loaves due at sunrise."

"Yeah." He said it the way he said a lot of things — like he was acknowledging her answer while simultaneously not believing a word of it. His gaze moved to the rolling pin sitting beside the prep table, and something in his expression shifted. "You were expecting someone else when I knocked."

There wasn't much point in lying about the rolling pin. He'd seen her reach for it, probably, and he was the kind of person who noticed things like that without making it a performance. She shaped the first loaf and set it in the pan and reached for the next piece of dough.

"I had a weird feeling," she said. "Someone watching through the windows. Maybe nothing."

The silence after that had a different quality.

"Amber." He said her name like a full sentence, low and serious, and she looked up. He'd pushed off the counter, and he was close now — closer than she'd registered — somewhere in the transit between the wall and the prep table while she'd had her eyes on the dough. The kitchen reorganized itself around the fact of him, warm and too-small and suddenly charged in a way that had nothing to do with the ovens. "You're not safe out here alone."

His voice was barely above a murmur, a gravelly rumble that she felt more than heard, vibrating somewhere below her sternum. She was looking up at him — he had five inches on her, minimum, and the set of his jaw was serious in a way that made her want to take a step back and a step closer simultaneously, which was not a sensation she had a good protocol for.

"I've been closing alone since October," she said.

"I know." His blue eyes held hers, and there it was again, that feeling of being read — not judged, just *read*, like he was taking inventory of something. His hands were at his sides, loose. He wasn't touching her. The air between them was doing something all on its own. "Doesn't make it smart."

She should have stepped back. The rational version of her, the careful two-years-in-Cherry-Creek version, understood this clearly. Instead she stayed exactly where she was, flour on her forearms, hair falling loose from the pencil, close enough to him that she could feel the warmth radiating off his chest and smell the night air cooling on his jacket.

"You came to drop off keys," she said. "At midnight."

"Finished late." His jaw shifted. His eyes dropped briefly, almost imperceptibly, to her mouth, and then came back up. "You were lit up like a target."

Something about the way he said it — not unkind, just raw and honest — made her breath catch. She could see the faint scar cutting through his left eyebrow, close enough now to trace it if she'd been that kind of reckless. She wasn't. She was the kind of person who kept her hands on the dough and her eyes level and didn't let herself want things she couldn't afford to want.

Except right now she was failing completely at all three.

He leaned in, slow and deliberate, one hand coming to rest on the edge of the prep table beside her, not touching, just bracketing, and she tipped her chin up and thought — clearly, with the part of her brain that was still functional — *this is about to happen, this is actually about to—*

The window exploded.

Not a crack. Not a chip. The sound was a full, violent crash, glass shattering across the tile of the storefront, a heavy something thudding across the floor in the dark. She flinched hard, her shoulder slamming back against the prep table, and Dalton was already moving — not away from the sound, *toward* it, which her brain flagged as significant even in the half-second she had to process anything.

"Stay back." He said it over his shoulder, clipped and absolute.

She didn't stay back. She followed him to the doorway between the kitchen and the storefront and stopped there, watching.

There was a hole in the front window, glass fanned out across the floor and the nearest table, a chunk of concrete block sitting in the middle of it all like it had always been there. The street outside was dark. The mist caught the corner lamp and turned it into a soft orange smear, and beyond that — nothing. No movement. No one running.

Dalton moved through the storefront like he'd changed into a different person. The unhurried, quiet man who'd leaned against her kitchen counter was gone. This version of him moved in a pattern that wasn't random — he kept low when he passed the window, angled wide, checked the blind corners first. His hand went to the back of his waistband and then stilled, like he'd reached for something out of habit and remembered it wasn't there. He went to the door, turned the lock, cracked it two inches, and scanned the street in a way that was methodical and fast and nothing like a man who fixed cars for a living.

"Gone," he said, after a moment that felt very long.

Amber looked at the concrete block on the floor. Something made her cross to it, picking her way through the glass carefully in her work clogs, crouching down. There was a piece of paper rubber-banded around it, and she pulled it free and unrolled it and read the words printed there in thick black marker.

Then she went to the window and looked out at the sidewalk.

Spray paint. Red, like something urgent, like something that couldn't wait for a more civilized medium. The letters were big enough to read from twenty feet away, which was probably the point: **SHARING ISN'T ALLOWED.**

Her stomach turned over hard and slow.

Dalton appeared beside her, and she heard the small, controlled exhale he made when he read it. She kept her eyes on the words and focused on breathing. The wet concrete smell from outside mixed with the cooling-butter smell from the kitchen and she focused on that, on the physical world, on staying in her body.

"He was watching us," she said. Her voice came out flat and strange. "Through the window. While we were—"

"Yeah."

The single syllable landed heavy. She turned to look at him and found him already looking at her, his expression doing something complicated — controlled, still, but underneath it something that looked a lot like fury and a lot like guilt, and she didn't know what to do with either.

"This isn't the first time," she said. She hadn't planned to say it. But he was standing in her kitchen at midnight with glass all over the floor and his eyes on hers, and she was so tired of carrying it alone. "There have been notes. And something left in my locker at work. And I think — I think he's been watching me for a while."

Dalton was quiet for three full seconds. Then: "How long?" "Since before I came here." She swallowed. "Maybe longer."

His jaw set. He looked back out at the red letters on the sidewalk, and something in his face went very still, the way a room goes still right before a storm decides what it's going to do.

"I need to go back out there," he said. "Check the alley, the side street. See if he left anything."

"He's gone. You said—"

"He's gone from the front." He looked at her directly. "Stay inside. Lock the door behind me."

She wanted to argue. She swallowed it, because he was right and she knew it and arguing just to prove she didn't need managing wasn't going to help either of them tonight. She followed him to the back door and turned the deadbolt after he slipped out, and then she stood in the kitchen with the smell of butter and yeast and the soft sound of the radio still playing — something slow and distant, some country station she'd tuned in for company — and she looked at her forty-eight loaves waiting to be shaped and thought: *he was out there the whole time.*

Watching her through the glass. Watching *them.*

The word *sharing* sat in her chest like a swallowed stone.

Dalton was back in six minutes. She knew because she counted, because counting was something to do. He came through the back door, relocked it, and stood in the kitchen with that particular stillness of someone who'd found nothing and wasn't happy about it.

"Nothing in the alley," he said. "No prints that'll hold, the mist got to them. He knew what he was doing." He looked at her. "You're calling the sheriff in the morning."

"I was planning to." "Tonight."

"It's midnight, Dalton."

"There's a shattered window and a message on the sidewalk." His voice was flat, no argument in it, just certainty. "That's not a morning problem."

She reached for her phone. He was right about that too, which was starting to be a pattern she found both reassuring and quietly maddening.

The deputy who came out was young and apologetic and took photos of everything with the thoroughness of someone who understood procedure but not urgency. Dalton stood off to the side with his arms crossed and watched the whole thing with an expression she couldn't fully read, and when the deputy suggested the window might be local kids getting rowdy ahead of the festival, Amber saw Dalton's jaw tighten in a way that meant he was making a deliberate choice not to say something.

She appreciated that more than she could articulate.

After the deputy left, she finished the remaining loaves on autopilot, working through the motions while Dalton sat on the stool near the back wall and didn't leave.

He didn't offer help. He didn't crowd her. He just stayed, a warm, solid presence in the corner of the room, his eyes moving occasionally to the boarded-up window the deputy had helped them cover with a piece of cardboard from the storeroom.

When the last tray was in the oven, she leaned back against the counter and looked at him.

"You don't have to stay," she said.

"I know." He held her gaze. "I'm staying."

She thought about the near-miss before the window shattered — his hand on the edge of the table beside her, the lean of him, the way the air between them had felt like something about to break open. She thought about the red letters on the sidewalk outside and the word *sharing* and the fact that someone had been watching long enough to feel ownership over something that wasn't even a thing yet.

She thought about how he'd moved through the storefront — low, angled, deliberate, checking corners in a sequence that wasn't instinct, it was *training*. The hand that had gone to his waistband and stopped.

She filed all of it away in the part of her brain that didn't sleep. "Thank you," she said finally. "For staying."

He nodded once. Looked at the oven timer, then back at her. "You should eat something," he said. "You've been in here for hours."

She almost laughed. She almost said *you sound like someone's dad*, but she didn't, because the kitchen was still warm and the night outside was still dark and she was standing four feet from a man who made her feel safer and more unsettled at the same time, and making a joke felt like the wrong way to spend whatever this moment was.

She pulled a croissant off the cooling rack instead and held it out to him. He took it without ceremony, and she took one for herself, and they stood in the hot little kitchen and ate in silence while the ovens hummed and the mist pressed against the boarded window and somewhere outside on the sidewalk, red letters dried slowly in the dark.

Sharing isn't allowed.

Whoever had written it was still out there. She knew that. Dalton knew it too— she could see it in the way his eyes moved to the door every few minutes, never fully at rest, always scanning. Like he was waiting for the next thing.

Like he already knew what it would be.

She watched him from the corner of her eye and told herself that the warmth in her chest was just the ovens, just the physical fact of a warm room on a cold night, nothing that meant anything or cost anything or would come back around to hurt her later.

She was getting pretty good at lying to herself. She'd had a lot of practice.

But her eyes stayed on him, and the night stretched long, and outside in the dark, the red words waited for morning like a promise someone had made without being asked.

4

A Ghost in the creek

Sheriff Tate Landry's office smelled like old coffee and the particular brand of indifference that came from behind a government-issue desk. Amber had been in rooms like this before. She knew the smell.

She sat in the hard plastic chair across from him and watched him review the photos on her phone — the spray paint on the sidewalk, the caved-in window, the concrete block — with the same expression a person wore when they were doing math they already knew the answer to. Slow. Polite. Unhurried by any actual concern.

"Festival weekend," he said finally, setting her phone on the desk and sliding it back to her. "Gets some yahoos riled up. We had a mailbox taken out on Birch Street just last Thursday. A mailbox." He said it like it was relevant.

Amber looked at him. "There was a message on the sidewalk."

"I saw the photo." He leaned back in his chair, the springs giving a tired groan. "Sharing isn't allowed. Kids get weird ideas from the internet. Could be anything."

"There were also notes," she said. "At least three. Delivered to my apartment and to my locker at work."

He picked up his pen. "You bring those in?"

"The last one, yes. I gave it to Deputy Marsh last night."

"Mmm." He wrote something, or pretended to. "You're new here, Ms. Rowan. Moved in — what, four months back?"

"Five."

"Right." He tapped the pen against his notepad. "Sometimes when people move to a new place, small-town folk can be a little — territorial. Prank stuff. Usually burns itself out."

She felt the old familiar sting of it, that particular dismissal that dressed itself up as reason. *Usually burns itself out.* That's what the detective in the city had said too, two years ago, sitting across from her in a room that also smelled like bad coffee and institutional carpet. *These things usually resolve themselves, Ms. Rowan. We'll be in touch.* They hadn't been in touch. Not once.

"This isn't local kids being territorial," she said. She kept her voice even, forcing the sharp, jagged retort that was clawing at her throat back down into her chest. She'd learned the hard way that emotion in rooms like this got labeled as instability, so she purposefully smoothed her expression into something blank and professional, refusing to let him see even a flicker of the frustration boiling beneath the surface.

Landry studied her for a moment, his steel-gray eyes doing a quick, professional read of her face. She watched him almost decide to take her seriously, and then watched him not.

"I'll have a talk with Marsh," he said. "Have him look into it. But I'd encourage you not to read too much into spray paint, Ms. Rowan. Small town. People notice newcomers." He stood, which was apparently her cue to leave. "You have any more incidents, you call us right away."

She stood. Picked up her phone. Smiled with her mouth only. "Sure," she said. "Thanks for your time."

Outside, the morning air was cool and thin, the kind that came after a night of mist and made everything smell faintly of wet bark and damp asphalt.

She stood on the sidewalk outside the sheriff's office and breathed it in and thought about the red letters drying on the pavement outside her workplace and the concrete block on the floor and Dalton's hand going to his waistband out of habit before he'd stopped himself.

She was so tired of being told her own experience was exaggerated.

She started walking. The diner was two blocks east; she needed coffee and something to do with the energy buzzing under her skin before she did something inadvisable, like going back inside and saying some very specific things to Sheriff Landry about what it felt like to watch your case get shelved while your attacker walked around free.

She made it about half a block before she almost walked directly into someone coming out of the hardware store doorway.

"Whoa." The woman caught herself on the doorframe, a paper bag tucked under one arm. She had platinum hair cut sharp at her jaw and icy blue eyes that assessed Amber in about two seconds flat. She was wearing a black leather jacket over a dress that was too short for the weather and not caring about it at all. "Watch where you're going, city girl."

Amber took a step back. "Sorry. I wasn't—"

"Amber Rowan." The woman said it like she'd been waiting to say it, which was immediately unsettling. "You work at the Roasted Bean."

"Yeah." Amber looked at her more carefully. She'd seen her around — behind the bar at the dive place on Route 9, usually, looking like she'd rather be somewhere else. "You work at Harley's."

"Nora Fisk." She shifted the paper bag. Up close, there was something underneath the sharp exterior — a tiredness, not the lazy kind but the kind that came from carrying something heavy for a long time. "I heard about your window."

"Word travels."

"Honey, this is Cherry Creek. Word doesn't travel, it teleports." She tilted her head, studying Amber with an expression that wasn't unfriendly, exactly, but wasn't warm either. "Can I buy you a coffee?"

Amber hesitated. Her internal alarm system, which had been humming at a low, jagged frequency for two years, spiked into a sharp, electric hum at the base of her skull. It did a quick, frantic scan of the woman—the way she held her shoulders, the lack of a wedding ring, the faint scent of stale cigarette smoke clinging to her leather—and came back with a messy, inconclusive ping: *not a threat, but definitely not neutral either.*

"Because I've got something to tell you and I'd rather not say it standing on Main Street." Nora glanced around, a fast, habitual sweep that Amber recognized because she did the same thing. "And because you look like you just got out of a room that disappointed you, and I know what that looks like."

The diner was warm and smelled like bacon fat and maple syrup. They took a corner booth. Nora ordered black coffee and Amber ordered the same, which seemed to earn some small increment of approval.

"My sister died three weeks ago," Nora said, without preamble, wrapping her hands around her mug. "Hit-and-run, out on Route 12. Sheriff called it an accident."

"I'm sorry," Amber said.

"Yeah." Nora's jaw worked. "The thing is, before she died — she was talking about you. A girl from the city who owed her money. She described you. Auburn hair, small, runs in the morning."

The coffee mug felt suddenly very cold against Amber's palms. "I don't know your sister."

"Maybe not by name." Nora's blue eyes held hers, steady and direct. "Her name was Cassie. Cassie Fisk. She was in the city two years ago. Tended bar off Delancey Street."

The room did something strange. Amber heard the clatter of dishes somewhere behind her and the muted conversation of other booths and underneath all of it, a high, thin ringing that lived in the space between a memory she had and a memory she didn't.

"Two years ago," she said carefully.

"She saw something," Nora said. "She told me once, drunk, that she'd seen something bad happen to a girl and she'd panicked and run. That she'd meant to come forward but then things got complicated and then more time passed and—" She stopped. Looked at her coffee. "She was scared. She wasn't a brave person, my sister. I loved her anyway."

Amber set her mug down. Her hands were not entirely steady. "She was a witness."

"I think so." Nora met her eyes again. "And now she's dead. And you're here getting your window smashed and messages spray-painted on the sidewalk." She paused. "You see what I'm seeing?"

Amber saw it. She'd been seeing the shape of it for weeks, in the dark, when her brain wouldn't stop assembling puzzle pieces she hadn't asked for. She just hadn't wanted to say it out loud because saying it out loud made it real and real meant she couldn't pretend anymore that this was containable.

"Why are you telling me this?" she asked.

"Because Cassie's dead and the sheriff thinks it's an accident and I've been sitting with it for three weeks trying to figure out who to tell." Nora's voice was flat and careful, the voice of someone who'd cried about this already and was past the point of doing it in public. "And because whoever scared her bad enough to stay quiet for two years is apparently still out there, and you seem like the kind of person who's going to keep walking straight into it whether I warn you or not."

Amber almost smiled at that. Almost. "That's an accurate read."

"I know." Nora pulled a business card from her jacket pocket — the bar's logo on it, her cell number written in black ink underneath — and slid it across the table. "You find out anything. You call me. Not the sheriff. He's not going to do a damn thing with it."

Amber took the card. She looked at it for a moment, at the neat handwriting, and thought about Cassie Fisk tending bar off Delancey and seeing something and running. She thought about what it must have cost Nora to sit across from a stranger and say all of this.

"Thank you," she said.

Nora picked up her coffee. "Don't thank me yet."

She took the shortcut home because she needed to think, and the shortcut ran along the edge of the woods behind the post office, a dirt path through a thin stretch of trees that shaved six minutes off the walk. She knew it was probably not her best decision, given the morning she'd had. She took it anyway. The path was familiar and daylight was still good and she needed the quiet of it, the cold air and the crunch of leaves underfoot and the way the trees opened up just enough to let in pale gray sky.

She was about halfway through when she saw it.

A flash of auburn caught against a low-hanging branch, maybe eight feet off the path. She stopped. Looked at it properly. It was a hair ribbon — thin satin, the deep red-brown color she'd stopped wearing after the incident because it had been part of a habit she'd wanted to leave behind, and then she'd started again sometime in September because it was just a ribbon and she was trying to stop letting objects have power over her.

She'd lost this one last week. She'd thought she'd dropped it at the bakery. Her brain worked through that very quietly.

She took one step off the path toward it. Then another. The ribbon was tied to the branch in a neat bow, deliberate, which meant it wasn't dropped. It was placed. She reached up and untied it slowly, the satin cool against her fingers, and stood holding it while her pulse did something unpleasant.

Four feet further into the trees, there was another one.

She should have turned around. She knew she should have turned around. Instead she followed it, moving through the trees with her phone in her hand, following the trail of small red-brown bows from branch to branch until the trees thinned into a small clearing she hadn't known was there, tucked back from the path and sheltered on three sides by old pines.

The clearing had a flat rock at its center. On the rock, arranged with a care that made her stomach turn completely over: photographs. Her photographs. Printed on regular paper, some blurry, all of them taken without her knowledge — her running on the morning path, her at the bakery window, her on her apartment steps in the early dark. Around the photos, a loose ring of objects she recognized: a coffee cup she'd thrown away, a grocery receipt, a sock she'd been missing for three weeks and had assumed went the way of all socks.

Her trash. He'd been going through her trash.

She stood at the edge of the clearing and looked at all of it and felt the bottom drop out of her stomach in a long, slow fall. This wasn't a note slipped under a door or spray paint on a sidewalk. This was a person who spent time here. This was a person who came back.

This was a person who thought of this as his.

She raised her phone and shot photos of everything, her hands steadier than she had any right to expect, and then she turned to go back to the path and that's when she heard it — a dry, definite crack of a branch somewhere behind her and to the left, in the deeper trees.

She ran.

Not a jog. Not a careful retreat. She flat-out ran, crashing back through the underbrush the way she'd come, branches catching at her jacket, her boots finding every root and uneven patch of ground that existed in those woods. Her lungs burned almost immediately from the cold air and she didn't care, she just kept moving, because every horror movie instinct she'd ever rolled her eyes at was apparently hardwired after all, and right now they were all screaming the same thing.

She hit something solid. Not a tree. A chest.

She reeled back, both hands coming up automatically, and then a grip closed around her upper arm — firm, controlled — and she looked up and it was Dalton.

He was in the woods. He was standing in the woods on the edge of the path she'd left, wearing his flannel and worn jeans and boots that were, she noticed with a lurch that bypassed every other thought in her head, dark with something that was not mud. His other hand was at his side, and in it, a hunting knife with a blade that was clean. The rest of him was not entirely clean. There was a smear along the side of his right boot, brownish-dark, and another on the hem of his jeans.

She stopped fighting his grip. She looked at his face, which was set in an expression she couldn't immediately name — controlled, hard, the jaw muscle jumping. His blue eyes swept over her quickly, checking, the way they always did, and then they went past her to the trees she'd come out of.

"Hey." His voice was low. "Hey, look at me. You're okay."

"There's a shrine," she said. Her voice came out strange, breathless and flat at the same time. "In a clearing back there. My photos. My trash. He built a — it's been there a while, it's not — someone made it deliberately, Dalton, it's been there—"

"I know." He said it quietly, and something in the way he said it made her go still.

She looked at him. At the knife. At his boots. "What are you doing out here?"

"Tracking a coyote." He said it evenly. "Been taking chickens from the Harmon place."

She looked at the blood on his boot again. It was the wrong color for an animal that size, and the wrong pattern — too much of it, and it hadn't dried the way mud dried. She'd grown up bouncing between enough different places to know what blood looked like when it was fresh enough to still be dark.

"That's not coyote blood," she said.

He didn't answer right away. His eyes came back to her face, and she saw something move through them — not guilt, exactly, but something in the same family. Something that knew it had been caught and was deciding what to do about that.

"Amber." He said her name the way he always did, like it meant more than she'd given it permission to mean. "You should go home."

"I just came from the sheriff's office," she said. "He told me the window was local kids and to relax. Then a woman told me her sister — a witness to my assault — is dead. And now you're standing in the woods next to a stalker's shrine with blood on your boots telling me to go home." She held his gaze. "So I'm going to need more than a coyote story."

The woods were quiet around them. A bird somewhere, the distant sound of a car on the main road, the creak of the pines in the light wind. Dalton looked at her for a long moment, and she watched him weigh something — she could see it happening, the internal calculation behind those blue eyes, the same controlled stillness she'd watched him use every time he was deciding how much to give her.

He hadn't put the knife away.

"I found the shrine three days ago," he said finally. His voice was quiet and careful. "I've been coming back to watch it. See if he returned."

"And did he?"

A pause that was its own kind of answer. "What did you do?" she asked.

"Made sure he knew the area wasn't unguarded," he said. It was the most careful sentence she'd ever heard, built specifically to avoid answering what she'd actually asked.

She looked at the blood on his boot one more time, and then back at his face, and the thing she felt wasn't fear, exactly. It was something more complicated than fear, something that lived in the same neighborhood as fear but also in the neighborhood of something she didn't want to name yet because naming it would require trusting her own judgment and her judgment had gotten her into serious trouble before.

"You should have told me," she said. "Yeah." He held her gaze. "I know."

The wind moved through the trees, cold and sharp, carrying the smell of pine and wet earth and underneath it, faint but unmistakable, something metallic that she didn't want to identify. She tucked the hair ribbon into her jacket pocket. Her photos were still back in that clearing on that rock, arranged by someone who thought of her as a collection rather than a person.

"Walk me home," she said.

He fell into step beside her without a word, the knife disappearing somewhere she didn't track. They walked out of the trees and onto the path and back toward the apartment in the thin morning light, and she was aware of every sound around them and aware of him beside her and aware that she still had approximately a thousand unanswered questions, and that the blood on his boots had not come from a coyote, and that she was choosing to walk beside him anyway.

She filed that choice away with everything else. There was getting to be quite a collection.

Behind them, the woods were quiet. Whatever had been watching had gone still. And somewhere in the clearing she'd left behind, her photographs sat on a flat rock in the pale light, patient as anything, waiting for someone to come back to them.

She didn't look back. But she felt it, the whole walk home. That particular feeling of being watched by something that believed it had a right to look.

It was a feeling she'd been living with for two years. She was starting to think she'd be living with it for a while longer yet.

5
The Wolf's Lair

She'd spent the whole walk home telling herself she wasn't going to do it.

She was going to take a shower, make coffee, sit at her kitchen table with her laptop, and do something sensible and grounded like pay a bill or look up the bus schedule to Albany. She was *not* going to spend the rest of her Tuesday fixating on the blood on Dalton Vale's boots, or the way he'd said *I found the shrine three days ago* like it was the most reasonable thing in the world, like he'd just casually decided to surveil a stalker's crime scene without telling her and that was totally fine.

She lasted about forty minutes.

The garage sat at the end of Birch Street where the road curved away from town proper, a converted two-bay structure with a hand-painted sign that read VALE AUTO above the roll-up doors. One door was halfway up when she arrived, letting out a wash of warm air that smelled like motor oil and rubber and something underneath it, something that she'd come to associate specifically with him — cedar, maybe, or just the particular warmth of a space that a person occupied enough to leave their trace on it.

She ducked under the door without knocking, because knocking felt ridiculous.

Dalton was under a truck, only his legs visible from the knees down, one boot crossed over the other in a way that looked almost relaxed. Classic rock drifted from a battered radio on a shelf near the wall, low enough to hear over but loud enough to cover the sound of her entrance. She stood there for a second, looking at the space — the neat rows of tools on pegboards, the stacks of tires along the back wall, and a small, meticulously maintained workbench dedicated solely to restoring old, discarded clockwork gears. It was a jarringly delicate hobby for a man with hands that looked like they were made for breaking things, the tiny brass components gleaming under a focused lamp. The smell of grease and old metal mixed with that cedar warmth, and she thought: *he lives here more than he lives in whatever apartment he actually sleeps in.*

"You want to start with the boots, or should I?" she said.

A pause. Then the low roll of wheels on concrete as he slid out from under the truck, blinking up at her from the floor with an expression that said he wasn't entirely surprised to see her. He sat up slowly. Wiped his hands on a rag he pulled from his back pocket. His flannel was pushed to the elbows, forearms streaked with grease, and he looked up at her with those blue eyes doing that thing they did, that careful, measuring assessment that she was starting to find deeply irritating because she could never quite read what it concluded.

"Amber." He got to his feet.

"Don't." She held up one hand. "Don't say my name like that and expect it to derail me. I want a straight answer about what happened in those woods."

He studied her. Looked like he was going to say something. Then his phone went off, buzzing loud from the workbench against the far wall, and he glanced at it, jaw tightening.

"Give me two minutes," he said. "I'll wait."

He crossed to the workbench and picked up the phone, turning his back to her, and she could hear the low rumble of his voice but not the words, could see the tension in his shoulders, the way his free hand pressed flat against the bench like he needed the contact. Whatever the call was about, it wasn't good news.

She didn't mean to snoop. That was what she would tell herself later, and it would be about seventy percent true. What actually happened was that she drifted toward the back wall where the tires were stacked, because she was restless and the call was taking longer than two minutes and she needed to do something with her hands, and when she leaned against the stack nearest the corner to wait, the top two tires shifted slightly, and she automatically grabbed them to stop them falling, and that's when she saw the floor beneath them.

A panel. Flush with the concrete, almost invisible, with a small recessed pull handle that would be totally hidden under a full stack.

She looked at Dalton's back. Still on the phone. His voice had gone quieter, sharper.

She looked back at the panel.

She hooked two fingers through the handle and pulled.

It came up on a hinge, smooth and well-maintained, revealing a steel safe set into the concrete below — maybe eighteen inches square, a combination dial on the face. It was closed but not locked; the dial was spun to zero and the handle turned freely in her hand. She told herself not to open it. Then she opened it.

Inside: a folded piece of paper. A burner phone, old, the kind you bought with cash. A folded utility knife. And a small velvet pouch, drawstring, the kind you got from a jewelry store when you bought something that came in a box.

She picked up the pouch. It weighed almost nothing. She loosened the drawstring, tilted it over her palm.

A silver locket slid out.

It was small and oval, the silver worn soft at the edges, with a tiny engraved pattern on the front that she'd traced with her thumbnail a thousand times. A bird in flight, wings spread. Her mother's locket — technically the only thing she had from her mother, because her mother had died without leaving much — and she'd worn it every day for six years until the night she'd lost it. The night she'd told herself it was just gone.

That things got lost in violence and you let them go or they dragged you under.

Her hand closed around it. The metal was cool against her palm and she stood there and felt the familiar weight of it and the whole world contracted down to that sensation, that specific small pressure, and her heart did something horrible against her ribs.

He had it. He had her locket. He'd had it for two years and he'd never said a word.

Her phone buzzed in her pocket.

She almost didn't look. When she did, the notification was from an unknown number — a link, private, no preview text. She clicked it, and her stomach dropped straight through the concrete floor.

It was a video feed. Live. High-angle, slightly fisheye, shot from somewhere near the ceiling in the corner of the garage. And in the center of the frame, standing over an open floor safe with a silver locket in her hand, was her.

She watched herself standing there for one surreal, nauseating second. Then the text came through below the link.

He didn't save you, Little Bird. He just moved you to a smaller cage.

She looked up at the ceiling. Found the camera in about four seconds — a small black disk, barely bigger than a smoke detector, nestled in the corner joint above a shelving unit. It had a clear sightline to the entire back half of the garage.

The hydraulic door groaned.

Loud, mechanical, the sound of heavy steel on track, and she spun around as the roll-up door she'd ducked under dropped the rest of the way to the floor with a solid, final bang. The radio cut out. The garage went dim, the only light coming from the fluorescents overhead and the pale strip of daylight under the side door, and the shadows jumped and settled and in the middle of all of it, Dalton stood at the door controls on the wall, his phone gone, his eyes fixed on the locket in her hand.

The silence lasted about three seconds. It felt longer.

"You weren't supposed to find that yet, Amber." His voice was flat. Not cold, exactly — more like a temperature that hadn't decided yet what it was going to become. All the quiet warmth she'd cataloged in him, the low careful way he spoke to her, the particular gentleness he deployed when she was scared — none of it was in his voice right now. He sounded stripped of it. "Not like this."

She took a step back. Her shoulders hit the edge of the workbench behind her, the metal cold through her hoodie, and she gripped the locket tighter and held her ground even though every self-preservation instinct she owned was running a very loud, very clear diagnostic that said *door, side door, now.*

"Then how?" Her voice came out steadier than she deserved. "When were you planning to tell me you had it? Next year? Never?"

He crossed the garage toward her, not fast, but the deliberateness of it was its own kind of pressure. He moved the way he always moved — quiet, controlled, like a man who'd spent years learning how to take up exactly as much space as he intended. He stopped about six feet away and just looked at her, and she looked back, and she was absolutely not going to let him see how hard her heart was slamming against her sternum.

"I found it at the scene," he said. "The night you were attacked." She heard that. She processed it. Then: "The night I was attacked." "Yeah."

"You were there."

Something moved through his expression, quick and controlled and gone before she could name it. "Yeah."

The workbench bit into her lower back. She was leaning into it without realizing it, putting as much distance as the space allowed between them while the information rearranged itself in her head. Dalton, in Cherry Creek, running a garage, showing up in her woods with a hunting knife and blood on his boots. Dalton, in New York City, two years ago, at the scene of her attack.

"Say all of it," she said. "Right now. All of it."

He looked at her for another long moment. Then he pulled one of the shop stools away from the workbench and sat down on it, forearms on his knees, like he was making himself smaller on purpose — like he understood that standing over her right now was not a great choice. She appreciated the gesture even while she was furious about needing it.

"I was in the city," he said. "Doing a job — private, not military, I was already out by then. I was cutting through that alley on my way back to my car. I heard you." He stopped. His jaw worked. "I heard him, first. And then you."

She didn't say anything.

"I intervened," he said. "He ran when I came in. I called 911 from a payphone two blocks away because I couldn't be the one who found you — I had a weapon on me that I wasn't supposed to have, and there were complications from the job I'd just come from, and if I'd stayed and the police had run my name, it would have—" He stopped again. "It would have been bad. For me and for other people. So I called and I left."

"You left me there," she said.

"I left you there," he said. No deflection, no softening. Just the words, sitting between them like a fact.

She thought about that. About waking up in a hospital with a two-hour gap where her memory should have been, with a nurse telling her that an anonymous caller had reported her and that the responding officers hadn't found anyone else at the scene. She'd spent months trying to figure out who that caller was. She'd stopped because the trying was destroying her.

"You took the locket," she said.

"It was in the dirt, about three feet from you. I picked it up. I don't know why— I just couldn't leave it there for the cops to bag and lose." He looked at his hands. "Evidence from cases like yours has a way of disappearing when the detectives aren't invested. I knew that. I thought I'd find a way to return it." He raised his eyes to her. "I didn't have a way to return it without explaining how I had it."

"So you moved to my town." A beat. "Not immediately." "But eventually."

"I kept track of you," he said. "After. I knew who he was — the man who attacked you. Rory Keane. I knew the cops weren't going to make anything stick. I knew he was going to come back around eventually, because men like him always do." His voice dropped a register. "When you moved here, I was already watching his movements. When he started moving toward Cherry Creek, I moved faster."

She stared at him. Her phone was still in her hand, the live feed still open, and she was standing in a locked garage with a man who had just told her he'd been watching her for two years, and she should be terrified, and she *was* terrified, but she was also — and this was the part that scared her most — she was also angry in a way that felt almost clarifying. Like it was burning off the fog she'd been living in and leaving something sharp behind.

"There's a camera up there," she said. She pointed at the corner. "Someone put a camera in your garage."

His eyes went to it, and something hardened in his face in a way she'd never seen before — not controlled, not measured, just cold and flat and very, very focused. He was on his feet before she'd finished pointing, crossing to the shelving unit, and she watched him scan the setup with the quick efficiency of someone who knew exactly what they were looking for.

"He's been in here," Dalton said. It wasn't a question.

"I got a live feed to my phone. A text with it." She turned her phone toward him. He read the message, and she watched something move across his expression that she'd only glimpsed before — a rage so tightly contained it barely registered on the surface, but she could feel the heat of it from where she stood.

"When did this come in?"

"About four minutes ago. Right after I found the safe."

He looked at the camera again. Then at her. Then at the locket she was still holding, and she realized her fist had been closed around it this entire time, the engraved bird pressing its shape into her palm.

"He's been watching this space," Dalton said. "Watching me. Watching you come here." He pulled out his phone and she watched him type something fast, then set it face-down on the workbench. "He knows you found it."

"Great," she said. "That's just great. So in addition to having a stalker who knows where I live and what I throw away and apparently how to install cameras in other people's garages, I also have—" She gestured at him, a sweep that encompassed the garage and the safe and all of the preceding conversation. "This."

"Amber."

"No." She pressed her free hand flat against the workbench because she needed something solid. "You don't get to say my name in that voice right now. You hid the fact that you were there. You hid the locket. You moved here and didn't tell me why and let me believe I was losing my mind, let me go to a sheriff who thinks I'm hysterical, and the whole time you knew exactly who was sending those notes because you already knew who he was." She pulled a breath. "How long were you going to let it go on before you told me any of this?"

He didn't look away. He didn't offer her anything easy. "I was trying to handle it before it got to you."

"Handle it," she repeated.

"End it," he said, and the flat simplicity of it landed like a stone in still water, and she understood clearly and completely what he meant and didn't ask him to clarify.

The garage was quiet around them. The fluorescents buzzed faintly overhead. She could smell motor oil and cedar and her own adrenaline, which she was pretty sure was a real thing, and she stood there holding her dead mother's locket and looking at this man who had saved her life and kept secrets from her for two years and locked her in a garage and was watching her with those blue eyes like she was the only thing in the room that mattered, and she thought: *I should hate this. I should be running.*

She wasn't running.

That was the part she was going to have to sit with later, the part that felt like the most honest and also the most alarming thing she knew about herself in this moment. She was backed against a cold workbench in a locked garage with a man who had just dismantled every assumption she'd built her sense of safety on, and she wasn't running. Her fear was real and her anger was real and underneath both of them, like a current she couldn't shut off, was something else entirely.

He stepped toward her. One step, slow, giving her every opportunity to tell him to stop.

She didn't tell him to stop.

He reached out, and his hand closed gently around hers — around the fist she'd made with the locket in it — and he didn't try to take it from her. He just covered her hand with his, warm and steady, and stood close enough that she could feel the heat off his chest and smell the cedar and grease and underneath it, faint, the particular scent of him that she'd been cataloging against her will for weeks.

"I'm sorry," he said. His voice was different now — lower, rougher, like something had worn through the careful surface of it. "I know that doesn't fix it."

She looked up at him. This close, she could see the faint scar through his left eyebrow, the shadows under his eyes that she'd stopped reading as general exhaustion and was now reading as something more specific. She could see the way he was watching her, that particular focused attention that she'd spent weeks telling herself meant nothing.

"No," she said. "It doesn't."

His thumb moved over her knuckles, once, slow.

"You should have told me," she said. Her voice came out quieter than she intended.

"I know." He didn't move away. "I know I should have."

Outside, a car passed on Birch Street, its headlights sweeping briefly through the gap under the side door. The sound of it faded. The garage settled back into its particular quiet, and she stood there with her hand in his and her heart doing something complicated and unreasonable, and she thought about Rory Keane somewhere in this town with a camera feed open on his phone, watching.

She thought about that message. *He just moved you to a smaller cage.*

She thought about Dalton's hands, and his boots, and the hunting knife, and the words *end it* spoken with such complete certainty.

She thought about the fact that she was still holding the locket. That she hadn't put it down.

She opened her hand. The small silver oval lay in her palm, the bird with its wings spread, and she looked at it for a moment and then she closed her fingers around it again, tucking it against her chest.

"Who else knows you were there that night?" she asked. "No one."

"Rory knows."

"Yeah." His jaw was tight. "He knows I intervened. That's why he's here. That's what the message means — he's not just coming back for you. He's coming for me too, and you're the leverage."

She turned that over. The shape of it, the logic of a man like that, the territorial ugliness of it. *He stole you from me. So I'll take you back and make him watch.* She'd been in this story before, on the other end of it, and she knew how men like that kept score.

"He's going to do something soon," she said. "Yes."

"Then we need a plan that isn't just you handling it in the dark and hoping I don't notice." She looked up at him. "I need to know what's happening. All of it, from here out. No more managed information."

Something shifted in his face. Not surrender — more like recognition. Like she'd said the one thing he hadn't let himself expect.

"Okay," he said.

"Okay," she echoed, and the word felt like the start of something she couldn't entirely name yet, something that lived in the same complicated territory as fear and fury and the warm, steady weight of his hand over hers.

She looked at the camera in the corner one more time. Somewhere on the other end of that feed, Rory Keane was watching her stand in Dalton's garage, holding her mother's locket, and thinking he understood what he was seeing.

He didn't understand what he was seeing. That, at least, she was sure of.

She pulled her hand back, tucked the locket into her hoodie pocket, and straightened up off the workbench. "You should take that camera down," she said. "And then you should tell me everything, from the beginning." She met his eyes. "I mean it, Dalton. Everything."

He held her gaze for a long beat. Then he nodded once, the way he did when he meant it, the way she'd learned to distinguish from every other kind of nod.

"Everything," he said.

The fluorescent light buzzed steadily above them. Outside, Cherry Creek went about its evening, quiet and ordinary and utterly unaware of what was being assembled in the dark at the end of Birch Street. And Amber stood in the middle of it all, heart hammering, locket warm in her pocket, and waited for the truth to finally find its way into the room.

6 The Truth in the Shadows

He kept his word.

That was the first thing she thought when he finally stopped talking, maybe an hour after she'd told him to say all of it. He'd sat on that shop stool with his forearms on his knees and he'd said all of it, and not once had he softened an edge or buried a detail or given her the managed version of events. He'd told her about Rory Keane's record, the assault charges that never stuck, the two women before her who'd recanted under pressure.

He'd told her about the private job that night — a corporate extraction, legal in the loosest sense, the kind of thing ex-special forces guys did for money when they couldn't figure out how to be civilians. He'd told her about the alley, about the sounds he'd heard, about the three seconds of pure animal decision-making that had ended with Rory running and Amber unconscious in the dirt and a locket in his hand that he hadn't meant to pick up but couldn't put back down.

And then he'd told her she was moving above the garage tonight.

She'd argued that for a solid twenty minutes. It hadn't changed anything.

The apartment above the garage felt tight and functional—one cramped room that doubled as a bedroom and living space, a narrow kitchen hugging one wall, and a bathroom with a showerhead that sprayed slightly sideways. It smelled like cedar and old timber and the faint ghost of motor oil that had worked its way into every surface of the building. There was one window facing Birch Street, with a clear sightline to the front of the property, and a second one on the side wall that Dalton had already covered with a blackout panel he'd screwed in from the outside. The bed was pushed against the far wall. Clean sheets, no headboard, a wool blanket folded at the foot of it.

"It's a box," she said.

"It's safe," he said, and carried her bag up the stairs without asking.

She'd stood in the middle of the room after he left and turned in a slow circle, taking inventory. A single lamp on a side table. A wooden chair by the kitchen. A shelf above the small counter with three canned goods and a box of crackers, like he'd made a half-hearted attempt at stocking the place before deciding she could handle one night without a full pantry. She'd found a mug in the cabinet and filled it with water from the tap and stood at the Birch Street window for a long time, watching the dark street below, before she finally sat on the edge of the bed and opened her fist and looked at the locket again.

The bird with its wings spread. Her mother's bird.

She clasped it around her neck and lay down without changing her clothes and didn't sleep for a long time.

When she did sleep, she didn't dream. That was almost worse.

Morning arrived gray and quiet, light filtering through the one uncovered window in pale strips across the floor. She registered the smell first — coffee, real coffee, not the weak stuff from the gas station on Route 9. Then sound: a soft, rhythmic clicking from below, mechanical and precise, punctuated by the occasional clink of metal on metal.

She sat up. Ran a hand through her hair, which had fully escaped whatever it had been doing yesterday and was now staging a small rebellion against her face. She pulled on her boots, didn't bother with a mirror, and went down the narrow interior stairs that connected the apartment to the garage.

Dalton was at the workbench. He'd pushed the clockwork gears aside to make room, and in their place he had a disassembled sidearm laid out on a clean cloth — barrel, slide, frame, spring, each piece in its own deliberate position. He was cleaning the barrel with a rod and a patch, slow and methodical, the same focused attention he gave the gear work, his flannel sleeves rolled to the elbows, coffee mug steaming near his right hand.

She stopped on the bottom step and looked at the scene. The soft gray light through the side door. The smell of coffee and gun solvent. His hands moving through the cleaning routine with the ease of something done a thousand times.

This is his morning, she thought. *This is just what it looks like.* "Coffee's on the counter," he said, without looking up.

She crossed to the small kitchenette space near the side wall, where a drip machine was finishing its cycle, and poured herself a mug. It was good coffee. Of course it was. She turned and leaned against the counter and watched him reassemble the gun with the same quiet efficiency he'd used to take it apart.

"You sleep with that?" she asked. "Usually."

"That's not at all alarming."

His mouth curved, just barely. "You want alarming, go look under the driver's seat of the truck."

"I'll pass." She wrapped both hands around the mug and let the heat work into her palms. "I need to go to the bakery."

The curve disappeared. He set the reassembled gun down on the cloth and finally turned on the stool to face her. "Not today."

"Dalton."

"He's been in this garage. He's had eyes on your apartment. He knows you found the locket — he watched it happen." His voice was level, but there was something underneath it that was not. "Going out alone right now is—"

"Is what I'm doing," she said. "I have a job. I have a life that I'm not handing over to Rory Keane on top of everything else he's already taken." She put the mug down. "I am not sitting in a room above your garage staring at the walls while you go handle things I'm not allowed to know about. We had a deal."

"The deal was I'd tell you everything. Not that you'd walk around town with a target on you."

"The deal was no more managed information." She crossed her arms. "Managing my movements is the same thing."

He looked at her for a long beat. His jaw was tight. She could see him running the argument in his head, testing the angles, finding the place where his position had a crack in it, and not liking it.

"Fine," he said at last. "I'll drive you." "I don't need—"

"I'll drive you," he said again, and it wasn't loud, but it also wasn't a suggestion, and she recognized the particular register of it — the one that meant he'd already bent as far as he was going to bend and she could push past it but it would cost her something she wasn't sure she wanted to spend. She picked her mug back up. Took a long sip.

"Fine," she said.

He drove her in his truck, the cab smelling like him and old leather, and he didn't talk, and she didn't either. He parked half a block from the bakery and she got out without saying anything, and when she glanced back before she pushed through the door, he was still sitting there. Watching.

She went inside.

The bakery was warm and flour-dusted and blessedly normal. The morning rush was thin — a Tuesday, overcast, the kind of day that kept people home with their own coffee. She tied on her apron, said hello to the woman who opened mornings, and put her hands in dough, and for about forty minutes she almost felt like a person who didn't have a stalker and a guardian angel with a disassembled handgun and a secret that had been sitting in a floor safe for two years.

Then Lila came in.

She didn't come in for coffee. She came in because Lila Beckett had a radar for human drama that could pick up a signal through three walls and a rainstorm, and she slid onto a stool at the counter with her caramel curls piled on top of her head and her cat-eye glasses slightly askew and she said, "Honey, you look like you got about four hours of sleep in a building that isn't yours."

"Good morning to you too."

"Did Dalton Vale drive you to work?"

Amber kept her eyes on the scone she was shaping. "I don't know what you're talking about."

"His truck's been parked on Elm for twenty minutes. I walked past it. He was just sitting there like a very large, very intense lawn ornament." Lila propped her chin in her hand. "Spill it."

"There's nothing to spill."

"Amber. Sugar. I've known that man since we were stealing apples from the Harlan property at age ten. He does not sit parked on Elm Street at eight in the morning for no reason." She paused. "He's watching this place, isn't he?"

Amber shaped the scone and didn't answer. Lila read the silence like a headline.

"Oh, it's like that," Lila said, quieter now. The teasing edge dropped out of her voice. "How bad is it?"

"I'm handling it." "Is *he* handling it?"

Amber placed the scone on the tray and finally looked up. Lila was watching her with those amber eyes that missed nothing, and there was no mischief in them right now, just a careful, steady attention that reminded Amber, not for the first time, that the brassy exterior was only one layer of what Lila Beckett actually was.

"Yeah," Amber said. "He is."

"And how do you feel about that?"

She thought about it honestly, which she hadn't really let herself do yet. How did she feel? Furious. Rattled. Relieved in a way that disgusted her, because she didn't want to be the woman who felt relieved because a man had decided to be her shield. And underneath all of that, something that had no clean name — something warm and terrifying and deeply inconvenient.

"Complicated," she said.

Lila nodded slowly. "He's looking at you different, you know. Has been for weeks. Like—" She paused, tilting her head. "Like you're the only stationary thing in a room that keeps moving."

Amber didn't say anything to that. She put the tray in the oven and checked the temperature and told herself she was not going to think about it.

She thought about it all day.

Every customer who came through the door got a half-second of her full threat assessment before she could stop herself — the scan she'd developed over two years, the automatic cataloging of height and hands and whether someone looked at her too long or in the wrong way. A man in a green jacket paid for his coffee and she watched his hands the entire time. An unfamiliar woman asked for a recommendation and Amber gave it, smiling, while her pulse ticked at the base of her throat. It was exhausting in a way that baking couldn't fix today, and by the time the afternoon light went gray and flat outside the windows, she was done.

Dalton was still there when she locked up. Different spot, same street, same stillness. She got in the truck without a word and he drove her back to the garage and she was grateful, on some complicated, reluctant level, that he hadn't asked how her day was.

That night she sat on the wooden chair in the small kitchen and ate crackers with canned soup she'd heated on the two-burner stove, and she listened to the sounds of the garage below — the occasional clink of metal, the low murmur of what might have been a phone call, his footsteps crossing the concrete floor. The building felt inhabited in a way her apartment never had. Lived-in. Like it had a heartbeat that wasn't hers.

She went downstairs at nine o'clock.

He was at the workbench again, the gear work in front of him this time, a small brass wheel held between his fingers while he examined it under the lamp. He looked up when he heard her on the stairs, and whatever he read in her face made him set the wheel down and give her his full attention without being asked.

"The extraction," she said. "The classified op you mentioned. The one that went wrong."

A pause. He leaned back slightly on the stool, arms crossing, and she could see him deciding how much of himself to hand over. She'd watched him make that calculation before. It always took longer than it should, and it always landed in the same place.

"Four-man team," he said. "We were pulling a civilian asset out of a situation in a place I'm not going to name. We had a twelve-minute window and we were at fourteen when the perimeter broke." He stopped. His throat moved. "I had to make a call. We couldn't carry everyone and make the exfil. I left two men behind to buy us time." He said it the same way he'd said *I left you there* — flat, no softening, the words just sitting there in their full weight. "They didn't make it out."

The garage was very quiet. She could hear the buzz of the fluorescent overhead, the distant sound of a car on the road outside.

"That's why you came back here," she said. "That's part of it."

"And me. I'm the other part."

He looked at her steadily. "You were in an alley and I made a call, and this time the person I left behind survived. And then she moved to a town forty minutes from where I grew up, and a man who wanted to finish what he'd started moved with her." He exhaled slowly through his nose. "I'm not looking for absolution, Amber. I know what I did. I know all of it — the alley, the locket, the two years of watching. I know how it looks."

"How does it look?"

"Like I traded my guilt for your safety and called it protection," he said quietly. "Like the math worked out better for me than for you."

She crossed the garage. Not fast, but deliberate, the way he moved, and she stopped close enough that she could see the exhaustion written into the lines of his face, the shadows under his eyes that she now understood had nothing to do with bad sleep and everything to do with a burden he'd been carrying alone for years. The scar through his left brow. The particular stillness of a man who'd learned to hold himself very still so the things inside him didn't show on the surface.

"It does look like that," she said. "Some of it." His jaw tightened.

"But you stayed," she said. "You could have walked away from the alley and never looked back and your life would have been easier. You didn't."

"That's not—"

"I'm not saying it makes everything okay," she cut him off. "I'm saying I see it. There's a difference." She held his gaze, and something in the air between them shifted, the way pressure shifts before a storm, something building and inevitable. "You should have told me sooner. You should have trusted me with it."

"I know."

"I'm telling you now — if you manage me again, if you hide one more thing from me, I will walk out of this garage and I won't come back."

"I know that too," he said, and his voice had gone rough at the edges, worn down to something unguarded that she'd never heard from him before. It moved through her chest like a key in a lock she didn't know she'd been keeping closed.

She kissed him.

Or he kissed her. She wasn't entirely sure where the line was. One moment there were six inches of charged air between them and the next his hand was cupping her jaw and her fingers were fisted in the front of his flannel and the kiss wasn't soft — it was desperate and bruising and real, the kind of kiss that came from too much accumulated tension and not enough anywhere to put it. He kissed her like he'd been holding his breath for weeks and she was the first clean air he'd found, and she kissed him back like she was angry about it, because she was, a little, even as her body registered the warmth of him and the specific solid reality of his chest under her hands and the low sound he made against her mouth that she felt in her sternum.

When they broke apart, she was breathing unsteadily. His forehead dropped against hers, his hand still cradling her face, thumb tracing her cheekbone once.

"Rory's going to make a move," he said against her hair. Low and rough, his breath warm at her temple. "Soon. I can feel it. He's been circling too long to wait much more."

"I know."

"If he touches you—" He stopped. She felt his hand tighten fractionally against her face before he controlled it. "If he gets anywhere near you, I will burn this entire town down to find him. I need you to know that."

She pulled back just enough to see his face. His eyes were blue and very serious and there was nothing performative in them, no attempt to impress her or scare her or play at being something he wasn't. He meant every word of it with a quiet, absolute certainty that should have frightened her.

The part that frightened her was that it didn't. "Then we'd better find him first," she said.

He studied her face for a long moment, like he was memorizing the angles of it. Then he nodded once, slow, and she recognized that nod. The one that meant he meant it.

"Together," he said.

Outside, Cherry Creek was dark and still and quiet, the way small towns went quiet at night — deeply, completely, like the dark was something it had always been comfortable with. Somewhere in it, Rory Keane was waiting. Planning. Nursing whatever twisted logic had convinced him that she was something he could own.

She stood in the warm light of the garage, her mother's locket cool against her collarbone, Dalton's hand dropping slowly from her face, and she thought about the woman who had woken up in a hospital with a two-year gap in her memory and fled to a small town to disappear. She thought about how that woman had spent every day since watching every door and every shadow and every stranger's hands, waiting for the next thing to take from her. She was done waiting.

7

The First Confession

She woke up to the sound of him cleaning a gun again.

Not the same gun. Different one, smaller, a compact she hadn't seen before, laid out on the kitchen table in its component pieces while the gray morning pressed flat against the single uncovered window. She registered it before she registered anything else — the smell of solvent, the soft metallic click of the cleaning rod working through the barrel, the particular quality of silence that surrounded Dalton when he was focused on something. Like the world agreed to quiet down for him.

She pulled herself upright on the narrow bed and scrubbed both hands over her face. Her hair was staging its usual mutiny. The locket was still around her neck, warm from sleep, and she touched it once before dropping her hand.

He didn't look up from the table. "There's coffee."

"There's always coffee," she said. "There's also always a disassembled weapon on whatever surface I'm trying to eat breakfast off of. Noticing a theme."

"You can eat standing up."

"I'm going to work," she said, and watched his hands go still.

He set the barrel down on the cloth and turned on the chair to face her, and she already knew the shape of this conversation. They'd had a version of it yesterday. They'd probably have another version tomorrow, and the day after that, until Rory Keane was no longer a problem or she lost her mind entirely from being cooped up in a room the size of a generous closet with a man whose gravitational pull was becoming genuinely inconvenient.

"Amber."

"Don't." She got up and crossed to the counter, poured herself coffee, and turned with the mug in her hands. "I know what you're going to say. He's circling. He's watching. It's not safe. I heard all of that last night and I understand all of that, and I'm still going to the bakery."

"He escalated. Watching your apartment was one thing — he left a live feed in your building. That's not curiosity, that's—"

"I know what it is." Her voice came out flat and certain, which surprised even her. "I also know that if I stop going to work, he wins a round. I lose my job, I lose my routine, I lose the last normal thing I have. And then what? I sit here while you handle it?" She took a sip of the coffee. "I already told you where that ends."

He stared at her. His jaw was doing that thing where it went tight and stayed there while he ran options in his head and didn't find any he liked. She was starting to be able to read him in a way that felt dangerous, mapping the small tells — the set of his shoulders, the way his breath changed when he was deciding something.

"I'll follow you," he said finally. "You walk in the front, I stay outside. You don't leave without telling me."

"You'll follow me," she repeated. "Like a very large, armed shadow." "Like someone who'd rather not scrape you off a sidewalk."

It wasn't funny. A jagged, hysterical sound clawed at the back of her throat, and she had to bite her tongue until she tasted copper just to keep the laugh from breaking loose. Her hands were vibrating, a fine, high-frequency tremor that made the ceramic mug rattle against her teeth. "Fine. But you stay out of the bakery unless I text you. I'm not having the whole town talk."

"The whole town's already talking."

"More, then." She set down the mug. "Give me twenty minutes."

He gave her twenty-two, and then they did the whole thing — the silent truck ride, the half-block parking spot, the way she didn't look back when she pushed through the bakery door but knew, without question, that he was still sitting there.

The bakery was warm and smelled like brown butter and cinnamon, and for about thirty seconds, her shoulders dropped and she felt like herself. Then the door opened behind her and a man she didn't recognize walked in, mid-forties, green coat, and her whole body went on alert before she'd made a single conscious decision about it. She watched his hands. Watched the way his eyes moved. He ordered a coffee and a croissant and left without ever once glancing at her, and she let out a slow breath and hated that she'd held it in the first place.

Lila came in just before ten.

She didn't bother with pretense, just climbed onto the counter stool and dropped her chin into her palm and watched Amber frost a tray of scones with the particular intensity of a woman who had decided something was going to be discussed whether or not the other party agreed to participate.

"He moved you in," Lila said. "Good morning, Lila."

"Above the garage. You slept there last night." It wasn't a question. "Honey, your shirt is one of his flannels. You didn't even notice, did you?"

Amber glanced down. She had not noticed. The flannel was soft from a hundred washes, faded to a gray-blue that probably used to be something more definitive, sleeves rolled twice to clear her wrists. She'd grabbed it off the chair in the dark that morning without thinking.

"It was cold," she said.

"Sure it was." Lila's knowing smirk was almost audible. "You want to tell me what's actually going on, or are we doing the thing where you say 'I'm fine' and I pretend to believe you for approximately forty seconds before calling bullshit?"

Amber set down the pastry brush. Outside the window, a woman walked past with a stroller, and Amber's eyes tracked the movement without her permission before she recognized her as someone's grandmother from two streets over and let herself blink again. "There's someone in town who shouldn't be. Dalton's making sure I don't get cornered alone until it's sorted."

Lila's smirk dissolved. "Someone dangerous." "Yeah."

"Connected to the notes?" "Yeah."

A pause. Lila's amber eyes went careful and steady, the way they did when she was thinking instead of performing. "And you and Dalton?"

"That's not—"

"Because the way you said his name just now?" Lila tilted her head. "That's not the voice of someone who's just grateful for the security detail, sugar."

Amber picked up the pastry brush again. "There's nothing to report."

"I've known Dalton Vale since we were ten years old stealing apples off Wes Harlan's property," Lila said, leaning forward. "I have never, in my entire life, seen him park outside a building for six straight hours voluntarily. He hates people. He hates sitting still. He especially hates small talk, which parking on a public street technically requires you to risk." She paused. "He'd walk through fire for you and you know it."

Amber didn't answer that, which was, of course, its own kind of answer. She was saved by a customer, and then another, and the morning rush carried her forward until Lila finally left with a coffee and one of the scones and a look that said *this conversation isn't over* in every language simultaneously.

The afternoon was worse. The paranoia didn't ease up — it layered, compounding with every unfamiliar face, every car that slowed near the window, every moment of quiet that felt like it was about to be broken by something she wasn't ready for. By three o'clock she was exhausted in the particular way that had nothing to do with physical labor and everything to do with running on cortisol and bad sleep and the specific mental toll of being afraid without being able to show it.

She was in the back, washing her hands at the utility sink, when she heard a sound from the front — a small crash, a sharp inhale from the woman working the register. Amber came through the doorway fast, wiping her hands on her apron, and stopped.

A small box sat on the counter. Brown paper, no label, the wrapping slightly damp at the corners like it had been carried in someone's hands on a cold day. The register woman, Patty, was backed against the far wall with her hands pressed to her mouth, staring at it.

"Where did that come from?" Amber asked, though something in her stomach already knew.

"A man," Patty said, and her voice cracked on it. "He just left it on the counter and walked out. I didn't — I opened it because I thought it was a delivery, and then—" She stopped. Her face was gray.

Amber crossed to the counter. She looked at the open box.

She'd seen a lot of things in two years of being afraid. She'd built up a pretty solid tolerance for things that should have broken her. But what was inside the box stopped her cold, turned the warmth of the bakery into something that felt like standing outside in January, and for a long moment all she could hear was her own heartbeat and the faint buzz of the refrigeration unit in the back.

She pulled out her phone and texted Dalton one word: *Inside. Now.*

He was through the door in under a minute, and she watched his face go from sharp attention to controlled stillness when he registered what was on the counter. He didn't touch the box. He looked at it, looked at her, looked at Patty still pressed against the far wall.

"You okay?" he asked Amber.

"No," she said honestly. "Call Landry."

Sheriff Tate Landry arrived twenty minutes later, which was fast for Cherry Creek. He filled the doorway of the bakery with his stocky frame and his starched uniform and his salt-and-pepper buzz cut, and he looked at the box on the counter the same way Dalton had — taking it in without reacting, cataloging the facts of it before he let himself have any feelings about them. He had a deputy with him who bagged it, gloves on, and took photographs, and Patty told her story twice while Landry listened with his arms crossed and his gray eyes moving between the three of them.

"You see the man who left it?" Landry asked Patty.

"Tall. Dark hair. He had a — a gold tooth, I think. He didn't say anything, just put it on the counter and left."

Landry wrote something in his notebook and then turned and looked at Dalton the way men look at things they've already decided are probably a problem. "Vale."

"Sheriff."

"You want to tell me why you were parked on Elm Street for six hours?" "Personal reasons."

"Personal reasons." Landry's mouth went flat. "There's a severed finger in a box in a bakery in my town, and you've been running surveillance on the building it was delivered to, and you'd like me to file that under personal reasons."

"I'd like you to run the print and find out whose it is," Dalton said. "I have a theory, but you'll want confirmation."

Landry stared at him for a beat that stretched long enough to be a statement on its own. Then he turned back to Amber. "Ms. Rowan. You know anything about who sent this?"

"His name is Rory Keane," she said. "He attacked me two years ago in the city. My case was dropped. He's in Cherry Creek." She said it flat and clean, the way she'd practiced saying hard things — not asking for sympathy, just laying out facts. "The notes I've been receiving have details from the attack that were never made public. It's him."

Landry's expression shifted by a fraction. Not much, but enough to tell her he was recalibrating. "You filed those notes with my office."

"I filed them. Nothing came of it."

His jaw worked slightly. "I'll need a formal statement. Both of you." He glanced at Dalton again, and something in his eyes said the statement was going to have a lot of questions attached to it, specifically for Dalton. "Don't go anywhere tonight."

They went back to the garage because where else would they go. Amber sat on the wooden chair in the small kitchen and didn't eat anything, because the thought of food felt impossible, and Dalton moved around below, the sounds of the garage rising up through the floor like a pulse. At some point he came upstairs, set a glass of water on the table in front of her, and sat down across from her without being asked.

"It was her," Amber said. "The woman who was found. Nora's sister." "Most likely."

"He left it in my workplace. In a bakery. Where people buy food and bring their kids." Her voice didn't shake. She was almost proud of that. "That's a message."

"Yeah." His voice was low and rough. "It is."

"He's telling me he can get to me anywhere." She looked up. "He's telling you that too. That he's not afraid of you."

Dalton's eyes went very still. Not cold — something hotter than cold, something contained and deliberate. "Let him not be afraid. Makes him sloppy."

"Dalton." She held his gaze, steady. "If he touches anyone else because of me — if someone else gets hurt because he's playing this game—"

"That is not on you." "You can't know that."

"I do know it." He leaned forward, forearms on the table, and his voice dropped to something that wasn't quite gentle but was as close as he got. "Rory Keane makes choices. His choices make consequences. None of that is yours to carry."

She pressed her lips together. The locket was cool and solid at her collarbone, and she pressed two fingers against it and breathed.

"If he gets near you," Dalton said, "I will burn this town down to find him. I told you that last night and I meant every word of it." He paused. "We find him first. That's the plan."

"Together," she said, because that was what he'd said the night before, and she'd meant it when she'd said it back, and she still meant it now.

"Together," he agreed.

There was a beat of quiet between them, real and unhurried, and she felt something settle fractionally in her chest — not relief exactly, not safety, but the particular calm that came from being in a room with someone who wasn't asking her to pretend any of this was fine. Who looked at the worst of it with her and didn't flinch. She reached across the table and touched the back of his hand. Not quite holding it

— just her fingers resting over his knuckles, light and deliberate. His hand turned under hers, and his palm pressed up against her fingers, and they stayed like that for a moment in the lamp-lit kitchen above the garage while Cherry Creek went dark and quiet outside and somewhere in it, Rory Keane waited with whatever came next already decided.

She pulled her hand back first. "I'm going to sleep."
"I'll be downstairs."

"I know." She stood. "Dalton." He looked up. "Thank you. For today. For all of it." She paused. "Don't make it weird."

The corner of his mouth moved, just barely. "Wouldn't dream of it."

She went to bed still wearing his flannel, and this time she didn't pretend not to notice.

8
Evidence of Malice

Landry called them in at nine the next morning.

Not a request. Amber had gotten enough of those in her life to know the difference between an invitation and a summons, and this was the kind that came with a deputy's voice on the other end of the line and a very particular emphasis on *both of you, please.* She pulled on her jacket and didn't bother with breakfast because the thought of eating anything in this particular moment felt like a terrible idea.

Dalton drove. She watched the storefronts of Cherry Creek slide past the window and thought about how strange it was, the way a town could look exactly the same from the outside while everything inside it had gone sideways. Hardware store. Diner. Flower shop with a handwritten chalkboard sign advertising autumn arrangements. All of it serene and golden in the early morning light, like something out of a postcard, like nothing bad had ever happened here or ever could.

She'd believed that once, when she first moved here. Two weeks in and she'd started thinking maybe she'd finally found a place where the past couldn't follow.

That felt almost funny now.

The sheriff's office smelled like burnt coffee and old paper. Landry met them in the hallway outside his office, and he did the thing he always did with Dalton — that slow, measuring look, the kind that communicated a complete editorial without a single word. He waved them both in, closed the door, and sat down behind his desk with his hands folded on the surface like a man who had decided to be deliberately calm about something that was irritating him considerably.

"DNA came back this morning," he said. "The print from the box matches a partial on file for a woman named Cassidy Fisk. Twenty-three years old, reported missing out of Albany six weeks ago." He paused. "Half-sister of Nora Fisk, currently residing on Maple Street."

Amber's chest went tight and cold. She'd already suspected it — Dalton had said *most likely* the night before with the particular certainty of a man who rarely said anything he wasn't sure of — but hearing it confirmed out loud was different. Cassidy Fisk was twenty-three years old and her sister ran a bakery three blocks from where Amber worked, and Rory Keane had left her finger in a box on a counter where people came to buy croissants and let their kids pick out cookies from the glass case.

"We're notifying next of kin this morning," Landry continued. "The town's being put on alert — nothing that'll cause a panic, but people need to know to report anything unusual." His gray eyes moved to Dalton, and they stayed there. "What I'd like to understand, Vale, is how you knew to be parked outside that bakery before the delivery happened."

"I didn't know about the delivery," Dalton said. "I knew Amber was in danger and I stayed close."

"Uh-huh." Landry opened a folder on the desk. He turned it so they could both see it, and Amber's eyes dropped to the page. "Here's what I'm looking at. Three unsolved disappearances in Cherry Creek over the last decade. Maria Hollins, 2015. Tim Brauer, 2018. Denise Cooke, 2021." He tapped each name as he said it. "All three cases went cold. All three of them — and I want you to pay attention here, Ms. Rowan — occurred within a six-week window when Dalton Vale was back in town between deployments or after his discharge."

The room got very quiet. Amber was aware of Dalton beside her, perfectly still, and she didn't look at him because she needed to hear this without his face in her peripheral vision pulling her toward the conclusion she already wanted to reach.

"That's a coincidence," she said.

"Could be." Landry's expression didn't change. "Three times is a lot of coincidence."

"You have evidence connecting him to any of those cases?"

"I have proximity and a pattern." He leaned back in his chair. "I'm not charging anyone with anything, Ms. Rowan. I'm showing you what I'm working with, because I think you deserve to know what's in this file before you go any further down whatever road you're currently on with this man."

She could feel Dalton's tension from six inches away, radiating off him like heat from a cast-iron stove. It hit her in waves, making the fine hairs on her arms stand up and sending a sympathetic prickle down her spine. Her own skin felt suddenly too tight, her nerves buzzing with the heavy, electric charge he was putting off. She kept her posture easy, kept her breathing measured, trying to keep her own pulse from galloping in sync with the violent stillness he was projecting.

"I didn't do it," Dalton said. Flat and clean, no decoration on it.

"He was interviewed in all three," Landry said. "Nothing stuck. But I've been doing this job for fifteen years, and when a name shows up three times in the same context, I write it down." He closed the folder. "I'm not telling you who to trust. I'm telling you to be careful."

She thanked him for the information and meant it, which was the complicated part. Because she did deserve to know. Even if it landed like a stone in still water, spreading rings she couldn't stop.

She didn't talk on the drive back. Dalton didn't push her to. He pulled up in front of the garage and put the truck in park and waited, engine idling, while she stared at the middle distance and tried to organize her thoughts into something she could actually use.

"Three disappearances," she finally said. "I know."

"Were you in town for all three?" A beat. "Yes."

"Did you—" She stopped, pressed her lips together. "Did you know any of them?"

"Hollins, no. Brauer, I'd seen him around. Cooke, I'd done some work on her car the summer before." He turned to look at her, and his expression was steady, not defensive. "I didn't hurt them, Amber. I can't tell you where they went, because I don't know. But I didn't touch them."

She believed him. That was the maddening thing — she looked at his face, the set of his jaw, the directness in his eyes, and she believed him down to her bones, and she couldn't decide if that was her gut working correctly or her heart doing the kind of stupid thing hearts did when they'd gotten attached to the wrong person. She'd been wrong before. She'd trusted a man who had secrets she hadn't discovered until it was too late.

She got out of the truck without answering him, and that felt like the most honest thing she could do.

Wes Harlan's property sat at the edge of the tree line on the north side of Cherry Creek, down a gravel road that wound through enough pines to make you feel like the town had never existed. She drove out there herself, midafternoon, because Lila had mentioned once that Wes had known Dalton's father, and right now she needed someone who could tell her something true without a personal stake in what she decided to do with it.

He was on the porch when she pulled up, pipe in hand, watching her park with the unhurried patience of a man who had very few places to be. He was big and broad, with a wild gray beard and the kind of eyes that had seen a lot and forgotten almost none of it. He didn't look surprised to see her.

"Figured someone'd send you up here eventually," he said. "Coffee's on."

The inside of his cabin smelled like woodsmoke and pine resin and something baking — a dense, dark bread from the look of it, sitting on the counter in a cast-iron pan. She sat at his kitchen table, and he poured two mugs and set one in front of her without asking how she took it, and she wrapped her hands around it and let the warmth work through her palms.

"Tell me about Robert Vale," she said.

Wes settled into the chair across from her with a slow exhale. "That's a hell of an opening."

"I'm running low on patience for the scenic route."

The corner of his mouth lifted under the beard. "Fair enough." He took a long pull of his coffee. "Robert Vale was a hard man. Not hard the way some men are hard — not from discipline or bad luck or the weight of years. Hard in the way that means he liked it. Liked making things smaller than himself." He turned his mug on the table, a slow rotation. "He put Dalton's mother in the hospital twice before she had the sense to leave. Dalton was fourteen the second time. He was the one who called it in."

Amber's throat tightened. She kept still.

"Robert had a temper that ran hot and a conscience that didn't run at all," Wes continued. "Mean streak a mile wide and the charm to cover it most of the time, which made it worse. Men like that — the ones who know how to turn it on and off — they do more damage than the ones who are just openly rotten." He paused. "You know the saying. Apple doesn't fall far from the tree."

"You think Dalton's like him," she said carefully.

Wes looked at her for a long moment. Outside, a crow called once from somewhere in the pines and went quiet. "No," he said. "I don't. And that's the harder thing to explain." He leaned forward, elbows on the table. "Dalton carried that man's legacy around like a stone in his pack from the time he was old enough to understand what it meant. Spent his whole life trying to be the opposite of it. The military was part of that — trying to build himself into something that used the instincts his father gave him for something other than cruelty." He set down his mug. "He's got a good soul, that boy. I've known him since he was twelve years old stealing apples off my property with Lila Beckett, and I'd stake my last dollar on his character." A beat. "That doesn't mean he's without shadows. It means he's fought them. There's a difference."

Amber stared into her coffee. "Landry showed me a file. Three disappearances."

"I know about those." "And?"

Wes picked up his pipe and turned it in his fingers without lighting it, a thinking gesture. "I don't know what happened to those people. I know Dalton wasn't the cause of it. But I also know that boy has spent years operating in spaces where things go wrong and people vanish, and I know Cherry Creek isn't as clean as it looks." He met her eyes. "Landry's not wrong to be cautious. He's just pointing the flashlight in the wrong direction."

She stayed another twenty minutes, mostly in comfortable silence, watching the pines shift in the afternoon wind and turning it all over in her head. When she stood to leave, Wes walked her to the door and stopped her with a hand briefly on her arm — not restraining, just present.

"Whatever you decide about him," he said, "decide it because it's what you see. Not because someone else told you what to see." He let go. "You've got good instincts, girl. Trust 'em."

She drove back through the pine road as the light started going amber and long, leaves catching the late sun and throwing it back in pieces. Her mind was still churning, cycling through Landry's file and Wes's words and the memory of Dalton's face in the truck when he'd said *I didn't hurt them* with that quiet certainty that didn't ask to be believed, just stated the fact and left it there.

She reached her car where she'd parked it at the edge of the gravel pull-off near the trailhead and stopped.

There was something on the windshield. Not tucked under the wiper the way parking tickets went — pinned through the center of a folded note with a knife. A bone-handled knife, blade sunk straight through the paper and into the rubber at the base of the glass, like a declaration.

She stood there for three full seconds, her whole body going cold and electric at once, before she pulled out her phone and photographed it from four different angles. Then she pulled the knife free with her sleeve over her fingers, careful not to smear anything, and unfolded the note.

The handwriting was block print, deliberate, each letter pressed hard into the paper.

He's a killer, Amber. Ask him about the third man in the room.

She read it twice. Then a third time, because the second time her vision had gone a little strange at the edges and she wasn't sure she'd taken it in correctly.

The third man in the room.

Her attack. The night she'd lost two years ago, the one that existed in her memory only as fragments — a sound, a smell, the particular quality of darkness in a place that should have been familiar, the sensation of a floor under her palms. The police report had documented her statement, such as it was, and her statement had been incomplete because her memory had been incomplete. She'd described one attacker. Rory Keane. The investigation had been built around one attacker.

But this note was talking about a third man. Not two — *third.* Which meant the writer knew there had been at least two people in that room with her, and they were telling her one of them was someone she hadn't accounted for.

Someone Dalton was protecting. Or hiding. Or both.

The pine road was quiet around her, nothing but wind and the distant sound of a truck on the highway half a mile away. She stood next to her car with the note in her covered hand and tried to think clearly through the noise in her chest.

Only two kinds of people could know that detail. The people who'd been there. Rory Keane had been there, so this could be Rory, feeding her doubt, trying to drive a wedge between her and the only person standing between him and access to her. That was one option, and it was a real one, and she turned it over carefully.

But there was another option. That it was true. That someone else had been in that room, someone her fractured memory hadn't managed to hold onto, and that Dalton Vale's presence in Cherry Creek wasn't just about redemption and guilt. That whatever he'd done that night — whatever intervention had saved her life — he hadn't done it alone, and the person he'd done it with was still a secret he was keeping from her.

She got in the car and sat there with the note on the passenger seat and the bone-handled knife wrapped in her sleeve, and she pressed her palms flat on the steering wheel and breathed until her pulse came back down to something manageable.

Dalton had said *together.* He'd said it twice, and she'd believed him both times, and she still wanted to believe him now. She did. She could feel the want of it like a physical thing, a pull in her sternum toward the version of this where he was exactly who she needed him to be and nothing else.

But the note was real. The knife was real. And the third man in the room was either a lie designed to break her or a truth that had been buried long enough to start rotting from the inside, and she didn't know which one yet, and that not-knowing was its own particular kind of terror.

She started the car and pulled back onto the road.

She was going to ask him. She was going to look him in the face and ask him about the third man, and she was going to watch what happened in his eyes when she did, because whatever Landry's file said and whatever Wes's careful words had and hadn't confirmed, she trusted herself to read that. She had to. It was the only thing she had left.

The sun finished dropping behind the hills as she drove. Cherry Creek spread out below her in the valley, its lights just starting to come on, warm and small against the early dark, looking like exactly the kind of place where nothing bad ever happened.

She didn't let herself find it comforting.

9
Storm Shelter

The storm rolled in from the west around nine, the way summer storms did in Cherry Creek — fast and mean, with no polite buildup. One minute the air was thick and heavy and electric, and the next the sky cracked open and the rain came down sideways, hammering the garage roof with a relentless, mechanical violence.

Amber stood at the window with her arms crossed and watched a trash can blow across the empty street below. The note was still in her jacket pocket. The bone-handled knife was wrapped in her sleeve on the passenger seat of her car, which was currently getting soaked in Dalton's lot. She'd driven straight here from the pine road, and she'd come in out of the rain and Dalton had taken one look at her face and not said a word, just handed her a towel and turned back to the engine he'd been working on, and she'd stood in the middle of the garage for a full minute trying to figure out how to start.

Ask him about the third man in the room.

She'd opened her mouth twice. Both times, Dalton had glanced up from under the hood, and the words had dissolved somewhere between her chest and her throat. Not because she was afraid of him. She was afraid of what she'd see when she asked. Because Wes had said he had a good soul, and Landry's file had said something else entirely, and the note had said something different from both of them, and she needed to know which version was true before she handed this man any more of herself than she already had.

Then the lights went out.

Not a flicker. A clean, total cut — garage, streetlights, the diner sign across the road, all of it swallowed at once. The only light left was the lightning, strobing white through the high windows in two-second intervals, throwing everything into brief, sharp relief and then taking it back again.

"Transformer," Dalton said from somewhere near the truck. His voice was calm, unhurried. "Whole block's out."

Amber didn't answer. She turned away from the window and tried to locate him in the dark.

She found him by sound — the quiet, deliberate movement of him crossing the garage floor — and then by the sudden warmth of him close behind her, near enough that she could feel the heat off his skin without him touching her. He reached past her and set a heavy flashlight on the workbench, clicked it on, and the beam threw a long wedge of yellow light across the concrete.

"Come upstairs," he said. Not a command, exactly. More like a fact he was laying down and leaving for her to pick up or not.

She picked it up.

His apartment was small — a kitchen, a living room that was mostly bookshelves and one battered leather couch, a bedroom with a window that faced the alley. He lit two candles on the kitchen counter and they threw warm, unsteady light over everything, softening the angles, making the space feel close and private in a way that had nothing to do with the square footage.

She should ask him now. She had the note in her pocket. She had the question ready.

Instead she sat on the couch and watched him pour two fingers of whiskey into a glass and set it on the coffee table in front of her, and the thunder rolled through the building in a long, bone-deep shudder, and she thought: *okay. Not yet. Just breathe.*

"You've been holding something since you walked in," he said. He settled into the chair across from her, his own glass in hand, elbows on his knees.

The candlelight caught the angles of his face and threw the shadows into deeper relief — the stubble, the faint scar through the brow, the blue of his eyes gone darker in the low light. "If you want to say it, say it."

"I found a note on my windshield." She reached into her pocket, set the folded paper on the table between them. "Pinned down with a knife."

He looked at it without touching it. Something moved across his expression

— controlled, contained, but there. His jaw tightened by a fraction.

"It says to ask you about the third man in the room." She kept her voice level. "The room being the night of my attack."

The silence stretched long enough that the rain filled it, hammering against the window in uneven bursts. Lightning whitened the room for a half-second and was gone.

"Amber." Her name in his mouth was rough and low, a sound like gravel shifting.

"Was there someone else there that night?" He set his glass down. "Yes."

The single syllable landed in her chest like something thrown hard. She'd expected it — she'd prepared for it, on the drive over, during the two hours she'd spent not asking — and it still hit like she hadn't.

"Who?"

He didn't answer immediately. He stood instead, moved to the window, stood with his back to her, and the rain blurred everything beyond the glass into gray streaks. She watched the tension in his shoulders, the way his hands closed at his sides and then opened again slowly, like a man counting to something.

"Dalton." Her voice was sharp this time. "Look at me."

He turned. And whatever he'd been working out in the twenty seconds he'd spent facing the window, he'd finished working it out, because when he came back to her there was nothing guarded left in his expression. Just something she didn't have a name for — stripped-down, braced.

He sat beside her on the couch, close enough that their knees nearly touched, and he leaned forward with his elbows on his thighs and said: "I'm going to tell you something, and I need you to hear all of it before you—"

"Just say it."

He exhaled. "I was hired. To be there that night." The room went very still, or maybe that was just her. "Hired," she repeated.

"There's an organization. They call themselves cleaners — fixers for people with money and problems they need made quiet. I was recruited out of the military. Wet work, mostly. The kind of jobs that don't exist in any official record." His voice was flat, not self-pitying, just laying it out. "I was sent to your apartment that night with another man. We were both contracted for the same job."

She already knew what the job was. She knew before he said it, because the math was simple and terrible and it had been sitting in the back of her skull since she read the note. But she needed to hear it from him.

"Say it."

"To kill you." He held her gaze without flinching. "That was the contract."

The candle nearest her guttered in a draft from somewhere, throwing shadows sideways across the wall. She was aware of her own breathing — slow, deliberate, the kind of controlled breathing she'd learned in the months after the attack when her therapist had shown her how to keep herself from flying apart.

"And?" she said.

"And I walked in and I saw you." Something shifted behind his eyes, a crack in the flat surface. "And I couldn't. That's the truth of it, Amber. I stoodin that room and I looked at you and I couldn't do it. The other man — he wasn't going to stop." A beat. "So I stopped him."

"You killed him." "Yes."

She pressed the heels of her hands against her thighs and stared at the floor between them. The storm outside was a low, constant roar, punctuated by lightning that turned the room white and gone in alternating heartbeats.

"Rory," she said slowly. "Rory Keane. He's connected to this."

"The man I killed was his brother." Dalton's voice dropped further. "The group — they don't forgive that kind of thing. Rory came after me first, and when he found out I'd been watching you, he shifted. Made it about you. About taking back what he thinks was stolen from him."

"The notes. The finger. All of it." She pressed a fist to her sternum, not because it helped with the physical ache there, but because she needed to feel something solid. "This has been a blood-debt the whole time."

"Yes."

"And you've been here. In Cherry Creek. Watching me. Since—"

"Since six months after that night." He didn't look away. "I needed to know you were okay. And then I couldn't leave."

She should have been furious. She was furious — it was there, hot and real, burning under her breastbone alongside everything else. He'd been contracted to end her life. He'd built a whole presence in this town around the guilt of it, and he'd let her fall toward him without telling her what he was, what he'd done, what she was orbiting without knowing it.

But she was also, in the same breath, alive. Because of him. Because he'd walked into a room with a contract and a partner and he'd chosen differently, and the cost of that choice had been following him for two years.

She didn't know what to do with all of it. So she sat with it, while the storm hammered the building and the candles threw their unsteady light and Dalton waited — still, patient, a man who had put the truth on the table and wasn't trying to manage what she did next.

She kissed him.

Not softly. Not tentatively. She crossed the distance between them and took his face in her hands and kissed him like it was the only honest response she had left, and he went very still for half a second — surprise, maybe, or the effort of not assuming — and then his hands found her waist and he kissed her back, and it was nothing like the controlled, guarded version of him she'd been navigating for weeks.

This was the thing underneath. The current that had been running beneath every interaction, every charged silence, every moment where he'd stayed close without touching — it was all of that, finally given permission.

He pulled her onto his lap with a quiet, firm certainty that left no room for hesitation, his hands sliding up her back, and she felt the full, solid warmth of him against her and something in her chest cracked open like a window she'd kept nailed shut for two years. His mouth was warm and demanding and thorough, and he kissed her like he was learning her, like he wanted to memorize the specific shape of this and keep it.

"Amber." He drew back just enough to say her name, his forehead dropping to hers. His breathing had gone rough. "You're sure."

"Don't ask me that again," she said, and pulled him back in.

He stood with her, hands sure and steady under her thighs, and carried her to the bedroom with the candle from the kitchen casting long shadows down the hallway. He set her on the bed with a gentleness that shouldn't have been possible given the intensity of everything preceding it, and he looked at her in the low amber light with an expression she recognized now— not calculation, not strategy. Just hunger, and underneath it, something reverent.

He took his time. That was the thing she hadn't expected — not with two years of tension stacked between them, not with the fury and the fear and the confession still fresh in the air. But he pulled back from every edge she expected him to rush past, his hands moving slowly, deliberately, over the curve of her shoulders, down her sides, learning the landscape of her with a patience that made her breath catch.

When her shirt came off, he stilled. His fingers traced the scar that ran along her left ribs — the one she'd stopped thinking about as a flaw somewhere around the one-year mark and started thinking about as simply part of the architecture of herself. He pressed his mouth to it, soft and unhurried, and the heat of it traveled up through her spine.

"You don't have to—" she started.

"I know," he said against her skin. "I want to."

She gave up directing things after that. Let herself be moved and held and taken apart slowly, methodically, with a focused attention that made her forget, for stretches of minutes at a time, that there was anything outside this room. He was commanding without being careless, and attentive in a way that felt less like performance and more like genuine, consuming interest — in her, specifically, in the particular sounds she made and the places that made her arch and the way her breathing changed when he found something that worked.

She pulled him up to her mouth and kissed him hard and wrapped herself around him and stopped thinking entirely.

Afterward, the storm was still going. She could hear it — the rain softer now but steady, the occasional low roll of thunder moving east. Dalton lay on his back with one arm around her, her head on his chest, his heartbeat slowing under her ear. His hand moved in slow, absent strokes up and down her arm, the way a person did when they'd stopped thinking and just let themselves exist.

She hadn't felt this in a long time. This specific quiet. Not the absence of noise, but the absence of vigilance — the particular exhaustion of a body that had finally put down something heavy.

Lightning filled the room in a sudden white flood, and she shifted against him, and her eyes dropped without intention to the angle of his inner thigh where the sheet had fallen away.

She went very still.

The tattoo was small, maybe two inches across — a symbol she'd seen before, rendered in clean, precise lines. Not ornate. Almost clinical in its simplicity. A specific shape she'd burned into her memory the afternoon she'd found the shrine in the woods, carved into the wood with the same deliberate precision as this ink.

The same mark. Exactly.

She didn't move. She lay there with her cheek on his chest and her eyes on that piece of skin and her mind doing the very slow, very cold work of slotting this into everything he'd just told her. The organization. The cleaners. The mark that had been carved into a shrine in the middle of the woods by someone who had been watching her, circling her, building an altar to an obsession she hadn't known existed.

Rory Keane. And Dalton Vale. And the same symbol on both.

He'd told her the truth tonight. She believed that. She believed he'd walked into that room and chosen differently, believed the guilt that lived in him was real, believed the way he'd kissed her wasn't a performance. She believed all of it.

But she also believed what she was seeing right now, and those two things were sitting next to each other in her chest like two live wires that hadn't yet touched, and she did not know what happened when they did. She kept her breathing even. His chest rose and fell beneath her ear, steady and slow, the rhythm of a man sliding toward sleep. His hand had stilled on her arm. Outside, the rain tapped against the glass in the patient, repetitive way it did when it had decided to stay awhile.

She stared at the ceiling in the dark and did not sleep. She was held in the arms of a man who had saved her life after being sent to end it, a man whose skin bore the same mark as the shrine built by the person hunting her, and she was warm and safe and terrified in equal measure, and she could not tell — could not yet tell — whether that mark was a brand from a past he'd left behind, or a thread still connecting him to something she hadn't fully seen yet.

She was going to have to ask. Tomorrow. When it was light and they were both clothed and she could watch his face without the dark hiding half of it.

But for now she lay still, listening to the rain and the low roll of retreating thunder, and she let herself stay in this complicated, unknowable place — tucked against the chest of a man who might be her salvation, or the most dangerous mistake she'd made yet, unable to move in either direction until she knew which one was true.

The candle in the hallway burned down to nothing sometime around midnight. The room went fully dark, and still she lay awake, and still she didn't know.

10
The Third Man

She left while he was still asleep.

That was the coward's way, and she knew it. But lying there in the gray pre-dawn light with that tattoo seared into her brain and his arm warm across her waist, she couldn't just keep waiting for morning to happen. She needed to move. She needed air that didn't smell like him, needed a space where she could think without his breathing in her ear, steadying her pulse when her pulse had no business being steadied.

She dressed in the dark, her jeans stiff from drying out overnight, her flannel hoodie pulled tight against the early chill. She slipped out the side door of the garage, checked both ends of the street the way she'd trained herself to, and walked the six blocks to Lila's diner. She sat at the counter with a coffee she didn't drink and stared at the laminate until the thought she'd been circling all night finally settled into something she could act on.

Nora Fisk.

The bakery opened at seven. Amber was there at five past, the bell above the door giving a bright, cheerful jingle that felt obscene given the occasion. Nora was behind the counter, sliding a tray of croissants into the display case, and she glanced up with the flat, assessing look she always wore before she'd decided whether a person was worth her energy.

"You look like hell," Nora said pleasantly.

"I need to ask you something." Amber set her palms on the glass top of the display case. "About your sister. About the people she worked with."

The pleasant look evaporated. Nora straightened slowly, a pair of tongs still dangling from one hand, and her icy eyes did a quick sweep of the bakery— empty, just the two of them and the smell of butter and hot dough and the distant clatter of someone in the kitchen.

"Backroom," Nora said. "Now."

The backroom was a narrow rectangle of flour-dusted shelving and a battered prep table. Nora set the tongs down, crossed her arms, and waited with the particular patience of someone who'd been expecting a conversation like this for longer than they'd admit.

Amber pulled up the photo on her phone — the one she'd taken of the shrine in the woods, zoomed in on the symbol carved into the wood. She held it out.

Nora's color drained. Not a gradual fade. A sudden, decisive blanch, like a switch had been thrown somewhere inside her.

"Where did you get that?" Her voice came out hushed and tight.

"Carved into a shrine in the woods outside town. And I've seen it somewhere else." Amber kept her voice level. "I need to know what it means."

Nora set the phone down on the prep table and took a step back, like the image had physical reach. She pressed her fingers to her mouth and stood there for a long beat, the kitchen sounds carrying through the wall — a mixer running, someone humming. Normal sounds from a world that felt very far away.

"It's a mark," Nora said finally. "For a group. My sister called them fixers, but that's a polite word for it." She paused. "They clean up problems for wealthy people. The kind of problems that need to disappear rather than just go away. My sister got pulled in about four years ago. She thought it was just courier work at first." A short, humorless breath. "It wasn't."

Amber's fingers were cold. She pressed them against her thighs. "Was she marked? The symbol?"

"Everyone who got past the outer ring got it." Nora's jaw tightened. "It wasn't a tattoo you got because you wanted one. "And the men she worked with. Were they all — would they all have it?"

Nora looked at her for a long, careful moment. "What are you actually asking me, Amber?"

"I'm asking if a man could have that mark and still have walked away from them."

The silence in the backroom was thick as the flour dust floating in the single stripe of morning light from the high window. Nora uncrossed her arms and picked the phone back up, looked at the image again, her expression doing something complicated.

"Walking away from that group isn't really a thing people do," she said slowly. "Not voluntarily. Not without consequences." She set the phone back down. "But there's another way to read it. If someone broke a contract. Refused a job. That would be considered a breach, and they'd be marked for collection." She met Amber's eyes. "Meaning the brand stays on your skin even after they decide you're the one who needs cleaning up."

Amber heard the blood moving in her ears. The smell of butter had gone sour on her tongue.

He was hired. To be there that night. His voice from last

night, flat and controlled, laying it out without flinching.

She'd believed him when he said he'd walked away. She still believed it. But believing it and understanding the full architecture of it were two different things, and standing in this flour-dusted backroom with Nora's pale face and the image of that carved symbol on the table between them, the architecture was becoming very clear.

Dalton Vale had never just been a stranger who happened to be nearby on the worst night of her life. He'd been sent there. He'd been part of the same machinery that had decided she needed to stop existing. And the tattoo on his thigh wasn't a relic or a ghost. It was a brand that meant the machinery still knew where he was.

She picked up her phone. Her hands were steady, which surprised her. "Thank you," she said, and she meant it.

Nora caught her arm before she reached the door. "Amber." Her grip was firm, her eyes sharp with something that might have been fear on Amber's behalf. "Whatever you're walking back into — be careful. That group doesn't send one man. They send two. Always two."

Amber looked at the hand on her arm. Then at Nora's face. "I know," she said. "He told me."

She walked back to the garage.

Dalton was awake. She could tell before she even pushed through the side door — the smell of coffee, the faint mechanical sounds from the workshop below. She stood at the top of the stairs, coat still on, and waited for him to appear in the kitchen doorway.

He did, a mug in hand, his flannel unbuttoned over a gray henley, his hair still rough from sleep. He read her face the way he always did, in that quick, quiet inventory that missed nothing, and whatever he found there made him set the mug down on the counter.

"You went to see Nora," he said.

"She confirmed it." Amber didn't take her coat off. She needed the layers right now, the physical weight of them. "The tattoo. The organization. All of it."

He nodded once, slow. Not surprised. Not defensive. Just absorbing the fact that the last wall between her and the full truth had come down.

"The man you killed," she said. "Rory's brother. Was he the one who hurt me that night? Before you—"

"Yes." The word landed hard. "He was the one who got to you first. I came in behind him. When I saw what was happening I pulled him back. He went for me instead. It happened fast." Something moved across his expression, brief and unguarded. "I've thought about the thirty seconds before I got through that door every single day for two years."

Amber pressed her palm flat against the kitchen doorframe. The wood was cool under her fingers.

"You should have told me," she said, and then stopped, because she'd banned herself from that line, and also because the honest truth was more complicated than that. He'd told her last night. He'd told her when the pressure of it had finally outrun his instinct to protect himself by staying silent. And she'd kissed him for it, which said something about her own complicated relationship with the truth.

"I know," he said quietly.

"I need to understand something." She met his gaze across the small kitchen. "The shrine in the woods. Was that Rory? Or was that you?"

"Rory." No hesitation. "He's been building that obsession for eighteen months. I found evidence of him watching your place three months ago, which is when I stopped staying at a distance." His mouth tightened. "I should have moved faster."

"But the symbol. Carved into the wood. Your symbol."

"It was a message. To me, not to you. He knew I'd find it eventually." A pause. "He was right."

She exhaled slowly. The cold knot that had been

sitting under her sternum since three in the morning loosened by a fraction. Not gone. But smaller.

"So when this is over," she said, "assuming we survive long enough for there to be an *over*— the organization still has your name. Because you broke the contract."

"That's a problem for after," he said. "Dalton—"

"One thing at a time." His voice was quiet but absolute. "Right now the problem is Rory. We deal with Rory, and then we deal with everything else."

She opened her mouth to push back on that, because *one thing at a time* felt like a very optimistic framework given their current circumstances, and she was about to say so when the workshop window exploded inward.

The sound was enormous — a crashing, splintering impact followed immediately by a whomp of ignition so deep she felt it in her chest before she registered it as sound. Orange light bloomed up through the floor grates. The smell hit her a half-second later: gasoline, burning rubber, and the chemical sweetness of something accelerating fast.

"Go." Dalton had her by the arm before she'd fully processed what she was seeing, steering her hard toward the stairs. "Now. Don't stop."

She went. The stairwell was already acrid with smoke, a thin layer of it sliding along the ceiling in a way that meant the fire below was eating through the workshop at speed. She hit the bottom step and felt the heat on her face like an open oven door, the fire already climbing the far wall where the supply shelves held every flammable thing a garage could hold.

"The door!" she shouted, but Dalton was already past her, shoulder into the side exit, the one that opened onto the alley. It blew open and cold night air rushed in, and she ran through it and kept running until the gravel of the lot was under her boots and the orange glow behind her was painting the alley walls in wild, shifting light.

She spun around. Dalton was three steps behind her, pulling the door shut on reflex even though it was already pointless. Through the high windows of the workshop, the fire was a living thing — fast and hungry, orange and white and hungry, feeding on two years of accumulated oil and gasoline and sawdust and the particular kind of mess that collects in a working garage.

He stood beside her and watched it for exactly two seconds. Then he looked away.

"Can you run?" he asked. "Yes."

"Rory's close. That throw was close-range." He was already scanning the alley, both directions, his body in that particular state of coiled readiness she'd come to recognize. "We can't be here when Landry shows up."

She understood what he meant. A fire at his garage, her present, his record— that conversation with the sheriff would take hours they didn't have and would end with Dalton in a room answering questions he couldn't answer without blowing the entire thing open.

"Wes," she said. He looked at her.

"Wes Harlan. He's far enough out of town, and he won't—" She stopped. "He won't ask questions he doesn't need the answers to."

Something shifted in Dalton's expression. Relief, maybe, or something adjacent to it. "You sure?"

"He told me himself you had a good soul." She almost laughed, except her throat was too tight from the smoke. "I think he'll survive the nuance."

Dalton grabbed her hand, and they ran.

His truck was parked two blocks over, which turned out to be just far enough. By the time they reached it, she could hear the first siren — distant, rising — and the orange glow above the rooftops was visible from the street. He drove without headlights for the first three blocks, then put them on once they hit the county road heading north.

She sat in the passenger seat with her hands folded in her lap and watched the dark fields slide past and thought about the fact that she was now technically fleeing a crime scene in a truck with a man who had, eighteen months ago, accepted a contract to kill her. She turned that thought over carefully, examining all its angles, and found that it didn't produce the emotional response she would have predicted twenty-four hours ago.

What she felt was tired. And angry. And also, underneath both of those things, something that refused to simplify into a clean narrative.

Dalton drove with one hand on the wheel, his jaw set, his eyes on the road. He hadn't spoken since the alley. She didn't push it. There was a specific kind of silence that was actually communication, and this was one of them.

She'd learned to read those silences over the past few weeks. That was the thing no one warned you about with dangerous men — the intimacy crept up on you sideways, through the small accumulated knowledge of their rhythms and tells, until you realized you could read them the way you read weather, the way you read roads.

She was in trouble, and not just the Molotov cocktail kind.

Wes Harlan's cabin sat at the end of a half-mile gravel track lined with old pines, and it was dark when they pulled up. Dalton had barely cut the engine before the porch light came on. By the time Amber's boots hit the gravel, Wes was in the doorway in a flannel robe and boots he'd clearly just shoved his feet into, his wild gray beard and the pipe clenched in his teeth giving him the look of a man who'd been awake long before they arrived.

He looked at them both. He looked at the smoke still faintly embedded in their clothes and the specific quality of their expressions.

"Get inside," he said. That was all.

He fed them. That was the first thing he did — reheated coffee and leftover stew from what smelled like earlier that evening, set it on the table without ceremony and let them eat while he settled into his chair by the woodstove and packed his pipe with the unhurried deliberateness of a man choosing not to speak until spoken to.

Dalton ate without appetite, methodical, refueling. Amber ate because her hands needed something to do. The stew was good — thick and heavy and real, the kind of food that made you remember your body existed.

Eventually Dalton pushed back from the table and looked at Wes. "I need to walk your perimeter."

Wes gestured toward the back door with two fingers. "Took the liberty. Motion sensors, northeast corner. Tripwire on the south trail. You'll want to note the third pine left of the shed — sight line's clear from there to the road."

Dalton studied the old man for a beat. Something passed between them that Amber didn't have the full vocabulary for — recognition, maybe, or the specific respect of one person who understood threat assessment toward another.

"I'll walk it anyway," Dalton said.

"Figured you would." Wes settled back. "Go on."

The back door opened and closed, and then it was just Amber and the old man and the tick of the woodstove and the smell of pine smoke and pipe tobacco, which was the smell of every cabin Amber had ever felt briefly safe in, which was not many.

"He tell you?" Wes asked. Not looking at her directly, just watching the stove.

"Everything," she said. "Or close enough."

"Mm." He took a long pull on the pipe. "How're you sitting with it?"

She thought about it. An honest answer felt overdue. "I don't know yet. I keep expecting to feel one clear thing, and instead I just feel all of them at once."

Wes nodded, unsurprised. "That's about right."

"He was sent to kill me," she said, and the words still had weight, still landed with a thud even spoken out loud for the second time. "That's not a small thing to sit with."

"No." Wes agreed easily, without minimizing it. "It isn't." "But he didn't."

"No. He didn't." The old man's brown eyes moved to her then, steady and patient. "You know what it means when a man breaks his programming? Not stumbles over it. Breaks it clean, in the worst possible moment, at the highest possible cost?"

She didn't answer, because she suspected he was about to tell her and she wanted to hear it without her own noise in the way.

"Means there was something in him that couldn't be trained out," Wes said. "All that conditioning, all that wet work, all those years of being told that people are problems and problems get solved — and he walked into a room and it didn't hold." He tapped the pipe against his knee. "That's not strategy, girl. That's not guilt after the fact. That's a man's actual nature asserting itself in the middle of everything built to suppress it." A pause. "I've known men who couldn't do that in a lifetime of trying."

Amber's throat was tight. "He still lied to me. For months."

"He did." Wes didn't argue it. "Fear'll make you do that. Not the coward kind of fear. The kind where you've finally got something real and you're convinced the truth will burn it down before it gets to grow." He turned back to the stove. "Doesn't make it right. But it makes it human."

She sat with that for a while. The woodstove ticked. Outside, she could hear the faint crunch of Dalton walking the perimeter — steady, methodical, the sound of a man who kept moving because stillness was where the ghosts caught up with you.

Eventually Wes pointed her toward the back bedroom with a jerk of his head and told her to sleep, that he'd take first watch, that the cabin had held through worse than this and so had the people in it. She didn't argue. Her body was running on fumes and adrenaline and she wasn't going to be useful to anyone by morning if she didn't close her eyes for a few hours.

She lay on the narrow cot under a heavy wool blanket and listened to the pines moving outside and the low exchange of voices from the main room when Dalton came back in — brief, quiet, the sound of two people who understood each other's economy of words.

She didn't sleep. Not fully. But she rested, which was different, and when the light at the window shifted from black to deep gray and then to the tentative, watery blue of very early morning, she got up and wrapped the blanket around her shoulders and went to stand in the doorway of the back porch.

The sunrise came in stages. First just a lightening of the sky above the tree line, the darkness thinning without committing to color yet. Then the first pale streak of gold, barely distinguishable from the gray. Then, slowly, the orange bleeding in at the horizon, warm and steady and indifferent to everything that had happened in the night below it.

Her fingers found the silver locket at her throat — an old habit, a reflex that lived in her hands independently of her thoughts. She held it between her thumb and forefinger, the metal warm from her skin, and she watched the light come up over Wes Harlan's pines and thought: *still here.*

The garage was ash by now. Rory Keane was still out there somewhere in the dark between the trees, carrying his dead brother's name and his blood-debt and whatever was left of his fractured obsession. The organization with their brands and their contracts was a horizon problem she hadn't even begun to map. Dalton was asleep on Wes's couch with a perimeter around the cabin and two years of guilt on his chest, and she was standing here with a blanket and a locket and no clear plan.

But she was still here.

That had to count for something. It always had.

She tightened her fingers around the locket, let the

metal bite slightly into her palm, and watched the sun finish arriving. It didn't offer answers. It didn't promise anything. It just came up the way it always did, reliable and ruthless, lighting everything it touched whether the things below were ready or not.

She thought she could work with that.

11
Ashes and Embers

The perimeter check took Dalton forty minutes. Amber counted them from the back porch, wrapped in the wool blanket, the locket still warm between her fingers. She heard him come in through the front, heard the low exchange with Wes, heard the couch creak under his weight. Then silence.

She went back inside and sat at the kitchen table with a mug of Wes's coffee — black, no apology for the strength — and watched the morning light fill the room in slow increments. The cabin smelled like pine resin and old wood and the ghost of last night's stew, and underneath all of it, faintly, the smoke that had followed them here from Cherry Creek like a thing unwilling to let go.

Wes was asleep in his chair by the woodstove. His pipe had gone cold in his hand, his chest rising and falling with the even rhythm of a man who'd trained himself to sleep when sleep was available, because the body kept its own ledger and the bill always came due. She studied his face for a moment — the deep lines, the gray beard, the particular stillness of a man who'd been in enough hard places that peace wasn't something he took for granted. He'd said what he'd needed to say last night and then let it be.

She respected that more than she could articulate.

She was on her second mug when Dalton appeared in the kitchen doorway.

He'd slept two hours, maybe three. It showed in the tightness around his eyes, but not in the rest of him. He moved the same way he always did — careful and deliberate, like every room was a space he was assessing before he committed his weight to it. He'd pulled on his boots and his flannel was buttoned, which meant he'd been awake long enough to have made decisions.

"Morning," she said.

"Coffee?" he asked. "Pot's still hot."

He poured a mug and leaned against the counter across from her, and they sat with that for a moment — the ordinary, surreal domesticity of it, two people who'd fled a burning building and were now drinking coffee in an old man's cabin while somewhere in the dark tree line, a man with a blood-debt and no brake pedal was waiting for his next move.

"I owe you an apology," Dalton said finally.

She kept both hands around the mug. "You gave me the truth last night. That's not nothing."

"I gave it to you too late."

"Yeah." She didn't argue that. "But you gave it to me. That's where we are."

He was quiet for a beat, watching her with that particular quality of attention that still made something tighten low in her chest—not fear, exactly, but a slow, heavy heat that crawled across her collarbone like a physical touch. It was the awareness of being truly seen, the weight of his gaze prickling against her skin until she felt the fine hairs on her arms stand up, an exposure that left her more breathless than the smoke ever had.

"A little." She set the mug down. "He told me about men who break their programming." She met his eyes across the narrow kitchen. "He seems to think it means something."

"And you?"

She turned that over carefully, the way she'd been turning it over since three in the morning when she'd first started trying to find the bottom of it. "I think I'm still deciding," she said. "But I'm here, which is its own answer."

Something shifted in his face — brief and unguarded, there and then locked back down. He nodded once, a small motion that carried more weight than it had any right to.

Wes stirred in his chair. His eyes opened with the immediate clarity of a man who didn't drift through waking up. He looked at them both, took in the scene — two people standing in his kitchen with coffee and the specific atmosphere of something newly fragile and newly chosen — and pushed himself to his feet.

"Eat first," he said. "Then we talk about what comes next."

What came next, it turned out, was a conversation Amber hadn't expected. Not the logistics — those she'd braced for, the where-do-we-go and the how-long-can-we-stay. What she hadn't braced for was Wes pulling a chair up to the kitchen table, planting his elbows on it, and looking at Dalton with the particular expression of a man about to say something that had been sitting in him for a long time.

"I know what you were," Wes said. Not an accusation. Just a fact, delivered flatly, the way you'd note the weather.

Dalton went very still. "How long?"

"Long enough." Wes picked up his pipe, turned it in his hands without lighting it. "Your father and I drank together for twenty years. He worried about you. Not the military part — the other part. The work that didn't have a name." A pause. "I didn't press him on the details. Didn't want them. But I knew the shape of it."

Amber watched Dalton's jaw work. He set his mug down on the counter with deliberate care. "Then you know what I did."

"I know what you didn't do," Wes said. "That's the part that matters to me."

The woodstove ticked. Outside, a wind moved through the pines, a low, rushing sound that came and went like breath. Dalton looked at the old man for a long moment, and the thing that moved across his face wasn't quite relief and wasn't quite shame. It was something between them, something that didn't have a clean name.

"We can't stay here and put you at risk," Dalton said.

"You'll stay until it's resolved." Wes's tone closed the door on that argument firmly. "I've got the land and the sight lines and two good rifles and a bad hip that makes me mean. You're not leaving me out of this." He glanced at Amber. "Either of you."

She almost smiled. "He does this," she told Dalton. "He makes decisions and then just presents them as weather."

"It's efficient," Wes said, unapologetic.

The morning moved at a different pace than the night had. Slower, more deliberate. Wes walked them through the cabin's defensive layout with the brisk, no-nonsense manner of a man for whom threat assessment was an old language he'd never quite forgotten — sight lines from each window, the approach from the road, the clearing to the south that gave anyone coming through the trees no cover for the last thirty yards. Dalton listened and added and questioned, and the two of them moved through the space with a shared vocabulary that Amber found herself learning in real time.

She wasn't passive about it. That was the thing she'd decided sometime in the gray pre-dawn, standing on the porch with the locket in her palm. She was done being the person things happened to. She'd spent two years being careful and quiet and small, and it hadn't kept the darkness from finding her. So she followed, and she asked, and she paid attention to everything.

They were outside by mid-morning, the air cold and sharp, the pine needles wet underfoot, the sky a flat, pale white that promised nothing but held a lot. Dalton was showing her the sight line from the tree line to the cabin's back porch, explaining where cover existed and where it didn't, and she was listening, and then she said: "Teach me to shoot."

He looked at her sideways. Not surprised, exactly. More like he'd been waiting for her to get there on her own.

"You sure?" he asked.

"I've never been more sure of anything in my life." Which might have been hyperbole, but it also might not have been.

Wes produced a .22 from the cabin without being asked, the kind of practical efficiency that made Amber like the old man more than she already did. They set up a line of tin cans on the old fence post at the edge of the clearing. Dalton stood behind her, close enough that she could feel the warmth of him against her back despite the cold, and he walked her through it — stance, grip, breath, trigger pull — with a patience she hadn't expected from him. His hands were steady and precise when he adjusted her grip, and his voice dropped low when he talked her through the mechanics, and there was an intimacy to it that had nothing to do with proximity and everything to do with trust. He was handing her something. She understood that. Not just a skill. Something larger.

The first shot went wide. The second clipped the fence post. The third took the can clean off.

The sound of it echoed through the pines and then died, and the silence that came after felt different than the silence before. Fuller, somehow. She lowered the gun and exhaled and felt something shift in her chest — small and solid and real, like a gear clicking into a slot it had always been meant for.

"Again," Dalton said. And there was something in his voice that she recognized as pride, which undid her slightly.

She shot until her hands were steady and her ears rang and she'd knocked down four out of six cans in a row, and then she handed the gun back to Wes and sat down on the porch steps and pressed her palms against her thighs and breathed. Dalton sat beside her. Not touching. Just present, which was its own kind of contact.

"When this is over," he said, "I meant what I said. Anywhere you want to go."

She turned her head. "You said that?"

"In the truck. I said it in my head." A beat. "Apparently I only got halfway there."

She let out a short, surprised laugh. It scraped past the tightness in her throat and came out rough, but it was real. "So say it now."

"When this is over—" he said it deliberately, making it an offering, "—I'll take you anywhere you want. Somewhere you haven't been. Somewhere without a history."

She looked at him for a moment, this man with his scarred eyebrow and his worn flannel and two years of guilt and a perimeter he'd just walked at five in the morning because the only way he knew how to care for someone was to put himself between them and everything that could hurt them.

She'd been so angry at him. She still was, underneath everything. But anger and want and trust weren't mutually exclusive. She was learning that in real time.

"Ask me again when we're not fugitives," she said. "Deal."

Wes fed them lunch. They didn't talk about Rory during it. The silence wasn't avoidance — it was the particular discipline of people who understood that the body needed a few minutes of ordinary before it could go back to the hard thing. Amber ate and listened to the wind and watched a crow land on the fence post where the tin cans had been and thought: *just a crow.* And then thought: *don't be naive.*

It was Dalton who found the bag.

He'd gone back out to check the south trail, the one with Wes's tripwire on it, and he came back twenty minutes later with a canvas pack that looked like it had been dropped in a hurry. Mud-smeared, one strap torn, the kind of bag you bought at an army surplus store and didn't care about losing. He set it on the kitchen table and they stood around it the way you stand around something you know is going to change the shape of things.

Inside: a burner phone with a cracked screen and a dead battery, three protein bar wrappers, a folding knife, and a hand-drawn map. Amber recognized the terrain on it — Wes's property, the county road, the tree line. Rory had been mapping the cabin. The routes in and out. He'd been here, close, possibly last night while Dalton was walking the perimeter and she was watching the sunrise.

Her stomach dropped.

But it was the map that made Dalton go quiet in a way that felt different from his usual quiet. She watched his expression as he traced the lines on it, and she saw the exact moment he found what she hadn't noticed yet.

"There," he said, and pointed.

In the lower corner of the map, small and neat, was a symbol. Not the carved mark from the woods — different. This one was a set of initials and a sequence of numbers that meant nothing to her. But alongside them, in handwriting that matched the map's rough lines, was a notation. An address in Cherry Creek. A meeting time, two days out. And below that, a single word that made the cold in the cabin feel sharper than it had any right to.

Confirmed.

Rory wasn't working alone. He had someone on the inside. Someone in town who'd confirmed information, confirmed timing, confirmed something that Amber couldn't fully read from the map alone but that felt, in the particular way that bad things always felt before they were fully understood, like the piece that changed everything.

"He's been communicating with someone," she said.

"Yes." Dalton's voice was flat and careful.

"Someone in Cherry Creek." She pressed her fingers to the address notation. "Do you recognize this?"

He was quiet for a beat too long. "It's near the sheriff's office."

The three of them looked at the map. Wes reached out and tapped the pipe against his palm, a slow, rhythmic motion that she'd come to recognize as the way he thought.

"Could be a lot of people," Wes said. "Could be a lot of things."

"Could be," Dalton agreed. But his eyes stayed on the map, and the muscle along his jaw had gone tight in a way that meant he was running through possibilities faster than he was speaking them.

Amber straightened. The locket was cool against her collarbone now, the morning warmth of it gone. She thought about Sheriff Landry and his weathered face and his steel-gray eyes and the way he'd looked at her the one time she'd tried to file a report — not hostile, exactly, but closed. Like a door with a lock she didn't have the key to.

She thought about other people too. Lila, who knew everyone. Nora, who had her own entanglements. The regulars at the diner who watched everything and said little. Small towns didn't keep secrets — they just passed them in a circle until everyone had held one.

"We need to know who it is before we do anything else," she said.

"Agreed." Dalton finally looked up from the map. "Two days is enough time to find out." His gaze moved to hers, and the blue of his eyes in the cabin's flat morning light was steady and certain and more than a little dangerous. "We're not going in blind."

Wes picked up the map, studied it, set it back down. "I'll make calls," he said. "Quietly. I've got ears in that town."

He glanced at Amber with an expression that was almost wry. "Some advantages to being old and forgettable."

She didn't think he was forgettable at all. But she let it stand.

The afternoon settled around the cabin like snow settling — slow and accumulative, the weight building without announcing itself. Amber helped Wes stack wood on the back porch while Dalton reinforced the south trail, and there was something almost meditative about the physical work, the solid knock of the logs, the cold air, the smell of pine and turned earth. Her body was tired in a deep, bone-level way. Her mind kept circling the map, the initials, the word *confirmed.*

She stacked the last log and straightened and looked out across the clearing toward the tree line, where the pines stood dark and close against the pale sky, holding whatever they were holding in their shadows.

Rory was out there. Mapped, connected, patient in the particular way that obsession made people patient — not because they were calm, but because they believed, with the unshakeable conviction of someone who'd made a thing the center of their whole meaning, that the end was already written. That she was already his. That it was just a matter of time.

She touched the locket. The metal was cold now.

Let him believe that, she thought. *Let him map all he wants.*

She turned back toward the cabin, where the light was warm in the windows and Wes was already moving toward the kitchen and Dalton would come back through the tree line in twenty minutes with mud on his boots and nothing in his expression except the particular focus of a man who'd decided that whatever it cost, she was worth the paying.

The hunt wasn't over. It had barely started. But for the first time in two years, she wasn't just the thing being hunted.

That felt like enough to build on.

12
The Hunter's Mark

The crows were there when Amber stepped off the porch at first light.

Not one or two. Seven. Lined up in a ragged, deliberate trail from the tree line to the bottom step, each one placed with its wings spread flat, its neck bent at an angle that didn't happen by accident. She counted them before she even registered what she was looking at, the way your brain catalogs a threat before your heart catches up. Seven dead crows, spread across Wes's frost-stiff grass like a message written in a language she hadn't wanted to learn.

Her stomach turned over.

"Dalton." Her voice came out steady, which surprised her. "Come look at this."

He appeared in the doorway behind her in under ten seconds. She felt his presence before she heard him move, that particular shift in the air that happened whenever he filled a space. He stepped past her and crouched at the bottom of the steps, studying the nearest crow without touching it. His jaw was set. His eyes moved from bird to bird, tracking the line back toward the trees with slow, methodical attention.

"He was here last night," she said. Not a question.

"Yeah." Dalton straightened. "This isn't just a warning. He's showing us he can walk up to the door." A pause. "He wants us to know how close he can get."

Wes appeared beside her, pipe cold in his hand, taking in the scene with the flat, unsurprised expression of a man who'd seen uglier. "Well," he said, after a moment. "That settles the question of whether he's patient."

"He's not patient," Dalton said. "He's theatrical. There's a difference. Patient people don't need an audience." He turned, and the look on his face was one she hadn't seen before: controlled, clean, stripped of everything except focus. It was a cold, tactical clarity that seemed to settle over him like armor, the kind of hard-wired instinct that only came from years of operating in the dark where mistakes were lethal. He was no longer just a man in a flannel shirt; he was a machine recalibrating for a mission. "He's escalating. Which means we don't have two days."

They moved fast after that.

Wes walked the property line while Dalton set tripwires along the south trail and the narrow deer path that cut through the pines on the east side.

Amber went with Dalton, handing him wire and stakes when he needed them, watching his hands work with a precision that was almost unsettling. He knew exactly how much tension to set, exactly where the trip point needed to be, exactly how to anchor it so wind wouldn't trigger a false alarm. She didn't ask how he knew. She'd stopped asking those kinds of questions. Instead she paid attention, because that was the most useful thing she could do.

"Six inches off the ground," he said, threading the wire around a pine trunk. "Anything taller, a deer sets it off.

Anything shorter, a person steps over without thinking." He glanced up. "You're remembering this."

"I'm remembering all of it," she said.

He tied off the wire and moved to the next anchor point without comment, but something in his posture eased fractionally, the way it did when she said something that landed right with him. She'd started noticing those small shifts. The way his shoulders dropped half an inch when the tension released. The way his hands slowed when he was thinking something through rather than reacting. She'd memorized the difference without meaning to.

By mid-morning, they'd covered every approach to the cabin that wasn't the front road. The cold had settled into Amber's fingers despite her gloves, and her breath made small, quick clouds in the air. Pine resin and damp earth and the faint metallic edge of the wire — that was what she'd remember about this day, she thought. The smell of preparation.

"Okay," Dalton said, when they'd reached the far edge of the property and he'd checked the last line. "Now we talk about what happens if he gets through."

She already knew what he was going to say. She'd known since yesterday, since she'd raised the .22 at those tin cans and felt something click into place inside her that had been loose for two years. "I want to keep practicing."

"I know." He was already moving back toward the cabin. "Wes has more ammunition."

Wes did. He also had a second firearm — a compact .38 revolver, heavier in the hand than the .22, with a shorter barrel and a different kind of authority. He set it on the porch railing without ceremony and said, "Time to graduate," and then went inside to make coffee, because Wes had an instinct for when two people needed space to do a thing without being watched.

Dalton set up new targets at the far end of the clearing: three tin cans and a piece of cardboard he'd sketched a rough outline on with a marker. Not a human shape, exactly.

Just a silhouette. Enough to shift the mental framing from sport to purpose.

He stood behind her again, not quite touching, close enough that she registered the warmth of him along her back, a contrast to the cold air pressing against her front. His hands came around to adjust her grip on the revolver, his fingers steady and deliberate over hers, and she was aware of him in that specific, full-body way that cut through every other thought — his breath near her temple, the rough edge of his flannel sleeve against her wrist, the low register of his voice when he spoke.

"This one kicks more," he said. "Don't fight it. Let your wrists absorb the recoil. If you tense up, your next shot goes wide."

"Don't tense up," she repeated. "Got it."

"Breathe out before you pull. The trigger takes more pressure than you expect. Don't jerk it — squeeze."

She exhaled. Squeezed.

The shot was louder than she'd braced for, the kick rolling up through her wrists and forearms in a sharp wave. The first can spun off the fence post and landed somewhere in the grass. She adjusted her stance without being told, exhaled again, and took the second one.

"There," Dalton said quietly. Just that. One word, and the weight of it.

She worked through the cylinder twice. By the end of the second round, her arms were burning and her ears were ringing and she'd hit the cardboard silhouette four times, center mass, which was what mattered. She lowered the gun and pressed her fingers to her sternum for a moment, feeling the thrum of her own pulse, and it struck her — not for the first time, but more clearly than before — that she was not the same person who'd moved to Cherry Creek two years ago with a duffel bag and a terror she couldn't name. That person had spent two years making herself small. This one was standing in a clearing in the cold, learning to put holes in things that threatened her, and feeling something that wasn't quite power but was adjacent to it. Something solid and earned.

Dalton came around to face her. His blue eyes moved over her face with careful attention, reading her the way he read everything — thoroughly, quietly, missing nothing. "How do you feel?"

"Honest answer?" "Only kind I want."

"Like I've been doing this wrong for two years," she said. "Running and hiding and waiting for somebody else to fix it." She turned the revolver over in her hands, then looked up. "I'm done with that version."

Something moved across his face, quick and unguarded, before he locked it back down. He reached out and took the revolver from her carefully, checked the cylinder, and set it on the porch railing beside the box of ammunition. Then he turned back.

"When this is over," he said, and his voice had dropped, the words deliberate and unhurried, "I meant what I said in that truck."

She crossed her arms against the cold. "You mean the thing you said in your head and only got halfway out?"

His mouth curved, brief and real. "I'll take you somewhere you've never been. Somewhere that doesn't have a single bad memory attached to it. You pick the direction."

She studied him — the scarred jaw, the worn flannel, the eyes that never quite stopped scanning even when the rest of him went still. Two years of guilt and another year of something he hadn't had a name for until she walked into his orbit. She was still angry at him, underneath everything. She'd probably be angry for a while. But she was also here, standing in his space in the cold, choosing not to run, and that said more than the anger did.

"Ask me again when we're not living in someone's survival plan," she said.

"Deal." He said it the same way he'd said it before, like it was a contract he intended to honor.

Wes had lunch ready when they came inside — canned soup, crackers, the particular efficiency of a man who fed people because it was practical and not because he needed to make a production of it. They ate. They didn't talk about Rory during the meal, and the silence was the functional kind, the kind that let the body bank some ordinary before going back to the hard thing. Amber ate the soup and listened to the wind move through the pines outside and thought about the map still sitting on the kitchen table. The initials. The address near the sheriff's office. The word *confirmed* in small, neat handwriting that made her skin crawl every time she pictured it.

After lunch, she went back to the table and spread the map flat again.

She'd been turning the question of the mole over and over since last night, running through faces. Sheriff Landry, with his steel-gray eyes and his bureaucratic distance. The regulars at the diner. The people who'd watched her settle into Cherry Creek with the particular, low-key intensity of small-town observers. She'd thought she was paranoid. Turns out she'd just been right.

Dalton came and stood beside her, arms crossed, studying the map over her shoulder. His chin nearly grazed her temple. She could smell him — flannel and cold air and a clean, warm male scent that shouldn't have been distracting under the circumstances and absolutely was.

"We still can't rule out Landry," she said.

"No," he agreed. "But that address is near a lot of things. The hardware store. The post office. The back parking lot where half the town cuts through." He pressed his thumb to the notation. "Someone confirmed Rory's intel on this cabin. That means someone knew we'd come here."

"Who knew?"

Dalton was quiet for a beat. "Wes. You. Me." He paused. "And whoever Wes called this morning."

From the doorway, Wes's voice came in flat and certain: "I called two people. Both of them I'd trust with my life." He moved into the kitchen, planted his hands on the table, and studied the map. "But I called from the cabin's landline, which is the same line I've had for thirty years. And landlines aren't as private as people like to pretend."

The three of them sat with that for a moment.

"It also could've been someone who spotted the truck on the road," Dalton said. "We weren't exactly invisible getting here. Small town, night of a garage fire — somebody saw us."

"So it narrows down to anyone in Cherry Creek with eyes and a phone," Amber said. "That's not actually narrowing it down."

"The initials narrow it," Dalton said. He pointed to the lower corner of the map. "Two letters. Not a lot of people those fit."

She stared at the initials. She'd been staring at them since last night. The shapes of them kept rearranging themselves in her head, trying to attach to a face, a voice, a name. Someone who knew this town. Someone Rory trusted enough to share coordinates with. Someone who'd been close enough to watch her without raising a single alarm.

She pressed two fingers to the paper and thought about who'd been there from the beginning. Who'd been warm and easy and immediately familiar. Who'd known where everyone was and what everyone did and had never once seemed suspicious because that was the whole point of a good cover— it looked like a personality, not a performance.

The thought arrived slowly, and then all at once, and she hated it the moment it landed.

She didn't say it out loud. Not yet. She needed more than a feeling and a pair of initials. But her chest had gone tight and her hands were flat against the table and the particular cold that settled over her wasn't the cabin air. It was the specific cold of suspecting someone you'd let yourself trust.

"We figure it out before we move," Dalton said. He straightened, and his voice carried the quiet authority it always did when he'd made a decision. "We don't go back to Cherry Creek blind. We don't reach out to anyone until we know." His eyes found hers across the table. "Two days."

She nodded. "Two days."

The afternoon was physical work: reinforcing the porch railing, adding a secondary wire across the east path, checking the sight lines from each window. Amber carried, hammered, held things steady while Dalton secured them, and the labor felt like it meant something — not busywork, but actual preparation, her hands doing something concrete in the face of a threat that had no concrete shape yet. Her muscles ached by the time the light started going gray in the sky, the flat white afternoon bleeding into early dusk.

She was at the kitchen sink washing the grit off her hands when the sound from outside stopped her cold.

Not a tripwire. Not a snap of branches. Something worse: footsteps on the gravel path, unhurried, and then a knock at the door.

Three knocks, deliberate. The kind that said *I'm not hiding.*

Dalton was already moving from the back room, the revolver in his hand, his entire body shifted into that predator stillness that meant every sense was up and live. He met Amber's eyes and held up one hand: *stay back.* She didn't move. Wes had gone for his rifle from the corner without a word, positioning himself at the side window where he could see the porch without being seen from outside.

Dalton crossed to the door. Amber held her breath. "Who's there," he said. Not loud. Not a question, exactly.

A voice came through the door — familiar enough that Amber's breath came back in a rush, and wrong enough that something at the base of her spine didn't settle the way it should have.

"It's Lila. Lila Beckett." A pause, and beneath the familiar brashness of the name, something that sounded raw and frightened. "Please — please just open the door. He found me. Rory found me and I barely got out and I didn't know where else to go."

Amber's hand went to the counter. Lila. Caramel curls and red lipstick and the particular energy of a woman who filled every room she walked into. Lila, who'd befriended her on her first day in Cherry Creek without being asked. Lila, who knew everyone's name and everyone's business and who'd slid into Amber's life so naturally that it had never once occurred to her to question the ease of it.

She moved toward the door. "Dalton—"

"Wait." His voice was flat. He still hadn't opened it. "It's Lila," she said. "I know her."

"I know." He didn't move. His eyes were fixed on the door with an expression that wasn't compassion. It was calculation, clean and cold, and it made something in her stomach turn. "Lila. Step back from the door and let me see your hands when it opens."

A beat. Then: "Okay. Okay, fine, just please—" He opened the door.

Lila stood on the porch, and she looked terrible. Bruises along her jaw and cheekbone, a split lip, her caramel curls wild and tangled around her face. Her jacket was torn at the shoulder. She was shaking — or doing something that looked exactly like shaking, the fine tremor of someone who'd been terrified and run hard and barely made it.

Amber's first instinct was to go to her. She took a step forward, and then she felt Dalton's arm come up across the doorway, not touching her but blocking the space, and she stopped.

He was still looking at Lila with that same flat attention. Not at the bruises. At her hands. At the way she was standing. At something Amber couldn't immediately name but that Dalton had apparently already cataloged and weighed and arrived at a conclusion about.

"Come in," he said, and his voice was perfectly neutral, which was the most dangerous thing about it.

Lila stepped inside. Her amber eyes moved around the cabin — quick, taking inventory, hitting the corners and the windows before they landed on Amber, and in that half-second before the warmth of recognition clicked back into her expression, Amber saw something cold.

She felt the bottom fall out of her chest.

Dalton had seen it too. She knew by the way his hand moved — slow, deliberate — toward the revolver on the side table. "Lila," he said quietly. "Those bruises look fresh."

"They are fresh," Lila said, and her voice had shifted, the frightened tremor dropping away like a coat she'd shrugged off. "But not for the reason you think, honey."

The tranquilizer pistol came up from inside her jacket in one smooth motion. She didn't aim at Dalton. She aimed at Wes.

The shot was soft — almost quiet, a compressed pop that didn't sound like what it was until Wes made a short, surprised sound and sat down hard in his chair, and then his head drooped, and the rifle slid from his hands.

"Wes!" Amber lurched toward him, and Lila's voice cut across the room, sharp and final.

"He's not dead. He'll sleep it off." A pause, and there was something in her tone that was almost apologetic, but not quite, the tone of a person who'd weighed a thing and made a choice and was now living on the other side of it. "I didn't want to do this the hard way. I really didn't."

Amber turned to face her. The woman standing in Wes's cabin wearing Lila's face was and wasn't the person she'd known. The posture was different. The eyes were different — not cold exactly, but stripped of the warmth that Amber had taken at face value, and she hated herself for that, for how completely she'd believed it.

"How long?" Amber's voice came out quiet and even, which was its own kind of fury.

Lila's mouth curved into something that was almost sad. "Since you walked into Cherry Creek. Since you sat down at the counter and ordered a black coffee and looked like someone who'd been running so long she'd forgotten what she was running from." She tilted her head. "I spotted you. That's what I do. That's what I've always done."

"For Rory."

"For the money Rory's people paid." She said it without flinching, which was somehow worse than if she'd been defensive about it. "I have debts, Amber. The kind that don't wait. The kind that have names and addresses and don't care about your feelings." Her free hand opened and closed at her side. "I didn't plan for you to matter. That part wasn't supposed to happen."

From outside, footsteps on gravel. Then the creak of the porch step under significant weight.

The door swung open behind Lila.

Rory Keane stepped in from the cold with a shotgun broken over his forearm and a gold-toothed smile that didn't reach his pale green eyes. He was muddier than Amber had imagined, his shaggy black hair plastered to his forehead, his jacket dark with pine resin and whatever he'd been moving through in the tree line. He looked at Amber the way someone looks at a thing they've been collecting, patient and proprietary, and her skin crawled straight off her bones.

"There she is," he said. Low and oily, like he was greeting someone who'd been late to a party he'd thrown in her honor. His eyes moved to Dalton, and the warmth evaporated. "You and me have a walk to take, Vale. All of us, actually." He raised the shotgun. "There's an old mine, twenty minutes through those trees. We're going to have a conversation out there where nobody can hear it." He smiled again. "Move."

Dalton didn't move immediately. He stood very still, and Amber could feel the calculation in him, the way he was running angles and outcomes and contingencies, doing the math on a situation that had exactly one variable he wouldn't gamble with: her. Rory read it too.

"She walks first," Rory said, and the smile dropped. "Or she doesn't walk at all."

That was the moment Amber understood the shape of it. Rory didn't want her dead. Not yet. He wanted Dalton to watch what came first. He wanted Dalton to know exactly how much power he'd lost, how completely the ground had shifted under the man who'd stolen what Rory believed was his.

Dalton's hands came up, slow and open, and he stepped back.

Amber's fingers tightened at her side. The revolver was on the side table, six feet behind her. The tripwires were outside. Wes was asleep in his chair with his chest rising and falling in the slow rhythm of the drugged. The locket was cold at her throat.

She looked at Dalton. He looked back, and in the half-second before he dropped his eyes and nodded toward the door, she saw it — not surrender, not defeat, but the deliberate, controlled choice of a man standing down in order to stay in the game. Buying time. Trusting her to do the same.

She turned toward the door. Rory stepped aside to let her pass, and she felt his eyes on her like a hand she hadn't consented to, and she kept her face empty and her spine straight and her breathing even.

The pines were dark ahead of them, holding their shadows, the mine somewhere in the cold distance beyond the tree line.

She stepped off the porch. The frost-stiff grass crunched under her boots. Behind her, she heard Dalton follow, and behind him, the sound of Rory's footsteps, unhurried and certain.

Twenty minutes through the trees. That was twenty minutes she intended to use.

13
Betrayal's Bloom

The trees swallowed the cabin light within the first two minutes.

Amber walked ahead, boots crunching through frost-stiff undergrowth, pine branches catching at her jacket sleeves like something trying to slow her down. The cold had teeth out here, away from the cabin's warmth, biting through her hoodie and settling into her collarbones. She kept her breathing even. She counted her steps the way she'd learned to count other things — threats, exits, the distance between herself and whatever was behind her.

Behind her: Rory, with his shotgun and his proprietary smile. And Dalton, hands raised, moving with the controlled stillness of a man conserving every ounce of himself for later.

Lila walked to Rory's left, her tranquilizer pistol still out, the torn jacket and the fake bruises a costume she'd stopped bothering to sell. She'd peeled off the frightened-woman performance the moment Wes hit the chair, and what remained underneath was something Amber was still trying to look at directly — the real face behind the caramel curls and the red lipstick and the brassy laugh that had made Cherry Creek feel almost like home.

Since you walked into Cherry Creek. That's what she'd said. *Since you sat down at the counter and ordered a black coffee.*

Amber had trusted her. She'd trusted her the way you trust someone who doesn't give you a reason not to — which, it turned out, was exactly the kind of trust that got you walked at gunpoint through a pine forest toward an old mine at dusk.

She cataloged the ground as she walked. A root system that broke the surface here, a depression in the earth there. A rusted fence post half-buried in dead leaves. Details. Dalton had drilled that into her over two days without ever saying the word — *catalog, catalog, catalog* — and so she did it now, mapping the terrain by feel and failing light, because twenty minutes was a long time if you used it right.

"Faster," Rory said from behind her. Not angry. Comfortable. Like he had all night and didn't mind reminding her that she didn't.

She moved faster.

Lila appeared at her left, close enough that Amber could smell her — the same vanilla body spray she'd always worn at the diner, which was maybe the most disorienting thing about all of this. She still smelled like someone Amber had liked.

"Don't do anything stupid," Lila said quietly. Not a threat, exactly. More like someone who'd already played out the scenarios and didn't want the cleanup.

"Wouldn't dream of it," Amber said.

Lila glanced at her sideways, and for just a second, something that might have been genuine regret moved through her expression. Then it closed off again, the way a window shuts against weather. "I meant what I said back there. About you mattering." She paused. "For whatever that's worth."

"Pretty much nothing," Amber said pleasantly. "But thanks."

The mine entrance appeared without warning — a black rectangle cut into a hillside, framed by crumbling timber supports and a rusted chain that someone had unhooked recently enough that the dirt around the post was still disturbed. The smell hit her before the shape fully registered: damp stone, old rust, something organic and cold and completely lightless. The kind of smell that made your body want to step back even when your brain was still deciding.

She didn't step back.

Rory produced a flashlight from his jacket — a big one, industrial, throwing a hard white beam into the dark. He swung it across the entrance like he owned the place, which maybe he did. The light caught rotting timber crossbeams, puddles of standing water, walls that wept with moisture. The mine swallowed the beam at about thirty feet and kept going.

"In," Rory said. And then, to Dalton specifically: "You first."

Dalton moved past Amber, and for one second, his arm brushed hers — brief, deliberate, the lightest possible contact — and she understood it. *I'm here. I'm still in this. Stay with me.*

She stayed with him.

Inside, the temperature dropped another ten degrees. The beam of Rory's flashlight carved shadows out of the walls, making the tunnel feel narrower than it probably was. Their footsteps echoed in a way that made it impossible to tell how many people were walking. Water dripped somewhere ahead, steady as a metronome, and the sound bounced until it seemed to come from everywhere at once.

Rory walked them about forty feet in before he told them to stop.

The tunnel opened into a small chamber here, wide enough for all of them without crowding. Old equipment rusted in the corners — a cart with a broken wheel, something that might have been a pulley system once, now just iron bones. Rory swept the light around and seemed satisfied with what he saw, which told Amber he'd been here before. This wasn't improvised. He'd chosen this place.

"Hands," he said, and Lila produced zip ties from her jacket pocket with the practiced efficiency of someone who'd packed for exactly this.

Amber's wrists got secured in front of her. Dalton's got secured behind his back, which was the smarter call, and Rory knew it — he watched Dalton's face while Lila did it, looking for the flinch of a man who understood he'd just lost his primary option. Dalton's expression gave him nothing.

Rory set the flashlight on the rusted cart, angling the beam so it threw dim, omnidirectional light across the chamber. Then he leaned against the wall and looked at Dalton the way someone looks at a bill they've been waiting to collect.

"Special forces," he said. "Recon. Extractions." He clicked his tongue. "Couldn't extract yourself from a one-room cabin with an old man and a scared girl." He tilted his head. "What happened to you, Vale?"

Dalton said nothing. His eyes moved — not to Rory, but around the chamber. Ceiling. Exits. The cart. Amber. Back to Rory. Still running the math.

Rory didn't like the silence. She could tell by the way he pushed off the wall and moved closer, the shotgun dropping to his side but not away. "You know what your problem is? You went and made it personal." He gestured loosely at Amber. "She was a job. A target. The boyfriend had something our people needed, and when he died before he could give it up, the trail went cold." He shrugged one shoulder, almost philosophical about it. "Then you showed up that night, played hero, and suddenly the girl's gone and you're playing house in Cherry Creek like that fixes anything."

Amber's chest clenched. *The boyfriend had something our people needed.*

She turned that over fast, turned it the way she'd been turning everything— the locket cold at her throat, the crescent moon tattoo on her wrist, two years of fractured nightmares she'd never been able to stitch into a coherent picture. Her ex, Marcus, who'd died in a car crash three weeks after the assault. Marcus, who'd kept secrets she'd chalked up to privacy and not thought hard enough about.

She pressed her bound wrists against her sternum and kept her face still.

"He's not going to answer you," she said. Her voice was steady, which surprised even her. "He's doing that thing where he's quiet so he can think. It drives me crazy too, honestly."

Rory's pale green eyes slid to her. He smiled the gold-tooth smile. "There she is. Lila said you had a mouth on you."

"Lila said a lot of things," Amber said. "Most of them turned out to be a performance, so I'd take her notes with a grain of salt."

From the edge of the chamber, Lila made a small, tired sound that wasn't quite a laugh.

Rory took a few steps toward Amber, and she made herself hold her ground, made herself keep her chin level and her breathing measured even as every instinct she had lit up at once. He was close enough now that she could smell him — cigarette smoke and pine resin and something chemical underneath, motor oil or solvent, the smell of a man who worked in a chop shop and didn't quite wash it off.

"You know what's funny?" he said, his voice dropping to something almost conversational. "The thing we're looking for — your boyfriend hid it.

Thought he was clever. Thought if he buried it somewhere personal, somewhere sentimental—" his eyes dropped to the locket at her throat "—we'd never think to look there." He reached out.

Amber jerked back. "Don't."

"Amber." Dalton's voice, quiet and very controlled.

She caught herself. Breathed. Rory's hand hung in the air between them for a moment, and then he pulled it back, unhurried, like he had all the time in the world and her resistance was mildly entertaining.

"I'm not going to grab it," he said. "Not yet. I want your boyfriend to watch that part." He glanced back at Dalton. "See, he went and fell for the target. Which means watching her lose things is going to hurt him a lot more than anything I could do to him directly." The smile widened. "So we're going to take our time."

Dalton's jaw tightened. Just slightly. Just enough.

Amber filed that away and kept talking, because talking was the only tool she had right now and she intended to use it like a crowbar. "So your whole organization — all this muscle, all these resources — and Marcus outsmarted you with a locket." She let the disbelief color her tone just enough. "That's embarrassing."

Rory's expression sharpened.

"I mean, really," she continued, pressing the advantage of his irritation the way she'd press a bruise to make sure it was real. "He wasn't exactly a criminal mastermind. He was a guy with a laptop and a gambling problem and an overinflated sense of his own cleverness. And you still couldn't get the thing back." She shook her head. "Your people must love working with you."

"Amber," Dalton said again, and this time it had a different texture — not a warning, but something else. Something that sounded, to her ears, like *keep going.*

She kept going. "Does Rory run point on all the jobs, or just the ones that go embarrassingly sideways? I'm asking for context."

Rory moved fast. He closed the distance and grabbed her arm, and she felt the grip of it, hard and furious, the specific anger of a man whose ego she'd just put her thumb into. "You think this is funny—"

The sound from behind him was barely a sound at all. A breath, a shift of weight, something plastic snapping.

Rory spun.

Dalton's hands were in front of him.

The zip tie hadn't broken — he'd slipped it, working the plastic over the heel of his hand with whatever he'd been doing while she kept Rory's attention forward, using the way his wrists were angled and the particular knowledge of a man who'd been restrained before and had spent time thinking about how not to stay that way. He'd been at it since the moment Lila put the ties on, slow and invisible, and she hadn't known for certain he was doing it, but she'd hoped, and she'd bought him every second she could.

Rory brought the shotgun up. Dalton was already moving.

What happened next was fast and brutal and not at all like the fights in movies, where people trade hits at a reasonable pace and everyone stays mostly upright. Dalton drove into Rory before the shotgun could level, both of them crashing into the wall of the tunnel with a sound that bounced off the stone and came back doubled. The shotgun went off — deafening in the enclosed space, the blast hitting the ceiling and raining grit and small stones down on everyone — and Amber's ears rang so hard the world went briefly white.

She spun toward Lila.

Lila was already coming at her, the tranquilizer pistol up, and Amber did the only thing available to her — she dropped. She went straight down, below the line of the shot, and felt the compressed pop of the pistol discharge just above her head, the dart skimming her hair. Then she drove up with both bound fists into Lila's forearm, throwing the next shot wide, and they went down together onto the wet stone floor in a tangle of elbows and knees and the specific, unglamorous physicality of two people fighting in a space too cramped for either of them.

Lila was stronger than she looked. Amber had known that, distantly, the way you know things about people and don't factor them in until it's too late. She'd spent years waitressing, carrying plates and hauling supply boxes, and she used that strength now, rolling on top of Amber and trying to pin her wrists. The vanilla body spray hit Amber in the nose, grotesquely familiar, and she used the spike of anger that came with it.

She bucked her hips and threw Lila sideways.

The tranquilizer pistol skittered across the stone and disappeared into the shadow somewhere to their left. Lila scrambled for it. Amber got there first— not to the gun, but to Lila's jacket, grabbing a fistful and dragging her back, and then they were grappling again, in the mud this time, both of them breathing hard, and somewhere behind them Dalton and Rory were still going at it, the sounds of the fight ricocheting off the tunnel walls in ways that made it impossible to track.

"Stop," Lila gritted out. "Amber, just stop—"

"No," Amber said, and it came out simple and flat, and she meant it with every bone in her body.

Her hands found something in the dark. Her fingers closed around it before her eyes confirmed what it was — a chunk of stone, fist-sized, dense enough that her bound hands could barely grip it. Old mine wall, broken loose at some point, sitting in the mud like it had been waiting. She closed both hands around it.

Lila saw her face and understood what was about to happen. "Amber—"

Amber swung.

The stone connected with the side of Lila's head — not as hard as she could have hit, not a kill shot, but hard enough. Hard enough that the fight went out of Lila all at once, her body going slack and dropping to the mud with a heaviness that meant unconscious, not dead. Her caramel curls spread across the wet stone. Her chest rose and fell.

Amber dropped the stone. Her hands were shaking. She pressed them flat against her thighs for exactly one second, let the shaking happen, and then she got to her feet.

The flashlight had rolled to a different angle during the struggle, throwing the chamber into tilted shadows, and it took her a moment to find Dalton and Rory in the dark. When she did, her breath stopped.

They were at the far end of the chamber, where the floor dropped away. She'd registered the vertical shaft earlier — a black circle in the ground, rimmed with rusted iron, the kind of drop that went down far enough that you couldn't hear the bottom. Rory had the shotgun again. He and Dalton were locked together at the rim, Rory's back to the shaft, Dalton's hands on the shotgun barrel, both of them fighting for control of the weapon with a grinding, desperate force that made the muscles in Dalton's forearms stand out even in the bad light.

She moved without deciding to move.

She crossed the chamber fast, grabbed the fallen zip tie off the ground — the one Dalton had slipped — and kept moving, and Rory didn't see her coming because every ounce of his attention was on the man trying to take the gun from him, on the specific terror of the shaft at his back and the knowledge that he was losing ground.

She got behind Rory and looped the zip tie over his head and pulled.

Not a garrote. Not enough tension for that. But enough to jerk his head back and break his concentration for exactly the second Dalton needed. Rory's grip on the shotgun faltered — just fractionally, just for a heartbeat— and Dalton wrenched it sideways and free, and then Rory was off-balance, arms windmilling, his boots scraping at the rim of the shaft, and Dalton grabbed a fistful of his jacket and yanked him back from the edge, away from the drop, and threw him down hard onto the stone floor instead.

Rory hit the ground and didn't get up right away. He lay there, chest heaving, the gold tooth catching the flashlight's beam, his pale green eyes blinking at the ceiling with the specific dazed expression of a man who'd just processed how close the other option was.

Dalton stood over him, the shotgun in his hands, his breathing ragged and controlled in equal measure. A cut above his ear bled steadily down his jaw. His flannel was torn at the shoulder. He looked at Rory on the ground for a long moment with an expression that had nothing soft in it, and then he stepped back.

"Don't," he said. One word. It carried everything it needed to. Rory didn't move.

Amber's legs chose that moment to inform her they were done being reliable. She sat down on the mine floor — not gracefully, just down, her back against the stone wall, her bound wrists in her lap, the cold and the dark and the ringing in her ears all arriving at once like they'd been politely waiting their turn. The locket pressed against her sternum. She wrapped both hands around it and held it there, this small cold weight that had apparently been the center of gravity for two years of her life without her knowing it.

Dalton crouched in front of her. He touched her face — one hand, careful, tilting her chin up to check her over in the dim light, his thumb swiping mud off her cheekbone. His eyes moved across her face the way they always did, thorough and quiet, looking for damage.

"You're okay," he said. Not a question.

"Jury's still out," she said. Her voice was steadier than she expected. "But probably."

He pressed her hands briefly between his, then stood, and the look he turned toward the mine entrance was the look of a man already calculating the next forty-eight hours. Rory on the ground. Lila unconscious in the mud. Wes asleep back at the cabin, drugged but breathing. The sheriff's number saved in a phone that was still in Amber's jacket pocket because nobody had thought to take it.

She pulled it out with her bound hands. Looked at the screen. One bar of signal, which was one bar more than she'd expected in the belly of an old mine.

She called Landry.

It rang four times. Then: "This is Landry."

"It's Amber Rowan," she said. "I need you to come to Wes Harlan's property. Bring people." She paused. "Bring a lot of people."

A beat of silence. Then the sheriff's gravelly drawl, stripped of its usual skepticism, replaced with something sharper. "I'm on my way. Don't you move."

She lowered the phone and let her head fall back against the stone wall. The mine breathed its cold, wet breath around her. Water dripped somewhere in the dark. Rory lay still on the ground, watching Dalton with the eyes of a man who'd run out of moves. Lila's breathing was slow and even in the mud a few feet away.

Amber closed her fingers around the locket and held on.

Twenty minutes through the trees, she'd thought when Rory marched them out of the cabin. Twenty minutes she intended to use.

Turns out that was exactly what it took.

14
The Mouth of the Mines

The mine didn't give a shit that they'd won.

That was the first thing Amber understood, sitting on the cold stone with her back against the wall and Rory zip-tied at the wrists and Lila still unconscious in the mud six feet away. The tunnel breathed its damp, rotting breath the same way it had when Rory was in charge of the flashlight.

Water dripped. The rusted cart sat in the corner like a shrug. The dark pressed in at every angle that the flashlight's tilted beam didn't cover, patient and absolute.

She was still holding the locket.

Dalton stood between her and Rory, the shotgun loose in one hand, blood drying down the side of his jaw from the cut above his ear. He'd used the zip tie Amber had looped around Rory's throat to secure the man's wrists instead, which she appreciated on a practical level even as her hands continued their low-grade trembling in her lap.

"Marcus hid a digital key in here," she said. Not a question. She'd been turning it over since Rory said it, pressing it like a bruise, and now she said it out loud to see if it held its shape in the open air. "In the locket. That's what this whole thing was."

Dalton turned from Rory. His eyes moved over her face with that methodical sweep she'd come to recognize — checking, cataloging, the same way she cataloged exits. "Yeah," he said. "That's what it was."

"Two years." She looked down at the small oval pendant, dull gold in the bad light, the crescent moon engraved on its face. She'd worn it because Marcus gave it to her. She'd worn it because it was the only thing of his she'd kept after he died. She'd worn it through a hundred nightmares and a hundred mornings of not knowing why she couldn't feel safe anywhere, and the whole time it had been carrying something that got people killed. "He hid a criminal organization's account key in my jewelry and didn't tell me. And then he died."

"The car crash wasn't an accident," Dalton said. Quiet. He said it the way he said things he'd been holding for a while, the words worn smooth from being carried.

She absorbed that. "I figured." She hadn't, not consciously, but some part of her had, the part that kept waking up at two in the morning with her heart already going and no dream to explain it. "And the assault."

"They went after you to find the key. They thought Marcus had passed it to you." He paused. "He hadn't. Or he had, without you knowing. We're still not sure which."

"We," Amber said.

Dalton's jaw tightened. "I had people looking into it. After that night."

From the floor, Rory made a sound that was half laugh and half contempt, muffled by the fact that he was face-up on wet stone with his hands bound and the specific dignity that left you. "Real touching reunion," he said. "You two want a minute?"

"You want another knock on the head?" Amber said pleasantly. "Because I've still got the rock."

She didn't. She'd dropped it in the mud after she hit Lila, and she couldn't see it from where she was sitting. But Rory didn't know that, and he went quiet again, which was the point.

Dalton crouched beside her. He set the shotgun across his knees and reached over, and she let him work the zip tie loose from her wrists, which took about thirty seconds of careful maneuvering and left red marks in the skin that she'd probably stop noticing in an hour. She rubbed her wrists on instinct and felt the crescent moon tattoo under her fingers, the small raised scar of it. Another thing she'd thought was just hers.

Funny, how much of your own life could turn out to be someone else's business.

"The sheriff's coming," she said. "I know."

"Landry's going to want to talk to you." "I know that too."

She looked at him — the blood on his jaw, the torn shoulder seam, the way he was still scanning the tunnel even crouched beside her, even in the aftermath, some part of him perpetually watching the angles. The scar through his left eyebrow caught the light. He looked like what he was: a man who'd been in a fight and won it by a margin too close to calculate.

"The organization," she said. "The one that wanted the key. Is this over, or is it just this chapter?"

He was quiet for a second. Honest quiet, not evasive. "The key changes things. If Landry gets the locket into the right hands, there's leverage. The kind of leverage that makes an organization decide the heat isn't worth the score." He met her eyes. "It's not over tonight. But it could be over."

"Could be," she repeated. "That's the most I've got."

She nodded. Looked down at the locket one more time, then reached back and unclasped it, the tiny mechanism stiff from cold and years of wear. She held it in her palm for a moment — this small thing, this weight she'd carried without understanding — and then she set it on the stone beside her, separate from her skin, and felt the absence of it like putting down something you'd been gripping for so long you forgot you were doing it.

Rory watched her do it. His pale green eyes tracked the locket like a man watching a door close that he'd been trying to reach for two years, and she felt a grim, clean satisfaction at that. Not triumph, exactly. Something quieter. Something that had her name on it.

"Your people are going to find out you failed," she told him, because she still had the mouth and she still intended to use it. "And you failed because you underestimated everybody in this room. Including Lila, honestly, because she could have gotten away clean if she'd just gotten on a bus instead of coming back to play the hero act." She tilted her head. "What was the plan there, anyway? Were you going to let her go once you had what you wanted, or were you always going to leave her in this tunnel with the rest of us?"

Rory's expression shifted. Something moved through it — not remorse, nothing that clean — but a flicker of something that told her the question landed exactly where she'd aimed it.

"That's what I thought," she said.

Lila stirred in the mud. A low sound, nothing coherent, just the involuntary noise of a body coming back online. Amber watched her for a moment — the caramel curls, the red lipstick smeared across her jaw from the fall, the rise and fall of her chest. Still alive. Still breathing. The same person who'd pressed a coffee cup into Amber's hands on her first morning in Cherry Creek and said, *You look like you could use a friend, honey*, and meant it, or something close enough to it that Amber had believed her. The person underneath the performance and the debt and the bad choices was still in there somewhere, probably. That didn't make any of it better. But it made it something other than simple.

Nothing about this was simple.

Dalton stood. He moved to check Lila's pulse, two fingers at her throat, and nodded at whatever he found there. Then he straightened and looked toward the mine entrance — the faint gray of the tunnel mouth visible in the distance, the outside air beginning to taste different from the trapped cold inside.

"Landry's going to have questions about the gun," Amber said. "I know."

"And about why you were at the cabin in the first place. And about the night of my assault."

"Amber." Her name in his mouth, not a warning this time, not a strategic redirect. Just her name, said with a weight that sat differently than everything else he'd said tonight. He turned from the tunnel mouth. "I'll answer his questions. All of them."

She studied him. Two years of a man-shaped gap in her memory, the outline of someone who'd been there when she was most broken, and she'd spent months in Cherry Creek filling that outline in from the edges without knowing that's what she was doing. The way he'd shown up. The way he'd known, always, exactly how afraid she was without needing her to explain it. The way he'd drilled her on exits and cataloging and the small survival habits that had just gotten her through the last hour alive.

"You were there," she said. "That night. You didn't just find me after. You were there during."

His silence was its own answer.

"You stopped them from finishing it," she said. "That's why I'm alive."

"That's why you're alive," he said. "And why they kept coming. Because I made it personal." He exhaled, short and controlled. "Rory wasn't wrong about that part."

She held that. Turned it around. A man who'd intervened in her worst night and then spent two years carrying the fallout of it, following her to a small town in upstate New York and positioning himself in her orbit, not because he was obsessed or territorial — or not only that — but because he'd set a machine in motion the night he stepped in, and the machine had her name on every moving part, and he'd decided that made her his responsibility.

His penance and his reason.

"You should have told me sooner," she said. "Yeah." He didn't dress it up. "I should have." "I'm still angry about that."

"I know."

"I'll probably be angry about it for a while."

"That's fair," Dalton said, and the corner of his mouth moved — not quite a smile, but the ghost of one, the dry flicker that was as close as he usually got. "I can work with angry."

Rory made another sound from the floor. Amber didn't look at him.

Outside — distant, muffled by the tunnel length and the hillside above them, but real — she heard the sound of vehicles. Engines, more than one, the crunch of tires on the dirt path that wound through Wes's property.

Headlights, probably, sweeping the tree line. She imagined Landry getting out of his truck with that weathered, skeptical face already shifting into the other mode, the one that meant he'd arrived at a scene and his brain had clicked over into whatever deputies and twenty years of law enforcement gave you when things stopped being theoretical.

"They're here," she said.

Dalton nodded. He looked at Rory on the ground, at Lila beginning to push herself up onto one elbow, at the locket sitting on the stone beside Amber. He looked at all of it the way someone looks at an ending — not with relief, exactly, but with the specific, bone-deep recognition of a thing finally being finished.

"Stay here," he said. "I'll go out, signal them in. Don't want Landry coming in blind with his hand on his weapon."

"Go," she said.

He moved toward the tunnel mouth. She watched him go, the broad set of his shoulders, the deliberate quiet of the way he walked even now, even after everything. The flashlight's beam caught him for a moment and then he was in shadow and then he was gone around the bend, his footsteps fading until she couldn't separate them from the water dripping somewhere deeper in the mine.

Lila had gotten herself to a sitting position. She pressed one hand against the side of her head, where the stone had connected, and didn't speak. Her mascara had cut dark lines down her cheeks, and her jacket was soaked through with mud, and she looked, stripped of the performance and the body spray and the brassy rapid-fire delivery, like exactly what she was: a woman who'd made a bad deal a long time ago and kept paying the premium on it long after she should have walked away.

Amber didn't say anything to her. Not yet. Maybe not tonight. There were things she'd want to say eventually — questions, accusations, the particular grief of finding out someone you trusted chose you as a mark — but right now the mine was cold and her wrists ached and the locket sat on the stone between them like a period at the end of a sentence.

She picked it up. Closed her fingers around it one more time. Then she set it back down and left it there.

Rory was watching her with those pale green eyes, the gold tooth hidden because he wasn't smiling anymore. He looked smaller on the floor than he had standing up. Most things did, she supposed, once they stopped moving.

"It wasn't supposed to go like this," he said. His voice had lost its oily confidence. What was underneath was flatter, younger-sounding, almost.

"No," Amber agreed. "It wasn't."

She could hear voices now — Landry's gravelly drawl, other voices she didn't recognize, the shuffle of boots on the tunnel floor approaching from the entrance. Flashlight beams strobed against the walls, multiple of them, and then a deputy appeared at the chamber entrance, hand on his weapon, sweeping the space, and behind him came Landry himself, his salt-and-pepper buzz cut and his weathered face and his steel-gray eyes that took in Rory on the floor and Lila against the wall and Amber sitting in the middle of it all with dried mud on her jacket and her hair in ruins.

"Well," Landry said, after a moment of taking stock. His voice had the tone of a man who had arrived at scenes that surprised him and had learned to absorb them before speaking. "You're not dead."

"Jury was out for a while," Amber said.

He looked at her for another second, something working in his expression that wasn't quite softness but wasn't his usual skepticism either. Then he nodded, once, and turned to his deputies. "Get him up. Her too, carefully — she may have a head injury." He moved into the chamber, pulling on latex gloves, and crouched beside the locket on the stone. "This it?"

"That's it," Amber said. "Don't open the clasp — there's a hidden panel on the back. I don't know what's on it exactly, but Rory's people do, and so does Dalton."

Landry looked at her over his shoulder. "Vale's outside. Told me quite a story on the way in."

"Did you believe him?"

The sheriff was quiet for a moment, studying the locket before he bagged it. "Believe enough of it to want the rest." He stood. "Which means you and me and him have a long night ahead of us."

"I know," she said.

She let a deputy help her to her feet, which she didn't particularly want but accepted because her legs had the structural integrity of wet cardboard and she wasn't going to prove a point by falling over. The chamber was suddenly full of people and light, radio static and the particular organized noise of law enforcement doing what it was built for, and

Amber let it move around her, let herself be still in the middle of it.

Outside the mine entrance, Dalton was waiting. He stood a few feet back from the deputies, his wrists not cuffed but not entirely free either — the particular in-between status of a man who'd cooperated and was being held cooperating until someone decided what to do with him. His eyes found her the moment she cleared the tunnel mouth, and something in his posture shifted, the coiled readiness in him loosening by about half a degree.

She walked to him. Not running, not dramatic. Just walked over and stood beside him, her shoulder against his arm, and he let out a slow breath that she felt more than heard.

"Wes?" she asked.

"Ambulance is at the cabin. He's awake. Pissed." A pause. "Called the deputy a 'wet-eared whelp,' apparently."

"That tracks," she said.

The night air hit her properly now, cold and clean after the mine's damp breath, and she pulled it in deep, feeling it reach the bottom of her lungs. Above the tree line, the sky had gone the deep blue-black of late evening, a handful of stars visible where the clouds had thinned. The pine trees stood in dark columns all around Wes's property, indifferent and enormous, the same trees that had watched all of this happen and would stand here long after every person involved had sorted themselves out or failed to.

She looked up at them for a moment. Then she looked down at her hands.

The crescent moon tattoo on her inner wrist caught a flashlight beam from somewhere behind her. She traced it with her thumb, the tiny familiar shape of it, and for the first time in two years it felt like just a tattoo. A thing she'd chosen. Hers, and only hers.

"Long night still ahead," Dalton said quietly.

"Yeah." She turned her palm up, and after a moment, his hand covered it, warm and certain. "But we're on the right side of it."

He squeezed her hand once. Didn't let go.

Landry appeared at the mine entrance behind them, the evidence bag with the locket in one hand and his radio in the other, and the look he gave them was complicated and knowing and didn't have a single drop of softness in it. But he didn't separate them either. He just said, "My truck. Both of you.

Now," and turned back toward the property without waiting to see if they'd follow.

They followed.

15
Subterranean Surrender

The chamber was small and dry, which was more than Amber had expected from a mine that seemed personally invested in making everyone inside it miserable.

She pressed her back against the rock wall and listened. Somewhere below them, deeper in the dark web of tunnels that branched downward from this level, she could hear Rory moving. Not gracefully. He was bleeding from where Dalton had caught him with the jagged end of a broken support strut — a solid hit to the shoulder — and whatever his tactical instincts might have been on a good day, a wounded Rory Keane crashing through century-old mine shafts was more noise than threat. For now.

Dalton stood at the chamber entrance, head cocked, listening to the same sounds she was. He'd stripped off his outer flannel shirt and knotted it around his forearm where Rory's blade had opened a shallow gash, and in the glow of the one small LED flashlight they'd recovered from the tunnel floor, he looked carved from the same rock that surrounded them. Jaw set. Eyes tracking. Blood dried in a dark line down the side of his neck that she kept trying not to stare at.

"He's moving toward the lower east shaft," Dalton said quietly. Not to himself. To her, which she was still getting used to — that he talked to her like she was part of the equation, not a variable to be managed.

"Is that bad?"

"For him? Probably. That section's been unstable since I was twelve years old." He turned from the entrance, and his gaze swept over her the way it always did — quick and thorough, checking for damage she might be minimizing. "You hurt?"

"Scraped. Bruised. Alive." She flexed her fingers, still feeling the ghost of Lila's jacket in her fists, the desperate grappling weight of another person fighting back. "I'm fine, Dalton."

"You keep saying that like I'm going to stop asking."

"You keep asking like I'm going to give you a different answer."

Something shifted in his expression — not quite a smile, but the suggestion of one, that dry flicker she'd learned to read like a second language. He crossed the small chamber and sat beside her on the low ledge of rock, close enough that his shoulder pressed into hers, warm and solid and exactly what her body needed to stop vibrating at a frequency she couldn't control.

For a minute, neither of them spoke. The mine settled around them, groaning faintly with the particular patience of something that had been here for a hundred years and intended to be here for a hundred more. Water dripped in slow percussion somewhere nearby. The air smelled of iron and cold stone and something faintly smoky from the flashlight's plastic casing, and underneath all of it, the warm, faint scent of Dalton — leather and skin and the copper bite of blood that she was choosing not to think too hard about.

The adrenaline had nowhere to go. That was the problem. Her hands were shaking with it and her heart was still running a sprint her body hadn't caught up to yet, and Dalton was right there, and they were alive, and she didn't know what to do with any of that except feel it.

She turned her face toward his.

He was already watching her. Of course he was.

"Hey," she said, which was an objectively stupid thing to say after everything, but it was what came out.

"Hey," he said back, and his voice did something low and careful that moved through her chest like a struck chord.

She kissed him. Not gently, and not with any particular plan — she just closed the three inches between them and pressed her mouth to his, and he made a low, guttural vibration against her lips, a sound that felt like the heavy thrum of a machine finally clicking into gear after a long, grinding stall. His hand came up to the side of her jaw, rough fingertips against her cheek, tilting her in, and she grabbed a fistful of his shirt and pulled him closer because she needed the weight of him, needed to feel that this was real and solid and not another fracture of nightmare.

"Amber." Her name in his mouth, pulled back just far enough to say it. "Don't stop," she said.

He didn't stop.

His hands moved to her waist and he pulled her into his lap with a controlled urgency that made her breath catch, her knees bracketing his thighs, the rock wall cold at her back and the length of him warm and immediate in front of her. She pushed his shirt up, needing skin, needing proof — her palms flat against his stomach, the lean muscle tensing under her touch, the small catch of his breath when her fingers grazed the gash on his ribs he hadn't mentioned.

"You're hurt," she said.

"I'm fine," he said, and the echo of her own words in his voice would have made her laugh if she'd had any breath left for it. His forehead dropped to hers. "We don't have to—"

"I know," she said. "I want to."

That settled it. He pulled her in again, slower this time but not gentle — there was nothing gentle in either of them right now, and that was fine, that was real, because what she needed wasn't softness. She needed the truth of him, the weight and the heat and the fact of Dalton Vale alive and here and choosing her in a way she could feel all the way down to the marrow.

She worked his belt with fingers that were still trembling faintly, and he unzipped her hoodie and pulled it off her shoulders and pressed his mouth to the side of her throat, and she felt his breath, ragged at the edges, and it undid something in her chest that had been wound tight for two years.

Maybe longer. She arched into him, and his hands moved with a certainty that told her exactly how much attention he'd paid to every small thing she'd ever given away, and she let herself be known by him in the dark of a mine shaft with Rory Keane bleeding somewhere below them and the whole fragile scaffolding of her survival still shaking.

It was desperate and it was raw and it was the most honest thing she'd done in as long as she could remember.

Afterward, she stayed where she was, her face pressed against his neck, both of them breathing hard. He had his arms around her, one hand spread warm between her shoulder blades, and she could feel his heartbeat — fast, then slower, then slower still, settling back into the steady drum she'd come to find more reliable than most things in her life.

"I love you."

He said it quietly. Not as a declaration, not as a performance — just as a fact he'd apparently decided to stop carrying alone. Like he'd set down something heavy and was surprised to find his hands empty.

She pulled back enough to see his face. In the thin light, his blue eyes were steady on hers, and there was no hedge in them, no strategic retreat. Just Dalton, waiting to see what she'd do with it.

Her throat did something complicated. "You pick the most insane timing." "I know."

"We're in a mine. There's a man bleeding somewhere below us who wants to kill me."

"I know that too."

"Dalton." She searched his face. She thought about all the ways he'd lied to her — by omission, by silence, by the careful architecture of everything he'd chosen not to say — and then she thought about every time he'd shown up. Every time he'd been there before she'd known she needed someone to be. The way he'd drilled her on exits, on cataloging, on the small survival habits that had just gotten her through an hour of being underground with a sociopath and a woman she'd thought was her friend. The way he'd looked at her in Landry's truck like her continued existence was the only thing he'd been planning around for two years.

She didn't say *I love you back*. Not yet. But she pressed her palm flat against his chest, over his heartbeat, and felt it move beneath her hand, and said, "You're the only person who ever actually fought for me. Not for the locket, not for the case. For me." She paused. "That's not nothing."

"No," he agreed. "It's not." "I'm still angry at you." "Yeah. You've mentioned."

"I'm going to stay angry for a while."

"I know." He covered her hand with his, pressing it more firmly against his chest. "I've got time."

She held that. Let it sit. Down below them, Rory's erratic movement had gone quieter, which was either better or worse depending on what he was doing, and she became aware that the window of relative safety they'd stumbled into wasn't going to hold indefinitely.

"Okay," she said. "Talk to me about the mine."

He shifted, and she moved off his lap to sit beside him again, both of them straightening, pulling back into operational mode with the ease of people who'd been doing that all night. He pulled the flashlight over and angled it at the rock floor between them, and his expression changed — the intimacy folding back into something focused and tactical, though his knee stayed pressed against hers.

"My dad used to do maintenance work up here in the eighties, before they shut the whole operation down," Dalton said. "I came with him sometimes when I was a kid. Mapped most of it in my head the way kids do, just because it was dark and enormous and I thought that made me brave." A beat. "I was maybe ten."

"So you know the layout."

"Enough. The upper chambers are solid — some of them are almost dry, like this one. But the lower east shaft, where Rory's heading?" He drew a rough shape with his finger on the rock floor. "It's been flooding seasonally for decades. The timber supports are rotted through. About sixty yards in, there's a section where the ceiling's been sagging for years. One wrong footfall, one wrong impact on the support column, and the whole thing comes down."

Amber studied the improvised diagram. "You want to lure him in there." "I want to lure him in there," he confirmed. "If he goes far enough, I can

trigger the collapse from the junction point. Stay back far enough, bring the

ceiling down on the far section, and he doesn't walk out." "How do you trigger it?"

"There's a secondary support beam at the junction. It's the only thing keeping the compromised section from going on its own. It's been like that since the nineties — I saw it last time I was down here, about three years ago. Hit it hard enough in the right spot and the whole cascade goes." He paused. "I need something heavy. And I need Rory far enough down the shaft that the collapse catches him."

"And you need him to go into the shaft in the first place." "That's where you come in."

She raised an eyebrow. "I love how casually you say that."

"You distracted him once already tonight. You're better at it than you think."

"I had a rock and the element of surprise. I'm not sure that translates to luring a deranged man into a collapsing mine shaft."

"It does," Dalton said, and he said it with the flat certainty he used for things he'd already worked out completely. "He's not thinking straight. He's bleeding, he's humiliated, and his whole plan has come apart. That makes him predictable. He wants you. That's been the only consistent thing about him from the beginning. Use it."

She was quiet for a moment. The mine breathed around them, damp and patient. "And if it goes wrong?"

"Then we improvise. We're good at that."

"Speak for yourself. I've been improvising for two years and it's exhausting." But even as she said it, she felt something settle in her chest

— not calm, exactly, but resolution. The particular clarity that comes when you've stopped running from the thing chasing you and turned around to face it. "Okay. Walk me through it."

He walked her through it. She listened carefully, asking questions, pushing back on the parts that seemed like they required more faith in her own steadiness than she was sure she had. He answered every question without condescension, adjusted the plan when she pointed out weak points, and treated her input like it was exactly as valuable as his own.

Which, she was realizing, was how he'd always treated her — she'd just been too busy bracing for the opposite to notice it clearly.

When they'd gone through it twice and she had it solid in her head, she looked at him. "If this works—"

"When this works."

"*When* this works," she amended, "we still have Landry waiting on the other side of this mountain with approximately seven thousand questions."

"I know."

"Are you ready for that?"

He was quiet for a second — not evasive, just honest. "I've been running from that conversation for two years. I think I'm done running." He picked up the flashlight, checked the battery indicator, and stood. "You?"

She stood with him. Her legs held, which she counted as a win. "I've been running since before that. I think I'm tired."

He reached out and brushed a strand of hair back from her face — just that, just the simple fact of his thumb against her cheek, gentle in a way that had nothing to do with tactics or plans or the next fifteen minutes. Then he dropped his hand.

"Let's go end this," he said.

They moved out of the chamber together.

The tunnels below smelled different from the upper levels — wetter, earthier, with a mineral bite that coated the back of her throat. The flashlight carved a thin path through the black and she stayed close behind Dalton, one hand on his shoulder, reading his pace and his pauses the way she'd learned to read everything about him: quickly, instinctively, with the specific attunement of someone who'd been paying attention even when she'd told herself she wasn't.

Rory's sounds came to them before they reached the junction point. Labored breathing, the scrape of boots on wet stone, a low stream of muttered profanity that she might have found almost funny under different circumstances. He was around the bend ahead, deeper into the east shaft, and the air there had a particular quality — a faint give to it, a subtle wrongness in the acoustics that told her the space above was not what it should be.

Dalton stopped at the junction. He pointed at the secondary support beam— a thick timber post, cracked along most of its length, wedged between the floor and a crossbeam overhead. She could see the ceiling above it, the way the rock had bowed downward in a long, patient curve that had taken decades to develop. She understood immediately what one solid impact would do to that column.

He pressed his lips close to her ear. "Twenty yards in, then call him. Keep him talking, keep him walking toward you. When he's past the third timber marker, I hit the column. You run."

"Back toward you." "Back toward me. Fast." "Got it."

"Amber." He held her gaze, just for a second, and what was in his face was not fear — Dalton Vale probably didn't do fear in any conventional sense — but something rawer. The particular expression of someone who's calculated the odds and doesn't love them but has no better option. "Fast," he repeated.

"I know," she said. "I'll be right behind you." She stepped into the east shaft.

The ceiling dropped almost immediately, the walls narrowing, the wet stone gleaming in the flashlight's beam where groundwater seeped through cracks that hadn't been there when the mine was operational. She counted timber markers — rough wooden posts spaced at intervals, most of them soft with rot, some of them already buckled. First one. Second. She stopped just past the second and killed the flashlight.

Darkness, absolute and immediate.

She waited for her breath to steady. It didn't, quite, but she worked with what she had.

"Rory." Her voice carried in the shaft — clear, controlled, the way she'd gotten at projecting calm she didn't feel. "I know you're down here."

Silence. Then the scrape of boots stopping.

"Come to beg?" His voice bounced off the walls, directionally confusing in the dark, but closer than she'd expected. He was moving toward her already. Of course he was. "Where's your guard dog?"

"Gone," she said. "He went back up. Left me here." She let a careful wobble into her voice, not much, just enough. "I found something you might want."

The quality of his silence changed. She could hear him breathing now, ragged with the effort of his wound. "What?"

"The locket. I still have it." She didn't. Landry had it, bagged and tagged, in an evidence vehicle on the other side of the hillside. But Rory didn't know that. "Dalton doesn't know. He thinks I gave it to the sheriff, but I kept it." She paused. "I want a deal, Rory. You take the locket, you walk away. You tell your people you got what they sent you for."

Footsteps. Getting closer. She tracked the sound, measured the distance, and stepped backward slowly, drawing him forward, keeping him moving.

"You're smarter than I thought," he said, and his voice had that oily quality back in it, the confidence of a man who believed he was winning. "I always said that. Told them you were smart."

"I'm practical," she said. "There's a difference."

She heard him pass the third timber marker — the faint creak of his shoulder brushing the rotted wood — and she spun on her heel and ran.

Behind her, a sharp, percussive crack rang out — Dalton, hitting the column with everything he had — and then the east shaft made a sound she felt in her teeth before she heard it, a deep, settling groan that started in the rock above and cascaded down through the timbers and into the floor under her boots, and she ran *hard*, back toward the junction, toward the faint shape of Dalton's silhouette visible at the turn.

Rory screamed. The sound cut off under something enormous.

She reached Dalton at the junction, and he caught her by the arm and hauled her clear as the east shaft behind them gave way in a roar of displaced air and falling rock that she felt in her chest like a physical blow. Dust billowed through the junction in a thick, choking wave. They pressed back against the wall, arms up over their faces, until the thunder of it settled into smaller sounds — rocks still shifting and settling, finding their new geometry in the dark.

Then quiet.

Amber coughed, lowering her arm. The dust was thick in the beam of the flashlight Dalton had clicked back on, particles suspended in the air like snow. The east shaft entrance was gone. Where the junction had opened into a passageway, there was now solid rock.

She stood there for a long moment, breathing through her sleeve. Her knees were doing something interesting. Her hands were scraped raw from the run, palms stinging where she'd caught herself against the wall at the turn, and she became aware of that slowly, the way you become aware of pain once the immediate crisis has stopped demanding all your attention.

Dalton put his hand on her shoulder. Steady. Present. "Done?" she asked.

"Done," he said.

She closed her eyes for exactly three seconds. Felt the cold air moving through the tunnel, felt the weight of the rock above them, felt the dull ache in her palms and the deeper, older ache of two years of running finally, finally coming to a stop.

Then she opened her eyes and looked at the man beside her, dust-covered and blood-streaked and absolutely, undeniably real, and said, "Get me out of this mountain."

He almost smiled. "Yeah," Dalton said. "Let's go."

They walked out together, his hand warm at the small of her back, the flashlight cutting through the dark ahead of them, and somewhere above, through a hundred feet of rock and timber and a century of silence, the world was waiting to start again.

16
The Weight of the Mountain

The mine gave one last shudder as they cleared the entrance, a deep subterranean groan that rolled up through the hillside and into the soles of Amber's boots like the mountain was settling into something final. She didn't look back. She'd looked back enough times in her life, and right now she needed to keep moving forward, one foot in front of the other, out into air that was cold and sharp and tasted like pine needles and wet earth and the particular sweetness of open sky.

The sun was coming up.

Not fully — just the first pale suggestion of it, a thin wash of gray-gold bleeding up behind the ridge to the east, softening the dark. The kind of sunrise that looks like an apology. She stopped walking when she felt grass under her feet instead of rock, stood there in the predawn half-light with her ruined hands hanging at her sides, and just breathed.

Dalton was a step behind her. He'd been limping since the beam. The beam. Right. She turned.

He was moving on his own, which she appreciated, but she'd seen the way his jaw had locked when she'd pulled the timber off his leg twenty minutes ago — thirty? time had stopped being a reliable thing underground — and the set of his mouth right now said he was doing math on the pain and deciding not to share the answer. Classic Dalton Vale, running the numbers and keeping the results to himself.

"Stop walking," she said. "I'm fine."

"You said that underground and I believed you because I had other things to worry about. Now I don't." She moved to his side, ducked under his arm without asking, and felt him exhale — not a protest, just a release. His arm settled across her shoulders and his weight shifted onto her, just enough. She was smaller than him by a significant margin and it was awkward and she didn't care. "Lean on me or fall down. Pick one."

He leaned.

They stood like that for a moment, both of them looking at the ridge going gold, and she became aware of things in sequence the way you do when the emergency switch finally flips off: her palms were shredded. Her knees were bruised from where she'd hit the tunnel floor during the run. There was dried blood on her forearm that she was fairly sure wasn't hers. Her hair was full of rock dust and she had a cut above her ear that had stopped bleeding sometime in the last hour but was going to be extremely unpleasant once the adrenaline wore off completely.

She was alive, though. She felt it in the sharp, icy burn of the mountain air in her lungs and the way her pulse throbbed with a heavy, rhythmic ache against the raw, shredded skin of her palms.

"He's not getting out of there," she said. It wasn't a question. "No," Dalton said. "He's not."

She nodded once. Filed it. There'd be time later to figure out what to feel about it — the fact that she'd kicked that beam, that she'd made the call, that somewhere in the east shaft of an abandoned mine Rory Keane had reached the end of whatever road he'd been on. Right now the only thing her brain was doing was noting that he was gone and she was here, and those two facts were the only two that mattered.

Below them, maybe a quarter mile down the slope, lights moved. Flashlight beams, then headlights, then the unmistakable sweep of a spotlight mounted on the roof of a vehicle. She heard voices, distant and fragmented, and then the specific crackle of a police radio cutting through the cold air.

"Landry," Dalton said.

"Yeah." She shifted under his arm. "Ready for that conversation?" "Ask me in about an hour."

"That's a no." "That's a not yet."

She almost laughed. It surprised her — the fact that her chest could still do that, make room for something as ordinary as almost-laughter, standing on a hillside at dawn with rock dust in her hair and blood on her hands. But there it was.

"Let's go," she said, and they started down toward the lights.

Sheriff Tate Landry saw them coming about fifty yards out and said something into his radio that she couldn't hear, then started up the slope toward them at a pace that was faster than his usual deliberate amble. He had two deputies behind him and a paramedic she didn't recognize, and when he reached them his steel-gray eyes did a fast inventory of them both — a lawman's scan, automatic and practiced — and whatever he clocked made the crease between his brows deepen.

"Jesus," he said. Not to anyone in particular. Just to the general situation.

"He's in the east shaft," Amber said. "The lower section. It collapsed." She paused. "He's not coming out."

Landry looked at her for a second, then at Dalton, then back at her. He had the particular expression of a man recalibrating something he thought he'd already figured out. "You two walk out of there on your own?"

"We did," Dalton said. His voice was even, controlled, the way it got when he was managing something — pain or the conversation or both.

"Vale, you're bleeding from about four different places." "Three," Dalton said. "The leg's just bruised."

"He had a beam fall on him," Amber said. "His leg needs to be looked at. Possibly his ribs too, he's been not mentioning those for a while."

Dalton gave her a sideways look that was approximately the expression of a man who'd been very politely betrayed.

"Sir," the paramedic said, stepping forward, and Dalton let himself be steered toward the ambulance with the resigned air of someone who'd lost the argument before it started.

Landry turned to Amber. He studied her scraped palms, the cut above her ear, the general state of her. His expression was complicated — not unkind, just weighted with the specific burden of a man who'd been wrong about something and knew it. "Miss Rowan."

"I'm okay," she said. "Relatively."

"I imagine." He pulled off his jacket and held it out. "You're shaking."

She was. She hadn't noticed. She took the jacket and pulled it around her shoulders and it was warm from him and smelled like coffee and gun oil, and the warmth of it hit her so hard she had to breathe carefully for a second to stay steady. "Thank you."

"Amber." Lila's voice, sharp and broken and entirely recognizable, cut through the ambient noise of the scene below, and then Lila herself was coming up the slope at a pace that was technically a jog but looked more like barely-restrained panic, her caramel curls wild from the night, mascara streaked in two dark lines down her cheeks. She hit Amber at full speed and hugged her so hard it hurt three separate bruises. "Oh my God. Oh my God, you absolute idiot, I thought—" She pulled back, holding Amber by both arms, looking at her face. "Are you okay? Are you hurt? Is that blood? Whose blood is that?"

"I'm okay," Amber said, and this time, with Lila's hands on her arms and the sunrise getting stronger behind the ridge, it felt almost true. "I'm okay, Lila."

Lila made a sound that was somewhere between a sob and a laugh and pulled her in again. "I've been standing down here for forty-five minutes not knowing and Landry wouldn't tell me anything and I swear to God I aged a decade."

"I'm sorry," Amber said into her shoulder. And she was. She was genuinely sorry for the forty-five minutes of not knowing, for all the months of half-truths, for dragging Lila into the gravity of something this dark. "I'm really sorry."

"Don't be sorry, be alive. Which you are." Lila pulled back and looked at her again, and her amber eyes were steady now, wet but steady. "It's over?"

"It's over," Amber said.

Over. The word sat strange in her mouth, like a word in a language she'd been studying for years and was finally hearing spoken aloud by a native speaker. She'd lived inside *not over* for so long that *over* didn't have a familiar shape yet. She'd have to learn it.

She found herself moving toward the ambulance.

Dalton was sitting on the open tailgate, shirt off, a paramedic doing something to his ribs that was making his jaw work. He had a blood pressure cuff on one arm and a flashlight being shone in his eyes and the patient expression of a man enduring necessary indignities. One of Landry's deputies stood nearby, which meant he was technically in custody, which Amber noted and put aside for the moment.

She sat down beside him on the tailgate. Not because there wasn't anywhere else to sit. He glanced at her sideways.

"Lila okay?" he asked.

"She's fine. Annoyed. Relieved." Amber looked at the paramedic. "How bad?"

"Two cracked ribs, probable," the paramedic said. "Leg contusion, deep but doesn't look fractured. Lacerations on the forearm and shoulder. He needs imaging." She looked at Amber. "You should let me look at those hands."

"In a minute." She turned back to Dalton. His ribs were wrapped now, white bandaging stark against his skin, and there was a rawness to him in the cold morning air — not vulnerability, exactly, more like a particular kind of exhaustion that had stripped away the outer layer of everything he usually kept between himself and the world. He looked tired. He looked real. He looked like a man who'd been carrying something for a very long time and had finally put it down somewhere it couldn't follow him home.

"Two cracked ribs," she said. "I've had worse."

"That's not the reassurance you think it is."

The corner of his mouth moved. "No, probably not."

Landry materialized at the tailgate. He had his notepad out and his recorder running, which meant this part was official. Amber appreciated the honesty of it. She'd been lied to by omission enough in the last two years to find the straightforward approach genuinely refreshing.

"I'm going to need statements from both of you," Landry said. "Full ones. Not tonight — you both need medical attention and I'm not an animal — but soon."

"You'll have them," Dalton said.

Landry looked at him for a long beat, the kind of look that comes from knowing someone most of their life and still not having them figured out. "Vale. I've got a collapsed mine shaft, a missing person who's probably under a few tons of rock, and more questions than I have answers for. But I've also got Lila Beckett who's been talking for an hour straight, and your girl here who just walked out of that mountain on her own two feet, and I'm starting to think the picture I had was wrong."

"I'll explain everything," Dalton said.

"See that you do." Landry closed his notepad. "Hospital first. My questions can wait till morning."

The drive down the mountain was quiet. Amber sat beside Dalton in the back of the ambulance and watched the trees go past through the small rear window, the sky getting lighter by degrees, and let herself be still. Her hands hurt. The paramedic had cleaned and wrapped them, and they throbbed in a steady, almost rhythmic way that was weirdly grounding. Pain that had a reason. Pain that was already on its way to healing. She could work with that.

Dalton's shoulder was warm against hers. Neither of them spoke, and it wasn't uncomfortable. It was the quiet of people who've run out of words not because there's nothing left to say but because some things don't need to be said immediately. They'd have time. For the first time in two years, she had the specific luxury of *later.*

The hospital was small the way everything in Cherry Creek was small — one floor, twelve beds, a staff that seemed to know everyone by first name. They took Dalton for imaging almost immediately, and Amber sat in a curtained bay while a nurse cleaned the cut above her ear and asked gentle questions she answered on autopilot. Yes, she was a local resident. No, she didn't have a regular doctor. Yes, she was sure she wasn't concussed, she'd know by now.

She was still in the same curtained bay, hands rewrapped and a cup of terrible coffee going cold on the tray beside her, when Nora Fisk walked in.

Amber registered her first by the smell — cigarettes and something floral underneath, the particular Nora combination — and then by the click of her boots on the linoleum. She came around the curtain looking like she hadn't slept, platinum hair disheveled in a way that was more real than her usual precision, leather jacket traded for a flannel that someone had clearly lent her. Her icy blue eyes were red-rimmed.

"You look terrible," Nora said.

"You look like you've been crying," Amber said. Nora's jaw tightened. "I don't cry."

"Sure." Amber gestured at the chair beside the bay. "Sit down, Nora."

Nora sat. She didn't say anything for a moment, just turned a lighter over and over in her fingers, the same nervous habit Amber had noticed the first time they'd talked. Then she set it flat on her knee and looked up. "I heard about the mine."

"News travels fast."

"Small town." A pause. "Is it true? He's gone?" "He's gone."

Nora exhaled. It was a long, slow release, the kind that's been held for a while. "Good," she said, flat and final. "Good."

Amber watched her. "You came here to tell me something. Not just to check."

Nora turned the lighter over once more. "My sister." She said it carefully, like testing weight on ice. "She wasn't — she wasn't a good person. I want to be clear about that. She made choices I tried to talk her out of, more than once, and she made them anyway because she thought she was smarter than the consequences." Her voice was steady but her knuckles were pale around the lighter. "But she was still my sister. And she's still dead."

"I know," Amber said quietly.

"What she told Rory — what she fed him, about you, about the details of that night — she didn't do it to hurt you specifically. She did it because she thought it was leverage on someone else. Rory convinced her it was just information. Just business." Nora's mouth twisted. "He was good at that. Making ugly things sound like transactions."

"She didn't know what he'd do with it."

"Maybe." Nora looked at her hands. "Probably not all of it. But she knew enough to know it wasn't clean, and she did it anyway." She paused. "I found the rest of her files. After she died, she had a drive — the digital key you've been hearing about. I gave it to Landry two hours ago." She glanced up. "Everything on it. The whole network, the contacts, all of it. It's Landry's problem now, and whoever Landry passes it to."

The words moved through Amber slowly, finding places to land. *The digital key. Gone. Landry's problem.* She'd been carrying the weight of that unnamed thing for so long — the sense that somewhere out there, something beyond Rory was watching, waiting, tracking her usefulness as a threat — and now Nora was sitting in a hospital chair at sunrise telling her it had been handed over, neutralized, passed up the chain to people with badges and jurisdiction and the actual authority to deal with it.

The weight lifted. Not dramatically, not all at once. But she felt it go, the way you feel a tension headache release — a slow, almost disbelieving easing. Her shoulders dropped half an inch.

"They won't come looking for me anymore," she said. It wasn't quite a question.

"Without the key and without Rory, there's no reason to," Nora said. "You're not leverage anymore. You're just a person." She paused. "A free person."

Amber stared at the curtain across from her for a moment. Just a person. Just free. She didn't know what to do with those words yet, but she was going to keep them somewhere safe and come back to them when the dust settled.

"Thank you," she said. "For the drive. For telling me."

Nora gave a short, humorless laugh. "Don't thank me. I should've said something sooner. About a lot of things." She stood, tucking the lighter into her jacket pocket, and for a second her expression cracked — not much, just a hairline fracture, enough to see what was underneath. "Take care of yourself, Amber."

"You too, Nora."

She left the same way she'd arrived — boots clicking, the faint smoke-and-floral scent trailing behind her. Amber watched the curtain settle in her wake.

Dalton was moved to a room around seven in the morning. Two cracked ribs confirmed, no fracture in the leg, four stitches in his forearm. The deputy who'd been shadowing him was parked outside the door, which Landry had apparently deemed sufficient oversight given that Dalton wasn't going anywhere fast with two cracked ribs and an IV in his arm. Amber walked past the deputy without making eye contact and pulled the chair up beside the bed.

Dalton looked at her. "You don't have to stay." "I know," she said, and sat down.

He let it go. She appreciated that about him — the way he'd stopped trying to manage her choices once he'd realized she was going to make them anyway. He was getting better at it. She was getting better at letting him be bad at it without taking it personally.

The room was small and smelled like antiseptic and the particular staleness of hospital air that never quite turns over. Morning light came through the blinds in pale stripes across the bed. Dalton had his eyes half-closed, not asleep but resting, and she sat beside him and drank terrible coffee and let the silence be quiet for once instead of loaded.

After a while, he said, "Nora came?" "She gave Landry the drive."

She watched the information move across his face. The slight release of something he'd been bracing against. "Good," he said. "That's good."

"Yeah." She set the coffee down. "Dalton. What happens now? With Landry. With the charges."

He was quiet, looking at the ceiling. "I'll answer his questions. All of them, this time. What I did two years ago, how I knew, why I didn't come forward. The vigilante stuff." A pause. "Some of that's going to cost me."

"I know."

"I'm not asking you to wait around for—"

"I know you're not," she said. "I'm telling you I'm going to anyway. Because I want to, not because you asked." She leaned forward, elbows on her knees. "I'm still angry, for the record. About the lying, about the two years of not knowing. That doesn't just dissolve."

"No," he agreed. "It doesn't."

"But angry and done are different things." She looked at him — the bruised jaw, the bandaged arm, the scar through his eyebrow catching the morning light. All of it worn and real and entirely his. "I'm angry. I'm not done."

His eyes found hers, and the expression in them was something she didn't have a clean word for — relief and gravity and something that might have been the particular feeling of a man who'd spent a long time believing he didn't deserve to be looked at without flinching. She held it, let him have it, didn't look away.

"Okay," he said. Just that. "Okay," she said back.

She settled into the chair, pulling her knees up, making herself comfortable in the way of someone planning to be somewhere for a while. Outside the window, the sky had gone fully blue. Cherry Creek was waking up — she could hear it distantly, the ordinary sounds of a small town starting its day, someone's radio, a truck engine, a dog barking once and going quiet. Sounds she'd spent two years barely registering, too tuned to the frequency of threat to hear much else.

She could hear them now.

She turned her rewrapped hands over in her lap and studied the bandages — white gauze, neat, functional. The scrapes underneath would heal. The scars from before, the older ones, the ones that lived somewhere further in than skin — those would take longer. She'd known that going in. She knew it now. But there was a difference between carrying damage that's still being inflicted and carrying damage that's finally, fully in the past tense.

The locket was gone. The key was gone. Rory Keane was buried under a mountain he'd chosen to walk into, and whatever came next — Landry's questions, the courts, the slow unglamorous work of rebuilding something from scratch — it would be hers to navigate. Not flee. Navigate. On her own terms, at her own pace, with her hands scraped raw and her chin up.

Dalton's breathing had steadied into sleep. She watched his chest rise and fall, the careful rhythm of it, and felt something settle in her own chest in response — not peace, exactly, not yet, but the precondition for it. The ground floor. The place you have to stand before you can build anything upward.

She'd start there. That was enough for today.

The sun climbed. The room stayed quiet. Amber Rowan stayed put, for the first time in two years not because she had nowhere to go but because she'd finally found somewhere worth staying.

17
Reckoning and Recovery

Landry came by the hospital room at nine-thirty in the morning with two coffees and the expression of a man who'd made a decision he wasn't entirely comfortable with but was going to stand behind anyway. He set one cup on the bedside table, kept the other, and pulled the chair from the corner without being invited. The deputy outside the door had been quietly reassigned about an hour earlier. Amber had noticed. She hadn't said anything about it.

"How's the leg?" Landry asked Dalton. "Functional."

"Ribs?"

"Worse."

"Honest." Landry took a sip from his cup, set it on his knee, and looked at the space between them rather than at either of them directly. "Lila Beckett gave a full statement this morning. Three and a half hours. My deputy's hand is going to cramp for a week." A pause. "She corroborated everything. The lair, the surveillance, what she saw. She also told me things about the night two years ago that she should've brought to me before now, and we're going to have a separate conversation about that." His jaw worked briefly. "But the picture she painted was thorough. Consistent with the physical evidence from the mine."

"What did you find in the mine?" Amber asked.

Landry turned to her. "Search team's been in there since dawn, the sections that are still accessible. We found the room. The whole setup — the files, the photographs, the monitoring equipment." He paused. "Keane wasn't operating alone. There was infrastructure in there that someone with resources built. We're working on tracing where the money came from." He looked at Dalton. "I think you can help me with that."

"I can," Dalton said.

"Good." Landry scratched the back of his neck in the way he apparently did when he was deciding how much to say out loud. "I've been doing this job for eighteen years. I've been wrong before. Not often, but I've been wrong." He didn't dress it up further or make a speech out of it. Just said it, flat and plain, and left it sitting there. "My office dismissed Miss Rowan's original case. That's on the record. I intend to fix what I can fix."

Amber held the coffee cup tighter. The warmth of it bled through the bandages on her palms and she focused on that, the steady, uncomplicated heat, while she took a breath. "I appreciate that," she said, and meant it in a way that didn't require elaboration.

Landry nodded once, then looked back at Dalton. "There are going to be charges, Vale. I can't make that go away, and I wouldn't if I could — that's not how this works. But the context matters. The fact that Keane is buried under a mountain and the network he was connected to is going to be handed to the state AG's office matters. How you cooperate matters." He stood, picking up his coffee. "Get your rest. We'll do this right."

He left. The room settled back into its quiet. Dalton stared at the ceiling for a moment, and Amber watched the tension in his jaw slowly, incrementally release.

"He's a fair man," she said. "Yeah," Dalton agreed. "He is."

She didn't push further. There was a version of this conversation that could

spiral into what-ifs and worst cases, and she'd done enough of that in her own head at three in the morning to know it wasn't useful. What came next would come next. She'd navigate it when it arrived.

Nora appeared around noon, and this time she didn't announce herself with boots on linoleum. She paused in the doorway instead, one hand on the frame, and looked at Dalton in the hospital bed with an expression Amber couldn't fully decode. It wasn't warm, exactly. It was something older and more complicated than warm.

"You look like hell," Nora said to him.

"You told me the same thing earlier," Amber said.

"It keeps being true." Nora stepped into the room and didn't sit, just stood with her arms crossed and her lighter nowhere in sight, which Amber had started to read as a sign that she was making an effort. "I came to say it to his face. The drive is with Landry. Everything on it." She looked at Dalton. "You knew about the key. You knew what it meant."

"I knew," Dalton said.

"My sister gave it to the wrong people." Nora's voice stayed level. "She knew what she was doing and she did it anyway. I've been going around with that for weeks, trying to figure out which part of it I'm supposed to be angry about and which part I'm supposed to grieve." She paused. "Turns out it's all the same part."

Neither of them said anything, because nothing needed to be said. The room just held it for a moment.

"She wasn't trying to get Amber killed," Nora continued. "I want to be accurate about that. She didn't hand Rory the information because she wanted someone hurt. She handed it over because someone told her it was collateral and she believed them, because it was easier to believe that." Her mouth pressed into a thin line. "She was wrong. That's the whole of it."

Amber had been listening to this and feeling something move around inside her chest — not forgiveness, not yet, maybe not ever in any clean complete way, but something adjacent to it. An understanding that the woman who'd fed Rory his ammunition hadn't been a villain so much as someone who'd made a catastrophic series of small bad choices, the way people usually did. It didn't excuse it. It just made it real in a way that pure malice somehow didn't.

"I'm sorry about your sister," Amber said. "Whatever she did. She was still yours."

Nora's expression shifted fractionally. Her arms dropped to her sides. "Yeah," she said, quiet in a way Amber hadn't heard from her before. "She was."

Dalton cleared his throat. "The organization — without the key, without Rory, without the leverage point — they're going to cut their losses."

"Already happening," Nora said, back to business. "The contacts on that drive are the kind of people who scatter when a light comes on. Landry's got it up the chain now. State level, maybe federal if the AG decides it's worth the paperwork." She glanced at Amber. "You're not a thread worth pulling anymore. There's nothing to gain."

Amber absorbed that. Just a person. Just free. She'd carried the weight of being useful to something terrible for so long that its absence felt strange, like putting down a bag you'd forgotten you were holding. Her shoulders ached from it. But the ache was the good kind — the kind you feel when the strain finally stops.

"Thank you," Dalton said to Nora. "For the drive. For coming here."

Nora made a sound that wasn't quite dismissive and wasn't quite accepting. "Don't make it a bigger thing than it is. I did what made sense." She moved toward the door, then stopped. "The bakery's opening next week. Soft launch." She didn't look back when she said it, like the information was incidental. "You should come by sometime. When you're not in the hospital."

"I'll be there," Amber said.

Nora left, and this time the click of her boots echoed slightly differently down the hall, like something had been put down that she'd been carrying

too.

Lila came in the late afternoon. She came with food from the diner — actual food, not hospital food, wrapped in foil and still warm — and she set it on the tray table and hugged Amber for the second time in twelve hours, and this time Amber just let it happen without cataloging her bruises. Lila smelled like coffee and the diner's particular brand of dish soap and something powdery underneath, and the familiarity of it hit Amber somewhere low and solid. This was what staying looked like, she thought. People you recognized by smell. People who brought you food when you were in the hospital because it was the obvious and correct thing to do.

"Landry talked to me for three and a half hours," Lila said, pulling back and straightening her polka-dot dress. Her eyes were clear now, the mascara long washed off, and she looked tired but steady. "I told him everything.

Everything I knew, everything I suspected, everything I should've said sooner." She looked at Dalton. "I'm sorry it took me this long."

"You were protecting people," Dalton said. "That's not a crime."

"No, but keeping my mouth shut when I knew something was off — that's something I have to live with." She said it simply, without wallowing in it. Classic Lila, Amber thought. She could name the thing and put it on the shelf and move forward in the same breath. "Anyway. I told him. The whole picture is out there now." She looked at Amber. "How are your hands?"

"They're fine." "Let me see." "Lila—"

"Let me see, Amber."

Amber held out her hands. Lila inspected the bandages with the focused, practical attention she gave to everything, and then she nodded and let go and didn't make a production of it. "Good," she said. "Keep them clean." She glanced between the two of them, Amber in the chair and Dalton in the bed, and her expression did something complicated before settling into something that was mostly fond and only a little rueful. "I'm going to go and let you two do whatever it is you do when nobody's watching." She picked up her purse. "Eat the food. Both of you. You look like survivors of something, which you are, but there's no reason to also look like you skipped dinner."

She left in the cheerful, efficient way she did most things, and the room felt warmer for having had her in it.

They ate. The food was good — diner chili and cornbread and something chocolate for after — and eating it in the pale hospital light, Amber felt something begin to approximate normal. Not the old normal, not the two-years-of-running normal. Something different. Quieter. More hers.

"Wes came by," Dalton said, after a while. "While you were with Nora this morning."

Amber glanced up. "I didn't know that."

"Didn't stay long." Dalton's expression was careful in the particular way it got when something had moved him and he was deciding how much to show. "He said he was making some calls. Old contacts. Said the fact that I helped take down Rory's network was worth something to the right people."

"What kind of calls?"

"The kind that get made when someone with Wes's history decides a situation needs informal pressure." A pause. "He thinks there might be room for a plea arrangement. Given everything. Given what Rory was connected to and what taking him down cost."

Amber set down the cornbread. Outside the window, the afternoon light was going golden, the kind of clean late-day gold that Cherry Creek did particularly well, slanting through the blinds and laying warm bars across the floor. She watched the light for a moment. "Will it work?"

"I don't know." He was honest about that, which she valued. He could've said probably, or almost certainly, and she'd have known he was managing her. "It depends on the prosecutor and how much the state wants the network information versus how much they want to make an example. Wes thinks the former outweighs the latter." He paused. "I think Wes is right, but I've been wrong before."

"So have I," she said. "Still here."

His eyes found hers across the narrow hospital room, and the weight in them was something she'd learned to sit with over the past months — this specific intensity of his, the way he looked at her like she was the fixed point he navigated by. It used to unsettle her. Now it just felt like being seen by someone who was actually paying attention, which was rarer than it should be.

"Whatever happens in a courtroom," she said carefully, "I want you to know that I'm not going anywhere. Not because I'm naive about what you did or because I've decided to pretend the hard parts weren't hard." She kept her voice steady. "Because I know what you chose that night. I know what it cost you and I know why you made the call you made, and I'm not interested in punishing you for being the reason I'm alive."

Dalton was quiet for a long moment. The monitor beside him beeped softly, steady and reliable. "You could argue the case the other way," he said. "That I made you a target by being there."

"I could," she agreed. "I've argued it at myself, actually, in the middle of the night more than once. But the argument keeps running into the same wall, which is that Rory would've found a target with or without you. That's just what he was." She paused. "You didn't make me a target. You made me a survivor."

Something crossed his face that she didn't have a clean name for, raw and unguarded in a way he rarely let himself be. He didn't say anything. He didn't have to.

"Sleep," she told him. "You have cracked ribs and you've been awake for approximately a hundred years. The charges will still be there tomorrow."

"That's also not the reassurance you think it is." "Stole that one from you. Payback."

His mouth moved. Not quite a smile but the architecture of one, which was close enough. He shifted against the pillow carefully, favoring his ribs, and she watched him settle and felt the quiet of the room rearrange itself around him as his breathing evened out.

She stayed. The chair wasn't comfortable and the coffee on the tray had gone cold again and her hands throbbed in a steady, manageable rhythm, and none of that mattered. She curled her feet up under her and watched the window go from gold to orange to the soft blue-gray of early evening, and listened to Cherry Creek outside doing its ordinary, unremarkable business. A car. A dog. Someone's radio playing something country and indistinct. The sounds of a town that didn't know it had nearly lost her and had no idea what it would've been missing.

She knew now. That was enough.

Whatever the courtroom brought, whatever Wes's old contacts managed to arrange, whatever version of the future assembled itself out of the rubble of the last two years — she'd meet it standing up. Not running, not hiding, not measuring the exits in every room she entered. She'd meet it with her scraped hands and her crescent moon tattoo and the full, clear memory of a woman who'd kicked a support beam in the dark and walked out of a mountain on her own two feet.

The nightmare was over. What came next was just life. Complicated, uncertain, occasionally terrible life, with the possibility — the actual, tangible possibility — of something worth having on the other side of the hard parts.

She could work with that.

18
The Plea

The county courthouse smelled like old carpet and recycled air and the specific anxiety of people who'd spent too long in waiting rooms. It was a thick, humid sort of tension that manifested in the rhythmic, wet tapping of a nervous man's shoe against the linoleum and the way the air seemed to vibrate with the collective holding of breath. Amber had been in three different waiting rooms over the past two days, and they all smelled the same — like documents and dread and weak coffee from a machine in the hallway that charged a dollar fifty and gave you something the color of dishwater in return.

She sat in the second row behind the defense table, close enough to see the tension in Dalton's shoulders through the back of his blazer. Someone had found him a decent one — dark navy, fitted enough to look intentional. He'd shaved, which changed his face in a way she was still adjusting to.

Without the stubble, the scar through his eyebrow was more visible, and his jaw looked harder, more deliberate. He looked like a man who'd made peace with whatever was about to happen. She wasn't sure she had.

His lawyer, a compact woman named Renata Marsh who wore her gray-streaked hair in a tight bun and spoke in the clipped, efficient rhythm of someone who billed by the hour, was talking quietly at the defense table. Dalton's posture was straight. He didn't turn around. He'd told her that morning not to watch him for cues, that whatever his face did in there wouldn't be useful information for her, and she'd told him she'd watch whoever she damn well pleased, and he'd almost smiled at that. Almost.

The prosecution's table held a man named Calloway, mid-forties, a little doughy around the middle, with the polished exhaustion of a prosecutor who'd been handling cases more complicated than he'd bargained for. He'd been talking to his assistant in low tones since they'd arrived, and twice Amber had caught him glancing across the aisle toward Renata Marsh with an expression she couldn't read from where she was sitting. Wary, maybe. Like he'd had a conversation that rearranged some of his assumptions.

Wes was three rows back. She'd spotted him when she came in — he didn't wave, just gave her the kind of slow, deliberate nod that meant *I'm here* in the language of people who didn't waste gestures. He was wearing a flannel she'd never seen on him before, which meant it was probably his version of dressing up. His pipe was nowhere in sight, which was its own kind of concession to the setting.

When her name was called to take the stand, her legs carried her there before her brain had fully agreed to it.

The courtroom wasn't full. This wasn't a high-profile trial in any dramatic sense — small county, limited press, a defense attorney who'd pushed hard to keep it quiet. But the seats behind the bar had enough people in them that the room felt present, watchful. Amber settled into the witness chair, adjusted the microphone, and looked out at the assembled faces. Calloway at his table, pen poised. Renata Marsh, one hand flat on the defense surface. Dalton, utterly still, his gaze finding hers for exactly one second before she looked away.

She'd practiced this. Not scripted it, because Renata had told her that scripted testimony always sounded scripted, and juries and judges could hear the difference. But she'd practiced the shape of it, the order of things, the way to say what she needed to say without losing the thread of it halfway through. She'd been over it in her head at two in the morning and in the shower and while staring at the ceiling of the motel room the night before, and now it was time to just say it out loud in front of strangers and let it land wherever it landed.

The prosecutor's questions started gently enough. Her name. Her residence. Her history prior to Cherry Creek. She answered in a steady voice, watching her own hands in her lap, the faint pink of the healing skin on her palms. Then the questions moved into the territory she'd been bracing for.

"Ms. Rowan, can you describe the events of the night in question, two years ago, as you remember them?"

She took a breath. Held it for a count of three. Let it go.

"I was attacked," she said. "In the parking garage of my apartment building. A man I didn't recognize grabbed me from behind. I fought him. I remember the smell of cigarettes and something chemical — like cleaning fluid. I remember the concrete against my face." She paused. "I remember the moment it stopped. The sound of it stopping. Someone else was there.

There was a struggle I couldn't fully see, and then there was quiet, and then someone was kneeling beside me." She looked at the judge briefly, then back at her hands. "That someone was Dalton Vale."

The room was absolutely still.

"He didn't call the police," she continued, keeping her voice even. "I've spent a long time being angry about that. Being confused about that. Thinking it meant something about his intentions toward me, or his character." She paused. "What I understand now — what I know, because I've pieced it together from what I've been told and what I've lived through — is that he made a calculation under duress. He made a call between securing evidence for a larger operation and ensuring my immediate survival. He chose my immediate survival." She let that sit for a moment. "He made that choice knowing it would cost him. Knowing that not completing his original mission meant exposure, meant consequences. He chose me anyway."

Calloway cleared his throat. "Ms. Rowan, the question of the defendant's intentions that night—"

"I know what the question is," she said, not unkindly. "You want to establish whether what he did was calculated self-interest or something else. I can't tell you what was in his head. I can tell you that the man who knelt beside me in that parking garage in the dark — who kept his voice low and his hands steady and talked to me until I stopped shaking — that man has spent the last several months putting himself between me and genuine danger at every opportunity, including being buried under several tons of earth, which is not something people typically do for calculated self-interest." She looked at Calloway directly. "Whatever the letter of the law says about his choices that night, I am alive because of those choices.

That's not a small thing. That's actually the whole thing."

She was aware of the shift in the room. Not dramatic, not the way movies did it, with people leaning forward and whispering. It was quieter than that. A kind of focused attention, like the room had been breathing at one rate and had adjusted to a different one.

She answered the rest of the questions. She described the messages, the escalation, the night in the mine. She described Rory Keane with the flat clarity of someone who had already processed every feeling she was going to process about him and arrived at the other side. She described what she'd found in that mine, and what Dalton had done when she found it. She kept her voice steady throughout, and when she finally stepped down from the stand and walked back to her seat, her legs were trembling slightly — not from fear, she realized, but from the particular physical exhaustion of having said true things out loud in front of people who needed to hear them.

She sat down. The woman beside her, a stranger, touched her arm briefly and then looked forward again without a word. It was one of the stranger kindnesses she'd received in a year full of strange kindnesses, and she filed it away.

The recess came around noon. Renata Marsh disappeared with Calloway and a court officer into a conference room down the hall, and Amber found herself in the corridor outside the courtroom, back against the wall, staring at the water-stained ceiling tiles and trying to remember how normal breathing worked.

"You did good, girl." Wes appeared beside her with the silent efficiency she'd learned not to be startled by anymore. He had his coffee in a styrofoam cup, and he offered it to her, and she took it and drank some without asking what it was. It was terrible. She appreciated it enormously.

"Did I?" she asked.

"Calloway looked like a man who'd driven to a destination and found the road closed," Wes said. "That's generally a good sign."

"What did you do, Wes?" She handed back the cup. "And I mean specifically. Because 'making calls' covers a lot of ground."

He was quiet for a moment in the way he got when he was deciding how much information was actually necessary versus how much was just satisfying. "I know some people," he said finally. "From before. People who operate in the kind of spaces where what Rory Keane was connected to — what that whole network was — becomes a matter of federal interest rather than county interest." He took a sip of the coffee. "Dalton's cooperation in dismantling that network carries weight with those people. I made sure the right ears knew exactly how much weight." A pause. "The prosecutor's office got a call from someone above their pay grade. The kind of call that clarifies priorities."

Amber absorbed that. "And Dalton knows?"

"He knows I was making calls. He doesn't know who I called." Wes's expression was unreadable in the comfortable way of someone who'd kept larger secrets for longer. "Some things are better left as general gratitude than specific debt."

"That's very convenient for you."

"I'm seventy percent convenience and thirty percent wisdom," he said. "The proportions shift depending on the situation."

She almost laughed. It came out as something shorter and shakier than a laugh, but the spirit of it was there. Wes seemed to count it as a win regardless.

The recess lasted forty minutes. When Renata Marsh came back down the hall, her expression was controlled but her step was slightly faster than it had been going in, which Amber had learned to read as the equivalent of a full grin on anyone else. She touched Amber's shoulder in passing and said, "It's moving in the right direction," and kept walking toward the courtroom doors, which told Amber exactly nothing and also everything.

They filed back in. Dalton was already at the defense table, and when Amber settled into her seat she was close enough to see the slight tension in his jaw, the way his thumb moved once against his knuckle and then stopped. He was holding himself very still in the particular way of someone who'd trained themselves not to show anything in high-stakes situations, and she thought about all the versions of high-stakes situations he'd navigated alone before she was part of the equation. All the rooms he'd sat in without anyone in the second row.

She wished she could tell him she was there. She settled for being there instead, which was the only version of the message that actually worked.

Renata Marsh rose to address the court, her voice carrying the calm authority of someone who'd won arguments in much more hostile rooms than this one. "Your Honor, in light of the defendant's substantial cooperation with the state Attorney General's office regarding the criminal network connected to the victim in this case, and in consideration of the compelling testimony of Ms. Rowan establishing both the circumstances of the original incident and the defendant's pattern of protective action in the two years since, the prosecution and defense have reached a proposed agreement."

Calloway confirmed it without looking thrilled about it, which told Amber that whatever pressure Wes's people had applied, it had arrived with enough weight to make this feel less like a choice and more like a foregone conclusion. She wasn't going to feel bad about that. She was going to feel exactly as relieved as she felt, which was considerably.

The judge, a woman in her sixties with close-cropped white hair and reading glasses she kept pushing up her nose, reviewed the paperwork with the unhurried thoroughness of someone who'd seen people try to rush her before and had found it unpersuasive. The courtroom waited. Amber's heart was doing something loud and inconvenient that she was reasonably sure the people on either side of her could hear.

When the judge finally looked up, she looked first at Dalton. "Mr. Vale. You've been offered a plea that reflects your cooperation and the extenuating circumstances of the original incident. You've agreed to its terms?"

"Yes, Your Honor," Dalton said. His voice was steady. Of course it was.

"Then let me be clear." The judge set her glasses down on the bench. "The court accepts this agreement with the understanding that it reflects a genuine weighing of facts, not a shortcut. The woman who testified this morning described events that this court takes seriously. You made choices that night that were outside the law. That those choices resulted in her survival and ultimately in the dismantling of a criminal network does not make them lawful." She paused. "It does, however, make them human. And this court is not in the business of ignoring humanity when it presents itself clearly." Another pause. "Time served, with five years of supervised probation. Conditions of probation will be provided in writing. You are to report as required, you are not to leave the state without prior approval, and you are to continue your full cooperation with the AG's office investigation." She looked at him steadily. "Do not waste this, Mr. Vale."

"No, ma'am," Dalton said.

The gavel came down. The sound of it moved through Amber's chest like a bell, clean and final and irrevocable.

She exhaled. It came out longer than she expected, and a little unsteady, and the woman beside her touched her arm again, and this time Amber turned and said, "Thank you," though she wasn't entirely sure what for.

Dalton was on his feet. Renata Marsh was shaking his hand and talking, but he wasn't looking at his attorney. His gaze had already cut across the low barrier, across the gap between the defense table and the second row, and when his eyes found Amber's face they held something that wasn't relief exactly, but was right next to it. Something that had been wound extremely tight for an extremely long time was releasing, and it showed in the slight drop of his shoulders, the way the hard line of his jaw softened a fraction.

She stood up. Moved through the small gate at the bar. And then she was close enough to him that she could smell the faint cedar of his jacket and the soap he'd used that morning, and she put both hands flat against his chest and tipped her face up toward his and said, quietly, just for him, "I told you."

His hands came up to her face — careful, deliberate, cupping her jaw with the kind of steadiness that made everything else feel less precarious. "You did," he said, equally quiet.

"I'm going to need you to remember that I was right. For future reference."

Something genuine and warm moved through his expression. "Noted," he said, and pressed his forehead to hers, and they stood like that for a moment in the middle of the courthouse with people moving around them, and the carpet still smelled like dread and recycled air, but it mattered considerably less than it had an hour ago.

Wes found them in the corridor afterward, pipe back in his teeth, flannel slightly rumpled from the proceedings. He shook Dalton's hand for a long moment without speaking, and Dalton gripped it back, and something passed between them that Amber understood was older and more layered than anything she'd been present for. She watched it and didn't interrupt. Some exchanges needed to be witnessed, not joined.

"Good," Wes said finally, which covered everything and needed nothing added to it.

"Thank you," Dalton said. "For whatever you did."

"General gratitude," Wes said, and glanced at Amber with a look that told her he hadn't changed the proportions on that calculation one bit. "Go home. Both of you. This building's done its job."

Outside, the afternoon had gone cool and bright, the kind of October clarity that made everything look slightly more resolved than it actually was. There were three reporters on the courthouse steps, which was two more than Amber had hoped for. One of them surged forward with a microphone extended, calling her name, and she felt Dalton's hand close around hers and his body shift, angling himself between her and the lens, moving her smoothly toward the parking lot with the quiet efficiency of a man who'd done extractions in considerably more chaotic environments than a county courthouse sidewalk.

"Mr. Vale, do you have a statement?" someone called after them. "No," Dalton said, without turning around, without slowing down.

His truck was at the far end of the lot. He unlocked it and opened the passenger door and she climbed in, and he rounded the front and got behind the wheel, and when he pulled out onto the main road the courthouse shrank in the side mirror and then disappeared behind a row of trees, and Amber tipped her head back against the headrest and closed her eyes.

The engine was steady under her. The seat was familiar. Outside the window, Cherry Creek went by in its ordinary afternoon way — the hardware store, the diner, the stretch of road that led out toward the lake and the hills beyond it. She knew this road now. She knew the way the light changed on it at different hours, the particular smell of the air when it came off the water, the sound of the town in the morning before it fully woke up.

She'd come here to disappear. Instead, she'd become someone who could stand in a courtroom and say true things out loud without flinching. She thought about the distance between those two versions of herself and felt something she hadn't felt in a long time, something quiet and slightly surprised.

Proud, maybe. Just a little. Just enough.

"Hey," Dalton said. His voice was low, unhurried, the particular register it went when the immediate danger had passed and he was just talking to her.

She opened her eyes. "Hey." "You okay?"

"I'm better than okay," she said. "I'm still figuring out what to call it."

He drove for a moment without answering. The road curved out toward the edge of town, and the trees thickened on either side, their leaves gone gold and amber and a deep russet that caught the late light like something on fire. "The judge was right," he said finally. "About what I did. It was outside the law."

"I know."

"I'm not asking you to—"

"Dalton." She turned to face him. "I testified to exactly what I believe. You don't have to walk it back for me. I meant it." She watched the muscle in his jaw move once. "You also don't get to spend the next five years of probation quietly punishing yourself for a choice that kept me breathing. That's not how this works."

A beat of silence. Then, quietly: "How does it work?"

She considered that seriously, because it deserved a serious answer. The trees flashed past. The light was going golden at the edges. "One day at a time," she said. "Like everybody else. Together, probably, if you can manage not to be insufferably cryptic about your feelings for more than forty-eight hours straight." She paused. "Which I'm not confident about, honestly, but I'm willing to give it a shot."

The sound he made was low and quiet and entirely real, and it settled somewhere warm in her chest. "I can work on it," he said.

"Good," she said. "Start now."

He reached across the console and took her hand, threading his fingers through hers with the steady deliberateness he brought to everything, and held on. The truck moved through the October afternoon, away from the courthouse, away from the trial, away from the last two years of running and hiding and holding her breath.

The road ahead was just road. Open and ordinary and entirely, mercifully unknown.

She held his hand back and watched it unspool in front of them, and for the first time in longer than she could name, she didn't count the exits.

19
Freedom's Price

The cabin smelled like pine resin and old wood smoke and something faintly mineral from the lake outside, and Amber stood in the middle of it for a full thirty seconds before she remembered how to move.

It wasn't much. One main room with a stone fireplace and a kitchen bolted onto the side of it, a bathroom with a clawfoot tub that had seen better decades, and a bedroom barely large enough for the queen-sized bed that took up most of it. The floors creaked. The curtains were the kind of faded plaid that meant someone's grandmother had picked them out in 1987 and nobody had seen any reason to replace them since. The porch looked out over a strip of gravel beach and then the lake, which at this hour was going flat and silver in the late afternoon light, the far shore just a dark smudge of trees.

Dalton dropped their bags by the door. He'd found the place through a guy he knew who'd served with him — a favor called in quietly, no names on any paperwork, just a set of keys left under a ceramic frog on the porch railing. Two days, maybe three. Long enough to breathe before they had to decide anything.

"It's perfect," Amber said.

He glanced around the room with the assessing efficiency of someone who'd slept in considerably worse conditions and thus calibrated their standards accordingly. "It's functional."

"That's what I said." She dropped onto the small couch and it exhaled a cloud of dust and she didn't even care. She tipped her head back and stared at the ceiling, which had a water stain shaped vaguely like a heron. "Nobody knows we're here."

"Nobody knows we're here," he confirmed, and his voice had that particular quality it got when the tactical part of his brain finally stood down — lower, slower, like he was letting the machinery idle for the first time in months.

She heard him moving around the kitchen, heard the tap run, heard the small sounds of someone figuring out what was in the cabinets. She didn't move. She let herself just be horizontal and safe and completely, blessedly nobody's problem for a minute.

The courthouse felt like it had happened to someone else already. The smell of that carpet, the sound of the gavel, the reporter's voice calling Dalton's name as they crossed the parking lot — all of it was already going soft at the edges, the way bad things did when you put enough distance and open road between yourself and them. She'd testified. The judge had ruled. Dalton had walked out of that building with her hand in his, and then the truck had eaten up the miles between there and here, and here was a cabin by a lake with a heron-shaped water stain on the ceiling and no messages waiting on her phone and no shadows in the parking lot.

She could feel the absence of fear like a physical thing. Like taking off a backpack you'd been wearing so long you'd forgotten it was there.

"There's soup," Dalton said, appearing in the kitchen doorway. "Canned. And crackers that are probably fine. And someone left a bottle of whiskey in the back cabinet that I'm choosing to interpret as a good omen."

Amber lifted her head. "Whiskey first, soup second." "That's a terrible order of operations."

"I just testified in open court about the worst night of my life and the man I love got handed five years of probation instead of a prison sentence. I'll have the whiskey first."

The word landed between them — not *love* exactly, but the architecture of it, the shape it made when she said *the man I love* out loud without flinching. She'd said it. Out loud. In a sentence. To him.

Dalton was very still in the doorway for a moment. Then he disappeared back into the kitchen, and she heard the clink of glasses, and when he came back he was carrying two of them with a reasonable pour in each, and he settled onto the couch beside her with the easy weight of someone who'd run out of reasons to keep his distance.

He handed her a glass. She took it. They sat there with their shoulders touching and the fireplace cold and unlit across the room and the lake going silver outside the window, and neither of them said anything for a while, and it was one of the more comfortable silences she'd ever been in.

"You said that on purpose," he said finally. "I say most things on purpose."

"Amber."

"Yes." She sipped the whiskey. It was decent. "I said it on purpose. You can say something back if you want. Or you can keep doing the stoic mountain man thing, I'm genuinely flexible on the format here."

He turned his head to look at her profile, and she could feel the weight of it even without turning to meet it. "I love you," he said. Just like that. No preamble, no hedging, no careful construction. Just the four words in his low, unhurried voice, like he'd decided the most efficient path was the direct one.

She exhaled. "See? That wasn't so hard." "Don't push it."

"I'm going to push it constantly, actually. You should know that about me going forward."

He made a sound that was almost a laugh, and then he took the glass out of her hand and set both of them on the floor and put his arm around her, and she turned into his chest with the specific relief of someone who'd been navigating by dead reckoning for a very long time and finally had a landmark to orient by. His hand moved up her back, slow and deliberate.

She could feel the warmth of him through the flannel, the steady pull of his breathing.

"Five years of probation," she said against his collarbone. "Five years."

"That's not nothing."

"No," he agreed. "It's not." "But it's not prison."

"It's not prison."

She pulled back enough to see his face. The scar through his eyebrow caught the fading light from the window. Without the courthouse blazer, without the razor-sharp tension of the last several days, he looked like himself again — the version she'd been building a map of these past months. Worn flannel, shadows under his eyes from poor sleep, jaw going stubbled again already. Steady. Present. Hers, if she wanted him, which she did, which she'd decided somewhere between the parking garage and the witness stand and this creaking couch in a cabin that smelled like pine and old smoke.

She kissed him.

Not the careful, deliberate kind of kiss they'd traded in high-stakes moments, where tenderness had to coexist with caution. This one had nothing to prove and nowhere to be, and she put her hand against the side of his face and felt the scratch of new stubble under her palm and kissed him slow and thorough and entirely without agenda, and felt him respond with a kind of focused attention that made her breath catch.

His hands moved. He drew her closer, shifting her weight until she was half across his lap, and his mouth was warm and tasted like whiskey, and outside the window the lake went from silver to pewter as the light dropped, and neither of them was paying attention to that anymore.

"Amber." His voice was lower now, roughed up at the edges. "We're celebrating," she told him. "Stop thinking."

"I'm not thinking." "You're always thinking."

"Less than usual, currently." His hands found the hem of her shirt and she felt the warmth of his palms against her sides, that particular heat of skin against skin that she'd cataloged and returned to in her memory more times than she'd admit. She pulled back and stripped the shirt over her head and dropped it somewhere, and the evening air in the cabin was cool against her shoulders until he pulled her back against him, his mouth finding the curve of her neck.

She made a sound she didn't bother to suppress. He responded to it with the attentiveness she'd learned to expect from him, following the sound to its source, his hands moving with that unhurried deliberateness that had always undone her faster than urgency would have. She worked at the buttons of his flannel and he let her, his mouth tracing down to her collarbone, and when she finally got the shirt off him she spread her hands across his chest and felt the terrain of him — the old scars, the muscle, the warmth — and it hit her somewhere behind the sternum that he was here and she was here and nobody was coming through the door.

That was new. That was genuinely new, and it made everything feel different, sharper, more present. No listening for footsteps. No corner of her brain running threat assessments. Just him and the cabin and the lake outside going dark and the fireplace they still hadn't lit.

"Hey," she said softly.

He raised his head. His eyes were dark and focused on her face. "I'm not scared," she said. "Just so you know. Not even a little bit."

Something moved through his expression — not surprise exactly, but something close to it, layered under something much warmer. His hand came up and pushed the loose hair back from her face with a steadiness that made her chest ache. "Good," he said.

She pulled him back down to her.

They moved to the bedroom eventually, and the mattress had its own opinions about being used but neither of them cared, and the October night pressed cold against the window glass while everything inside was warm and slow and unhurried in the way that only happened when there was nothing left to run from. He was careful with her in places and not careful at all in others, and she was equally unsubtle about what she wanted, and the whole thing had the quality of something being celebrated rather than survived — which was, she thought distantly, entirely the point.

Afterward, she lay in the dark with her head on his chest and his arm heavy and warm across her, and listened to the lake. It made a small sound against the gravel beach, repetitive and steady, like something breathing.

The cabin had gone fully dark except for the thin strip of moonlight under the curtain edge.

"I want to reopen the bakery," she said. His chest moved under her cheek. "Okay."

"Not here, necessarily. I mean — I don't know yet. Maybe here. Maybe somewhere else." She traced an absent shape against his ribs. "I just know I want to do it. I was actually good at it. And I liked it. And I don't want Rory Keane to be the reason I stopped baking, because that's insane and I refuse to let that be the narrative."

"Smart."

"Don't patronize me."

"I meant it." He shifted slightly, and she felt his chin against the top of her head. "You're actually good at it. Those scones were objectively the best thing I've eaten in three years." She snorted. "High bar."

"I'm serious."

"I know, that's what's funny." She was quiet for a moment. The lake breathed outside. "What about the garage? Is there anything left to go back to?"

He considered that in the way he did — not stalling, just actually thinking it through before he answered. "There's the lot. The foundation. The equipment that was in storage off-site." A pause. "It's rebuild-able. If I wanted to rebuild it."

"Do you?"

"I think so." He said it like he was testing the weight of it, checking whether it held. "Cherry Creek's home. Has been, even when I wasn't making a great argument for it." Another pause, longer. "I'd want to do it right. Not just a garage. Something that's actually — worth staying for."

She lifted her head to look at his face in the dark. The moonlight caught the angle of his jaw. "Worth staying for," she repeated. "Is that what I am? A reason to stay?"

"You're the main reason," he said, with the blunt simplicity of someone who'd decided to stop being cagey about it. "Yeah."

She held his gaze for a beat, then laid her head back down. "Good," she said. "Because I think I might want to stay too. I haven't decided yet. But I think so."

"Take your time."

"We have some of it now, apparently." "We do."

She closed her eyes. The lake kept its steady rhythm outside. His hand moved slow against her arm, absently, like he wasn't entirely aware he was doing it. She thought about the girl who'd driven into Cherry Creek eight months ago with a car full of boxes and a white-knuckle grip on the steering wheel, scanning every mirror, counting exits. That girl had been running so long she'd forgotten what she was running toward.

She wasn't that girl right now. She wasn't sure she was done being her entirely — trauma didn't clean itself up that neatly, and she had enough self-awareness to know that the nightmares would come back sometimes,

and the flinching, and the moments where shadows did something wrong in her peripheral vision and her body made its own decisions before her brain caught up. That was just the arithmetic of surviving something real. But she was also the woman who had stood in a courtroom and spoken the full truth out loud, without script and without apology, and watched it land, and walked out on the other side of it still intact.

Those two things could coexist. She was learning that.

She fell asleep to the sound of the lake and Dalton's steady breathing and the occasional pop of the cabin settling in the cold, and she didn't dream about parking garages or fluorescent lights or the chemical smell of cigarettes. She dreamed about something warm and formless that she couldn't name when she woke up, which was fine. Some things didn't need to be named.

Morning came in through the gap in the curtains, sharp and bright and completely indifferent to how tired she still was. She lay still for a while, cataloging the sounds: birds somewhere close to the water, the lake still doing its steady thing, the distant percussion of Dalton in the kitchen. The smell of coffee crept under the bedroom door, which was the single most persuasive argument for getting up she'd ever encountered.

She pulled on his flannel from the floor and padded out.

He was at the small stove in yesterday's jeans and nothing else, and the morning light came through the kitchen window and landed across his shoulders in a way that was genuinely unfair. He had two mugs ready on the counter. He handed her one without turning around, which meant he'd heard her coming, which was just who he was.

"It's better than the courthouse machine," he said.

"That's an extremely low bar, but thank you." She wrapped both hands around the mug and leaned against the counter beside him and looked out at the lake, which was doing something spectacular in the early light — gone gold and glassy, the tree line on the far shore reflected perfectly in it, the whole thing looking more like a painting than an actual place. "God."

"Yeah," he said.

They stood there for a while. The coffee was good. The light kept moving across the water in slow, shifting bars. A heron — an actual one, not a water stain — landed on the gravel beach and stood there with the particular stillness of a creature that had nowhere to be and knew it.

"We should stay two more days," Amber said. "Agreed."

"And then we should go back and figure out what's next." "Agreed."

"And you're going to promise me something."

He turned to look at her. She kept her gaze on the heron.

"When it gets hard — and it will get hard, because probation is a process and rebuilding takes time and I'm going to have bad weeks and you're going to have bad weeks and neither of us is particularly evolved at asking for help — you have to actually tell me. Not go silent and manage it alone in the dark like some kind of emotionally constipated wilderness hermit." She finally turned to meet his eyes. "Deal?"

His mouth did something that was fully a smile this time. Not the almost-version, not the restrained flicker she'd cataloged through the harder months. An actual smile, small and real and directed at her, and it rearranged his whole face in a way that still managed to surprise her. "Emotionally constipated wilderness hermit."

"It's accurate and you know it."

"It's accurate," he conceded. He set his mug down and took hers from her hands and set that down too, and then he pulled her against him with both arms, and she went, tucking her chin against his shoulder. He was warm from the stove and he smelled like coffee and sleep and the particular clean scent of him underneath everything else. "Deal," he said. Into her hair, quiet and sure. "Deal."

She held on. Outside, the heron lifted from the gravel in one slow, unhurried arc and disappeared over the tree line, and the lake settled back into its gold and glass silence, and the morning kept coming in through the window, and it was so ordinary and so completely fine that she felt something loosen in her chest that she hadn't even known was still wound tight.

Not everything had to be survived. Some things could just be lived.

"Okay," she said. She pulled back and picked up her coffee. "I'm going to go sit on that porch and drink this and look at the lake and not think about anything important for at least an hour."

"I'll make eggs."

"You can make eggs?"

"I've been feeding myself for thirty-two years." "That's not actually an answer to the question."

He picked up his mug and turned back to the stove with the particular composure of a man who had decided the conversation was over. She watched him for a second, this man who'd walked out of a courthouse with five years of probation and driven them four hours to a lake cabin and made coffee in the morning and promised to stop going silent in the dark, and she thought: *okay.* Just that. Just the quiet, settled weight of it.

Okay.

She pushed open the porch door and stepped out into the cold October morning, and the air hit her face sharp and clean and smelling like pine and lake water, and she sat down in the wooden chair that faced the water and pulled the flannel tighter around her shoulders and drank her coffee.

The lake was still doing its gold and glassy thing. Somewhere across it, a loon called — that long, strange, lonely sound that wasn't actually lonely if you knew what it meant, which was just: *I'm here, I'm here, I'm here.*

She leaned back in the chair. The wood creaked under her. She had no messages to check. No shadows to count. No exits to map. Just the lake and the trees and the sound of Dalton in the kitchen and the cold bright morning pressing itself against everything like it had all the time in the world.

She let it.

For a long time, she just let it.

20

The Darkness We Fell Into

They drove back into Cherry Creek on a Tuesday afternoon, and the town looked smaller than Amber remembered it. Not in a bad way. Just smaller, the way a thing shrinks once you've stopped being afraid of it.

She rolled the window down a few inches as Dalton pulled onto Main Street, and the air that came in smelled like wood smoke and early November and the particular damp-leaf scent of a small town settling into winter. The hardware store had a new hand-lettered sign in the window. The diner's lights were on. A kid was kicking a soccer ball against the fire station wall with the determined, joyless repetition of someone who'd run out of better options. Ordinary. All of it just ordinary, and she was so grateful for ordinary she could have cried.

She didn't cry. She pulled the window back up and leaned her elbow on the door and watched the street go by.

"Quiet," she said.

"It's always quiet on Tuesdays." Dalton made the left turn toward the far side of town, toward the garage lot, without her asking. He knew that was where she wanted to go first. That was the thing about him — he paid attention in a way that still caught her off guard sometimes, that quiet precision of a man who'd spent years reading environments for threat and had started turning that same careful attention toward her instead.

The garage was gone. Obviously she'd known that, but seeing the empty lot in the cold daylight was a far cry from just knowing it. Without the rush of adrenaline or the haze of urgency, the reality of the loss finally had room to breathe. Dalton parked at the curb and they both got out without discussing it.

The foundation was still there, the concrete outline of what had been, the footprint of the building's whole life. Someone had cleared the worst of the debris. The charred skeleton beams were gone, hauled off at some point while they'd been at the cabin or at the courthouse or in between. What remained was the concrete floor, the lot's gravel perimeter, and the long autumn sky above it doing that particular thing where the light came in at an angle and turned everything slightly golden.

Amber walked to the center of the slab and stopped.

The smell was still there, faintly — that specific, acrid note of fire damage that didn't entirely leave a place for months. But underneath it, or maybe through it, there was something else. Damp earth. The mineral cold of the concrete. And then she saw it.

There, in a crack running along the near edge of the slab where the foundation met the soil, a single green shoot had pushed its way through. Thin as a finger, improbably vivid against the gray. She crouched down and looked at it without touching it, this ridiculous, stubborn little thing growing out of the ash-stained ground like it hadn't gotten the memo about what had happened here.

"Hey," she said, mostly to herself.

Dalton came to stand beside her. She could feel his presence without looking — the warmth and solidity of him, the way he occupied space. He looked down at the sprout for a moment.

"Huh," he said.

"That's all you've got? *Huh?*" "It's a plant."

"It's a plant growing out of a burned building." She straightened up and turned to face him. "That's something."

One corner of his mouth moved — not quite what anyone would call a smile, but the bones of one, the suggestion of it. "Yeah," he said. "It's something."

She turned back to the lot. Standing there, with the cold November air on her face and the smell of old smoke and new earth rising around her, she felt something settle into place in her chest. Like a joint clicking back into alignment after weeks of being slightly wrong. She'd been running the question in her head for days — *stay or go, stay or go* — and she'd thought maybe she'd need more time, more distance, more of the lake's gold-glass certainty before she could answer it.

She didn't, as it turned out. "I want to stay," she said.

Dalton was quiet. Not the processing kind of quiet, not the hedging kind. Just still.

"I'm not going to let Rory Keane's ghost decide where I live," she continued. "I'm not going to let any of it do that. This is where I landed, and it's where I baked my first good croissant in two years, and it's where Lila called me honey before she even knew my last name, and it's where you found me." She paused. "Or I found you. I'm still fuzzy on the mechanics."

"Little of both," he said.

"Little of both." She nodded once, decisive. "So I want to stay. I want to reopen the bakery. Here. In Cherry Creek." She turned to look at him directly. "Tell me that's not insane."

Dalton crossed his arms, not in the defensive way, just the thinking-it-through way. He studied the lot for a moment, then her. "It's not insane," he said. "I already told you I want to rebuild the garage."

"And I'm telling you I want the bakery next to it."

"The corner lot's for sale," he said, like he'd already looked it up. Which, knowing him, he had. "Two units. Good bones. It'd take work."

"I like work."

"I know you do." He came to stand beside her again, shoulder-to-shoulder, and they both looked out at the concrete slab and the green shoot and the whole blank, possible lot. "I'll build you the best bakery this state's ever seen."

She glanced sideways at him. "That's a big promise."

"I keep my promises."

She knew that. She'd seen it in a hundred small ways — the coffee ready before she said she wanted it, the quiet steadiness in the courtroom, the deal he'd made on a cabin porch with his chin against her hair. She knew it. "Yeah," she said. "You do."

They stood there a little longer, not talking, the November light moving slow across the empty lot. Then she bent down and touched the green sprout with one fingertip — just barely, just a brush — and straightened up.

"Okay," she said. "Let's go get our stuff."

Lila found them at the apartment two hours later, while Amber was pulling boxes out of the closet and Dalton was loading the truck with the particular systematic efficiency of someone who'd moved under worse conditions than this.

The knock was three fast raps followed by the door opening before Amber could answer it, which was the signature Lila Beckett method of announcing herself. She came in with a casserole dish covered in foil and her caramel curls piled up in a catastrophic bun, cat-eye glasses slightly askew.

"You're back," Lila said. It wasn't a question. She set the casserole on the counter and crossed the room and pulled Amber into a hug that smelled like fried food and raspberry hand lotion and had the quality of someone who'd been holding that hug in reserve for weeks.

Amber hugged her back, hard. "We're back."

"I heard," Lila said, pulling away and looking her over with the frank assessment of someone checking for damage. "Tate called me. Said you'd been spotted on Main Street." She paused. "He also said — and I quote — 'about damn time,' which is the most emotional he gets, so you know it counts."

"I'll take it."

"There's a chicken and rice situation in that dish. Don't argue with me." Lila glanced at the boxes, then at the window, then back at Amber. "You're staying?"

"We're staying."

Lila pressed her lips together. Her eyes went bright and glassy for approximately two seconds before she tipped her chin up and recalibrated into her natural mode, which was brassy and forward and extremely loud about it. "Obviously. I mean, obviously. Where else would you go? The city?" She waved a hand dismissively. "Please. The city can keep itself."

"The city can absolutely keep itself," Amber agreed. "And Dalton's rebuilding the garage?"

"And I'm opening the bakery."

Lila's whole face went incandescent. "Oh, *honey.* I have opinions about the menu that I have been sitting on for months."

"I know you do."

"The lavender scones alone—" "I know."

"I have *notes.*"

"Lila." Amber grabbed her by both arms, grinning in spite of herself. "I know. We'll do the lavender scones. We'll do all of it. But right now I have to finish packing this apartment, so if you want to be useful—"

"I was born useful," Lila said, and picked up a stack of books.

They packed for an hour, the three of them, Dalton moving with quiet purpose between the apartment and the truck and Lila talking with the comfortable, machine-gun rhythm of someone who'd been storing up conversation for weeks. She had opinions on the corner lot Dalton had mentioned. She had opinions about the zoning. She had somehow already mentally arranged the display cases and the seating area and had a strong preference for exposed brick if they could manage it. Amber let her talk, carrying boxes and half-listening, watching through the window as the afternoon light slanted lower across the street.

There was nothing threatening about the street. A few cars. A woman walking a dog. The hardware store still with its hand-lettered sign. She watched it all and felt nothing except a kind of quiet, provisional warmth. She was allowed to be here. She'd decided that. She was staying, and the past was a thing that had happened to her, not a thing that still owned her, and she was *staying.*

The apartment was mostly cleared by four. Dalton closed the truck's tailgate and came back inside, and the three of them ate Lila's chicken and rice standing around the kitchen counter because there was nowhere left to sit, and it was good — properly good, the kind of food that meant someone had put time and care into it — and Amber said so, and Lila preened appropriately.

"You're going to be okay," Lila said, when she was leaving, casserole dish tucked under her arm, hand on the door. She said it directly, without her usual decorative layer of sarcasm. Just flat and sure and true.

Amber met her eyes. "Yeah," she said. "We are." They went to the lake that evening.

Not the cabin — they'd given the keys back, left the plaid curtains to their perpetual grandmother-aesthetic existence. But Cherry Creek had its own lake, a twenty-minute walk from town, and Dalton knew the path without thinking about it. She followed him through the trees as the last of the afternoon light failed, the ground under her boots soft with fallen leaves, the air sharp and clean and smelling of pine resin and cold water.

The shore was a narrow strip of flat rock, the lake spreading out from it in the fading light. The water was dark now, the far bank just a shadow, the sky above it going from pale gold to something deeper, the first stars just starting to show at the horizon's upper edge. A cold wind moved off the water. Amber pulled her jacket tighter and stepped to the shoreline, where the water came in small, quiet increments against the rock.

Dalton came to stand beside her.

She thought about the girl who'd driven into Cherry Creek eight months ago. The white-knuckle grip on the wheel, the constant mirror-checking, the way she'd sat in the new apartment and counted the exits before she'd even unpacked a box. That girl had been so thoroughly convinced that survival was a solo endeavor, that needing someone was the same thing as being vulnerable, that love was just another word for leverage in the wrong hands.

She'd been wrong about so much.

"I keep thinking about that girl," she said. Dalton waited. He was good at waiting.

"The one who moved here. She was so sure the darkness was going to swallow her. Like it was just a matter of time." She watched the water move against the rock, that patient, repetitive motion. "It didn't, though. That's the thing. We fell into it — all of it, the bad stuff and the really bad stuff — and it didn't swallow us. It just..." She paused, searching for the right word. "Changed the shape of things."

"Forged," Dalton said. Low, quiet. Not correcting her, just offering it. She considered that. "Yeah," she said. "Forged. That's better."

He shifted beside her, and then his arm came around her from behind, pulling her back against his chest, his chin dropping to the top of her head. He was warm. Solid. Present in the specific way that she'd stopped trying to explain or qualify or be suspicious of, because she knew it now in her body the same way she knew the smell of good bread or the sound of rain — as a simple, true thing. She let herself lean into him.

The lake went darker. The stars multiplied. Somewhere across the water a loon called — that long, strange, carrying sound — and she felt his arms tighten slightly in response, that unconscious reflex of protection, and she smiled at the water because she loved him for it even though she didn't need it.

That was the part she hadn't expected. That she could love the protection without requiring it. That she could take it as a gift instead of a lifeline. That was new. That was, she thought, the actual thing that had changed.

"I'm not who I was when I got here," she said. "No," he agreed. "You're not."

"I'm not the girl who escaped. I'm the woman who stayed." She said it out loud to hear how it fit, and it fit fine. Better than fine. "And fought."

Dalton pressed a kiss to the top of her head. Not the urgent, loaded kind; just slow and deliberate and warm, the kind that meant *I hear you* and *I'm here* in the same breath. She felt it all the way down.

She turned in his arms until she was facing him, his hands resting at the small of her back, the lake at her back and his face above her in the early starlight. The scar at his brow was a pale line in the dimness. His eyes were steady on her face. This man who'd walked out of a courthouse with five years of probation and no apologies and driven them to a lake cabin and made eggs in the morning and meant every word he'd said in the dark — she held his gaze and felt, for the first time in longer than she could accurately remember, the specific, uncomplicated peace of being exactly where she was supposed to be.

"The darkness didn't win," she said.

"No." His thumb traced a slow circle at the base of her spine. "It didn't." "We did."

"We did."

She kissed him then, with the cold air on her cheeks and the lake at her back and the stars coming in over the tree line, and he kissed her back with that unhurried, focused attention that still managed to rearrange her thinking every single time. His hands pulled her closer and she went, wrapping her arms around his waist, her fingers finding the warmth of him under the flannel, and it was slow and deliberate and tasted like the cold and the night and something she'd spent two years not knowing she was looking for.

When they broke apart, she pressed her forehead against his jaw and felt his chest rise and fall under her palms.

"Best bakery in the state," she said.

His chest moved on something she was choosing to classify as a laugh. "Told you."

"I'm going to hold you to that." "I know you will."

She pulled back and looked at the lake one more time — dark and wide and completely, blessedly ordinary, doing nothing except being itself, which was more than enough. The loon called again from somewhere she couldn't see. A long, echoing note that moved across the water and dispersed into the trees.

I'm here, I'm here, I'm here.

She took his hand. He took hers back, fingers interlacing with the easy certainty of people who'd stopped pretending they didn't need each other.

"Let's go home," Amber said.

Dalton squeezed her hand once. "Yeah," he said. "Let's go home."

They walked back through the trees as the night settled fully around Cherry Creek, and the town's lights came through the branches ahead of them, warm and small and steady, and the path was dark but she knew every step of it, and she wasn't afraid of the dark anymore.

She was the woman who'd walked through it. That was enough. That was everything.

21
Fresh Paint and New Blood

The bakery smelled like wet plaster and fresh paint and underneath all of that, faintly, like smoke. Three weeks of scrubbing and primer and two full coats of eggshell white hadn't entirely erased what had happened here, and Amber had stopped pretending it would. You couldn't paint over a thing and expect it to be gone. You could just make it livable.

She dragged a box of dishware across the concrete floor, the scrape of cardboard loud in the empty space, and stopped to check the placement of the second industrial oven against the back wall. It was heavy and silver and almost comically large for a bakery that didn't have a single customer yet, but she'd ordered it anyway. Go big or go back to the city, she'd told Lila. Lila had said something about exposed brick and high ceilings being wasted on self-doubt.

The brick was still unpainted. She liked it that way.

From somewhere behind the partial wall that would eventually be the service counter, she could hear Dalton working. The low percussion of a wrench turning, a joint being tested, the occasional deliberate silence that meant he was reading the situation before he acted. He'd been at the plumbing since seven in the morning, which meant he'd been up since at least five, which meant he hadn't slept well again. She'd noticed. She was getting better at noticing the things he didn't say.

She crouched down to check the oven's leveling feet and decided two of them needed adjusting. Her knees ached from the concrete floor, a dull, biting throb that signaled just how little insulation was between her and the frozen ground. The bakery was a tomb of stagnant air — November in Cherry Creek was being its usual relentless self, a damp, bone-deep chill that seeped through her thick leggings and made her joints feel like they were filled with grit. Every time she exhaled, her breath bloomed in a ragged, silver fog that hung in the air for a second too long, a ghostly reminder of how hard her lungs were working just to stay warm.

Dalton appeared around the partition wall. His flannel was pushed up to the elbows, forearms streaked with grease and something that looked like joint compound, and there was a smear of eggshell white paint drying across his left shoulder that he clearly didn't know about. He looked at the oven, then at her crouched position, then at the oven again.

"Rear foot's off by about a centimeter," she said before he could offer to do it himself.

He leaned against the partition. "I can—"

"I have it." She adjusted the leveling foot, checked it with the small level she'd tucked into her back pocket, and stood up. "Plumbing?"

"Pressure's good. Hot water line needed rerouting but it's done." He wiped his hands on a rag that had seen better days. "The sink basin's coming in Thursday."

"Thursday works." She surveyed the room, hands on her hips, doing the mental math she'd been doing every day since they'd signed the lease. Display cases along the front windows. Prep tables center. Cold storage to the left. Seating, eventually — six small tables, nothing fussy — once the floors were refinished. It was going to be good. She could feel it in the specific way she felt good bread, something bone-deep and certain. "We need to talk about the front shutters."

"Already ordered them."

She turned. "I didn't pick shutters yet."

"I know." He tucked the rag into his back pocket and crossed his arms, and there was something in the set of his jaw that was different from the project-management look he'd had on all morning. Careful. Measured. "I

ordered them two days ago. Heavy gauge. They'll be here by the end of the week."

Amber put the level down on the counter. "Dalton. What kind of shutters?"

"The kind that stop a crowbar," he said, and left no room in his tone for a follow-up joke.

She opened her mouth, and then didn't say anything, because outside, past the fresh paint and the half-hung pendant lights and the glass door she'd been so proud of, a black car sat at the curb. Not parked the way people parked when they were running into the hardware store or grabbing a coffee. Just sitting. Windows tinted dark enough that she couldn't see a driver. She'd noticed it an hour ago and told herself it was nothing. It had been there for three hours.

"Yeah," Dalton said quietly, watching her register it. "I know." "How long have you been watching it?"

"Since it pulled up."

"You didn't say anything."

"I was hoping it was nothing." He paused. "It isn't nothing."

She crossed her arms over her chest, the cold air suddenly sharper. "Okay," she said. "Okay, so what do we-"

A knock at the door. Crisp. Professional. The kind of knock that didn't expect to be ignored.

Dalton was already moving toward the door before she finished turning, and she let him, because arguing about it right now would be a waste of the seconds they had. He opened it without hesitating. A courier stood on the step, young, bored-looking, a flat white box tucked under one arm and a digital signature pad in his other hand. He held up the box.

"Delivery for Rowan?"

Amber stepped forward. "That's me."

The courier handed over the pad, she signed, and he passed her the box and was already turning back toward the curb before she'd finished. The black car was still there. He didn't look at it. She watched him not look at it, and that was its own answer.

She set the box on the counter and opened it.

White lilies. A dozen of them, pristine and waxy and smelling like funeral parlors, arranged with the kind of precision that said this wasn't sentiment, this was a statement. Her stomach turned over slowly, the way it did on the top of a roller coaster, that suspended moment before the drop. Tucked among the stems was a card, heavy stock, embossed in a font that cost money. She pulled it free.

She read it once. Then again. Then she put it down on the counter without saying anything and let Dalton read it over her shoulder.

The Vane Collective. Formal letterhead. Precise, bloodless language about outstanding obligations and unrecovered assets. The word *stolen* appeared once, clinical and deliberate. A forty-eight-hour window for voluntary compliance.

The bottom of the card had a small, printed emblem. A geometric shape she didn't recognize, but something about it made the back of her neck prickle.

"They know the key didn't burn in the mine," she said. Her voice was flat. She was proud of how flat it was.

"Yes." Dalton picked up the card and turned it over. The back was blank. He set it down again.

"Rory was working for them."

"Rory was a contractor. Bottom of the chain." He looked at the lilies. "This is the chain itself."

Amber thought about the black car still idling at the curb. "The car."

"Message delivery. They wanted us to see it first, then the flowers. So we'd understand the sequence." His jaw was tight. "So we'd know they're organized."

"Are they?" she asked. "Organized?"

The look he gave her said *don't make me answer that*, which was itself an answer. He was already moving to the corner of the room where he'd left his equipment bag — she'd stopped asking why he brought it every day — and pulling out a device she recognized as a signal detector from the one time he'd explained it to her. He swept it methodically, starting at the door, working inward.

"Dalton." She watched him move. "Talk to me."

"The Collective doesn't leave a job unfinished." He moved along the front windows, the device held steady. "They especially don't leave it unfinished when someone who worked for them goes rogue. There are principles involved. Reputation." He said the word the way other people said *disease.* "Once they send the letter, the clock is real."

"What happens at forty-eight hours?" "They stop asking."

She sat down on the edge of the counter because her legs had decided they'd rather not stand. The lilies were right there, close enough to smell, that thick sweet rot of white petals that she was never going to be able to separate from threat for the rest of her life. She pushed the box away from her. "We don't have the key."

"They don't know that." "Then we tell them."

"People like this don't take our word for it." He swept the storage room doorway, then stepped inside. She heard the device's quiet electronic stutter change pitch.

She was off the counter before she'd consciously decided to move, crossing the room and stepping into the storage doorway. The storage room was narrow, shelves along both walls, three fifty-pound bags of flour she'd ordered last week stacked in the corner. Dalton was crouched in front of them, the signal detector resting on the floor, his hands careful around the top bag.

"Don't," she said sharply.

"I've got it." He peeled back the bag's folded top with two fingers, looked inside, and reached in with the kind of deliberate precision that made her chest seize. When his hand came back out, he was holding something the size of a large coin. Matte black. A small red indicator light, barely visible, pulsing slowly.

A listening device. In a sealed bag of flour she'd personally ordered from a supplier two towns over.

The silence in the storage room lasted exactly four seconds.

"They were already in here," she said. "Before the flowers. Before the car." "Yes."

"Someone got into this bakery." She looked around the small room, the shelves, the back wall with its single high window. "Someone got in here and put that in my flour and we were working ten feet away and we didn't

—"

"Amber." His voice was low and steady and she hated how much she needed that right now. "Look at me."

She looked at him. He was still crouched, the device balanced on his palm, and his blue eyes were the only still thing in the room.

"They want us scared," he said. "That's the point of all of this. The car, the flowers, the bug. It's psychological. They want us reactive, not rational."

"Great," she said. "I am both of those things simultaneously."

He set the device carefully on the shelf and stood up. The storage room was small enough that he was close, and she could smell sawdust and machine oil and the faint chemical bite of primer. She'd stopped cataloging those things as comfort and started cataloging them as just *him*, which was either progress or a different kind of danger.

"This ends now," he said quietly. "The open-door situation. The unlocked windows. The assumption that Cherry Creek is small enough to hide in." He held her gaze. "I'm putting up cameras tonight. All four corners, motion-triggered, encrypted feed direct to my phone. And the shutters I ordered — reinforced steel, motorized. They'll be mounted by Friday."

"You already had all of this planned," she said. "I was hoping I was wrong to plan it."

She crossed her arms. The anger was there, just below the fear — not at him, exactly, but at the shape of this, the way safety kept receding every time she thought she'd found solid ground. "You can't just — Dalton, you can't install a military bunker in my bakery without telling me what you know. That's not protective, that's just you making decisions in a room I'm not in."

Something shifted in his expression. Not defensiveness. More like acknowledgment, the kind that cost something. "You're right."

That stopped her.

"I've been running threat assessments since before we signed the lease," he said. "I told myself it was standard precaution. I told myself I didn't want to alarm you until I had something concrete." He paused. "I was also telling myself I could handle it before it became your problem."

"It is my bakery," she said. "It's already my problem."

"I know that." He scrubbed a hand through his hair, leaving it worse than before. "I know. That's — I'm aware that's not a good reason."

She studied him for a moment, this man who'd rebuilt a garage and now had plans to fortify her dream like it was a forward operating base, and she felt the anger soften slightly at its edges. Not disappear. Just become less sharp.

"Okay," she said. "So tell me what you know. Right now. All of it."

"The Collective is not local," he said. "They're organized, they're patient, and they have reach. The key was only part of what Rory was supposed to deliver. There were documents — financial records, account routing, names of people who'd rather not be named. Rory was skimming. When he went off-script, he became a liability, and then I removed him from the equation, and now there's a hole in their operation that they need closed." He looked at the listening device on the shelf. "They're not going to let that go."

"And they've been listening," she said. "Which means they know we don't have the key."

"It means they know everything we've said in this room for however long that thing has been planted." He picked it up again, turned it over. "I'd guess four days, based on the battery signature. They know about the shutters. They know about the cameras." A beat. "They know we're not running."

The red light pulsed steadily. Patient. Amber reached out and took the device from his palm, looked at it for one long moment, and then carried it to the back of the storage room and dropped it into the industrial floor drain in the corner. It made a small, anticlimactic sound when it hit the bottom.

Dalton watched her do it without saying anything.

"Okay," she said, dusting her hands on her jeans. "Then let's be very clear about what they're going to find when they come looking." She turned to face him. "They're going to find the cameras you're installing tonight.

They're going to find the steel shutters. And they're going to find us still here." She held his gaze. "Put up your cameras, Dalton. Put up all of them. And then tell me what else we need."

He was quiet for a moment, reading her the way he always did, that careful attention that wasn't surveillance anymore, just — knowing her. "You're sure."

"I'm not sure of anything," she said honestly. "But I'm staying. So make the bakery safe enough to stay in."

Outside, the black car finally pulled away from the curb. She heard it through the wall — the low purr of an expensive engine, unhurried, as if it had all the time in the world. Which, she supposed, from their perspective, was exactly right. Forty-eight hours was generous for people who operated on the principle that patience was just another form of pressure.

Dalton went back to his equipment bag and started pulling out camera housings. She watched him work for a moment, the systematic efficiency of it, and then she turned back to the bakery floor and the oven that still needed its second leveling foot adjusted and the shelves that weren't going to organize themselves.

The lilies sat on the counter in their white box, pristine and cold and fragrant.

She picked up the box, walked to the back door, and set it outside on the step. She didn't throw it. She didn't need to make a production of it. She just put it where it belonged, which was outside of the thing she was building, and then she came back in and picked up her level and got back to work.

The bakery smelled like paint and plaster and the faint ghost of smoke. It also smelled like sawdust and machine oil, and the particular clean bite of cold air coming through the gap under the door. She breathed it in and held it and let it be complicated, because that was what it was. Complicated and hers and worth protecting.

Above her head, Dalton mounted the first camera in the corner above the front door, the bracket clicking into place with a sound like a lock engaging.

Good, she thought. Lock it all down. She wasn't going anywhere.

22
The Name on the Ledger

Wes's cabin smelled like woodsmoke and old coffee and the particular kind of damp that settles into a place after decades of hard winters. Amber had been here once before, briefly, and she'd thought then that it looked like a man who'd decided the world could take a flying leap. She thought the same thing now, standing in the doorway while Dalton ducked under the low frame behind her, except now she understood that choosing to opt out wasn't weakness. Sometimes it was survival strategy.

Wes was in his armchair by the woodstove, a wool blanket over his lap and his left leg propped on a milk crate. The bruising had faded to greenish-yellow at his temple, but he was still moving like every joint needed permission first. He waved them in without getting up, which told her more about how bad he was feeling than anything else could have.

"Sit down," he said. "Coffee's on the stove. Help yourselves."

Dalton poured two mugs and handed one to Amber, then pulled a wooden chair close and sat with his elbows on his knees, the way he always sat when he was bracing for something. Amber took the other chair and wrapped both hands around the mug. The cabin was warm, almost too warm, and the fire popped and hissed in a way that should have been comforting but wasn't.

Wes looked at Dalton for a long moment, then at Amber, then back to Dalton. "You show her the letter yet?"

"She knows about the Vane Collective," Dalton said. "That's not what I asked."

A beat of silence that had weight to it. Amber watched Dalton's jaw tighten, a slight pull of muscle beneath stubble, and filed that away.

"Tell me what you found," Dalton said.

Wes reached under the blanket and pulled out a manila folder, thick with printed pages and a few handwritten notes in his cramped, slanted script. He set it on the crate next to his leg. "Been making calls since before your bakery got its first coat of paint," he said. "Old contacts. People who owe me things. The Collective's been operating for about twelve years. Started as a private security outfit, legitimate on paper, shifted to asset recovery and enforcement around year four." He opened the folder. "Julian Vane runs it. Forty-one years old, no criminal record, because he's got six lawyers and a very careful paper trail. Operates from upstate, has reach across the Northeast, couple of tentacles into Canada." He paused. "He's not Rory. Rory was a dog on a leash. Julian Vane's the one holding it."

"We know all that," Dalton said. "What did you find that I don't know?"

Wes looked at him steadily. "The man you killed. The third one, night of Amber's assault." He let the sentence sit there. "That was Elias Vane. Julian's younger brother."

The fire popped. Outside, a branch scraped the cabin window.

Amber turned to look at Dalton slowly, the way you turn toward a sound you're not sure you heard correctly. His face hadn't moved. That was the thing — it hadn't moved at all, which meant he'd already known. The realization settled through her like cold water finding the lowest point.

"You knew," she said.

Dalton didn't answer immediately, which was its own answer.

"Dalton." Her voice was careful in the way she made it careful when she was working very hard not to let it crack. "Did you know who he was?"

"Not that night," he said. "I found out two days later. Ran the prints through a contact." He set his coffee mug down on the floor. "Elias had a record.

Small stuff, but it was enough to ID him." "And you didn't tell me."

"No."

She stood up. Not because she had anywhere to go in the small cabin, but because sitting still wasn't possible anymore. "So this whole time — the letter, the forty-eight hours, the listening device in my flour — all of it is happening because Julian Vane thinks I'm the reason his brother is dead, and you knew that and didn't say anything to me."

"You weren't a reason," Dalton said. "You were a location. Elias was there because the job sent him there. He died because of choices he made before I ever walked through that door."

"That is not the point."

"I know it's not." He looked up at her, and his eyes were steady in that way she sometimes hated, because it felt too much like control when she wanted him rattled. "I didn't tell you because it would have meant explaining that the reason a syndicate was now actively hunting us was directly connected to you being attacked. I didn't want you carrying that."

"That's not your call." The words came out sharper than she intended. "Dalton, that is not your call to make. My safety, my life, the thing that is actively trying to kill me — I get to know. All of it. You don't get to decide what information is too heavy for me."

"I know," he said quietly.

"Stop agreeing with me, it's making it harder to be angry at you."

Wes made a sound that was almost a laugh. Both of them looked at him. "Don't mind me," he said, and nodded at the folder. "There's more."

Amber sat back down, not because she was done being furious, but because the folder was the more immediate problem and she'd learned over the past several weeks that rage was a luxury she had to schedule carefully. She'd deal with Dalton's omissions later. Fully. At length. Elias was Julian's only blood family," Wes continued. "Their parents died when Julian was nineteen. He raised Elias himself, built the Collective around protecting him. Elias was his second in command, his proof that what he'd built was worth something." He closed the folder. "To Julian, this isn't a business dispute. It's a blood debt." He fixed Dalton with the look of a man who'd seen enough wars to know how they ended. "He's not going to send another letter."

Dalton nodded once, the sharp downward motion of someone confirming what they'd already calculated. "Timeline's collapsed."

"Forty-eight hours was theater," Wes said. "He's already moving."

Amber's fingers tightened around her mug. The coffee had gone lukewarm, and the ceramic felt rough against her palms, a small scratchy anchor. "So what do we do?"

Before Wes could answer, the small television on the shelf in the corner of the cabin caught her eye. The sound was low, almost inaudible under the crackle of the woodstove, but the crawler at the bottom of the screen snagged her attention the way bad news always did, like it had a hook in it. Local news. A live feed from what she recognized as the county jail, all blue and white official lighting, a reporter in a heavy coat speaking into a microphone with the expression people wore when they were professionally neutral about something terrible.

"Wes," she said. "Turn that up."

He grabbed the remote from the side table and raised the volume.

—found unresponsive in her holding cell early this morning. Officials are calling it an apparent suicide, though the family has not been notified pending confirmation of identity. The victim, a Cherry Creek resident being held on charges related to an ongoing investigation—

Amber was on her feet again, moving toward the television, her whole body gone cold in a way that had nothing to do with November. The reporter kept talking, words like *pending investigation* and *no further comment from the sheriff's office*, and then there was a photograph on the screen.

Caramel curls. Red lipstick. A smile that threw itself wide open and didn't hold anything back.

Lila.

The sound that came out of Amber was small and involuntary and she pressed her hand over her mouth and held it there. Behind her, she heard Dalton stand up. She heard the wooden chair scrape the floor. She didn't turn around.

"That's not a suicide," Dalton said. His voice was very low and very flat. "That's a cleaning."

"Lila was in custody," Amber said, and her voice was strange to her own ears, scraped thin. "She was supposed to be safe. That's why she was in custody."

"She was a loose end," Dalton said. "She knew too much about the operation, about Rory's connection to the Collective. They couldn't let her testify." A pause. "Julian doesn't leave loose ends."

"She has a son." Amber's hand was still pressed to her mouth. She made herself lower it. "She has a kid, Dalton. He's seven years old and she —" She stopped. Swallowed. Tried again. "She bought me a coffee my first week here and told me I looked like I needed a friend. That's — that's who she was."

Nobody said anything. The television reporter moved on to weather, cheerful and oblivious. Wes reached over and turned it off.

The silence was different now. Heavier, and with a specific shape to it. Amber stood with her back to both men and breathed through it, the grief and the fury tangling together in her chest until she couldn't cleanly separate them. Lila had been loud and brassy and unashamedly nosy and she'd pushed Amber to eat pie and talk about her feelings and she'd been so *alive*, the kind of alive that other people caught like a cold, and now she was a photograph on a television screen with a caption underneath.

Amber turned around. "We're done hiding," she said. Dalton was already watching her. "Yes," he said. "We are."

Wes shifted in his chair and reached under the side table, lifting a worn leather satchel onto his lap with effort. He unzipped it and pulled out a manila envelope, thicker than the folder, which he held out to Dalton. "Financial records. Account routing. Three shell companies traced back to Julian's primary offshore account. I had a friend in banking pull strings she probably shouldn't have pulled." He exhaled through his nose. "That's your leverage. If you can get it to the right people —"

"I know who to get it to," Dalton said, taking the envelope.

"Sheriff Landry's going to be a problem," Wes said. "He's already sniffing around the Lila situation. He's not stupid. Give him enough to work with without getting yourself arrested for the parts of this story that don't reflect well on you."

"Noted," Dalton said, and the word carried a dry, humorless weight. Wes looked at Amber. "You holding up?"

"No," she said. "But I'll save the falling apart for later."

He nodded like that was the only acceptable answer. "Good girl." He paused. "Lila would've liked knowing you were still standing."

That hit somewhere tender, and she let it. She didn't look away from it or smooth it over. She just held it.

They were outside in the cold, gravel crunching under their feet as they walked to Dalton's truck, when he stopped and opened the passenger door and then, instead of waiting for her to get in, turned and faced her. He reached into the inner pocket of his jacket and pulled out a small flip phone, matte black, anonymous. He set it in her palm. "Burner," he said. "Untraceable. That's the only number in it." He met her eyes. "Mine. You hit one and call, I answer. Doesn't matter where I am."

She folded her fingers around it. The plastic was cold and slightly rough in her grip.

Then he reached into the back of his waistband and produced a small pistol, compact and dark, and held it out to her grip-first. She stared at it.

"I know you know how to shoot," he said. "You told me about the range sessions after the assault." His voice was steady but she could hear something underneath it, something tightly controlled. "This is a .380. Light, easy to conceal. There's one in the chamber and seven in the magazine." He paused. "I'm not giving you this because I think you can't handle yourself. I'm giving you this because I can't be in every room."

She took it. It was heavier than it looked, the weight of it settling into her palm with a kind of grim pragmatism. She checked the safety the way the range instructor had shown her two years ago, muscle memory surfacing through everything else.

"The time for staying quiet is over," Dalton said. "Julian thinks grief makes him righteous. It doesn't. It just makes him dangerous. And dangerous is something I know how to deal with."

"We," she said.

He raised an eyebrow.

"Dangerous is something *we* know how to deal with," she said. "Because I am done being the person things happen *to*, Dalton. That stops right now. We go after this together or I go after it myself, and I promise you, you would prefer the first option."

Something moved through his expression — not quite a smile, not quite relief, somewhere in between, like a knot releasing. "Yeah," he said. "I would."

The drive back toward Cherry Creek was quiet, the kind of quiet that isn't empty but full, packed tight with everything neither of them had finished saying. The trees along the road were stripped bare, gray and skeletal against the late-afternoon sky, and the light had gone flat and pewter, that particular November light that felt like the world was conserving itself.

Amber held the burner phone in one hand and watched the road.

"You should have told me about Elias," she said. Not accusatory this time. Just true.

"Yes," he said.

"I understand why you didn't. I don't agree with the reasoning, but I understand it." She turned to look at his profile, the clean line of his jaw, the small scar through his left eyebrow. "No more of that. Whatever you know that touches my life, I need to know it too. Even if it's ugly."

"Especially if it's ugly," he said. "Especially," she agreed.

They passed the diner. The lights were on inside, the warm yellow spill of it across the wet asphalt, and Amber saw a handwritten sign in the window that said *Closed for Family* in Nora's rounded script. She looked at it until they were past it, until it was just a yellow smear in the side mirror.

Lila had called her *hot stuff* the first time they'd met, and it had made Amber laugh despite herself, and she hadn't expected to love that diner or the woman who worked it, but she had. She did. Past tense now, and the past tense of it was going to take a while to get used to.

She tucked the pistol into the inner pocket of her jacket and felt it settle against her ribs. Cold metal and hard purpose. Julian Vane thought a blood debt made him the most dangerous person in this equation.

Amber Rowan had survived worse than a man with a ledger and a grudge, and she was done pretending otherwise.

"We need to call Landry," she said. "Tonight," Dalton confirmed.

"And we need to look at those financial records Wes pulled." "Tonight," he said again.

"And you're going to tell me everything else you know. All of it. Whatever's still sitting in that head of yours that you've been deciding I can't handle." She kept her voice even. "I want it all on the table."

He glanced at her sideways, just for a second, and she saw it — the cost of what she was asking, how much of his armor she was requesting he set down. He looked back at the road.

"All of it," he said.

The truck moved through Cherry Creek's main street, past the closed hardware store and the dark windows of the insurance office and the gas station with its buzzing fluorescent lights. The town looked the same as it always did. Quiet. Small. The kind of place that minded its own business until it couldn't anymore.

Amber thought about Lila's kid, seven years old and waiting for a mom who wasn't coming home, and she felt the grief sharpen into something harder and more useful. Not rage, exactly. More like resolve. The kind that doesn't announce itself, just settles in and starts building.

Julian Vane had a ledger with Dalton's name on it. He'd sent flowers and couriers and listening devices, and he'd reached into a jail cell and silenced a woman who'd done nothing worse than know too much.

He thought that made him untouchable.

Amber pressed her palm flat against the pistol through her jacket and breathed out slow and steady through her nose.

Let him think that. Right up until he couldn't anymore.

23
Worship in the Dust

The bakery smelled like sawdust and sugar and the sharp chemical bite of new wiring, which was not the most romantic combination in the world, but Amber had stopped requiring romance from the universe somewhere around the third week of her life going completely sideways.

It was past eleven. The security installer had packed up his van and left two hours ago, and the overhead lights were off, everything running on the work lamp Dalton had rigged in the corner while he crouched behind the counter panel checking the camera feeds on his laptop. Amber had been wiping down the new shelving units for the past twenty minutes, which was technically productive and also gave her hands something to do besides shake.

"Feed's clean on the east wall," Dalton said. "Northwest corner still has a dead zone. Six inches, maybe eight."

"Can we fix it tonight?"

"Already ordered the bracket. Tomorrow morning." He typed something, scrolled, typed again. The blue light of the screen caught the underside of his jaw, the stubble there, the faint tension in the muscle. "Come look at this."

She came around the counter and crouched beside him, close enough that her shoulder pressed into his. The laptop showed a grid of camera feeds, each one a crisp gray rectangle of empty street, empty alley, empty parking lot behind the bakery. Everything quiet. Everything still. She was aware of his warmth against her arm, the particular solidity of him, the way he smelled like motor oil and cold air and something underneath that was just *him*—a scent that hit her like a physical blow to the solar plexus. It wasn't just smell; it was a sensory trigger that sent a phantom shiver racing down her spine, a flicker of a memory of a night she couldn't quite see but could suddenly feel in the way her skin prickled. It made her mouth go dry and her heart hammer a frantic rhythm against her ribs, a primal recognition that this man was both the storm and the shelter from it, and she had not been this close to him since Wes's cabin, since the drive home, since all of it had settled on them like snow — heavy and quiet and impossible to ignore.

"We've got good coverage," he said. "Perimeter's solid. If anyone moves within forty feet of the building, we get an alert."

"Good." She wasn't looking at the screen anymore. She was looking at his hands on the keyboard, the knuckles, the faint scar tissue across two of his fingers from something she hadn't asked about yet. "Dalton."

"Mm."

"Stop looking at the cameras for a second."

He went still. Not the tense, combat-ready stillness she'd learned to read as danger, but something different. Slower. He closed the laptop halfway and turned his head.

She kissed him.

Not gently. Not the soft, tentative kind of kiss that asks permission. She grabbed the front of his flannel shirt and kissed him like she was furious at him and in love with him and terrified she might not get another chance, which was more or less exactly how she felt, so she figured the honesty was appropriate. He made a sound low in his chest and his hand came up to cup the back of her head, fingers threading into her hair, and he kissed her back with the same intensity she'd given him, matched it and exceeded it until she couldn't tell anymore who was leading and who was following.

They ended up in the backroom.

It wasn't graceful. They knocked into a shelf and sent a bag of flour skidding, and she laughed, breathless, and he pressed her back against a stack of supply crates and didn't look even slightly apologetic about it. The room smelled like raw wood and unground grain and the faint vanilla ghost of tomorrow's prep work. A single work lamp burned in the corner, casting everything in warm amber.

"The cameras," she said against his mouth.

"Interior's off," he said. "I turned them off two minutes ago." A pause. "I was optimistic."

"Were you."

"Had a feeling," he said, and his hands found her waist, sliding under the hem of her hoodie, and the contact of his palms against her skin made her breath catch in a way that felt embarrassingly immediate.

She pulled the hoodie over her head and dropped it. His eyes moved over her, slow and deliberate in a way that made her want to cover herself and stand straighter at the same time. She did neither. She reached for his shirt instead.

"All of it," she said.

He obliged. The flannel hit the floor and then the henley beneath it, and she let herself look, let herself put her hands on him — the flat planes of his chest, the ridge of a scar along his ribs that she'd seen before but never touched. She traced it with her fingertips, and something in his expression went fractured and open in a way she'd only seen a handful of times. Like she was reaching somewhere he didn't let people reach.

"Does it hurt?" she asked. "Not from you," he said.

She pressed her mouth to it. Felt the tension move through him, the long exhale, his hands gripping her hips like she was the only solid thing in the room. She understood that. He felt that way to her too — like a fixed point when everything else was spinning.

He walked her backward until her knees hit a folded tarp on the floor, the kind the painters had left behind, and then they were down, and his weight settled over her in a way that should have felt suffocating and instead felt like a wall between her and everything outside this room. His hands were everywhere, deliberate and thorough, like he was memorizing her — the curve of her shoulder, the hollow of her collarbone, the place under her jaw where her pulse jumped when he pressed his lips there.

"Dalton," she said. Just his name. It was enough.

"I've got you," he said. His voice was rough, stripped down to its bottom register. "I've got you, Amber."

She believed him. That was the terrifying part — she actually believed him.

He took his time with her in a way that felt almost cruel given the state she was in, given the weeks of tension and fear and wanting that had been building between them like pressure behind a dam. His mouth moved down her throat and she arched into it, her fingers curling into his hair, and when she tugged he made a sound she felt more than heard, a low vibration against her skin. She was dimly aware that they were on a painter's tarp in a bakery backroom surrounded by fifty-pound flour sacks, and she could not have cared less.

When he finally moved over her fully, his eyes found hers in the amber half-light, and he waited. A beat. Two. Checking.

"I'm here," she said. "Don't stop." He didn't.

It was fierce and close and raw in a way that had everything to do with Lila's photograph on a television screen and a blood coin from a man who thought he owned the world and the burner phone in her jacket pocket and the pistol against her ribs. It was their bodies saying the thing their mouths couldn't quite manage: *I choose you. I choose this. Even knowing everything it costs.* His hands gripped her like she was something he was refusing to let the world take, and she gripped him right back, and they burned through the worst of the fear the only way they could, skin against skin in the dark.

Afterward, they lay on the tarp with their clothes half-retrieved, her head on his chest, his arm across her back. The work lamp hummed. Outside, somewhere distant, a car passed on Main Street. She could hear his heartbeat slowing back to normal under her ear, steady as anything, and she focused on that rhythm and let herself just exist for a minute without thinking about blood debts or dead women or the forty-eight hours that had already started counting down.

Dalton broke the quiet first.

"There's something else," he said. "Something I told Wes I'd tell you when the time was right."

She lifted her head. His profile was angled toward the ceiling, jaw set, the particular look of a man who's already decided to do something hard and is just getting through the opening of it. "Tell me," she said.

He exhaled. "My father was in the Collective." She went very still.

"Not a foot soldier," he continued. "He was one of the founding members. Before Julian Vane restructured it, before it had a name anyone outside would recognize, my father was in the room where it started." His voice was flat but not empty — the flatness of something that had been worked over many times in private. "He recruited men with military backgrounds, specialized skills. Extraction, surveillance, wetwork. He built the infrastructure. Julian Vane walked in and monetized it."

Amber sat up slowly. The flour-dusty air of the backroom thickened around them, pressing against her skin with a new, heavy density.

"He didn't leave," Dalton said. "He died. Heart attack, when I was twenty-two. I was two years into my service contract." He turned his head to look at her, and his eyes were the particular shade of blue that appeared when he wasn't guarding anything. "I found out what he'd been doing about six months after he died, when a contact of his reached out to me. Thought I'd want to step into his role." A pause. "I didn't."

"But that's why they know you," she said. "That's why Julian Vane knows your name, why you're not just some random man who interfered in a job. You're the son of one of the men who built what he runs."

"Yes."

"And when you killed Elias—"

"It wasn't just a soldier of the Collective taking out one of their own," he said. "To Julian, it was the betrayal of a legacy. The founder's son, raised inside the same world, choosing the wrong side." He sat up, elbows on his knees, head angled down. "I was raised to be exactly what Julian is. My father made sure of it — the discipline, the skills, the particular way of seeing people as assets or threats. He was grooming me before I even knew what grooming was." He stopped. "I chose the military instead because I needed to believe there was a version of what I was good at that wasn't just organized crime with better paperwork."

She reached out and put her hand on his arm. She felt the muscle there, the tension. He didn't pull away.

"I'm not just protecting you from Julian Vane," he said quietly. "I'm trying to undo something. My father helped build the machine that sent men to your apartment two years ago. That sent Rory to make your life a nightmare.

That killed Lila." His jaw tightened. "I can't fix that. I can't reach back and make him into someone different. But I can make sure the thing he built doesn't get to take anything else from you. That's — that's what this is. All of it."

Amber looked at him for a long moment. The work lamp threw shadows across his face, and she thought about what it would do to a person to spend thirty-two years believing they came from something rotten, to carry the weight of a legacy they never chose. She thought about her own fractured childhood, the foster homes, the particular loneliness of not belonging anywhere, and how she'd spent years running from what she'd come from too.

"You're not your father," she said. "I know that."

"Do you?"

He was quiet for a moment. The kind of quiet that meant the question had landed somewhere it needed to land. "I'm working on it," he finally said.

"Good." She moved closer, pressed her shoulder into his. "Because what you just told me doesn't make me want to run. I want you to know that. It makes me understand you better, and those are not the same thing as being scared of you." She paused. "I'm scared of Julian Vane. I'm scared of what he's going to do when the clock runs out. But you? No." She tilted her chin up. "You are the least frightening thing in my life right now, and I mean that as the compliment it is."

Something in his face unlocked — just a fraction, the way a window cracks open and suddenly the whole room can breathe again. He put his arm around her and pulled her into his side, and she let him, and they sat there on the painter's tarp in the flour-scented dark and she listened to him breathe.

"The audit," she said after a while. "Wes said the forty-eight hours was theater. That Julian was already moving." She looked up at him. "What if the audit isn't about the financials at all? What if it's a distraction?"

She felt him go alert under her, the subtle shift of his body from still to ready. "Say that again."

"The official audit notification, the inspector coming day after tomorrow — Julian controls enough of the local administrative structure to fake that kind of paperwork. We know that from Wes's financial records." She thought it through, the pieces clicking into a shape she didn't like at all. "We've spent two days getting ready for an audit. Pulling records, making sure the bakery's books are clean, being here late running security checks. We've been *here*. Stationary. Predictable." She pulled back enough to look directly at him. "He's not coming for the ledger through a legal mechanism. He's using the audit to keep us in one place while he sends someone to take me."

Dalton's expression went very hard and very still. She watched him run it through — she could almost track it, the tactical part of his brain pulling up the scenario and testing it against what he knew. Then he picked up his phone from the floor beside the tarp and pulled up something, scrolling fast.

"The inspector's name," he said. "Wes's contact pulled the county records when the audit notice came in. Gerald Marsh, twenty-two years with the state, no flags." He scrolled further. "But the request that triggered the audit

— it was filed from a shell address. One of the three Wes traced." His head came up. "Son of a bitch. You're right."

"The audit was never real."

"It's a containment strategy. Pin us down, make us concentrate our energy on defense, and send someone in under cover of the inspection." He was already standing, reaching for his shirt. "He'd want it clean. Quiet. A woman goes missing from her bakery during a state inspection — chaos, confusion, conflicting accounts. By the time anyone figures out what happened, she's gone."

Amber stood up. Her legs were steady, which surprised her a little. "So what do we do?"

"We don't show up for the audit," he said. "We don't give him the stationary target." He pulled his phone out, typed a short message — to Wes, she assumed, or maybe his contact at the county — and pocketed it. "We need to move."

"Move where?"

He looked at her, and his eyes were calculating and certain all at once. "Wes has old logging trails behind his property. Fifteen miles of them, back into the state forest. His cabin's at the edge of a grid that hasn't been mapped digitally — old survey lines, pre-GPS. I know those trails." He paused. "Julian Vane is a city operator. He works through infrastructure, through systems, through people who owe him money. He doesn't do wilderness."

"You want to disappear into the woods."

"I want to take you somewhere Julian Vane's reach doesn't extend," he said. "Take away his leverage, his ability to predict where you'll be. Make him come out into the open to find us instead of setting a trap and waiting." His voice was steady but underneath it she could hear the urgency, controlled and pointed. "He thinks he's hunting. I want to reverse that."

Amber picked her hoodie up off the floor and pulled it on. She could feel the cold settling back in as the warmth between them faded into the larger cold of the room, the building, the November night pressing against the new windows. She thought about the burner phone in her pocket and the pistol in her jacket and the financial records in Dalton's truck and Lila's son, seven years old, waiting for a mother who'd been made into a loose end.

"Okay," she said. "Okay?"

"Okay, we go." She grabbed her jacket from the supply shelf where she'd dropped it and checked the inner pocket — pistol, present and accounted for. "But we call Landry first. We give him enough to work with. Not everything, but enough that if something happens to us in those woods, he knows where to point." She met his eyes.

"Lila deserves someone who's going to answer for what was done to her. I want that on the record before we go dark."

He studied her for a second. Then, quietly: "All right."

"And Dalton?" She zipped her jacket, collar up. "Whatever else is in your head — whatever other pieces of this you've been sitting on — you tell me on the trail. All of it, while we walk." She looked at him squarely. "No more deciding what I can handle. Deal?"

He picked up his flannel and shrugged it on, then his jacket over it, and he looked at her the way she'd come to understand meant he was making a decision that cost him something. "Deal," he said.

She turned the work lamp off. The backroom went dark, lit only by the faint ambient glow bleeding under the door from the security system's standby light. The flour sacks and raw wood shelves disappeared into shadow, and the room became just a shape, a space where something real had happened that she'd carry forward with her.

She pushed through the door. Dalton was right behind her, close enough that she could feel the warmth radiating off him even through two layers of jacket, and she thought: *this is what I'm choosing. Him. The whole complicated, dangerous, legacy-haunted mess of him.*

She'd made worse choices. She couldn't think of any right now, but she was fairly confident she had.

The bakery was dark and quiet around them as they moved toward the back exit, past the new counter and the display cases and the chalkboard menu she'd written in her neatest handwriting four days ago like she was building something permanent. Maybe she still was. Maybe the permanence was just going to have to wait a little longer.

Dalton pushed the back door open and the cold hit her, clean and sharp and smelling of frozen ground and pine from somewhere uphill. His truck was parked in the alley, dark and anonymous. Above the buildings, the sky was clear for once, a hard glittering spread of stars that didn't care at all about Julian Vane or blood debts or any of it.

She got in. He got in. The engine turned over, low and reliable. "Call Landry," he said. "Then we move."

Amber pulled out the burner phone, clicked on the single contact that wasn't Dalton — she'd added Landry's direct line yesterday, just in case — and pressed call. It rang twice.

"Landry," the sheriff's voice came through, gravelly with late-night fatigue.

"It's Amber Rowan," she said. "I know it's late. I need twenty minutes and I need you to listen to all of it."

A pause. She heard him shifting, the creak of a chair. "Go ahead," he said.

Dalton pulled the truck out of the alley and headed north, toward the dark tree line at the edge of town, toward Wes's logging trails and the fifteen miles of unmapped forest that Julian Vane didn't know existed. She talked. The heater kicked on and filled the cab with warmth and she talked steadily, calmly, giving Landry exactly enough to do his job while Dalton drove them toward the only kind of safety left: the kind you make yourself, out of nothing but nerve and the particular stubbornness of people who've already survived the worst and decided they're not interested in doing it again.

The town lights fell away behind them. The trees rose up on either side of the road, tall and dark and indifferent. Amber kept talking, and Dalton kept driving, and the night held them both in it, and somehow that was enough.

24
A Gentleman's Threat

The soft opening wasn't supposed to happen until ten.

Amber had the chalkboard sign flipped to OPEN at nine forty-seven because the cinnamon rolls needed to come out of the oven and she needed something to do with her hands, and the morning had that particular quality of false calm she'd learned not to trust. The kind where the light was clean and the street outside was just a street and nothing felt wrong yet.

Lila's replacement, a quiet twenty-year-old named Meg who wore her hair in two braids and asked very few questions, was stacking paper cups beside the espresso machine. Dalton was in the back, supposedly reviewing the delivery schedule, actually watching the rear camera feeds on his laptop. Amber could hear the occasional quiet tap of keys.

The bell above the door rang at nine fifty-two.

The man who walked in was not from Cherry Creek. She knew that immediately, the way you know a wrong note in a familiar song before you can name what's off. He was tall, silver-haired, wearing a suit the color of storm clouds that fit him the way expensive things fit men who've always had money. No briefcase. No tourist energy. He paused just inside the door and let his eyes move around the room with a kind of unhurried assessment that had nothing to do with deciding between a latte and a cappuccino.

He chose a table near the window. He sat down, folded his hands, and waited.

Amber took his order herself. She didn't know why. Some instinct pulled her forward when Meg started to move, and she stepped in front of her and said, "I've got it," and walked over with her order pad like this was a completely normal Tuesday.

"Black coffee," he said. His voice was smooth. Cultured. The kind of voice that made pronouncements sound like observations. "And one of those cinnamon rolls, if they're fresh."

"Just out of the oven," she said.

"Wonderful." He smiled. It was a practiced smile, the kind politicians deploy on rope lines. "You're Amber Rowan."

She kept her face neutral. "You have me at a disadvantage." "Julian Vane," he said. "I believe you've heard the name."

She had. She'd heard it in the dark of Wes's cabin, in Dalton's flat voice, in the county financial records spread across a folding table. The name had clawed at the edges of her nightmares for weeks, attached to words like syndicate and blood debt and founder. But hearing it from his own mouth, seeing it delivered with that calm, social smile, made the name hit like a physical blow to the solar plexus, knocking the air right out of her lungs. It wasn't just a word anymore; it was a threat given flesh and bone, standing right in the middle of her sanctuary.

"I'll get your coffee," she said.

She walked back to the counter at a normal pace. She did not run. She pushed through the door to the back room and found Dalton already standing, laptop closed, jacket on. His eyes found her face and whatever he read there made him move immediately toward the door to the front.

"Julian Vane," she said quietly. "Table by the window."

Something moved across his expression. Not surprise. More like the confirmation of a thing he'd been bracing for. "Stay behind the counter," he said.

"Not a chance."

He didn't argue. He pushed through the door and she followed him out.

The temperature in the room dropped about ten degrees the moment Julian Vane registered Dalton's presence. Not literally, but it felt that way. Meg, behind the espresso machine, went very still the way animals go still when something unfamiliar enters their space. Julian looked up from his folded hands and his smile didn't waver, but his eyes recalibrated, sliding from Amber to Dalton with the smooth adjustment of a man who'd expected this variable and simply filed it under *as anticipated.*

"Dalton," Julian said. "You look well. Better than the last time I saw you, actually. That was Elias's funeral, if I'm not mistaken. You weren't there in person, of course, but I saw the surveillance." He tilted his head slightly. "You looked tired."

Dalton pulled out the chair across from Julian and sat down. He didn't ask permission. He put his forearms on the table and his voice, when it came, was the kind of low and even that meant he was working very hard to stay exactly that. "What do you want, Julian."

"I already told the young lady. Coffee. Cinnamon roll." He glanced toward the counter. "Still waiting on both, actually."

Amber poured the coffee. Her hands were steady. She carried it to the table and set it down and stayed standing, close enough to hear everything and far enough that Meg, who was pretending to wipe the espresso machine, wasn't directly in the blast radius of whatever this was.

"I came to offer a resolution," Julian said. He wrapped both hands around the coffee cup in a gesture that managed to look almost friendly. "I'm a businessman, Dalton. I'm not interested in theater. Theater is expensive and messy and the people who make the most noise about it are usually the ones with the least leverage." He paused. "I have leverage."

"Say what you came to say," Dalton said.

"The digital key," Julian said. "The one your father's asset passed to the girl's boyfriend two years ago, before things went sideways. I want it returned. Along with Miss Rowan's cooperation in an upcoming deposition, which will be brief, procedural, and handled by attorneys rather than law enforcement." He lifted the coffee cup, drank, set it down. "Do those two things, and I walk out of this town and you both live long, unremarkable lives. I give you my word."

"Your word," Dalton said.

"I know how that sounds to you. But consider the alternative, which involves a great deal more inconvenience for everyone involved, and ends only one way." Julian's eyes moved to Amber. "For what it's worth, Miss Rowan, I hold no personal grievance against you. You were a circumstance. You still are."

Amber pulled out the chair next to Dalton and sat down. She was not going to stand over this conversation like a bystander at her own life. "What's on the key?" she said.

Julian regarded her with what might have been mild approval. "An encrypted ledger. Twelve years of financial transfers tied to political contributions in six states. Names, amounts, dates. The kind of documentation that tends to complicate careers at fairly senior levels of government." He folded his hands again. "Your boyfriend, Max, stole a copy of it from one of my associates. He intended to use it as a bargaining chip. Leverage to buy himself a position in my organization."

The room was very quiet. Amber heard the espresso machine hiss softly from across the room.

"Max," she said. The word came out flat.

"He was enterprising," Julian said. "I'll give him that. He identified an opportunity and he moved on it. The problem was that he miscalculated his own value to us, and he miscalculated the cost of the security he believed you provided him." Julian's tone didn't change, didn't soften, didn't sharpen. It stayed exactly the same, which was somehow worse. "He positioned you as his insurance policy. If anything happened to him, you would go to law enforcement with what you knew. Except you didn't know anything, did you? He never told you. You were simply the threat he waved in the room."

Amber said nothing.

"He didn't love you," Julian said. "I want to be precise about that, because I think you deserve precision. He saw you as a useful asset. The relationship was real enough on the surface, but its function in his planning was purely strategic. You were the human shield he'd built himself over two years." A pause. "I'm sorry. That's a genuinely unpleasant thing to learn."

The cinnamon roll was still on the counter, untouched. Amber stared at the table surface. She was aware of Dalton beside her, the coiled stillness of him, and she was aware that she should be feeling something larger than what she was currently feeling, which was a cold, spreading numbness that started in her chest and radiated outward.

She'd known, on some level. She'd known when the memories surfaced in fragments, when the pieces refused to arrange themselves into a story where Max was the good guy. She'd known the way you know a thing you aren't ready to admit out loud yet. And still, hearing it stated in a stranger's polished voice in her own bakery at nine fifty-five in the morning hit like a door swinging open on an empty room.

"You should eat your cinnamon roll," she said. "You paid for it."

Julian smiled. Genuinely, this time. "You're remarkable," he said. "I can see why Dalton is invested."

"Don't," Dalton said. The word was quiet and final and Julian apparently understood the perimeter it drew, because he moved on.

He reached into the inner pocket of his jacket and produced a small silver coin. He placed it on the table between them, in the center, equidistant from both sides. It was old, or looked old, worn smooth on the face. "The blood coin," he said. "You've heard of it. The debt is active. It will remain active until the key is returned." He pushed back his chair and rose, unhurried, buttoning his jacket. "I'm staying at the inn on Prospect Street. You have until midnight to contact me with an answer. After that, the terms change, and I stop being civil." He glanced down at the coin. "I do enjoy being civil. I find it makes everything go more smoothly."

"We'll be in touch," Dalton said.

"See that you are." Julian picked up the coffee cup, finished it, and set it back on the table. He nodded once to Amber, politely, the way you acknowledge a host when leaving a dinner party, and walked to the door. The bell rang. He was gone.

Amber looked at the silver coin.

Meg materialized beside the table with the cinnamon roll on a plate, looked at both of their faces, set the plate down without a word, and retreated back to the espresso machine. Smart kid.

"He's not going to wait until midnight," Amber said.

"No," Dalton agreed. "He's not. He came in here in broad daylight in a town where he has no cover because he wanted us rattled. He wanted you rattled." He didn't reach for the coin. Neither did she. "The offer is real but the timeline is theater. He's already running the next move."

"He wanted me to know about Max." "Yes."

"Because a woman who just found out the last two years of her life were a

lie is a woman who's off-balance." Amber picked up the silver coin and turned it over once in her fingers. It was heavier than it looked. "He thinks if he breaks the story I've been telling myself about why any of this happened to me, I'll be easier to manage."

Dalton watched her without speaking.

"He's not wrong that it lands hard," she said. "I want to be honest about that. It lands hard." She set the coin back down. "But he's wrong about what it does to me. He thinks it makes me less. It actually just makes everything simpler." She pressed her index finger against the coin for a moment, then lifted it. "Max is gone. Whatever he intended to use me for, it doesn't matter anymore. The only thing that matters is that Julian Vane is in Cherry Creek and we have until dark before he stops pretending to be reasonable."

"We need to move," Dalton said. "Now. While he's back at the inn playing the waiting game."

"The logging trails."

"Wes's property, back into the state forest. I texted him twenty minutes ago when you came to get me. He'll have the secondary cabin stocked." He paused. "Julian operates through infrastructure. Phones, money, systems, people who owe him. He doesn't know those trails exist. They predate satellite mapping."

Amber stood up. She glanced at Meg, who was definitely listening while pretending to clean the steam wand. "Take the rest of the day," she said. "Paid. Lock up at noon and don't come back until I call you."

Meg looked up, and her expression had that particular quality of a person who'd correctly assessed the situation but was too sensible to ask about it. "Okay," she said. "You want me to take the rolls out of the case so they don't go stale?"

"Yes," Amber said. "Take them home."

She went to the back room and pulled her jacket off the hook. Pistol in the inner pocket, present. Burner phone in the outer pocket. She picked up her bag from the shelf, checked it out of habit, then came back through the door.

Dalton was standing at the counter with his jacket on and the laptop bag over one shoulder. The silver coin was no longer on the table.

"Did you take it?" she asked.

"Evidence," he said. "Landry's going to want to see it eventually."

She looked at the window, at Main Street outside, at the ordinary Tuesday morning happening beyond the glass. A woman walked a dog. A teenager cut through the parking lot on a bicycle. The inn on Prospect Street was four blocks north, and Julian Vane was presumably sitting in it right now, doing whatever men like him did while they waited to see if the people they'd threatened would fold before the deadline.

"He said Max never loved me," she said. She wasn't talking to Dalton specifically. She was saying it out loud to hear what it sounded like, now that she had a minute to listen. It sounded like a fact. Cold and specific and already past. "Two years. I thought he was the person I'd built something real with, and the whole time I was just the contingency plan."

"Amber."

"I know." She zipped her jacket. "I'm not falling apart. I'm filing it. There's a difference." She moved toward the back exit. "I'll fall apart later, somewhere that isn't Julian Vane's preferred location for watching me do it."

Dalton held the door. She went through it into the cold alley, and his truck was right there, dark and reliable, exactly where it had been at eleven last night when they drove north toward the tree line.

She got in. He got in. The engine caught on the first try.

"The key," she said as he pulled out of the alley. "The encrypted ledger. We need to talk about where it actually is."

"We do," he said. "On the trail. All of it, while we walk. Your words." She almost smiled. "Yeah. My words."

Main Street slid past outside, the storefronts and the diner and the hardware store and the ordinary daylight life of Cherry Creek, which had no idea that a man in a charcoal suit had just bought a coffee and laid a blood coin on a table and given two people until midnight to decide whether they wanted to keep living. The town looked exactly like itself. It always did.

Amber watched it pass and thought about the coin's weight in her fingers, and about Max's face in the fragments she'd been piecing together for two years, and about the particular silence of a love story that turned out to be something else dressed up in the right clothes.

The trees came up on both sides of the road, tall and dark and exactly the same as they'd been last night. Dalton drove north without speaking, and she appreciated that. She didn't need him to say anything. She needed the truck to keep moving and the distance from Julian Vane to keep increasing and the woods to close in around them the way they had last night, indifferent and solid and entirely outside the reach of men who operated through systems.

"He underestimates you," Dalton said eventually. "Julian. He thinks the thing about Max breaks you."

"I know he does."

"It's going to cost him."

Amber settled back against the seat and watched the tree line thicken. "Yes," she said. "It is."

25
The Ghost of a Boyfriend

The secondary cabin was smaller than Wes's main place, older too, with a wood stove instead of a fireplace and a single cot shoved against the east wall. It smelled like pine resin and old wool blankets and the particular cold that settles into a space when no one's been using it for months. Amber stood in the center of it and took stock: two windows, both low, both facing the trees. One door. A hand-pumped water basin. A Coleman lantern on a shelf next to a box of matches and three cans of beans.

"Wes stocked it," Dalton said from behind her, setting down the supply pack. He moved directly to the windows, checked the angles, pulled the shutters closed on the one facing north. "Blankets in the trunk under the cot. There should be a two-way radio on the shelf, up high."

She found it behind the lantern. It was old, military-looking, with a rubberized grip worn down at the edges. She set it on the small table beside the stove and looked at Dalton. "Now what?"

"Now we sleep in shifts." He said it the same way he might say *now we eat* or *now we drive*. Like it was the obvious next step and the fact that neither of them had slept more than three hours in the last forty-eight was a detail too minor to acknowledge. "You take the cot first. I'll take the first watch."

"Dalton."

"Amber." His voice carried no give in it.

She sat on the cot. Not because she was complying exactly, but because her legs had made the decision independently. The wool blanket scratched the back of her wrists when she pulled it up. The wood stove ticked and popped as the metal heated. Outside, the forest was dark and completely silent, the kind of silence that had weight behind it.

She didn't sleep. She thought she might lie there and stare at the ceiling planks and cycle through Julian's polished voice telling her things she already knew on some level but hadn't yet named out loud. *He positioned you as his insurance policy.* She'd expected the memory of those words to do what they'd been doing since nine fifty-five this morning, which was sit in her chest like a stone she couldn't put down.

Instead she fell into the kind of sleep that isn't really sleep at all, more like a door falling open without warning, and on the other side of it she was somewhere else entirely.

The apartment. Max's apartment in the city, the one with the big windows that looked over the street and the radiator that clanked every night at two a.m. She knew this place. She'd spent two years trying to remember what happened inside it, and now she was standing in the hallway outside the kitchen, and she could hear voices.

Max's voice, urgent and low: "Just take it. That's what we agreed."

Another voice, clipped and cold. She didn't have a face to put to it then, but she knew it now: Elias Vane. Younger than Julian, with a jawline so sharp it looked carved from granite, the kind of man who treated every conversation like a transaction with a predetermined outcome.

"The terms changed," Elias said. "You understand what that means."

"I understand that I delivered what you asked for. The ledger. The whole ledger. That was the arrangement."

"The arrangement," Elias said, "assumed you were the only person who knew about it."

Silence. Then the sound of something being set down on the counter. Small. Hard. She knew what it was before she saw it, the way you know things in dreams: the locket. The one she'd found later in her jacket pocket, not understanding how it got there, not understanding what it meant. Max had put it there. He'd pressed it into her hand, or her pocket, at some point in the night she couldn't hold onto, and she'd woken up with it days later in the hospital.

"She doesn't know anything," Max said. "She's clean. She's the clean version of this."

"She's a liability," Elias said. "You made her one the second you brought her into your cover story."

The sound that followed was not a negotiation. It was the end of one.

In the dream she moved, the way you move in nightmares, through hallways that are longer than they should be, toward a room she couldn't reach fast enough. She heard Max shout, one short, furious syllable that wasn't her name. It was the sound of a man realizing he'd been outplayed, not afraid for her, not afraid for himself in the way a person is afraid when they love something. Just angry. Incandescently, purely angry that the deal had gone sideways. That the payday was gone.

That was the sound that broke her open, even in the dream. Not fear. Rage at a lost transaction.

Then there was someone else in the room. She felt him before she saw him, a shift in the air, the specific quality of someone moving through a space with absolute intention and zero noise. She turned in the dream and there was Dalton, younger somehow, or maybe just less worn down, crouched low beside the doorframe with that particular stillness that meant he'd already mapped every exit and every threat and every second of what was about to happen.

His eyes found her across the room and he said, very quietly: "Get down." She woke up screaming.

Or not screaming, exactly. The sound that came out of her was too jagged to be a scream, more like a gasp that tore itself loose on the way up. She was sitting upright on the cot with both hands gripping the blanket and the wood stove was still ticking and Dalton was right there, crouched in front of her with one hand on her shoulder and the other braced against the cot frame.

"Hey," he said. "Hey. You're here. Secondary cabin, Wes's property, north trail. You're here."

She pressed the heel of her hand against her sternum and breathed. Once. Twice. The pine resin smell came back. The cold came back. She was here.

"I remembered," she said.

Dalton didn't move. He stayed right where he was, close enough that she could see the tension in his jaw, the careful way he was holding himself steady for her to use as a reference point. "What did you remember?"

"The apartment. That night." She swallowed. "Max handed over the locket. To Elias. And then Elias decided to cut losses, both of us. And Max, when he realized what was happening, he wasn't scared for me. He was furious about the deal. That's what I heard in his voice. Not fear. Not me." She exhaled slowly. "You were there. You came in through the door and you told me to get down."

Dalton's jaw moved. Something crossed his face that wasn't guilt exactly, more like the expression of someone carrying a weight they'd stopped expecting to ever set down. "Yeah," he said. "I was there."

"You'd been tracking Elias." It wasn't a question; she was putting pieces together out loud and she needed him to let her finish before he explained anything. "Not just that night. For weeks."

"Six weeks," he said. "He was moving assets for Julian, skimming off the transfers. The Collective wanted it documented, not stopped. They wanted the full picture before they acted." He paused. "My orders were to observe the hand-off. Confirm the ledger changed hands. Let it happen and report back."

The word *orders* landed with particular clarity. "But you didn't." "No."

"Because Elias was going to kill us both."

"Because Elias was going to kill you," Dalton said. "Specifically. Max was negotiable to him. You were loose ends." He shifted slightly, settling his weight back on his heels. "I'd been watching the apartment for three nights. I knew your routine. I knew you had nothing to do with the ledger or Max's play. You were exactly what he told Elias you were: clean. And Elias did not care."

Amber sat with that for a moment. "You defied your orders." "Yes."

"For a woman you didn't know."

"For a woman who was about to be killed for being someone's cover story." His voice was flat. Matter-of-fact. "That's not a complicated calculation."

She looked at him, really looked, at the steadiness of him in the dark with the lantern throwing low gold light across one side of his face. She'd spent weeks trying to work out whether Dalton was something she should be afraid of, whether the protective intensity that pulled her in was the same thing that made him dangerous. And now, sitting in a cold cabin with the memory of that night finally solid and real inside her, she understood that those two things weren't in conflict. He was dangerous. He was also the reason she was alive to be afraid of anything at all.

"The Collective punished you for it," she said.

"They discharged me. Called it conduct unbecoming." A short pause. "I called it the right call."

"It was," she said quietly. "For what it's worth."

He didn't say anything. He reached out and his hand covered hers where it was still gripping the blanket, warm and steady, and she turned her palm up and held on. The fire ticked. The forest pressed against the shuttered windows, dark and close and indifferent, and she let herself lean into his shoulder and stay there while the last of the nightmare drained out of her and something else moved into the space it left behind. Not peace, exactly. But solid ground after a very long time without it.

"I'm not afraid of what you did," she said. "I know that's what you've been waiting for me to say, even if you'd never ask."

She felt him exhale, slow and controlled, like releasing pressure from something that had been sealed for a long time.

"I know," he said.

"Good." She straightened, pulling herself upright. "So now we're on the same page about all of it. The whole thing. No more pieces you're holding back."

"No more pieces."

"Then we figure out how to not get killed by Julian Vane's people, because I am genuinely not interested in surviving two years of Max's bullshit only to get taken out in the woods by a man who wears tailored suits to intimidation meetings."

That cracked something loose in Dalton's expression. Not quite a laugh, but close to one, and she felt it in her chest in a way she didn't examine too carefully.

The sound hit without any warning at all.

It was low at first, a mechanical hum she registered as distant, then it wasn't distant, it was directly overhead, a buzzing oscillation that made the lantern light seem to flicker just from the vibration traveling through the cabin roof. Amber was on her feet before she'd consciously decided to stand. Dalton was already across the room, hand on the lamp, killing the light.

Darkness. The hum, steady and circling.

"Drone," Dalton said. His voice was completely level, which Amber had learned meant the situation was serious enough that he'd moved past the point of letting his voice carry any information about it. "Thermal imaging, probably. Military-grade if Julian's using it."

"He found us." She kept her own voice low, almost no volume at all. "How? The trails predate satellite mapping, you said."

"They do. But a drone doesn't need a trail." A pause. He was listening, tracking the sound. "It's doing a grid pattern. Not random. Someone is flying it deliberately, watching a screen somewhere. We have maybe three minutes before whoever's on the other end confirms our heat signatures and radios a position."

Amber moved to the pack on the floor and started pulling what she'd need. Jacket, already on. Boots, already on. She grabbed the secondary flashlight and checked it without turning it on. "He's not waiting until midnight," she said. "He wasn't waiting when he walked into the bakery this morning and he's not waiting now."

"No," Dalton agreed. He was pulling on his tactical vest in the dark, moving by memory. "He's running attrition. Wear us down, flush us out, make us run into whatever he's positioned on the perimeter." He buckled something. "He's not improvising. He had this ready before he even sat down at that table."

The hum shifted, tightened its circle. Closer. "What do we do?" Amber asked.

"We move," he said. "Now. Out the south window while it's on the north pass. We get into the tree cover before it completes the loop. Once we're under the canopy, thermal reads get cluttered by the forest."

She was already at the south window, easing the shutter open with both hands, slow enough that it made no sound. Cold air flooded in, sharp and smelling of pine needles and wet bark. The forest beyond was complete darkness, no moon through the cloud cover, no ambient light from anywhere.

"I can't see anything," she said.

"Ten feet to the first tree line. Straight out. I'll be right behind you." He pressed something into her hand. A small compass, old, analog. "North is uphill. Stay south."

She went out the window feet first, dropped the short distance to the ground, and moved. The cold hit her face like a flat palm. Behind her she heard Dalton come through the window, heard the soft controlled landing of someone who'd done this kind of thing on surfaces a great deal less forgiving than pine-needle ground. The drone hum peaked, loud and directly above, and then she was under the trees and the sound became muffled and broken up by the canopy and she stopped moving and pressed her back against the nearest trunk and breathed through her nose.

Dalton materialized at her shoulder fifteen seconds later. He put his mouth close to her ear. "It's still circling. But the cabin's empty now. When it confirms no signatures inside, whoever's flying it will report back." He was barely audible. "That buys us time, but not much. They'll know we moved."

"Then they'll come into the trees," she whispered back. "Yes."

She thought about Julian Vane, sitting somewhere warm, watching a thermal feed on a screen with that calm, patient expression, and the cold fury that moved through her was clean and useful. She took it and set it aside to use later.

"He's not going to stop," she said. "Even if we give him the key. He's going to clean the slate. Like Elias was going to."

"I know."

"So the midnight deadline was never real."

"No." A pause. "He came to the bakery to see what we were. Whether we'd fold or run. We ran, which tells him we're not going to give him what he wants voluntarily. So now he skips the civility."

Above them, faintly, the drone hum shifted direction, moving away in a slow arc toward the northwest. Amber watched the darkness between the trees and kept her breathing even. Julian Vane had resources, a drone, mercenaries presumably, and the patience of a man who'd been running a shadow organization for twelve years. What they had was this forest, the two-way radio she'd grabbed from the table before the light went out, and Dalton, who had spent years learning how to disappear into terrain exactly like this one.

She put her hand on his arm. "What do you need me to do?" she asked.

He was quiet for a beat, listening to the forest. Then: "Stay close. Watch the angles I can't. If you see movement, two taps on my shoulder. Don't call out." He shifted, orienting himself without the compass. "We're going to move north-east, toward the ridge. Higher ground, more cover, and there's a rock formation up there that breaks thermal even without canopy." He paused. "It's going to be rough terrain in the dark."

"I'll manage," she said.

He moved, and she followed, and the forest swallowed them both whole.

They moved in silence for twenty minutes, picking through undergrowth that grabbed at her boots and over roots she felt rather than saw. Dalton set the pace, unhurried but relentless, and she matched him step for step and did not complain about anything. The cold was a fact. The dark was a fact. Julian Vane's drone was a fact. She filed them all and kept moving.

At some point she pulled out the two-way radio, clicked it to the frequency Dalton had shown her earlier, and pressed it against her ear. Static. Then, faint but unmistakable, a voice she recognized even through the distortion.

She touched Dalton's shoulder. He stopped.

She held the radio up. Julian's voice came through, clipped and precise, mid-sentence: "...confirm the cabin is clear. Redirect team two to the eastern perimeter. And send word to the Cherry Creek unit. The audit proceeds at dawn. Start with the bakery."

Static. Then nothing.

Amber lowered the radio. Her mind was already doing the math, running the names, running the faces. The bakery. Nora Fisk had been talking about stopping by in the morning to drop off the invoice for the rye flour order. The construction crew had a seven a.m. start time. Meg, who'd taken the cinnamon rolls home and been told to come back when Amber called.

She looked at Dalton in the dark. She could barely see him, just the shape of him, but she could feel his attention fully on her.

"He's sending people to Cherry Creek," she said, her voice barely a thread of sound. "To the bakery. At dawn."

A long pause. Not hesitation; calculation.

"Nora," she said. "She doesn't know any of this is coming." "I know."

"We can't just stay in these trees while Julian's people walk into town and hurt someone who has nothing to do with the ledger." She kept her voice steady by force of will alone. "We can't do that."

"No," he said. "We can't." He took the radio from her hand, studied it for a moment in the dark like he was reading something she couldn't see. "We need to split our focus. Keep Julian's people busy out here and get word to Landry before dawn." He handed the radio back. "Can you reach the sheriff on the burner?"

She checked her pocket. The burner was still there, battery still reading two bars. "If I can get a signal."

"The ridge," he said. "We go up. You get signal, you call Landry. I deal with whatever Julian's sent into these trees." He said it with the same matter-of-fact certainty he used for everything else, as if *dealing with mercenaries in a dark forest* was a logistics problem rather than a mortal one.

Amber gripped the radio and the compass and kept pace as he started moving again, uphill now, the ground steepening under her boots. She thought about Julian Vane's smooth voice on the radio and the word *audit* and what it meant when men like him used clean corporate language for things that weren't clean at all.

The ridge was up there somewhere in the dark. Landry's number was in the burner. Nora was in Cherry Creek, completely unaware, and dawn was coming whether they were ready for it or not.

She climbed.

26
Marked for Audit

The ridge was steeper than it looked from below.

Amber climbed with both hands when she had to, her fingers cramping as she clawed at slick roots and jagged outcroppings. Every time her boots sought purchase, the wet rock felt like greased glass, sending a jolt of alarm up her spine as she nearly slipped on the loose, saturated soil. Her lungs burned with the effort, the physical strain of the incline making her muscles scream in protest. Dalton moved ahead of her without effort, like the incline was a minor inconvenience rather than a forty-degree scramble in the dark. She followed his silhouette and didn't waste breath on talking.

They reached the top of the ridge just before four in the morning. The tree cover thinned up here, replaced by granite shelf and wind, and the sky above them had lightened from black to the kind of dark gray that meant dawn was an hour out, maybe less. Below, the forest spread in every direction, indistinguishable from this angle, all shadow and canopy and the occasional pale gleam of a creek catching what little light existed.

Amber pulled out the burner phone. Two bars. She dialed Landry's number from memory.

He picked up on the second ring, which told her he hadn't been sleeping either.

"Rowan."

"Julian Vane is sending a crew to Cherry Creek," she said. No preamble, no explanation. There wasn't time for either. "The bakery. Dawn. They're calling it an audit, which in Julian Vane's vocabulary means something considerably worse than an accountant with a clipboard."

A pause. She could hear him sit up, heard the particular sound of a man recalibrating. "How many?"

"I don't know. We picked up a radio transmission from one of the men Julian deployed out here. He's running two operations simultaneously." She pressed the phone harder against her ear against the wind. "Nora Fisk may be heading to the bakery in the morning. The construction crew has a seven a.m. start."

"I'll have people there by five-thirty," Landry said. His voice had gone flat and professional, the skepticism stripped clean out of it. "What about you?"

"Working on it," she said. "Don't let anyone into that building who isn't one of yours."

She ended the call before he could ask the follow-up questions she didn't have answers to. Dalton was crouched at the ridge's lip, scanning the tree line below through a pair of compact binoculars he'd pulled from the tactical vest. She moved to him and dropped to a crouch beside him.

"Landry's handling Cherry Creek," she said.

"Good." He passed her the binoculars without lowering his gaze from the tree line. "Three o'clock from the big hemlock. Movement."

She found the hemlock, a massive tree at the base of the ridge, and shifted right. For a long moment she saw nothing. Then she caught it: a shape that didn't match the surrounding stillness. A man, moving low through the brush, wearing dark tactical gear that read as a slightly different texture of darkness against the trees. He was moving slowly, methodically, sweeping wide.

"I see him," she murmured. "He's moving parallel to the ridge. Not coming straight up."

"Flanking," Dalton said. "There'll be at least two more. Julian wouldn't send a single man into terrain he doesn't know." He rose into a low crouch, already recalibrating. "They're going to try to bracket us."

She kept the binoculars up, scanning. "Second one, nine o'clock. Further back, moving slower."

"Good eyes."

"I had a good teacher," she said, which was charitable given that her training had consisted of approximately twenty minutes of whispered instruction while climbing through a dark forest.

Dalton was already moving, not down toward the mercenaries but laterally along the ridge, staying below the skyline. She followed, keeping low, and he stopped after thirty yards at a place where the granite shelf gave way to a steep gully choked with undergrowth.

"Wait here," he said. "Absolutely not," she said.

He turned. In the gray pre-dawn she could see his expression clearly enough to read it: not irritation, exactly, more the look of someone who had anticipated this answer and was deciding how much time to spend on it.

"I need someone watching the ridge," he said. "If there's a third man I haven't spotted yet, he'll come up from the east. You see him, two taps on the radio." He pressed the recovered radio into her hand. "You don't move, you don't call out, you don't do anything except watch and signal."

She took the radio. "And if the third man spots me before I spot him?"

"He won't." A brief pause. "Stay below the rock shelf, keep the granite at your back. You'll be invisible from below and you'll have line of sight east. Trust the position."

She trusted the position. What she didn't entirely trust was the part where Dalton walked down into that gully alone to do whatever he was about to do to two armed mercenaries in the dark, but she understood the logic, and she understood that arguing further would cost them minutes they didn't have. So she got into position behind the rock shelf, set her back against the cold granite, and raised the binoculars.

Below, Dalton disappeared into the gully like he'd stepped through a door and closed it behind him.

The next eight minutes were the longest of her life.

She watched the tree line and kept her breathing steady and tried not to think about what was happening in the undergrowth she couldn't see. She tracked the second mercenary until he passed behind a dense stand of spruce and she lost him. The first man had stopped moving entirely, which was either because he'd gone to ground or because something had happened to him and she had no way to know which.

Then, from below and to her left, the unmistakable sound of something heavy hitting the ground. Once. Then silence.

She gripped the radio and kept her eyes moving.

The second mercenary emerged from the spruce stand and immediately changed direction, angling toward the sound. He was moving faster now, less careful, which meant he'd heard it too and had made a decision about what it meant. Amber watched him cross a gap in the canopy and then she saw Dalton, already repositioned, already waiting, and what happened next was quick and deliberate and not remotely hesitant.

The man went down hard. Dalton was on him for three seconds, and then it was done.

She exhaled slowly and kept scanning east. Nothing. No third man from that direction, at least not yet. She clicked the radio twice anyway, because Dalton had told her to signal on sighting and she figured one click for clear was useful information too.

He came back up the gully five minutes later. There was a cut along his jaw that hadn't been there before, and his knuckles were scraped raw, and he moved like a man whose ribs were protesting something but who had filed that complaint for later.

"Two down," he said. "Third one is still out there. He's moving wide, trying to circle around." He held up a compact radio unit he'd stripped from one of the downed men. Different from the one she was holding. Newer. "This was on the second one."

She watched him tune the frequency, and a burst of static resolved into a voice, low and clipped: "Team one, report. Team one."

Silence from team one, for obvious reasons.

Then a different voice came through, and Amber's spine went rigid, because she knew that voice. She'd been sitting across a table from it less than twenty-four hours ago.

Julian Vane's voice was precisely as composed on a tactical radio as it had been over coffee. "Team two, redirect to the ridge. Team one has gone dark." A brief pause, the kind that contained a calculation rather than an emotion. "And confirm the Cherry Creek unit is in position. I want the bakery secured before six a.m."

Amber lowered the radio. The cold fury she'd filed away on the forest floor came back, sharper now, with a specific target.

"He's not going to stop," she said. "Even if we deal with every man he sends into these trees tonight, he's still got people heading to Cherry Creek, and he'll send more, and he'll keep escalating until we either hand over what he wants or we're not a problem anymore."

"I know," Dalton said.

"We can't fight a war on two fronts indefinitely. We don't have the resources and he does." She turned the radio over in her hands. "He's using the town as leverage. Forcing us to split our attention, wear down our options, make us feel like we have to keep reacting instead of acting."

Dalton studied her. The gray dawn light was spreading now, slow and flat, and she could see the focused attention in his face, the way he was tracking not just what she was saying but where she was going with it.

"So we stop reacting," he said.

"We stop reacting." She pulled her jacket tighter against the wind coming off the ridge. "Landry has Cherry Creek. That's handled as well as we can handle it from here. Which means we focus on what's in front of us." She looked down at the tree line, where the third mercenary was somewhere in the dark, circling wide. "How many traps did you set before we came up here?"

A pause. "Four. Pressure-trigger lines, cable snares at knee height, one noise-maker rigged to a tripwire near the creek crossing. Nothing lethal, but they'll stop a man and they'll make noise." He checked the position of the sky, reading something from it she couldn't. "The third man is going to hit the creek crossing if he keeps on the route he's taking."

"When?"

"Ten minutes. Maybe twelve."

She raised the binoculars again and scanned east, then swept back toward the creek. The forest below was lightening incrementally with the dawn, shapes acquiring edges. She found the creek by the pale glint of moving water and tracked the bank, looking for movement.

"There," she said. "Crossing further upstream than you expected. He adjusted."

Dalton was already moving before she finished the sentence, back down into the gully, using the terrain the way she was slowly learning he used everything: with complete economy, no wasted motion, each step placed with the same care as the last.

She tracked the third mercenary through the binoculars. He crossed the creek and moved uphill, angling toward the ridge from the northeast. He was good; he moved quietly and checked his angles. But he didn't know this terrain, and Dalton did, and she could see the moment the man's rhythm broke, one foot going down wrong, a brief stumble. He recovered fast, but fast wasn't the same as unaffected.

The tripwire hit him thirty seconds later. It wasn't subtle. The noise-maker Dalton had rigged cracked through the pre-dawn quiet like a gunshot, and the man reacted on instinct, going low and pivoting toward the sound, which meant he was looking the wrong direction when Dalton came out of the brush to his left.

It was quick. It was efficient. It was also the most unambiguously violent thing Amber had ever watched happen in real time, and she kept the binoculars up through all of it, because she needed to see it clearly, needed to understand without flinching what Dalton was and what he was capable of, and what that meant about who they were to each other.

What she found, watching it, was not what she'd expected. She wasn't repelled. She wasn't scared of him. What she felt, pressing cold and solid against the granite with the binoculars at her eyes, was something closer to relief. The kind of relief that comes from understanding that the person standing between you and something terrible is genuinely capable of the job.

She put the binoculars down and waited.

Dalton came back up the ridge alone. He was breathing harder than before, and there was a new tear in his jacket sleeve, and he moved with the particular deliberateness of someone managing pain without acknowledging it. He dropped down beside her against the rock shelf and took the radio she held out.

"Three," she said. "Three," he confirmed.

She watched his profile in the growing dawn light. "You thought showing me that would change something between us. "He was silent for a moment, not evasive, more like someone choosing words with care. "It's a reasonable concern."

"It didn't," she said. "For the record."

He exhaled once, short and controlled, and she let it sit without pressing on it further. Some things didn't need to be pulled apart.

The radio in his hand crackled. Julian's voice came through again, still unhurried, still precise. "Team two, confirm status. I'm seeing no movement on the ridge feed." Another pause. "Team one and two, check in."

Silence from both teams, which was going to tell Julian something specific and actionable within the next sixty seconds.

Dalton pressed the transmit button and held the radio up. "Your teams are done, Julian," he said. "All three."

A long pause. Then: "Dalton. I should have known you'd be thorough." The composure was intact. It was genuinely unnerving. "That changes the timetable but not the outcome. You understand that."

"I understand you've still got people heading to Cherry Creek," Dalton said.

"The audit proceeds regardless of what happens in those woods. That's the point of redundancy." A brief, almost clinical pause. "Tell me, how is Miss Rowan holding up? The woods at night can be quite unsettling for someone with her history."

Amber reached over and pressed the transmit button herself. "Miss Rowan is fine," she said. "Miss Rowan has also been on the radio with Sheriff Landry for the past twenty minutes. Your crew is walking into a welcoming committee, Julian, not a bakery."

The silence on the other end was different this time. Not long, but different in quality.

"That was resourceful," Julian said, and the composure had a new texture to it, something colder underneath. "It doesn't change the fundamental position. I have resources you don't, time you're running out of, and leverage you haven't fully accounted for yet."

"The ledger," Dalton said.

"The ledger," Julian agreed. "You have something I need. I have something you want to protect. That's a negotiation, not a war. I'd prefer to conclude it before anyone else gets hurt."

The transmission ended. The static filled the space it left behind.

Amber put her hands flat on the cold granite and looked out at the forest below, where three of Julian's men were incapacitated and the dawn was coming up pale and flat through the trees. She thought about Cherry Creek, about Nora Fisk stopping by in the morning with a flour invoice, about the construction crew pulling up at seven a.m. to a building surrounded by Landry's deputies. About Julian Vane sitting somewhere warm and organized, running attrition with the patience of a man who'd done it before and won.

She thought about all of it, and then she thought about what Julian had said. *Leverage you haven't fully accounted for.*

"He thinks we don't have the ledger," she said slowly. Dalton turned toward her.

"He thinks we're running because we don't have anything to use against him. He thinks the leverage only runs one direction." She pressed her fingers against her sternum, feeling the cold through the jacket fabric. "But if we had a copy of the ledger, the whole thing, that changes the math completely."

"We don't," Dalton said carefully.

"No," she agreed. "But he doesn't know that for certain, and the fact that he wants to negotiate instead of just eliminating us outright means he's not entirely sure what we have." She pushed off the granite and stood up, facing the gray dawn. "We're going back to Cherry Creek. We're done running circles in these woods while Julian holds the town over our heads."

Dalton rose beside her without argument. He looked at the tree line one more time, checking for movement out of pure habit, and then he looked at her with an expression she was starting to recognize: the one that meant he'd already reached the same conclusion and had been waiting to see if she'd get there herself.

"We go back," he said, "we do it on our terms. Not because he pushed us out."

"Exactly," she said. "He wants to dictate the pace. So we take it from him." She zipped her jacket up to her chin against the morning wind. "Call it a counter-audit."

Something shifted at the corner of his mouth, brief and dry. "Let's move," he said.

They went down the far side of the ridge together, into the cold gray morning, with the radio and the compass and the burner phone and nothing else except the particular clarity that comes from having nothing left to lose except the things worth keeping.

Below them, Cherry Creek was waking up. Above them, Julian Vane was recalculating. And somewhere between those two facts was a window, narrow and closing, and Amber intended to walk through it before it shut.

27
The Ranger's Trap

They came down out of the hills as the storm rolled in from the northwest, the kind of front that arrives without negotiation, sky going from pale gray to a solid, churning dark in the time it takes to cross a ridge. The rain started before they reached the tree line. Not the tentative kind, either. Sheets of it, cold and driving, cutting visibility down to maybe thirty feet and turning the leaf litter underfoot into a silent, sodden carpet that swallowed their footsteps completely.

Amber pulled her jacket collar up and kept moving. The rain was miserable and she was grateful for it anyway. Julian's people couldn't see through it any better than she could.

Dalton navigated by something she'd stopped trying to understand and just accepted as a functional instinct. He moved through the dark and the downpour like he'd memorized the topology of this land years ago and kept it filed somewhere useful. Maybe he had. He'd grown up here. These were his woods before they were anyone's threat.

They hit the town's outskirts just past two in the morning. The streets were empty and slick, the streetlights casting orange halos through the rain, every surface reflecting back the same wet, fractured light. Cherry Creek looked abandoned. That was the first wrong note. Even at two a.m. on a Tuesday, there was usually someone: a night-shift worker, a porch light, a dog walker. The kind of ambient human noise a small town produces without thinking about it.

Right now there was nothing. The town felt held very still. "Too quiet," she murmured.

"Yeah." Dalton pressed her back against a wall, scanned the street in both directions, and tilted his chin toward the bakery two blocks east. "Count four positions. One on the corner, one in the alley mouth, two covering the front. They're not hiding. They want us to see them."

She looked. He was right. Julian's men weren't making much effort at concealment, which meant either they were confident or they wanted her rattled. Possibly both. "Landry's people?"

"Should be, but I'm not seeing any sheriff's presence." His jaw was tight. "Either Landry got here and Julian's crew already moved on them, or Julian got ahead of the call."

She processed that without panicking, which was progress. "Back entrance."

"Through the alley off Maple. But there's a man on the alley mouth." "One man," she said.

He gave her a flat look. "You're not suggesting you take a trained mercenary in a dark alley."

"I'm suggesting you draw his attention from the front while I go around the block and come in through the loading dock. There's a panel in the baseboard next to the proofing oven. I never got around to fixing it, which turns out to be a design feature." She watched the sentry on the corner shift his weight, bored and wet. "I know that building better than they do."

A pause, long enough that she felt him calculating risk against necessity.

"You see anything that isn't a clear path, you pull back," he said. "You don't engage if you can avoid it."

"Understood."

"I mean it, Amber."

"I know you do." She checked the direction of the rain. "Give me ninety seconds to get around the block before you move."

She went before he could add anything else to the list of things she'd promised not to do.

The block took sixty seconds at a run, staying close to the building faces, using the downpour as cover. The loading dock behind the bakery was a concrete platform with a rusted steel door, and the padlock on it was the same one she'd installed when she took over the lease, which meant she had the key in her jacket pocket, which she'd thought about before she left and felt quietly smug about now.

The lock opened. The door swung inward with a groan she winced at, but the rain swallowed it. She slipped inside.

The bakery in the dark smelled like flour and sugar and the faint chemical tang of cleaning solution. Familiar. She let her eyes adjust, moving past the prep tables and the cold storage unit, past the proofing rack, toward the front of the shop.

She found Nora Fisk in the front room, bound to a chair with zip ties at her wrists and ankles, a strip of duct tape across her mouth. Her platinum hair was disheveled and her mascara had tracked down both cheeks in a way that suggested she'd been crying and was now just furious about it. She looked up when Amber came in and her eyes went wide with something that wasn't quite relief, more like desperate recognition.

Amber pressed a finger to her lips and crossed to her. She pulled the tape free in one sharp motion because slow was crueler. Nora hissed in a sharp breath and said nothing, which was impressive self-control. The zip ties were harder. Amber grabbed a bread knife from the rack by the prep table and worked at the plastic until it gave.

"How many?" Amber breathed, barely any sound at all.

"Four outside, two came in with me." Nora's voice was a thread. "One left to check the perimeter twenty minutes ago. One is still here. He's in the back hallway."

"Can you walk?"

"My ankles are numb but yes." Nora rolled her wrists, grimacing. "Amber. There's something you need to know. They went through everything. They went through the storage room, the dry goods, all of it. They were looking for something specific."

Something cold moved through her chest. "The flour tins." Nora stared. "How did you know?"

Amber crossed to the storage shelving faster than she should have, moving without caution in a way she'd specifically promised not to do, and it was the speed of her that saved her, in a backwards sort of way, because the man who stepped out of the back hallway was expecting someone moving carefully. He wasn't expecting her to already be three feet to his right with a bread knife in her hand and absolutely nothing to lose.

She got one clear second of him: big, close-cropped dark hair, tactical vest, the kind of build that said he did this professionally and had for years. He recalibrated fast. Too fast. He had her wrist before she could drive the knife home and wrenched it sideways, and the knife clattered off the prep table and hit the floor.

She hit him instead. With her elbow, across the nose, because Dalton had shown her that particular move on the second day she'd spent in his company and she'd thought at the time that it seemed excessive and now she wanted to go back and thank her past self for paying attention. The cartilage crunched. He grunted and released her wrist, which was all she needed.

She grabbed the cast iron skillet off the hook above the prep station and swung it like she meant it.

It connected with his shoulder instead of his head, which was less ideal, but it knocked him hard into the shelving unit, and two twenty-pound bags of bread flour fell off the top shelf and hit him on the way down, which was not a move anyone could have planned but which Amber was going to count as intentional.

He came back up fast and shook flour out of his face and looked at her with an expression she read clearly: surprise, recalibration, the shift from dismissive to serious. He was reaching for the sidearm at his hip when the back door opened and Dalton came through it.

Whatever happened in the next ten seconds was fast and efficient and conclusive, and when it was done the man was on the floor and not getting up under his own power.

Dalton straightened. There was a dark patch spreading through the shoulder of his jacket, visible even in the low light, and he was holding that arm differently than the other one. Controlled. Careful.

"You're shot," Amber said.

"Caught a graze on the corner sentry." His voice was even. "It's through-and-through. I've had worse."

"That is genuinely not the reassurance you think it is."

"Amber." He said her name the way he sometimes did, low and precise, meaning *I hear you and we're moving past this for now.* He crouched beside the man on the floor, checking his tactical vest, his pockets, the radio clipped to his chest plate. "Nora. You okay?"

Nora was standing at the prep table holding the bread knife Amber had dropped, which, honestly, fair. "Define okay," she said. "Because I've been zip-tied to a chair for three hours, so the bar is on the floor."

"Can you move?" "Yes."

"Then get behind the prep counter and stay down until I tell you otherwise." He wasn't unkind about it. He also wasn't negotiating. Nora went behind the counter without further discussion, which said something about the current state of everyone's priorities.

Amber crossed to the storage shelving. She found the flour tins on the third shelf, right where she'd put them, and pulled them down one by one. The second tin from the left was lighter than the others. She'd weighted it with a handful of dried beans and a folded piece of oilcloth, and inside the oilcloth was a small USB drive she'd found in the lining of Marcus's old jacket pocket two months after he died, which she'd told herself meant nothing and stored in the most innocuous place she could think of because she hadn't been ready to look at what was on it.

She'd never looked at it. She'd carried it around like a pebble in her shoe, ignoring it, because pulling at that thread meant pulling at everything else attached to it.

The drive was still there. Small and flat and unremarkable, the kind of thing you'd miss if you weren't looking specifically for it.

She closed her hand around it and stood very still for a moment.

"That's it," Dalton said, from behind her. He'd moved without her hearing him, which she was mostly used to by now. "Isn't it."

"I think so." She turned around. "I didn't know what it was. I mean, I suspected it was something. But I filed it under things-I'll-deal-with-later and apparently later is now."

He was studying her face rather than the drive. "You've had it this whole time."

"Yes." She didn't apologize for it. She'd had her reasons, even if they weren't good ones. "Marcus gave me the jacket two weeks before he died. He said he wanted me to have it because the lining was warm. I thought that was just him being him. I didn't find the drive until I was going through the pocket seams to mend them."

A beat of silence. Then Dalton exhaled and let it go, which she appreciated more than she had words for.

The man on the floor made a sound, low and involuntary, the sound of someone coming back to awareness with a great deal of reluctance. Dalton crouched beside him again, and the shift in his posture was something she'd seen exactly once before, on the ridge in the dark, and it meant a specific thing about what was going to happen next.

"Dalton," she said.

"I need Julian's location." His voice was quiet and entirely serious. "He's not going to give it freely."

She pressed her lips together and didn't look away. "Make it fast."

What followed was not something she watched directly. She kept her gaze on the storage shelves and the flour tins and the small drive in her palm, and she listened to the sounds from behind her, which were methodical and deliberate and at one point involved the man on the floor saying something through clenched teeth that ended in a number of words she'd rather not repeat. Nora, behind the prep counter, was very quiet. The rain hammered the roof and the windows and the back door and provided more ambient noise than any of them needed.

It took four minutes. She knew because she counted.

"Courthouse," Dalton said. He straightened up. She could hear it in his voice, the particular flatness of someone who has done something necessary and put it away. "The old county courthouse on Birch. He's got the main hall secured."

Amber turned around. The man on the floor was breathing, both hands pressed against his ribs, not going anywhere under his own power for a while. She filed the rest of her observations under *do not dwell on this right now.*

"The courthouse," she repeated. "Where you were sentenced."

Dalton's expression didn't change. "He picked it deliberately. That's what Julian does."

"Right." She tucked the drive into her inner jacket pocket, next to her chest, where she could feel it. "Nora. Is there a first aid kit anywhere in this building?"

"Under the sink in the bathroom," Nora said, coming out from behind the counter with somewhat more composure than Amber would have managed in the same situation.

"Get it, please." She crossed to Dalton and put a hand on his uninjured arm. "You're not going anywhere until that shoulder is wrapped. Don't argue with me about this."

He looked down at her hand, then up at her face. "I wasn't going to argue." "Good. Because I have a cast iron skillet and I know how to use it."

Something moved across his face, brief and genuine, not quite amusement but close enough to its neighbor. He let her steer him to the prep table without resistance.

While Nora retrieved the kit, Amber carefully worked the jacket off his injured shoulder, which required patience and a steady hand and the deliberate suppression of every instinct that wanted to react to the dark red stain spreading through the flannel of his shirt. The wound was what he'd said it was, a through-and-through graze along the outer muscle of the shoulder, ugly and painful but not structurally catastrophic. She'd seen enough of his old scars by now to understand that his body had absorbed worse and kept moving.

That didn't make it easier to look at.

She cleaned it, packed it, wrapped it with the compression bandage from the kit. He sat very still through all of it, watching her work with an attention that had nothing clinical about it.

"The ledger," he said, while she taped the bandage. "If it's on that drive, it changes everything. We don't have to get within ten feet of Julian. We upload it, get it to Landry, get it to someone at the federal level who isn't already in Julian's pocket, and the Collective starts crumbling from the inside out."

"Which is why he's been desperate enough to send mercenaries into the woods and a crew to terrorize my bakery at two in the morning." She pressed the last piece of medical tape flat and stepped back. "He knows the ledger exists. He's not entirely sure we have it. And he's running out of time before someone figures out his crew just assaulted a woman and held her at gunpoint in a small-town bakery, which is the kind of thing that attracts exactly the kind of attention he can't manage."

"He's cornered," Dalton said. "Cornered men are the most dangerous version."

"I know." She handed him his jacket back. "Which is why we're not charging into that courthouse tonight with four sentries still somewhere in this town and your shoulder wrapped in medical gauze." She held up a hand before he could respond. "We're going to contact Landry and tell him exactly where Julian is. We're going to get this drive to someone who can verify what's on it. And we are going to do it right, because we did not survive two days in the woods to get careless now."

He studied her for a long moment, his blue eyes steady and serious.

"You're not the same person who walked into these woods two days ago," he said.

"No," she agreed. "I'm also not the same person who found that drive and put it in a flour tin because she was scared of what it meant." She pulled her jacket closed over the inner pocket, over the small hard shape of the drive pressing against her sternum. "I've had the leverage this whole time. I just wasn't ready to use it."

Nora, who had been listening to all of this with the expression of someone reassessing several things simultaneously, cleared her throat. "I hate to be practical, but there are still armed men outside this building."

"There are," Amber said. "Which is why we're calling Landry right now." She pulled the burner phone out and dialed the number she'd already memorized, because memorizing it was the kind of thing that felt excessive until it wasn't.

He picked up on the first ring. "Rowan. Where are you?"

"The bakery. Nora Fisk is with me, she's okay. Dalton has a shoulder wound, non-critical." She kept her voice low and steady. "Julian Vane is at the county courthouse on Birch Street with what I'm guessing is a personal security contingent. We also have four of his men still positioned around the bakery exterior, and one incapacitated inside." A pause. "We also have the ledger."

The silence on the other end had a very particular quality to it. "Say that again," Landry said.

"We have the ledger files. On a drive. I've had it for two months without knowing what it was." She pressed her fingers over the pocket. "Bring enough people for the courthouse. And Tate, bring someone you trust absolutely, because some of what's on this drive is going to have names in it that will make your job very complicated."

Another silence, shorter this time. "Sit tight. Don't let anyone in or out. Twenty minutes."

The call ended. Amber set the phone on the prep table and looked at the two people with her in the dark, rain-hammered bakery, her whole body running on something that wasn't quite adrenaline anymore, something steadier and colder and more purposeful than that.

She'd been running from this for two years. From Marcus's death, from the assault, from the fractured dark of that night, from the knowledge that somewhere in the gap of her missing memory was a truth she'd been terrified to find. She'd come to Cherry Creek to disappear, and instead she'd found Dalton Vale, and a stalker with a grudge, and a flour tin full of consequences.

The drive was a hard little rectangle against her ribs. Evidence. Leverage. The thing Julian Vane had sent men into the woods to prevent her from using.

She was going to use it.

"Twenty minutes," she said. "Nora, is there anything left in this building to drink? Because I could genuinely use a cup of coffee."

Nora let out a laugh that was slightly unhinged around the edges and entirely understandable given the circumstances. "Honey, after tonight, I'll make you a whole pot."

28
Shattered Knees

Landry arrived in nineteen minutes with four deputies and a county detective she didn't recognize, a lean woman with close-cropped silver hair who took one look at the blood-spattered flour bins and the enforcer groaning on the floor and simply adjusted her glasses, her expression as flat and bored as if she were checking a grocery list. They cleared the exterior in under eight minutes. Amber heard it through the bakery walls: the brief radio chatter, two sets of boots on the loading dock, the muffled sound of Julian's remaining sentries being secured with significantly less ceremony than they'd extended to Nora.

Dalton stood near the prep table with his injured arm held carefully at his side, watching the detective move through the space with the practiced efficiency of someone logging every detail. He didn't volunteer anything. He didn't need to. Amber did the talking, which felt appropriate given that it was her bakery, her flour tin, her drive.

Landry took the USB in a gloved hand and turned it over twice. "Two months," he said.

"Two months," she confirmed. "I didn't know what it was."

He studied her face the way he sometimes did, looking for the crack in the story. He didn't find one, because there wasn't one. He pocketed the drive. "Vane's at the courthouse. You're certain."

"The man in the back hallway gave us the location." She didn't elaborate. Landry didn't ask her to. His eyes moved briefly to Dalton and then moved away, which was its own kind of answer about what the sheriff suspected and had decided to set aside for now.

"My people will take the courthouse," Landry said. "You two are done for the night."

Dalton said nothing to this, which was not the same as agreeing to it.

Nora was already giving her statement to one of the deputies, arms crossed over her chest, mascara tracks dry on her cheeks now, voice steady and precise. She caught Amber's eye across the room and tipped her chin up, a small, sharp gesture that said *I'm fine, go.* Amber nodded back.

The detective sealed the bakery as a scene, which meant everyone who didn't have a badge was no longer welcome in the front room. Landry directed them toward the loft stairs at the back of the building with a look that was more instruction than suggestion. "Rest. Both of you. I'll have someone outside the building."

The loft was a narrow space above the storage room that the previous tenant had used as an office and Amber had never fully converted to anything. A futon against one wall, a standing lamp she'd hauled up because the overhead bulb was burned out, a wooden crate serving as a side table, a spare blanket folded over the back of a chair. The window at the far end looked out over the alley and the back of the building across the street, both of them currently invisible behind sheets of rain hitting the glass in uneven waves.

Dalton sat on the futon and let her deal with his jacket. Getting it off had been easier in the bakery below with the first aid kit open beside her. Up here she had to work more carefully around the wrapped shoulder, peeling the flannel back without disturbing the bandage. He sat with his hands loose on his thighs and let her do it, which she'd learned by now was not something that came naturally to him.

"Landry said his people will take the courthouse," she said. "Yes."

"You're not planning to let that happen without us." A pause. "No."

She folded his jacket and set it on the crate. Outside, the rain intensified briefly, a hard gust driving it sideways against the window, and then it settled back into its steady rhythm. The lamp cast a warm, low circle of light that didn't reach the corners of the room. The whole space smelled like the bakery below: flour, yeast, the faint sweetness of sugar, and underneath all of it the sharper notes that didn't belong, rain-soaked clothing, blood-copper from his shoulder, the particular exhaustion that settles into a body after two days of running through wet woods on bad sleep.

"We should try to sleep," she said. She didn't move. "Amber."

"What."

He reached up with his uninjured arm and took her wrist, not pulling, just holding. His thumb pressed gently against the crescent moon tattoo she'd gotten at twenty-two, during what she'd described to Nora last week as her 'brief phase of making impulsive decisions,' which she was currently reconsidering the accuracy of given that the last two years of her life had been nothing but impulsive decisions of escalating consequence.

"Come sit down," he said.

She sat beside him on the futon. The frame creaked. The rain kept going. Below them, she could hear faint movement, Landry's people finishing their sweep, the occasional murmur of a radio.

Dalton's hand moved from her wrist to her jaw, slow and deliberate, tilting her face up. His blue eyes were steady on hers. He'd been shot in the shoulder four hours ago and he still looked like the most certain person in the room, which was both comforting and slightly maddening.

"We're not going to sleep," he said. Not a question. Not an accusation. Just a statement of fact that he was laying out for both of them to look at.

"No," she agreed. "Probably not."

He kissed her, and it was nothing like the desperate, adrenaline-burned thing that had happened between them in the woods two nights ago. This was slower. More deliberate. The kind of kiss that takes its time because the person doing it is paying attention to every second of it, filing it somewhere careful.

She pulled back just enough to breathe. "Your shoulder." "I know where my shoulder is."

"I'm serious. Don't use that arm."

A brief silence. "You're trying to give me instructions right now."

"I'm trying to keep you from tearing open a wound I just spent ten minutes cleaning and wrapping, yes."

He made a sound low in his chest, something between acknowledgment and amusement, and shifted so his injured arm rested along the back of the futon, out of the way. "Better?"

"Marginally." She reached up and pressed her palm flat against his sternum, feeling the steady, heavy beat of his heart under the flannel. Still there. Still going. She'd been acutely aware of that fact for the last four hours, in the way you become aware of something only after you've come close to losing it. "I keep thinking about the courthouse," she said. "What Julian's going to do when Landry's people show up."

"He'll have a contingency. He always does." Dalton's hand moved up her spine, slow and warm through the fabric of her jacket. "Which is why we're not leaving it entirely to Landry."

"No." She leaned into him carefully, resting her cheek against his uninjured shoulder. "We're not."

They stayed like that for a moment, just the rain and the lamp and the sounds of the building below them, and she let herself have it, this small, quiet space between the last thing and the next thing, because she'd learned in the last forty-eight hours that these spaces were where you stored your courage for later.

Then she tilted her chin up and kissed him again, and this time neither of them pulled back.

He was careful with her in a way that had nothing clinical about it. Every movement was measured, unhurried, like he was reading a text he intended to memorize. His one good hand traced her collarbone, her throat, the curve of her shoulder, and she felt herself unwinding under it, the coiled tension of two days of running and fighting and being afraid releasing in slow increments. The lamp threw warm light across his face when she pulled back to look at him, and she could see the faint scar through his eyebrow, the stubble dark against his jaw, the particular way his eyes went when he was focused entirely on her, which was a way she'd cataloged sometime in the last two weeks without deciding to.

"I need you to know something," she said.

He waited, which was one of the things she'd come to rely on about him, the way he never rushed her into words.

"If the courthouse goes wrong," she started. "It won't."

"Dalton. If it does." She put two fingers against his jaw to keep him from redirecting. "If something happens to me, you release the drive to the FBI. Not to Landry first, directly to the federal level. There's a name in those ledger files, I don't know who yet, but Julian's been protecting someone significant, and if Landry takes point without federal oversight, that person can bury it." She held his gaze. "Promise me."

The muscles in his jaw shifted under her fingers. "Nothing is happening to you."

"Promise me anyway."

A long beat, the rain filling the silence between them. Then: "I promise." The words were quiet and absolute, the kind you can't take back, and she could tell from the way he said them that he knew it. "Your turn," he added, after a moment.

"My turn what."

"If something happens to me." His eyes were steady. "You take the drive, you walk out, you don't look back. You don't try to finish it yourself."

She considered lying to him. She decided against it. "I can't promise that." "Amber."

"I can promise I'll release the files. I can promise I'll call Landry and stay behind his people and not do anything reckless." She paused. "I can't promise the part where I don't look back. That part's not available."

Something crossed his face, brief and complicated, and then he exhaled and let it go, the same way he'd let go of the two months she'd carried the drive without telling him. "All right," he said.

"All right?"

"You're the most stubborn person I've ever met. I'm choosing to find it useful."

She laughed, short and genuine, and it surprised her, the way laughter sometimes does when you're not expecting to be capable of it. He was watching her when she looked back up, with an expression she didn't have a clean word for, warm and serious at the same time, like the two things weren't in conflict.

"Tell me something," she said. "Something you haven't told anyone."

He was quiet for a beat. Outside, the rain shifted again, coming in heavier, drumming hard against the window glass. "There's a name I've had picked out since I was nineteen," he said finally. "For a daughter. My mother's middle name was Elise. I always thought, if I had a kid, that was it. Elise."

He said it flatly, like a fact, not sentiment. "Nobody knows that. I've never said it out loud."

She absorbed this. The lamp flickered once, steadied. "Elise," she repeated, trying it out. "That's a good name."

"Your turn."

She'd been thinking about it since he started talking. She knew what it was before she said it. "Thomas. After my foster father in the second home I was placed in. He was the only one who bothered to learn how I took my coffee." She picked at a thread on the futon fabric. "He died when I was sixteen. I never told anyone that I still think about him when I smell black coffee."

Dalton's hand moved to cover hers, stilling the thread-picking. He didn't say anything, and she was grateful for it. Some things don't need a response. They just need to be heard by someone who isn't going to flinch.

Later, with the rain still going and the lamp still burning low, he lay on his back along the futon with his injured arm settled carefully and his other arm around her, and she had her cheek against his chest and could feel the rise and fall of his breathing evening out. Not sleep, she didn't think either of them slept, but the body's version of it, the metabolic descent that comes after the adrenaline burns off and there's nothing left to run on.

She stared at the ceiling, listening to the rain and his heartbeat and the occasional radio murmur from below, and ran through it methodically. Julian at the courthouse. The ledger on the drive in her jacket pocket, which she'd moved to the inner chest pocket before coming upstairs. Landry with four deputies and a detective. Dalton with a wrapped shoulder and the particular, controlled focus of someone who'd been trained to function hurt. Herself, with a bread knife she'd already used once tonight and a cast iron skillet she'd used to considerable effect.

It wasn't a reassuring inventory. It was, however, an honest one.

Sometime around four in the morning, she heard his breathing change and knew he was fully awake again.

"We should go soon," she said, to the ceiling.

"Yeah." His arm tightened briefly around her. "Twenty more minutes." She didn't argue with twenty minutes. She took them.

They dressed in the low light, pulling on dark layers, moving around each other in the narrow space with the practiced efficiency of people who'd been sharing close quarters for two days and had learned each other's movements. She helped him with his jacket again, working it over the wrapped shoulder. He checked the suppressed sidearm he'd carried out of the woods, cleared it, re-seated the magazine. She watched him do it and felt the shift in the air between them, the specific gravity of a room when two people are about to walk toward something they both know could go wrong.

"Hey," she said.

He looked up from the weapon.

"Elise is a good name," she said again. "I just wanted to say that twice."

His jaw moved. Not quite a smile, but the muscle grouping that preceded one. "Thomas is a solid name too."

"Yes. It is." She pulled her jacket closed, pressed her hand flat over the inner pocket, felt the hard edge of the drive through the fabric. Still there. Still hers to use. "Okay," she said. "Let's go end this."

She went down the stairs first. Below, the bakery was quieter, most of Landry's people having moved to stage near the courthouse, one deputy left at the loading dock with instructions to keep the scene secure. He looked at them coming down the stairs and at the weapons and at Dalton's wrapped shoulder, and he made a decision that Amber respected: he stepped aside and looked at the wall.

The loading dock door swung open onto the alley. Cold air hit her, rain-washed and clean, the storm still running but gentler now, a steady drizzle replacing the earlier sheets. The streetlights reflected off the wet pavement in long orange ribbons. Cherry Creek at four-fifteen in the morning, wiped clean and quiet, the town holding its breath the way it had when they'd arrived three hours ago, except now she understood that the stillness wasn't menace. It was just the town, being a town, indifferent and small and ordinary in the way she'd come here looking for.

She'd found a lot more than ordinary. She was starting to think that was fine.

Dalton moved up beside her, close enough that his arm pressed against hers. He scanned the alley in both directions. "Ready?"

The courthouse was four blocks north. Julian Vane was waiting in it, probably confident that Landry's approach would be the end of the game and that the ledger was either in his hands or destroyed. He hadn't counted on her. That was the thing about people like Julian: they underestimated the stubborn ones. The ones who survived by being too irritating to put down cleanly.

"Ready," she said.

They stepped out into the rain together and moved toward Birch Street without looking back.

One Last Night

The loft stairs were narrow enough that she had to turn sideways to carry the two mugs of water she'd grabbed from the small shelf near the landing. Dalton was already up there, standing at the rain-blurred window with his good arm braced against the sill, watching the alley below. His jacket was over the chair. The bandage on his shoulder showed through the henley fabric, a small dark bloom at the center where the wound had seeped through the gauze.

She set the mugs on the wooden crate and stood behind him for a moment, close enough to feel the warmth radiating off his back. Outside, the rain kept coming, steady and gray, the alley pavement shining under the single working streetlight. Nothing moved down there. Landry's deputy was still at the loading dock. Everything was exactly as it had been ten minutes ago.

"You should sit," she said. "I've been sitting."

"You've been standing at a window for twenty minutes."

He turned. His blue eyes moved over her face with the particular attention he gave to things he was trying to memorize, which she'd noticed he did more in the last twelve hours than in the entire two weeks before them. "Come here," he said.

She went. It wasn't a decision so much as a fact, the way gravity isn't a decision. Her body simply recognized its center and tilted toward it, her shoulder brushing his chest before she even realized she'd moved. It was a magnetic, involuntary pull, a physical surrender that left her leaning into his heat as if her bones were made of iron and he was the only pole that mattered. He pulled her in with his good arm, and she tucked herself against his uninjured side, and they stood there together watching the rain hit the glass.

"I keep running the courthouse layout in my head," she said. "Stop."

"I can't just stop."

"I know." His hand moved up her spine, slow and deliberate. "Do it anyway. Give yourself twenty minutes."

She exhaled against his chest. The bakery smell clung to the loft, yeast and sugar and the faint warmth of the ovens two floors below, and underneath it the rain and the copper-sharp note of his bandaged shoulder, and underneath all of that, him. Warm flannel and skin. She'd been cataloging that particular combination without deciding to, the way you absorb things you're afraid of losing.

"Twenty minutes," she agreed.

He kissed the top of her head, and she felt the tension in his jaw, the controlled steadiness of a man running on discipline instead of sleep, and she thought: *me too.*

Somewhere in the next few minutes, they moved to the futon. Not urgently. It wasn't desperation that moved them; it was something slower and more certain, the way water finds its level. He sat and she was beside him, and his good hand curved around her jaw, and she turned her face into it, pressing her cheek against his palm the way she'd been wanting to since they came up the stairs.

"Hey," she said softly.

"Hey." His thumb brushed her cheekbone.

She kissed him first this time. Soft, deliberate, no urgency in it, just the press of her mouth against his and the slight exhale that moved through him when she did. His hand shifted to her hair, fingers working through the tangled mess of her ponytail until it came loose, and she felt the heavy weight of it fall against her shoulders and didn't care.

They took their time with each other's clothing. She worked his henley up carefully, avoiding the bandaged shoulder, and he let her manage it without protest, which she understood was its own kind of trust from him. She spread her palm flat on his bare chest, feeling the steady thud of his heart, the muscle and warmth of him, the realness of it after two days of running through rain and cold and dark. Still here. Still beating.

"Your shoulder," she murmured against his jaw. "It's fine."

"I just re-wrapped it."

"I know where it is," he said, echoing himself from earlier, and there was a dry warmth in it that made her press her forehead against his cheek and breathe for a second.

He was careful with her in a way that wasn't clinical and wasn't cautious. It was considered. Every movement was something he chose to make, deliberate and unhurried, like the next few hours weren't waiting on the other side of the window. His good hand traced her throat, her collarbone, the soft inside of her wrist where the crescent moon tattoo sat, and he pressed his lips there, warm and still, and she felt something in her chest loosen by several degrees.

She pulled his face back up to hers and kissed him harder this time, her fingers working into his hair, and he made a low sound against her mouth that she felt more than heard. They moved together onto the futon, finding the configuration that worked around his shoulder, and she ended up with her knees on either side of his hips, looking down at him in the low lamplight, his dark blond hair messed up and his blue eyes fixed on her face with the kind of focus that had unsettled her the first time she saw it and now felt like the steadiest thing in her world.

"You're staring," she said. "Yes."

"It's unnerving."

"You'll survive it." His good hand curved over her hip, unhurried. "You survive everything."

She leaned down and kissed him again, and this time it was slower, deeper, the kind that takes inventory. She felt his pulse at his throat under her lips, his collarbone, the flat muscle of his chest. She bit down gently at his shoulder, the undamaged one, and felt his hand tighten on her hip in response. She did it again, a little less gently, leaving a mark she could see in the lamplight, and something about that felt necessary, like signing something.

"Amber," he said, low.

"I want to remember every part of this," she said against his skin. "When it's over. I want to know I was here."

His arm pulled her closer. He rolled them carefully, keeping his weight off his shoulder, and looked down at her with an expression she'd spent two weeks trying to find a clean word for. She still didn't have one. Serious and warm in the same breath, like they were the same thing and always had been.

"You're going to be here," he said. "When it's over. You're going to be right here."

"I know," she said. "I just wanted to say it out loud."

He kissed her jaw, her throat, the place where her pulse beat fast under her skin, and she arched into him and let herself stop running the courthouse layout through her head, stop counting minutes, stop tallying what could go wrong. For the next twenty minutes, there was only this. The lamplight. The rain. The weight and warmth of him and the slow, consuming certainty of every movement between them.

She raked her nails down his back when she needed to hold onto something, and he exhaled hard against her throat and said her name like it was the only word he had. She dug in again, deliberate, marking him the way he'd marked everything about the last two weeks on her, leaving evidence. He answered by pressing his lips to her temple, her cheek, the corner of her mouth, the careful tenderness of it contrasting with the grip of his hand on her hip, and she thought: *this is what it is, then. All of it at once. The softness and the force of him, and somehow both of those things are the same person.*

They were quiet afterward, the futon frame creaking as they settled, his good arm around her, her cheek against his chest. The rain hadn't let up. Below them, the bakery was still. The deputy at the loading dock coughed once, audible through the floorboards, and she heard his boot shift on the concrete, and the ordinary mundaneness of that sound, someone standing a post, bored, shifting his weight, almost made her laugh.

"What," Dalton said.

"The deputy just coughed." A pause. "And?"

"Nothing. It's just very normal. While we're up here being very not normal." She pressed her fingers against his ribs, feeling him breathe. "I'm not complaining."

His arm tightened around her, brief. She felt him exhale slowly above her head.

"I want you to set up a dead man's switch," he said, after a moment. His voice was quiet, even.

She lifted her chin to look at his face. "For the drive?"

"If we both go in and neither of us comes out, the files need to reach the FBI regardless. There's a federal field office in Albany. I can give you an email address for a contact there, someone I worked with after my discharge." He paused. "You schedule the email with the files attached and set it to send at six in the morning unless you manually cancel it. If one of us is alive and able, we cancel it and hand it off directly. If neither of us can cancel it, it goes automatically."

She sat up. The lamp threw warm light across the futon, across his bare chest, across the bandaged shoulder and the mark she'd left on the other side. "You have a federal contact."

"I have several. I've been careful about not using them until I had something substantial enough to be worth the exposure." His eyes were steady on her. "The ledger is substantial enough."

"What's his name? Your contact."

"Reyes. Special Agent Marco Reyes. Tell him Vantage sent the files. He'll know what that means."

She filed it. *Reyes. Vantage. Albany field office. Six a.m.* "You've been carrying around a plan for this whole time."

"I've been carrying around contingencies. There's a difference." "Is there?"

He almost smiled. Not quite, but close. "A plan implies I knew how it would go. Contingencies just mean I thought about the ways it could go wrong." He shifted, wincing slightly as his shoulder adjusted. "Get your phone. I'll give you the email."

She dug her phone out of her jacket pocket, opened the mail client. He gave her the address from memory, a federal domain that looked legitimate, and she drafted the email, attached the ledger file from the copy she'd sent to her cloud backup the night before, and set the scheduled send for six a.m. Her thumb hovered over the confirm button.

"If I cancel this at five-fifty-nine and we're both fine," she said, "I'm going to feel extremely dramatic."

"You can feel dramatic at five-fifty-nine. Set it."

She confirmed the send. The phone showed a small clock icon next to the draft. Scheduled. Done.

She set the phone on the crate and looked back at him. He was watching her with the same focused attention as before, and she recognized that he was also memorizing this.

Her, in the low light, hair loose, phone in hand, the small decisive motion of setting a trigger that would detonate the Vane Collective's records into federal hands if they weren't alive to do it themselves.

"Thomas," she said. He blinked. "What?"

"Our son. If we have one." She pulled her knees to her chest, sitting cross-legged on the futon. "I said it before, but I want to say it again when we're both awake and it counts. Thomas."

Something moved across his expression, unguarded and brief. He cleared his throat. "Thomas Vale," he said, trying it out.

"Thomas Vale Rowan," she corrected. "Hyphenated."

"Thomas Vale Rowan." A pause. "That's a lot of name for a kid." "He'll grow into it."

"He will." Dalton's voice was quieter now, carrying something under the dry precision of it. "Elise," he said. "Elise Vale Rowan."

"Elise Vale Rowan." She repeated it and felt the weight of it, two names for people who didn't exist yet, spoken in a bakery loft in the middle of a rainstorm before they walked toward a man who'd tried to have her killed twice. It was either the most reckless thing she'd ever done or the most courageous, and she was finding it increasingly difficult to tell the difference. "That's a good name," she said. "It sounds like someone who knows what she wants."

"She'll have your stubbornness. God help everyone."

"She'll have your tendency to stand at windows staring at nothing for twenty minutes at a time. That's worse."

He let out a low sound, half exhale and half laugh, and she felt it all the way through her chest. She leaned over and pressed her mouth to his jaw, felt the stubble rough against her lips, stayed there for a second. His hand came up and held the side of her face, thumb at her cheekbone.

"We're coming back from this," he said.

"I know." She pulled back just enough to find his eyes. "I know we are. I'm not doing this because I think we're going to die. I'm doing it because I want it to be real. The names. The switch. All of it." She held his gaze. "I want it to be real before we go out there, not after."

The muscle in his jaw shifted. He nodded once, the kind of nod that meant he understood, actually understood, not just the words but the specific shape of what she was telling him. She'd learned to read that nod over the last two weeks. It was one of her favorite things about him, though she hadn't told him that yet.

Maybe after. She'd tell him after.

They dressed in silence, the comfortable kind. She pulled on the dark layers she'd set aside, laced her boots, checked the inner pocket of her jacket for the drive. Hard and present, right where it should be. She watched Dalton work his jacket over his wrapped shoulder with the practiced economy of someone who'd dressed in the field enough times that injury was just a variable to route around. He checked his sidearm with the fluid attention of someone for whom that motion was as automatic as breathing, cleared it, seated the magazine, holstered it.

She checked her own piece, the compact pistol she'd collected from the bakery's back room where Dalton had stashed it the previous evening. She ran through the same sequence: clear, load, holster. Her hands were steady, which still surprised her a little. Two months ago, she'd shaken every time she opened a note from Rory. Now she was checking a firearm in a bakery loft at four in the morning and her hands were steady.

People changed under pressure. She was starting to understand that wasn't always a bad thing.

"Remember the ventilation access on the east side of the courthouse," Dalton said, pulling his jacket closed. "Second floor, above the old records room. The duct runs up to the clock tower. Julian will have men on the stairs, but he won't have covered the vents. It's not a path most people would know about."

"I know about it because I spent three weeks doing deliveries to the county clerk's office," she said. "And because I'm nosy and I looked at the building map on the public records site when I had nothing to do."

"That's why you're useful."

"I'm going to need you to elaborate on 'useful' at some point." "You're invaluable," he said, dry and even. "Is that better?" "Marginally." She zipped her jacket. "You'll take the ground floor?"

"Lower two floors. Smoke grenades to pull his men down. You use the confusion to get to the east side access while they're looking at the ground floor." He paused. "You go up, you get eyes on Julian, you wait for my signal before you move."

"And if I can't wait for your signal?"

He looked at her. "Then you don't wait."

"Okay." She straightened her collar. "Good talk."

She picked up her phone from the crate. Six a.m. scheduled send. Clock icon, steady and small. She showed it to him once more, confirming, then tucked it back into her jacket.

"Reyes," she said. "Vantage. Albany. Six a.m." "Correct."

"I'm not going to need it." "No," he agreed. "You're not."

She moved to the stairs and stopped, turning back. He was standing in the

low lamplight, jacket on, shoulder wrapped, blue eyes catching the warm glow, and she looked at him for two full seconds and stored it somewhere she wouldn't lose it. The specific way he looked in this specific light on this specific night. The scar through his eyebrow. The stubble. The bandage. The mark she'd left on his shoulder, invisible under the fabric but there, permanent and hers.

"Hey," she said. "For the record. You're not a monster."

His expression didn't shift, exactly. But something behind his eyes did. "You don't know everything I've done."

"I know enough." She held his gaze for another beat. "You're the man who picked a daughter's name at nineteen and never told anyone. That's not a monster. That's just someone who needed the right person to tell it to." She turned back toward the stairs. "Come on. Let's go."

The loading dock door opened onto the alley, and the cold air came in fast, rain-washed and sharp, carrying the smell of wet pavement and the faint diesel trace from the delivery lane. The drizzle had settled into something fine and constant, not the earlier sheets but a steady mist that sat on every surface and turned the streetlights into soft, blurred halos. Cherry Creek at four-fifteen in the morning was utterly, completely quiet, the storefronts dark, the sidewalks empty, the traffic lights cycling through their colors for no one.

Dalton moved up beside her and scanned the alley in both directions. She watched his eyes track left to right, methodical and quick. He gave a single nod.

The courthouse was four blocks north, its clock tower visible above the roofline, pale stone against the dark sky. Julian Vane was up there, probably running his own calculations, probably certain that Landry's approach would be enough of a distraction, probably not accounting for the fact that Amber Rowan had spent two years surviving things she wasn't supposed to survive and had recently developed a taste for not cooperating with other people's plans for her.

She pressed her hand once over her jacket pocket, feeling the drive through the fabric. Still there.

"Ready?" Dalton said.

She thought about Thomas and Elise, two names spoken in a lamplit loft, real now in the way that spoken things become real. She thought about the email sitting in her drafts with a six a.m. send time and hoped to God she'd be canceling it with coffee in hand and Dalton's shoulder properly healing and Landry somewhere nearby being professionally grumpy about paperwork.

"Ready," she said.

They moved out into the rain, heading north on Birch Street, two figures in dark jackets on a wet empty road. The mist settled on her hair and her lashes and the collar of her jacket, cool and clean, and she let it. The courthouse clock showed four-eighteen. Forty-two minutes before dawn started graying the sky.

Plenty of time.

29
One Last Night

The loft stairs were narrow enough that she had to turn sideways to carry the two mugs of water she'd grabbed from the small shelf near the landing. Dalton was already up there, standing at the rain-blurred window with his good arm braced against the sill, watching the alley below. His jacket was over the chair. The bandage on his shoulder showed through the henley fabric, a small dark bloom at the center where the wound had seeped through the gauze.

She set the mugs on the wooden crate and stood behind him for a moment, close enough to feel the warmth radiating off his back. Outside, the rain kept coming, steady and gray, the alley pavement shining under the single working streetlight. Nothing moved down there. Landry's deputy was still at the loading dock. Everything was exactly as it had been ten minutes ago.

"You should sit," she said. "I've been sitting."

"You've been standing at a window for twenty minutes."

He turned. His blue eyes moved over her face with the particular attention he gave to things he was trying to memorize, which she'd noticed he did more in the last twelve hours than in the entire two weeks before them. "Come here," he said.

She went. It wasn't a decision so much as a fact, the way gravity isn't a decision. Her body simply recognized its center and tilted toward it, her shoulder brushing his chest before she even realized she'd moved. It was a magnetic, involuntary pull, a physical surrender that left her leaning into his heat as if her bones were made of iron and he was the only pole that mattered. He pulled her in with his good arm, and she tucked herself against his uninjured side, and they stood there together watching the rain hit the glass.

"I keep running the courthouse layout in my head," she said. "Stop."

"I can't just stop."

"I know." His hand moved up her spine, slow and deliberate. "Do it anyway. Give yourself twenty minutes."

She exhaled against his chest. The bakery smell clung to the loft, yeast and sugar and the faint warmth of the ovens two floors below, and underneath it the rain and the copper-sharp note of his bandaged shoulder, and underneath all of that, him. Warm flannel and skin. She'd been cataloging that particular combination without deciding to, the way you absorb things you're afraid of losing.

"Twenty minutes," she agreed.

He kissed the top of her head, and she felt the tension in his jaw, the controlled steadiness of a man running on discipline instead of sleep, and she thought: *me too.*

Somewhere in the next few minutes, they moved to the futon. Not urgently. It wasn't desperation that moved them; it was something slower and more certain, the way water finds its level. He sat and she was beside him, and his good hand curved around her jaw, and she turned her face into it, pressing her cheek against his palm the way she'd been wanting to since they came up the stairs.

"Hey," she said softly.

"Hey." His thumb brushed her cheekbone.

She kissed him first this time. Soft, deliberate, no urgency in it, just the press of her mouth against his and the slight exhale that moved through him when she did. His hand shifted to her hair, fingers working through the tangled mess of her ponytail until it came loose, and she felt the heavy weight of it fall against her shoulders and didn't care.

They took their time with each other's clothing. She worked his henley up carefully, avoiding the bandaged shoulder, and he let her manage it without protest, which she understood was its own kind of trust from him. She spread her palm flat on his bare chest, feeling the steady thud of his heart, the muscle and warmth of him, the realness of it after two days of running through rain and cold and dark. Still here. Still beating.

"Your shoulder," she murmured against his jaw. "It's fine."

"I just re-wrapped it."

"I know where it is," he said, echoing himself from earlier, and there was a dry warmth in it that made her press her forehead against his cheek and breathe for a second.

He was careful with her in a way that wasn't clinical and wasn't cautious. It was considered. Every movement was something he chose to make, deliberate and unhurried, like the next few hours weren't waiting on the other side of the window. His good hand traced her throat, her collarbone, the soft inside of her wrist where the crescent moon tattoo sat, and he pressed his lips there, warm and still, and she felt something in her chest loosen by several degrees.

She pulled his face back up to hers and kissed him harder this time, her fingers working into his hair, and he made a low sound against her mouth that she felt more than heard. They moved together onto the futon, finding the configuration that worked around his shoulder, and she ended up with her knees on either side of his hips, looking down at him in the low lamplight, his dark blond hair messed up and his blue eyes fixed on her face with the kind of focus that had unsettled her the first time she saw it and now felt like the steadiest thing in her world.

"You're staring," she said. "Yes."

"It's unnerving."

"You'll survive it." His good hand curved over her hip, unhurried. "You survive everything."

She leaned down and kissed him again, and this time it was slower, deeper, the kind that takes inventory. She felt his pulse at his throat under her lips, his collarbone, the flat muscle of his chest. She bit down gently at his shoulder, the undamaged one, and felt his hand tighten on her hip in response. She did it again, a little less gently, leaving a mark she could see in the lamplight, and something about that felt necessary, like signing something.

"Amber," he said, low.

"I want to remember every part of this," she said against his skin. "When it's over. I want to know I was here."

His arm pulled her closer. He rolled them carefully, keeping his weight off his shoulder, and looked down at her with an expression she'd spent two weeks trying to find a clean word for. She still didn't have one. Serious and warm in the same breath, like they were the same thing and always had been.

"You're going to be here," he said. "When it's over. You're going to be right here."

"I know," she said. "I just wanted to say it out loud."

He kissed her jaw, her throat, the place where her pulse beat fast under her skin, and she arched into him and let herself stop running the courthouse layout through her head, stop counting minutes, stop tallying what could go wrong. For the next twenty minutes, there was only this. The lamplight. The rain. The weight and warmth of him and the slow, consuming certainty of every movement between them.

She raked her nails down his back when she needed to hold onto something, and he exhaled hard against her throat and said her name like it was the only word he had. She dug in again, deliberate, marking him the way he'd marked everything about the last two weeks on her, leaving evidence. He answered by pressing his lips to her temple, her cheek, the corner of her mouth, the careful tenderness of it contrasting with the grip of his hand on her hip, and she thought: *this is what it is, then. All of it at once. The softness and the force of him, and somehow both of those things are the same person.*

They were quiet afterward, the futon frame creaking as they settled, his good arm around her, her cheek against his chest. The rain hadn't let up. Below them, the bakery was still. The deputy at the loading dock coughed once, audible through the floorboards, and she heard his boot shift on the concrete, and the ordinary mundaneness of that sound, someone standing a post, bored, shifting his weight, almost made her laugh.

"What," Dalton said.

"The deputy just coughed." A pause. "And?"

"Nothing. It's just very normal. While we're up here being very not normal." She pressed her fingers against his ribs, feeling him breathe. "I'm not complaining."

His arm tightened around her, brief. She felt him exhale slowly above her head.

"I want you to set up a dead man's switch," he said, after a moment. His voice was quiet, even.

She lifted her chin to look at his face. "For the drive?"

"If we both go in and neither of us comes out, the files need to reach the FBI regardless. There's a federal field office in Albany. I can give you an email address for a contact there, someone I worked with after my discharge." He paused. "You schedule the email with the files attached and set it to send at six in the morning unless you manually cancel it. If one of us is alive and able, we cancel it and hand it off directly. If neither of us can cancel it, it goes automatically."

She sat up. The lamp threw warm light across the futon, across his bare chest, across the bandaged shoulder and the mark she'd left on the other side. "You have a federal contact."

"I have several. I've been careful about not using them until I had something substantial enough to be worth the exposure." His eyes were steady on her. "The ledger is substantial enough."

"What's his name? Your contact."

"Reyes. Special Agent Marco Reyes. Tell him Vantage sent the files. He'll know what that means."

She filed it. *Reyes. Vantage. Albany field office. Six a.m.* "You've been carrying around a plan for this whole time."

"I've been carrying around contingencies. There's a difference." "Is there?"

He almost smiled. Not quite, but close. "A plan implies I knew how it would go. Contingencies just mean I thought about the ways it could go wrong." He shifted, wincing slightly as his shoulder adjusted. "Get your phone. I'll give you the email."

She dug her phone out of her jacket pocket, opened the mail client. He gave her the address from memory, a federal domain that looked legitimate, and she drafted the email, attached the ledger file from the copy she'd sent to her cloud backup the night before, and set the scheduled send for six a.m. Her thumb hovered over the confirm button.

"If I cancel this at five-fifty-nine and we're both fine," she said, "I'm going to feel extremely dramatic."

"You can feel dramatic at five-fifty-nine. Set it."

She confirmed the send. The phone showed a small clock icon next to the draft. Scheduled. Done.

She set the phone on the crate and looked back at him. He was watching her with the same focused attention as before, and she recognized that he was also memorizing this. Her, in the low light, hair loose, phone in hand, the small decisive motion of setting a trigger that would detonate the

Vane Collective's records into federal hands if they weren't alive to do it themselves.

"Thomas," she said. He blinked. "What?"

"Our son. If we have one." She pulled her knees to her chest, sitting cross-legged on the futon. "I said it before, but I want to say it again when we're both awake and it counts. Thomas."

Something moved across his expression, unguarded and brief. He cleared his throat. "Thomas Vale," he said, trying it out.

"Thomas Vale Rowan," she corrected. "Hyphenated."

"Thomas Vale Rowan." A pause. "That's a lot of name for a kid." "He'll grow into it."

"He will." Dalton's voice was quieter now, carrying something under the dry precision of it. "Elise," he said. "Elise Vale Rowan."

"Elise Vale Rowan." She repeated it and felt the weight of it, two names for people who didn't exist yet, spoken in a bakery loft in the middle of a rainstorm before they walked toward a man who'd tried to have her killed twice. It was either the most reckless thing she'd ever done or the most courageous, and she was finding it increasingly difficult to tell the difference. "That's a good name," she said. "It sounds like someone who knows what she wants."

"She'll have your stubbornness. God help everyone."

"She'll have your tendency to stand at windows staring at nothing for twenty minutes at a time. That's worse."

He let out a low sound, half exhale and half laugh, and she felt it all the way through her chest. She leaned over and pressed her mouth to his jaw, felt the stubble rough against her lips, stayed there for a second. His hand came up and held the side of her face, thumb at her cheekbone.

"We're coming back from this," he said.

"I know." She pulled back just enough to find his eyes. "I know we are. I'm not doing this because I think we're going to die. I'm doing it because I want it to be real. The names. The switch. All of it." She held his gaze. "I want it to be real before we go out there, not after."

The muscle in his jaw shifted. He nodded once, the kind of nod that meant he understood, actually understood, not just the words but the specific shape of what she was telling him. She'd learned to read that nod over the last two weeks. It was one of her favorite things about him, though she hadn't told him that yet.

Maybe after. She'd tell him after.

They dressed in silence, the comfortable kind. She pulled on the dark layers she'd set aside, laced her boots, checked the inner pocket of her jacket for the drive. Hard and present, right where it should be. She watched Dalton work his jacket over his wrapped shoulder with the practiced economy of someone who'd dressed in the field enough times that injury was just a variable to route around. He checked his sidearm with the fluid attention of someone for whom that motion was as automatic as breathing, cleared it, seated the magazine, holstered it.

She checked her own piece, the compact pistol she'd collected from the bakery's back room where Dalton had stashed it the previous evening. She ran through the same sequence: clear, load, holster. Her hands were steady, which still surprised her a little. Two months ago, she'd shaken every time she opened a note from Rory. Now she was checking a firearm in a bakery loft at four in the morning and her hands were steady.

People changed under pressure. She was starting to understand that wasn't always a bad thing.

"Remember the ventilation access on the east side of the courthouse," Dalton said, pulling his jacket closed. "Second floor, above the old records room. The duct runs up to the clock tower. Julian will have men on the stairs, but he won't have covered the vents. It's not a path most people would know about."

"I know about it because I spent three weeks doing deliveries to the county clerk's office," she said. "And because

I'm nosy and I looked at the building map on the public records site when I had nothing to do."

"That's why you're useful."

"I'm going to need you to elaborate on 'useful' at some point." "You're invaluable," he said, dry and even. "Is that better?" "Marginally." She zipped her jacket. "You'll take the ground floor?"

"Lower two floors. Smoke grenades to pull his men down. You use the confusion to get to the east side access while they're looking at the ground floor." He paused. "You go up, you get eyes on Julian, you wait for my signal before you move."

"And if I can't wait for your signal?"

He looked at her. "Then you don't wait."

"Okay." She straightened her collar. "Good talk."

She picked up her phone from the crate. Six a.m. scheduled send. Clock icon, steady and small. She showed it to him once more, confirming, then tucked it back into her jacket.

"Reyes," she said. "Vantage. Albany. Six a.m." "Correct."

"I'm not going to need it." "No," he agreed. "You're not."

She moved to the stairs and stopped, turning back. He was standing in the

low lamplight, jacket on, shoulder wrapped, blue eyes catching the warm glow, and she looked at him for two full seconds and stored it somewhere she wouldn't lose it. The specific way he looked in this specific light on this specific night. The scar through his eyebrow. The stubble. The bandage. The mark she'd left on his shoulder, invisible under the fabric but there, permanent and hers.

"Hey," she said. "For the record. You're not a monster."

His expression didn't shift, exactly. But something behind his eyes did. "You don't know everything I've done."

"I know enough." She held his gaze for another beat. "You're the man who picked a daughter's name at nineteen and never told anyone. That's not a monster. That's just someone who needed the right person to tell it to." She turned back toward the stairs. "Come on. Let's go."

The loading dock door opened onto the alley, and the cold air came in fast, rain-washed and sharp, carrying the smell of wet pavement and the faint diesel trace from the delivery lane. The drizzle had settled into something fine and constant, not the earlier sheets but a steady mist that sat on every surface and turned the streetlights into soft, blurred halos. Cherry Creek at four-fifteen in the morning was utterly, completely quiet, the storefronts dark, the sidewalks empty, the traffic lights cycling through their colors for no one.

Dalton moved up beside her and scanned the alley in both directions. She watched his eyes track left to right, methodical and quick. He gave a single nod.

The courthouse was four blocks north, its clock tower visible above the roofline, pale stone against the dark sky. Julian Vane was up there, probably running his own calculations, probably certain that Landry's approach would be enough of a distraction, probably not accounting for the fact that Amber Rowan had spent two years surviving things she wasn't supposed to survive and had recently developed a taste for not cooperating with other people's plans for her.

She pressed her hand once over her jacket pocket, feeling the drive through the fabric. Still there.

"Ready?" Dalton said.

She thought about Thomas and Elise, two names spoken in a lamplit loft, real now in the way that spoken things become real. She thought about the email sitting in her drafts with a six a.m. send time and hoped to God she'd be canceling it with coffee in hand and Dalton's shoulder properly healing and Landry somewhere nearby being professionally grumpy about paperwork.

"Ready," she said.

They moved out into the rain, heading north on Birch Street, two figures in dark jackets on a wet empty road. The mist settled on her hair and her lashes and the collar of her jacket, cool and clean, and she let it. The courthouse clock showed four-eighteen. Forty-two minutes before dawn started graying the sky.

Plenty of time.

30
The Final Reckoning

The courthouse clock read four-forty-one when Amber pulled herself up through the ventilation access on the second floor.

The duct had been exactly where she'd remembered it from three weeks of delivery runs to the county clerk's office: a louvered panel above the old records room, half-hidden behind a filing cabinet that hadn't moved since the nineties. She'd wedged herself in sideways, hauled herself up by her forearms, and crawled in near-total darkness with the smell of decades-old dust and the distant, muffled percussion of Dalton's smoke grenades going off somewhere below her. Two quick concussive thumps, then a third.

Voices shouting. Boots on tile, going the wrong direction.

Good. They were looking at the ground floor.

The duct ran up at a thirty-degree angle, then leveled out for six feet before angling up again. Her shoulders scraped the sides. She kept her breathing shallow and her elbows moving, pushing herself forward in the dark by increments, counting the cross-joints by feel. Four joints from the records room brought her to the main shaft. From there, the shaft ran vertical for two stories before opening into the clock tower's mechanical room.

She climbed. Hand over hand, boots finding purchase on the riveted seams. Her jacket caught once and she yanked it free without stopping. Her shoulder burned. She climbed anyway.

The mechanical room hatch gave with a dull click when she pressed her palm against it, and she eased it open slow enough that it didn't squeak, then pulled herself through and crouched on the concrete floor in the dark, listening.

Footsteps. One set, steady and unhurried, moving in a slow circuit around the perimeter of the floor above.

She drew her pistol, checked the chamber by touch, and found the access stairs to the clock tower's upper level. They were wood, old, and she tested each step before she trusted it with her weight. Twelve steps. She counted them.

At the top, she stopped.

The clock tower's main room opened around her, pale stone walls and four enormous clock faces letting in the pre-dawn gray in thin bars of light. The gears and counterweights hung in the center of the room, a tangle of old iron and chain that hadn't moved in years. In the far corner, Sheriff Landry sat zip-tied to a support column, his uniform jacket gone, his face bearing a cut above his left eye that had bled down his cheek and dried there. He was conscious. His eyes found her immediately.

She pressed one finger to her lips. He gave a single, almost imperceptible nod.

Julian Vane was standing at the east clock face, his back to the stairs, looking out through the clock's numerals at the square below where the smoke from the grenades was still drifting up in pale ribbons. He wore a dark coat, his posture completely unhurried, his hands clasped behind his back. He looked like a man watching a delayed train from a platform, slightly bored, entirely certain it was coming.

"Amber," he said, without turning around. "You're three minutes slower than I estimated. The duct runs steep, I suppose."

She came fully into the room and kept her gun up. "Where are your men?"

"Downstairs, dealing with your friend's theatrics." He turned then, unhurried, and faced her. Julian Vane was handsome in the way that certain objects were beautiful without being warm: clean jaw, silver at his temples, pale eyes that moved over her with an assessment so clinical it made her skin tighten. "I didn't call them up here. I knew they wouldn't be necessary."

"You knew I was coming."

"I knew *he* would send you up the back way while he handled the front." Julian tilted his chin slightly. "Dalton's been running that playbook since his extraction days. Diversion at the primary entry, secondary asset through the quiet route. I know his methods rather well. I funded them for three years." He paused. "The drive, please."

"I don't have it."

"You do. Inner jacket pocket, left side. You've touched it twice since you entered the room." His expression didn't shift. "Please don't waste my time with misdirection. You're not bad at it, but you're not trained for it either."

From the corner, Landry made a sound, something low and warning. Julian didn't look at him.

"Here's what I think happened," Julian said, moving a few steps to his right, circling toward the center of the room with the same easy patience. "You survived something terrible. You ran. You built yourself a quiet little life in this quiet little town, and then Dalton found you, and you decided that he was the safe one. The strong one. The person standing between you and the dark." He paused. "You traded one predator for another, Amber. That's all. You just chose the one who held the door open instead of blocking it."

She kept the gun level. "That's a nice speech." "It's an accurate one."

"Maybe." She took one step forward, weight balanced, exactly the way Dalton had drilled into her in the garage three weeks ago when she'd asked him to stop treating her like something to protect and start treating her like someone who needed to know how to fight. "But here's the thing about your theory. You're right. I did find a predator." Another step. "I just didn't hide behind him."

Julian's brow moved slightly. A small adjustment, like a recalculation.

"I learned to hunt," she said.

The door below the stairs exploded inward.

Dalton came through it with exactly the kind of controlled violence that didn't announce itself ahead of time. He had Julian's nearest man down before the man's radio hit the floor, and then he was up the stairs in four strides and through the tower doorway, his sidearm up, his eyes moving across the room in the practiced sweep that took in Landry, Julian, her, the geometry of the space, all in under two seconds.

Julian moved faster than she'd expected.

His hand came out of his coat pocket with a black device, small and rectangular, a detonator with a red safety cap already flipped open. His thumb hovered over the trigger. "The building's support columns," he said, his voice entirely steady. "Four charges. Enough to bring the east wing down inside six seconds. The sheriff dies in the rubble. You both die in the rubble. I walk out in the confusion." He looked between them. "Or you give me the drive and I disarm it."

Dalton had gone completely still. Not the stillness of hesitation; the stillness of a man calculating trajectories.

Julian's eyes moved to him. "Put it down, Dalton. This isn't a battlefield. There are no extraction protocols for this scenario."

"You're right," Dalton said. "There aren't." He kept his gun exactly where it was.

Julian's thumb pressed against the detonator's trigger, not depressing it, just making the contact clear. "I'll count to three."

Amber didn't wait for three.

She shot Julian Vane twice in the chest.

The sound was enormous in the stone room, both reports cracking off the walls and the iron gears and the clock faces so that it seemed to come from everywhere at once. Julian's expression registered something, not quite surprise, more like the look of a man updating a spreadsheet with an unexpected figure. His hand opened. His body went backward, two stumbling steps, and then the east clock face gave way behind him, the old glass and iron frame that had been weakening since the last hard winter, and he went through it and out into the pre-dawn air above Cherry Creek's main square.

The detonator fell from his open hand.

Dalton caught it at knee height, one-handed, his fingers closing around it before it cleared eighteen inches of drop. He straightened, checked the safety cap, flipped it back closed, and pressed the disarm sequence on the side panel. Somewhere below them, four soft clicks sounded in sequence as the charges disengaged.

The room went quiet except for the sound of the wind coming through the broken clock face and the distant shout of someone in the square below, someone who'd just seen something fall.

Amber stood with her gun still raised, pointing at the empty space where Julian had been.

She lowered it.

Her hands were steady. She noted this with the distant, slightly detached clarity of someone running a post-event check, the way Dalton had taught her. Hands steady. Breathing fast but controlled. No tunnel vision. She was fine. She was completely fine.

"Amber." Dalton was beside her, his hand on her arm, not gripping, just present. "You good?"

"Yes." She clicked the safety on and holstered the pistol. "Get Landry."

He produced a folding knife from his jacket and crossed to the corner in four strides. Landry was already working his wrists against the zip ties, and Dalton cut through them in two quick strokes. The sheriff stood up with the careful movement of a man taking inventory of his own body, rolled his shoulders, touched the cut above his eye, and then looked at Amber with an expression she couldn't immediately categorize.

He'd watched the whole thing. Every bit of it. "You shot him," Landry said.

"Yes."

"Twice."

"That's generally the recommended minimum."

Landry was quiet for a beat. Outside, the square was getting louder, voices multiplying, the distant rise of a siren starting up somewhere south of Main Street. The sheriff looked at the broken clock face, at the gray morning sky showing through the gap, then back at Amber. His expression had settled into something she recognized now: the look of a man who'd revised his opinion of someone and was deciding whether to say so.

He decided not to say it. He just gave her a short nod, the kind that carried weight precisely because it wasn't elaborated on.

"Deputy's going to be up those stairs in about ninety seconds," Landry said. He reached into his jacket and produced his badge, checking it automatically like he needed the familiar weight of it to reorient. "Both of you stay exactly where you are when he comes through. Hands visible, weapons holstered. Let me do the talking."

"Sheriff." Dalton's voice was even. "The detonator. There are four charges on the support columns."

"Locations?"

"Southwest, northwest, northeast, and the main load-bearing column in the east hall. I can walk your bomb unit to each one."

Landry absorbed this without blinking. "Do that," he said. He straightened his jacket, which had blood on the collar from the cut above his eye, and positioned himself near the stairs. "And Vale. For the record." He paused. "I'm not blind. I haven't been blind for a while."

Dalton didn't respond to that. But something in his posture shifted, a fraction of tension releasing from his shoulders, barely visible, the kind of thing she'd only notice because she'd spent two weeks learning the specific language of how he carried himself.

The deputy came through the door at a run, badge out, voice already going, and Landry stepped forward to intercept him and took over the room with the authority of someone who'd been running crisis scenes since before the deputy was old enough to drive.

Amber stood at the broken clock face and looked out at Cherry Creek's main square in the early morning light.

Below, Julian Vane lay in the square. People were keeping their distance, a loose ring forming on the cobblestones, and the siren was closer now. The mist was still coming down, fine and constant, settling on the old stone buildings and the storefronts and the bare-limbed trees along the sidewalk, and the town looked exactly like itself: small and specific and very much still standing.

She pressed her palm flat against the stone wall beside the broken frame. Cold, rough, solid. She felt it under her hand and breathed.

Dalton came and stood beside her. Close enough that his arm pressed against hers. He didn't say anything.

"I canceled the email," she said. "I figured."

"I was going to do it dramatically, with coffee, like I said." "You can still do that part."

"The coffee part. Yeah." She exhaled. "It's over."

He was quiet for a moment, watching the square below where the first official vehicles were pulling up. Then: "It's over."

She turned away from the window. Her phone showed five-nineteen a.m. Thirty-one minutes before the scheduled send. She pulled up the draft, found the scheduled email with its small clock icon, and canceled it. The icon disappeared. The draft sat empty and inert in her folder, nothing attached, nothing dangerous, just a blank message waiting to be deleted.

She deleted it.

"Reyes is still going to get the files," she said. "I'll send them manually. Today, when this is done. The right way."

"I know." Dalton's hand moved briefly to her shoulder, a firm, grounding pressure, then dropped. "Come on. Landry needs us downstairs."

She followed him toward the stairs. At the top step, she paused and glanced back at the room: the iron gears, the pale stone, the broken clock face with the morning light coming through it in gray bars, and the empty space where Julian Vane had been standing twenty minutes ago, certain he held all the relevant variables.

He hadn't accounted for her. That had always been his mistake, and everyone else's before him. She was done being the variable people forgot to factor in.

She went down the stairs.

The lower floors of the courthouse were controlled chaos by the time they reached the main hall: Landry's deputies securing Julian's men, two of whom had surrendered without much argument once the smoke cleared and the man giving their orders stopped being a factor. A bomb unit van was pulling into the east lot. Someone had brought Landry a first-aid kit for the cut above his eye, which he was ignoring while talking on his radio.

He waved Dalton over to walk the bomb unit to the charge locations without breaking his radio conversation.

Amber sat on a bench in the courthouse hallway and waited, and for the first time in two years, the waiting didn't feel like dread. It felt like the pause between one thing ending and something else not yet named.

A deputy she didn't recognize brought her a paper cup of water. She drank it. It tasted like a courthouse water cooler, which was somehow the most normal thing that had happened to her in weeks, and she almost laughed at that, almost, and then did laugh, quietly, into the empty cup, because there was no one close enough to hear it and she had earned the right to laugh at whatever she needed to.

Dalton came back twenty minutes later. He sat down beside her on the bench, leaned his head back against the wall, and closed his eyes. He looked exhausted in a way that the dark and the movement had been covering up, and now that they'd stopped moving, it was right there on his face.

"Charges are all disarmed," he said. "Building's clear."

"Good."

"Reyes is going to want a full debrief. Probably today, once Landry makes the call."

"I know." She turned the paper cup in her hands. "I'm ready for that."

He opened his eyes and tilted his chin slightly toward her. His face was close, angled her way, with the cut on his jaw from two nights ago still healing and the stubble grown out past the point where it was intentional and the blue of his eyes gone soft with exhaustion and something else, something that had been living in there for weeks and had stopped pretending it wasn't.

"Hey," he said. "Thomas Vale Rowan."

She felt the words settle somewhere specific in her chest. "Elise Vale Rowan," she returned.

He nodded once, slow. "Still real." "Still real," she agreed.

Landry appeared at the end of the hallway, moving toward them with his badge clipped back on and the first-aid kit someone had pressed on him now apparently having been accepted, a strip of medical tape holding the cut closed. He stopped a few feet away, planted his boots, and looked between the two of them with his hands on his hips in the posture she'd learned meant he was about to say something he'd already decided on.

"Vale," he said. "I need a full statement. Everything you know about the Vane Collective's operations in this county, and I mean everything, before Albany gets here and I lose jurisdiction over my own town." He paused. "Rowan. Same."

"Yes, sir," she said.

Landry's jaw shifted. He looked at her for two seconds with the same revised-opinion expression from the clock tower, and then he said, gruffly, "You did good up there. In case nobody gets around to saying that in an official capacity today, which they probably won't, given the paperwork situation." He turned back toward the main hall. "Statement room's down the left corridor. Take five minutes."

He walked away.

Amber looked at Dalton. "Did he just compliment me?" "Close enough."

"I'm putting that in my statement." "Don't put that in your statement."

She almost smiled. She let herself, actually, fully, and it felt strange on her face the way things feel when you haven't used them in a long time and the muscles have to remember. Outside, the square was fully lit now, the morning having arrived without ceremony while they were in the courthouse dealing with the end of something that had started two years ago in a city she'd tried to outrun. The mist had thinned. The storefronts along Main Street were starting to show their lights.

Cherry Creek was waking up.

She stood, smoothed her jacket, and pressed her hand once to her inner pocket out of habit. The drive was there. It would go to Reyes today, properly, with a phone call first and Dalton on the line as her corroborating witness, and then the ledger would be someone else's weapon to use, in the hands of people whose job it actually was to use it.

She'd carried it long enough.

Dalton got up beside her, and they walked down the left corridor toward the statement room, their boots quiet on the old tile floor, the courthouse settling around them in the early light. At the door, she stopped with her hand on the frame.

"For the record," she said, and her voice came out steadier than she felt, which was saying something because she felt fairly steady, steadier than she'd been in two years. "I knew what I was doing up there. When I pulled the trigger. I want that on record. I made the choice."

Dalton stopped beside her. "I know you did."

"I'm not saying it for you. I'm saying it because I need to hear myself say it." He was quiet for a moment. Then: "Noted."

She pushed the door open and went in. Outside, through the narrow

window at the end of the room, the clock tower was visible against the morning sky, its east face broken open, pale stone bright now in the early light. The clock hands were frozen at four-forty-eight, the moment the frame had given way. They'd have to repair the face, pull in a restoration crew, probably make the local paper.

Cherry Creek, she suspected, had more than enough to talk about for a while.

She pulled out a chair, sat down, and folded her hands on the table. Dalton took the chair beside her, close enough that his knee was a few inches from hers, and she felt the warmth of him there and let it be exactly what it was: solid, present, and hers.

When Landry's deputy came in with a recording device and a yellow legal pad, she was ready.

31
Ashes to Orchards

The bakery smelled like brown butter and cardamom, and Amber had stopped jumping every time the front door opened.

It had taken three weeks to get there. Three weeks of flinching at the bell above the door, of tracking every customer's hands before their faces, of keeping the phone face-up on the counter within arm's reach. But this morning, when the door swung open and a gust of October air blew in a woman she'd never seen before, Amber had glanced up, registered "stranger, no visible threat, wants coffee," and gone right back to piping buttercream onto a cinnamon roll without missing a stroke. That felt like something worth noting. She noted it, and then she filled the order, and then she noted it again on the walk home that evening, quietly, without making a whole thing of it.

The new windows were the first thing people mentioned when they came in. Tempered, shatterproof, low-reflection glass, fitted in the same old wooden frames so the place still looked like itself from the street. Nora had pointed at them on opening day with her coffee cup raised like she was toasting them. "Bulletproof chic," she'd said. "Very now." Amber had laughed, which was also something she was doing more of, the kind of laugh that came up without her having to let it.

The opening had been a Tuesday, which felt exactly right. Not a Friday with balloons and fanfare. A Tuesday, because Tuesdays were just regular days, and that was the whole point.

Nora had brought her half-sister's favorite song on a playlist, played it through the small speaker above the display case at low volume, and neither of them talked about it. They didn't need to. Amber had squeezed her wrist once, Nora had refilled the coffee, and that was the memorial service, conducted over croissants and the sound of Main Street traffic. Clean. Honest. Theirs.

By noon on opening day, they'd sold out of the cardamom rolls and most of the tarts. A woman Amber vaguely recognized from the hardware store bought four scones and told her the old bakery on Miller had never done lavender shortbread, so she'd be back Thursday. Amber wrote "Thursday, shortbread" on the whiteboard behind the counter and felt something she didn't have an immediate word for. Not happiness exactly, but something adjacent and more durable.

Lila showed up at two in the afternoon with her son on her hip and a bottle of champagne she'd wrapped in a dish towel because she hadn't had time to get a bag. "It's technically prosecco," she announced, setting it on the counter. "Don't be a snob. Where's the man with the sling?"

"He said he'd stop by after the garage closed."

Lila pressed her lips together in a smirk that carried an entire conversation inside it. "Uh-huh. And how's that going, the man-with-the-sling situation?"

"Lila."

"I'm just asking."

"You're never just asking."

"Fine." Lila set her son down and watched him immediately lunge for the display case. "I'm asking with full investment and zero apology. How is it?"

Amber was quiet for a second, arranging the last of the afternoon pastries into the takeout box she was putting together for Wes, who'd said he didn't need anything and meant the opposite. "It's good," she said. "It's actually good."

Lila's smirk softened into something real. "Yeah. I can tell."

Dalton came in at four-fifteen with his arm in the sling and sawdust on his jacket and the look of someone who'd been doing more with one arm than most people managed with two. He stopped inside the door, took in the room, the new windows catching the late afternoon light, the display case, the little chalkboard menu Amber had written herself in her distinctly imperfect handwriting, and he didn't say anything for a moment. He just looked at it the way people look at things they've been worried about and can now see are okay.

"Sold out of the cardamom rolls," Amber told him from behind the counter. "Already?"

"By noon."

He crossed the room and leaned against the counter, and she came around to his good side without thinking about it, and he tucked her under his arm, which she had also stopped thinking about. She'd stopped cataloging the specific ways his presence felt like solid ground. It just did. She'd let it be a fact rather than a mystery.

"Prosecco?" she offered, nodding toward the bottle Lila had abandoned on the counter when she'd left to retrieve her son from the back room where he'd discovered the commercial mixer.

"I'll pass."

"Smart. It's technically terrible."

He pressed a brief, warm kiss to her temple and she felt it down to her collarbone. "You did good," he said.

"We're not done yet. Sheriff Landry said he'd swing by for coffee."

Dalton's expression did the slight shift she'd come to recognize as his version of amused. "Landry. Voluntarily. In a bakery."

"He's branching out."

The sheriff came in at half past four, still in uniform, badge catching the light. He stood in the doorway for a second the same way Dalton had, surveying the room, then stepped inside and let the door close behind him. He looked at the new windows first. Then the display case. Then Amber.

"Coffee," he said. "Milk? Sugar?"

"Black." He pulled out a stool at the counter and sat down with the deliberate care of a man whose knees had logged too many miles. "Place looks good. Windows are good. Sensible." He said it the way he said everything: like a brief filed report, clipped and final.

Amber poured his coffee and slid it across the counter. He wrapped both hands around the mug and exhaled through his nose.

"Heard from the task force this morning," he said. "Vane family assets are formally under seizure. The property portfolio, the shell accounts, the Collective's operational funds. Takes a while to move through the federal process, but it's moving." He took a sip of the coffee. "Substantial portion's being directed into a victims' compensation fund. Families affected by the Collective's operations over the last decade. The task force's language, not mine, but the short version is the money goes to the people it was taken from."

Amber set her hands flat on the counter. The crescent moon tattoo on her inner wrist was visible, that small impulsive mark she'd gotten at twenty and never regretted. "All of it?"

"Not all of it. Federal seizures never work that clean. But a meaningful portion." Landry looked at her across the counter. "You handed them a complete ledger. Twenty years of transactions. That doesn't happen. That's the kind of thing people spend careers trying to build, and you walked it in on a flash drive." He paused. "What you gave them mattered. I want that said clearly."

She hadn't expected that from him. She should have, maybe, after the clock tower. But she still hadn't fully updated her read on Landry, and his directness caught her off guard in a way she appreciated more than she'd say out loud. "Thank you," she said.

He nodded once, drank his coffee. Dalton had come to stand at the end of the counter, and the two men existed in the same space with the specific quiet of people who'd stopped circling each other.

"Vale," Landry said. "Sheriff."

"Garage doing okay?" "Busy enough."

Landry turned the mug in his hands. "Henderson's transmission finally

went. He's going to need the full job. Mentioned he'd been putting it off because he didn't want to bother you."

"He can bring it in Monday."

"I'll tell him." Landry finished the coffee and set the mug down with a small decisive click. He reached into his jacket pocket and produced a folded sheet of paper, which he slid across the counter to Amber without ceremony. "Task force sent that through my office. Official confirmation that your case from two years ago has been formally reopened and reclassified. Your original report is part of the federal record now." He stood up from the stool. "Nobody can quietly close it again."

She picked up the paper. It was official letterhead, dense with bureaucratic language that somehow, underneath all of it, said: *we see you now*. "How much do I owe you for the coffee?" she managed.

"On the house," he said, which they both knew was backwards. He buttoned his jacket. "Good coffee. Make sure the Henderson kid doesn't park on your curb when he comes to pick up his order. He'll do it if nobody tells him not to."

He left, the door closing firmly behind him.

Amber looked at the paper in her hands. She folded it carefully and tucked it into the pocket of her apron. Dalton watched her do it without commenting, which was one of the things she'd come to rely on, his ability to let her have a moment without filling it.

"Justice," she said, testing the word. It felt strange in her mouth, too large and too simple at the same time. But accurate. "That's what that is."

"Yeah," he said. "That's what that is."

She untied her apron and folded it over the counter. Outside, the October light had gone amber and low, the kind of afternoon that tips toward evening without warning, and the street was quiet in the specific way of small towns at the end of a workday. She looked at the room again: the windows, the chalkboard, the display case with its few remaining pastries, the stool where Landry had just been sitting.

The cemetery was a ten-minute walk from the bakery, east along Miller and then up the low hill where the oldest part of Cherry Creek's history was laid out in rows. She'd thought about going alone. She went with Dalton.

His arm was still in the sling, but he walked at her pace without making a production of it, hands in his jacket pockets, breath visible in the cooling air. They didn't talk much on the walk. They didn't need to fill the quiet the way she used to, compulsively, to keep the fear from pooling in the gaps.

Rory Keane's grave was in the newer section, near the back fence, a simple marker with his name and dates. No flowers. No evidence of recent visitors. The grass around it was still settling.

She'd stopped at the gas station two blocks over and bought a single white lily, the only one they had, a little travel-worn but intact. She held it by the stem and looked at the marker for a long moment. There was nothing she wanted to say to him. She'd run through every version of that imaginary confrontation in the months of nightmares and the weeks of waking fear, and none of it needed to be spoken aloud now.

She set the lily at the base of the marker. Not for him. For the fear he'd been, which was real, and which was finished.

Dalton stood a few feet behind her, giving her space without retreating.

"I don't forgive him," she said. It wasn't directed at the grave. It was just a fact she wanted on record. "I'm not here for that."

"I know."

"I just needed to put it somewhere." She straightened. "The flower. The whole thing. I needed to put it somewhere outside of me."

He came forward and stood beside her, the two of them looking at the simple marker in the late afternoon light. His good hand found hers, fingers threading through, solid and warm. She didn't catalog it this time. She just held on.

"It's done," she said. "It's done," he agreed.

She turned away from the grave without looking back. They walked out of the cemetery through the iron gate, which swung closed behind them with a soft clang of metal on metal, and the sound of it felt like punctuation. The right kind. A period, not a question mark.

The town spread out below the hill in the early evening light, rooftops and storefronts and the steeple of the church on Fourth, and beyond the east end of Main Street, the clock tower of the courthouse, its east face still boarded over with fresh plywood while the restoration crew waited on the period-appropriate glass. She'd read in the local paper that it would take six weeks. The clock hands were still frozen at four-forty-eight. The paper had called it a "historical incident." She'd read that phrase three times and then put the paper down and made herself a very large cup of coffee.

Dalton's thumb moved across her knuckles. She felt it the way she felt most things now: fully, without the instinct to deflect.

"Lila called this morning," Amber said as they started down the hill. "She wants to do a second opening. A Friday one, with actual champagne this time. Real champagne." "Of course she does."

"She's already made a list. There are seventeen items on it and one of them is a fog machine."

"A fog machine." "For atmosphere."

He made a sound that was definitively a laugh, low and brief, and she felt it against her shoulder where his arm pressed against hers. "You're going to let her do it," he said.

"I'm absolutely going to let her do it." Amber glanced sideways at his profile, the stubbled jaw and the faint scar through his brow, the particular way he scanned a space even when he was relaxed, a habit so deep it was just part of him now. "She's earned the fog machine."

They came down off the hill and onto Miller Street, and the bakery was visible at the far end of the block, its lights still on, the new windows catching the last of the evening gold. From this distance it looked settled. Permanent. Like it had been there for years rather than weeks.

Amber thought about the first time she'd seen it, boarded up and smelling like old flour and closed-down things, and how she'd stood on the sidewalk and tried to talk herself into believing it could be something. She'd been so tired then. The kind of tired that isn't about sleep.

She wasn't tired like that anymore. There were other kinds of tired, the ordinary exhaustion of a fourteen-hour opening day, the specific fatigue of too many early mornings back to back. Those she could work with. Those were just the cost of a life that was actually being lived.

"Wes left a message," Dalton said. "Wants to know if we're coming out to the cabin Sunday."

"Tell him yes. Tell him I'm bringing the scones he pretended he didn't want."

"He'll say he doesn't need them." "And then he'll eat four of them."

"Yeah." Another brief, quiet laugh. "Yeah, he will."

They stopped in front of the bakery. Through the window she could see the display case, mostly empty now, and the chalkboard, and the little corner she'd set up with two chairs and a low table for people who wanted to sit. A woman she didn't recognize was in one of the chairs, reading something on her phone, a coffee cup on the table beside her. Just a person, in a chair, in a bakery, on a Tuesday evening in October. Nothing more than that.

Nothing required to be.

Amber fished her keys out of her jacket pocket. "I need to close up and get the morning prep started." She looked at the keys in her hand. "You don't have to stay."

"I know," he said, and stayed.

Inside, the woman with the phone finished her coffee and left with a quiet thank-you and a wave. Amber locked the door behind her and flipped the sign to Closed, and then it was just the two of them and the smell of the day's baking and the last of the evening light coming through the shatterproof glass in long, flat rectangles across the floor.

She started on the morning prep. Dalton sat at the counter and kept her company, not hovering, not filling the silence unnecessarily, just present the way he'd been present in courthouse hallways and clock towers and all the dangerous spaces between then and now. She measured flour and thought about the cardamom rolls, how she'd tweak the ratio slightly for Thursday, more cardamom and a little less brown butter because the sweetness had tipped slightly over. Small corrections. That was what tomorrow was for.

"Hey," he said at one point, from his stool at the counter. She glanced up from the bowl.

"The town doesn't feel like a cage anymore." He said it simply, like he was confirming something he'd been sitting with. "Does it."

She considered that. The town outside the windows, with its storefronts and its steeple and its slow Tuesday evening, and the cemetery up on the hill with its fresh plywood and its white lily, and the sheriff who'd drunk her coffee and left her a piece of paper that said *we see you now.*

"No," she said. "It doesn't."

He nodded, satisfied with that, and she went back to the flour, and the bakery settled around them in the early dark, warm and specific and solid, smelling like everything she'd built one careful Tuesday at a time.

Outside, Cherry Creek went quietly about its evening. The clock on the courthouse was still frozen, but the town wasn't waiting for it to move. Neither was she.

32
The Darkness We Keep

The house smelled like pine and lake water and the particular kind of quiet that only exists when the air finally stops vibrating with the expectation of a blow. Amber felt it in the way her shoulders had finally dropped from her ears, the tight coil in her lower back unspooling until she was actually leaning into the doorframe rather than just using it for cover. For the first time in two years, her lungs didn't feel like they were trying to expand against a cage of iron bands; she just took a breath, deep and easy, and let it out without checking the shadows for a reason to hold the next one.

Amber had noticed it two weeks after they moved in, the silence. Not the hollow, waiting kind she'd lived inside for two years, the kind that felt like a held breath, like something crouching just outside the frame. This was different. Settled.

The silence of a place that had absorbed enough ordinary living to stop feeling temporary.

She stood at the kitchen window with her second cup of coffee and watched the lake do what it did in the hour before the light tipped into gold. The surface was calm. A single heron stood in the shallows near the far bank, very still, completely unbothered. She'd started noticing the heron about a week ago. It seemed to have a schedule. She respected that in a bird.

The porch door opened and Dalton came through it with the specific unhurried quality of a man who'd spent most of his life moving fast and had only recently decided to stop. He'd been out since early, something about the dock needing a board replaced before the temperature dropped enough to make it a real problem. He had sawdust on his forearm and a smear of something dark near his elbow that she hoped was wood stain and not motor oil, because she'd just washed that flannel.

"Dock's good," he said, by way of greeting.

"I was not worried about the dock."

"I know. I was." He reached past her for the coffee she was holding, took a sip without asking, handed it back. That small casual theft was something she'd come to accept as a character defect she was choosing not to address. "Heron's back."

"He never left. He has a whole situation going on over there." She tipped her chin toward the far bank. "I think he has a spot."

"Animals are territorial."

"So are some humans I know."

Dalton looked at her with the particular kind of dry patience he deployed when she said something true that he didn't intend to argue with. He took the mug again, finished the coffee, and set it on the counter. "Sunset's going to be good tonight. That cloud cover will do something interesting."

She'd learned to trust his weather instincts the same way she'd learned to trust his read on a room. Both came from the same source: years of paying close attention to things most people glanced past. "Then we should be on the porch for it," she said.

"That was the plan."

She went back to the bedroom to pull on an extra layer because the evenings had been getting into the low fifties and she was stubborn about her comfort, not about the cold. The bedroom still had that slightly unsettled feeling of a room that hasn't fully become itself yet. Some boxes were stacked in the corner, books mostly. She'd been unpacking in stages, a habit she'd developed across too many apartments where she'd kept things boxed as a kind of exit strategy, just in case. She was trying to break it. The books would be on shelves by the end of the month.

She grabbed the heavy cream-colored cardigan from the hook on the back of the door and shrugged into it. In the mirror above the dresser she registered herself the way she sometimes did now, without the immediate inventory of damage. The faint scar along her collarbone. The shadows under her eyes, lighter than they used to be. The crescent moon tattoo on her wrist, visible below the cuff. She looked like herself. That used to be a complicated thing to feel.

When she came back out, Dalton was on the porch, his jacket on, two glasses of the red wine Lila had brought over last week sitting on the small table between the two chairs. The sunset was doing what he'd predicted. The cloud cover had broken in horizontal bands, and the light coming through was the kind of orange that looks slightly unreal, like someone had turned a saturation slider too far and then decided it was correct after all.

The lake held it. That was the thing about water at that hour: it didn't just reflect the sky, it made the sky more specific, more concentrated. The color on the surface was deeper than the color above it, and the heron stood in the middle of it all, perfectly indifferent.

She sat. He sat. She took her glass. They watched.

This was something they were still learning, the two of them. How to be in a place without it being tactical. How to sit outside and watch a sunset without scanning the perimeter, without calculating exits. They weren't entirely there yet. She noticed him clock the tree line twice in the first five minutes, a reflex so ingrained it probably wasn't fully voluntary. She noticed because she'd done the same thing, her gaze snagging on the gap between the birch trees to the south before she'd consciously redirected it. Old training. They were both reprogramming.

She sipped the wine. It was decent. Lila had described it as "aggressively drinkable," which was an accurate assessment.

"I talked to Wes this morning," Dalton said. "How's the hip?"

"He says it's fine. He also says the same thing about his back and his knee, so I'm choosing not to believe him on any of those." He turned the glass in his hand. "He liked the scones you sent."

"He texted me a thumbs up, which from Wes is basically a standing ovation."

Dalton's mouth shifted in a way she'd cataloged extensively enough to recognize as affection. "He wants to come out and see the house before the snow."

"Tell him to come for dinner. I'll make the lamb thing he pretends he doesn't care about."

"He'll say he doesn't want the fuss."

"And then he'll eat two servings and ask if there's enough for a plate to take home."

"Yeah." A pause. "Yeah, he will."

The light shifted. The orange went deeper, started pulling toward rose at the edges. The heron moved, took two deliberate steps to the left, and resettled. Amber tracked it for a moment and then let her attention go back to the water.

She heard Dalton move. Not away, but the specific adjustment of someone reaching into a jacket pocket, deliberate, with intention. She glanced sideways.

He was holding something small. He turned toward her and held it out on his palm, and she saw the chain first, fine silver, and then the locket, round and simple, warm-toned gold, no bigger than a quarter.

She recognized the shape. She'd had one before, a long time ago, and then it had become evidence in a federal case, tagged and bagged and photographed with a little numbered placard beside it. She'd last seen it across a conference table under fluorescent lights. She didn't need it back. She'd been clear about that, and they'd been clear they understood.

This was not that locket.

"Open it," Dalton said.

She took it from his palm and worked the tiny clasp with her thumbnail. Inside, behind a small oval of protective glass, was a photograph. She tilted it toward the remaining light to see it properly.

It was the two of them. Opening day at the bakery, taken from outside the window by someone who'd been walking past, she had no idea who, but whoever it was had caught them at the right angle. Dalton with his arm still in the sling, leaning against the counter. Amber beside him, mid-laugh at something, her head tilted back slightly. The new windows behind them catching the afternoon light. The chalkboard visible in the corner of the frame.

She recognized the laugh because she remembered what had caused it. Lila's son had knocked the prosecco off the counter and it hadn't broken, it had just rolled under the display case, and the kid had gone after it at full speed on his hands and knees, and the look on Dalton's face when a toddler disappeared under the pastry display had been genuinely priceless.

She'd been happy in that moment. Specifically, measurably, without caveat. "Where did you get this?" she said.

"Lila. She said someone texted it to the diner's community board. She had it printed."

"Of course she did." Amber ran her thumb across the glass. The chain pooled in her other hand, cool and light. "Dalton."

"It's not a piece of anything," he said. "It's just a picture."

She understood what he meant. The first one had been a piece of the past, a piece of evidence, a piece of a story that had other people's hands all over it. This was theirs. Specific and ordinary and theirs.

She closed the locket and held it out toward him. "Put it on me."

He took it, and she turned in the chair and lifted the curtain of her hair away from her neck, and he reached around and fastened the clasp. His fingers were warm against the back of her neck, and he took a second longer than necessary. She didn't rush him.

When she turned back, the locket rested just below her collarbone, against the cardigan. She pressed two fingers to it briefly and then let her hand drop.

"Thank you," she said, simply.

He looked out at the water instead of answering, which was its own kind of response from him, the kind that meant it had mattered enough that words felt insufficient. She'd learned to read that too.

The rose at the horizon was bleeding into purple now. The lake had gone darker, the surface still, the heron a motionless silhouette in the shallows. Somewhere across the water, something moved in the brush on the far bank and then was still. Amber tracked it, assessed it as animal and small and nothing, and let it go. The assessment had taken maybe two seconds. Progress.

She pulled her knees up to her chest in the chair, an ungainly maneuver in a piece of outdoor furniture not designed for it, but she made it work. The cardigan was doing its job. The wine was doing its job. The night was coming in from the east, slow and without drama.

"I keep thinking about what Landry said," she said. "About the compensation fund. The families."

"What about it?"

"I don't know. I just think about it sometimes. That there are people somewhere who are going to get something back, and they don't know yet that it's coming." She watched the water. "That's a strange kind of thing to be part of."

"A good kind," Dalton said.

"Yeah." She exhaled. "Yeah, I think so."

The first star appeared above the eastern tree line, faint and then more definite, the way they always come in, tentative at first until they realize they have the field to themselves. She watched it for a moment.

"I used to think about leaving," she said. "Not Cherry Creek specifically. Just, in general. I'd lived with one foot already out the door for so long it felt like posture. Like my natural stance." She tipped her head back against the chair. "I don't think about it now."

"No?"

"No. I think about whether we should get a dog. And whether the cardamom ratio in the rolls is right. And whether Wes is actually fine or whether I need to drive out there and check on him myself." She paused. "Normal things."

Dalton was quiet beside her, the good kind of quiet that didn't require filling. He'd put his feet up on the porch railing, crossed at the ankle, his glass resting on his knee. From this angle she could see the scar through his eyebrow, the one from the bar fight he'd told her about in that flat, factual way he described most of his history, as a series of events that happened, neither romanticized nor regretted.

"We're staying," he said. Not a question. A statement of fact he was putting into the air to let it exist outside of his head.

"We're staying," she confirmed.

More stars now, the sky committing. The purple at the horizon had gone to dark blue and was moving toward black at the zenith. The lake had absorbed the last of the light and was reflecting stars at its edges, the water so still it was nearly impossible to tell where the surface ended and the sky began.

Dalton set his glass down on the table and turned in the chair to face her. He had that look, the focused, unhurried one that meant he was about to say something he'd been sitting with for a while. She'd learned not to preempt it.

"I will never stop," he said. "You understand that. Whatever comes. I'm not going anywhere."

She knew what he meant. The guardian thing, that particular quality of attention he'd turned on her since long before she'd given him permission, since before she'd understood it wasn't a threat. She'd fought it for months, called it controlling in the privacy of her own head, tried to outmaneuver it because she'd needed to prove she didn't need it. She still didn't need it.

But she'd stopped confusing needing with wanting, and she'd stopped treating wanting as a weakness.

"I know," she said. "And I'm not going to pretend I don't want that."

He reached across the space between the chairs and took her hand. His fingers were rough from the dock work, the skin at his knuckles weathered. His grip was steady without being tight.

"I'm your partner," she said. "Not just the person you're protecting. Both things."

"Both things," he agreed, without hesitation, which was the part that mattered.

She turned her hand over in his and threaded her fingers through, and they sat like that while the night finished arriving. The stars multiplied. The heron, invisible now in the dark water, made a single low sound from the shallows, something between a call and a complaint, and then went silent.

"About the dog," she said. "We can get a dog."

"You didn't even ask what kind." "Doesn't matter."

"It might matter. Some dogs are a whole thing."

"Whatever you want," he said, with the particular calm of a man who'd survived classified operations and therefore had accurate perspective on what actually constituted a problem. "I'll build it a house if it needs one."

She laughed, and it came up clean and real, the kind that doesn't require setup. "Okay. But I get to name it."

"Non-negotiable." "Good."

He shifted in the chair and she felt the movement before she saw it, his arm coming around her shoulder, pulling her sideways toward him. It was a slightly ridiculous configuration, two adults trying to share a single porch chair, but she tucked herself against his side and he adjusted until it worked, his chin resting briefly on the top of her head before she tilted her face up and found his jaw instead. The stubble. The warmth of his skin in the cooling air.

She pressed her lips to the angle of his jaw, unhurried, just contact, just the fact of him being there and solid and real. He turned his head enough to drop a kiss to her temple, then her cheekbone, his mouth moving slow and deliberate in the way that had always undone her, that particular patience of his that she'd once read as control and now understood as attention, as the specific care of someone who was paying close attention and had nowhere else to be.

His hand moved up her arm, over the cardigan, warm even through the wool. She turned further into him, her palm flat against his chest, and felt his heartbeat, steady and present. He kissed her properly then, his mouth on hers, warm and unhurried, tasting of red wine and something underneath it that was just him, familiar in the way that had become necessary. She kissed him back with the same quality of attention, no urgency, no desperation, just the full acknowledgment of each other in the specific dark of a night they'd both gotten to keep.

When they broke apart she stayed close, her forehead against his cheek. His hand rested at the curve of her waist, heavy and warm.

"The scars," she said, after a moment. She wasn't sure exactly what she meant by starting there, but he waited. "The ones that are still there. I've stopped being angry at them."

"Yeah?"

"They're just information now. They're just what happened." She pressed her palm a little harder against his chest. "We don't have to be people who weren't touched by it. We just have to be people who kept going."

He didn't say anything. He turned his head and pressed his lips to her hair, and she felt the exhale, long and quiet, against her scalp. That was enough. That was the whole answer.

The cool was settling in properly now. The lake made a small sound against the dock, water moving against wood, rhythmic and low. Above them the stars were fully committed, dense across the center of the sky where the light from Cherry Creek's main street was far enough away to stop competing. She'd never lived anywhere she could see this many stars. She was still getting used to it.

She felt the locket against her sternum, a small pressure, a small weight. Not evidence. Not a piece of a case. A Tuesday in October, a laugh she hadn't been forcing, a man with his arm in a sling looking at a room she'd built and finding it good. That was what was inside it. That was what she was carrying.

She could live with that. She intended to.

The night air was cold against her cheeks and warm everywhere else. Dalton's arm was solid across her back, his hand at her side, his heartbeat under her palm. The lake held the stars at its surface, patient and still. The heron, somewhere in the dark of the shallows, settled into its own silence.

She didn't need a life untouched by everything that had happened. She just needed this: the cool air, the warmth of him, the specific weight of a locket that was only ever going to be what it was. Her thumb moved across his knuckles and his fingers tightened briefly in response, one small press of acknowledgment.

Outside, Cherry Creek was exactly what it had always been. A small town at the edge of a lake, going quietly about its evening. And inside that, at the very edge of the water, on a porch with two glasses and a fading sunset and enough stars to make the sky feel like a different kind of country, the two of them held on.

The cold deepened, the stars multiplied, and neither of them moved to go inside.

AUTHOR'S NOTE

P. Hartwell is an author of mystery and romantic suspense, with a signature blend of atmospheric tension, emotional depth, and a whisper of the uncanny. Drawn to the places where history falters and secrets endure, he crafts stories that linger in the charged space between beauty and terror, love and fear, truth and illusion.

Raised along the windswept shores of Lake Erie and shaped by global travels, ancestral lore, and a reverence for forgotten histories, Hartwell brings a cinematic sense of place to his work. His novels unfold in immersive, shadow-laden landscapes where grief stirs beneath the surface, the past refuses to stay buried, and every silence speaks volumes.

With a keen eye for psychological nuance and elemental unease, Hartwell invites readers into worlds rich with tension, secrets, and haunting echoes—where every clue carries weight, and nothing stays hidden for long.

Acknowledgments

Writing The Darkness We Fell Into has been a descent into the shadows, and I couldn't have emerged without the light of so many incredible people. First, to my readers, your hunger for stories that push boundaries fuels every word I write. This book is for you, the ones who crave the dark with me.

To my editor, your sharp eye and fearless feedback carved this story into

something raw and real. Thank you for seeing the heart in the horror. To my beta readers, your late-night notes and honest reactions shaped Amber and Dalton's world. Your passion kept me going.

To my family and friends, thank you for the space to chase these ghosts, for the encouragement when doubt crept in, and for loving me through every deadline.

And to everyone who believes love can be both salvation and sin—thank you for diving into the depths with me.

With gratitude,

P. Hartwell

Made in United States
Cleveland, OH
14 June 2026

37900530R00204